# DAUGHTER OF DIAMONDS

LUCK GODS SERIES BOOK 3

J. GABRIEL GATES

Steed Publishing and Media, LLC
Michigan
Steedpublishing.com

Book Cover Design by ebooklaunch.com

Interior illustration by Etheric Designs

This is a work of fiction. Any resemblance between characters and real persons, living or dead, is coincidental.

**1**

---

## AGGIE

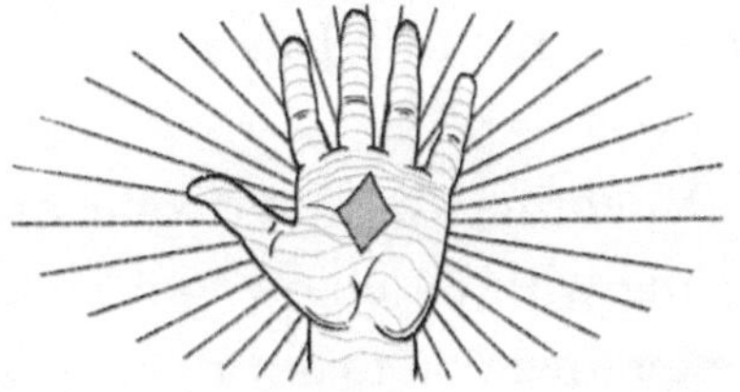

A roll of the dice. The flip of a coin. The flicker of a random thought. I am queen of these things. I could make you fall in love with your worst enemy, turn your nightmares to dreams, or make your grandmother's cancer disappear. I also made up an extremely dorky rap about the periodic table of elements which allowed me to rock AP Chemistry freshman year, but that's another story.

Currently, I stood amid a jostling crowd outside a municipal building in downtown Detroit. A protest leader stood next to the iconic Spirit of Detroit statue, yelling into a microphone about standing up to hate. Impassioned and eloquent as her words were, my attention drifted to the statue behind her. It depicted a kneeling man the green color of oxidized bronze, wearing only a loin cloth. His arms were outstretched to either side like the arms of a scale. In one hand he held a few small, golden people who reached up to him in supplication. In the other, he held a golden sun. It had no idea what the statue was meant to symbolize, but I somehow related anyway.

*A minor deity weighing the needs of family versus the demands of power? I feel you, green man. I feel you.*

As if in response, my pips—glowing, heart-shaped marks on the palms of my hands—sent a burning, restless energy humming through me. It was that feeling that had drawn me here, the pull of *the work*. There was some good luck I needed to dole out, some task I needed to do. I just had to figure out what it was.

Deuce, the Valentine four and one of my very best friends, nudged me with an elbow and nodded toward the Renaissance Center tower off to our right.

"You think the Diamantes will show up?" he asked. The Diamantes—the Diamonds—were our fellow red-suit good luck gods. Their Midwest headquarters was located in the penthouse of the Ren Center. Danusia, the Jill of Diamonds, might well be sitting way up there on her balcony, watching us like ants from behind the lenses of Chanel sunglasses. But I doubted it. As their name suggested, the Diamonds more interested in stock buybacks and corporate mergers than in social justice movements.

"You wish," Mina teased. She was the Valentine eight, and my other best friend in the suit. It was a fair assumption that Deuce might pine for Jill of Diamonds, since Danusia Diamante was a stunning, literal goddess with a flawless body, airbrush-perfect face and platinum blonde hair. But Deuce only grunted his displeasure.

"Yeah, right. I'm not interested sloppy seconds from..." his eyes flicked to me and he let the thought die.

"It's fine," I said. "You can say his name. Jack. Jack, Jack, Jack, Jack. See? I'm fine. No spontaneous combustion or anything. I'm not even dolorous about him."

"Dolorous?" Mina laughed.

"Oh, you haven't heard?" Deuce said. "Her Royal Highness is prepping for the reading and vocab portion of the SAT. She had me up until three AM the other night doing flash cards."

"Doing flash cards, eh?" Mina teased, her eyes narrowing. I knew what she was insinuating, but I wasn't taking the bait. Even if I was interested in Deuce that way, he was like my best friend. And Jack.... I didn't even know how to finish the thought. Instead, I said:

"You and Galen were up pretty late the other night, too. What were the two of you up to?"

At this Mina's eyes got big, her cheeks got pink, and her lips clamped tight. She gave me a warning look that said: *shut up.*

I was about to tease her more, but the crowd surged, taking us with them as they began marching north, up Woodward Avenue.

"Where are we going?" I asked.

"Weren't you listening?" she Mina. "To confront the other group in Campus Martius Park."

The *others* were neo-Nazis who'd come to town to stage a rally. The group we walked among had gathered as a counter protest. It didn't take a master of deductive reasoning to determine things might get ugly, and judging from the police in riot gear who marched alongside us, we weren't the only ones who suspected there might be trouble. But the police were few and the protesters many. *The work* had probably led us here to protect people and the keep the violence in check.

Forward we marched amid the chants and shouts, the chatter of maracas and the blaring of airhorns. My hands slipped to the weapons concealed beneath my hoodie: a long dagger and a very charmed revolver that had once belonged to Annie Oakley—who, fun fact, was a nine of Hearts in her day. No wonder she was such a good shot.

Checking my weapons made me think of Jack, and my eyes scanned the crowd for probably the hundredth time, looking for his breath-stoppingly handsome face. When I didn't find him, I scanned once more, looking for Mom. I caught myself searching for both of them all the time, so much that it was almost another OCD compulsion to add to my collection. But for the past couple of months, there'd been nothing. Zero sightings.

When I didn't find them, I began nervously counting the faces that were not theirs, ticking them off by touching my thumb to a different finger with each number—another of my OCD tics.

A gentle hand closed on my arm. Deuce watched me, concern in his usually mischievous brown eyes. "You okay, my queen?"

That was all it took, a touch, a look, and the spell was broken. I forgot what number I was on and the counting compulsion released me from its talons. For the moment.

"Yeah. Fine." I said, my voice a little breathy between the walking and the anxiety. "And I told you, don't call me that."

It wasn't that the title was inaccurate. I was the Queen of

Hearts, the highest regent of the Valentine suit of Luck Gods. Sure, I experienced heavy doses of impostor syndrome daily, along with crushing amounts of guilt and self-doubt. I was seventeen. I had no business commanding the type of power I now possessed, and I could think of probably twenty people off the top of my head who deserved it more than me. When Deuce said *my queen* teasingly or with a quirk of irony, that was fine. It was moments like this, when he said it in earnest, that made me uncomfortable.

But I had no time to think about our suit's power dynamics. Ahead, protesters were beginning to cross the street and make their way into the park, an oval-shaped, grassy space encircled by Woodward Avenue. Office buildings towered around us, some art deco reminders of Detroit's glorious past, others gleaming, glass blades that evoked the future. A war memorial sat at the south end of the park, and the throng of protesters split as they reached it, some going left, others right. I tapped Mina on the shoulders and gestured left.

"You and Deuce go that way. Meet back at the memorial if there's trouble," I said, and they both nodded as we parted ways, them heading to the left, me to the right.

Spread out we'd have a better chance of diffusing our charm into the crowd and quashing trouble no matter where it started. And it seemed we wouldn't have long to wait. Already shouts echoed up ahead. One man shoved another down. I jumped at the crash of a thrown bottle shattering on pavement. My hand went to the hilt of my dagger, and the yearning for *the work* pulsing in my hands grew stronger.

As I strode onto the green, another feeling washed over me. The prickly, shivery foreboding of bad luck. But I couldn't turn back, even if I wanted to. The crowd lurched forward, carrying me with them, as inexorable as the gravity around a black hole.

A low stage stood at the park's north end and a youngish man with a shaved head paced atop it, brandishing a noose and shouting into a bullhorn. As my group drew nearer, I counted the man's followers. Twenty-three is my OCD number of completion, and I came up with two sets of twenty-three plus a handful more—it was hard to tell exactly with the crowd milling and shifting. Most of the demagogue's followers wore red shirts, and for some reason they brandished brooms. The brooms were meant to symbolize something, I guessed, but already they were being used as weapons. The Nazis near the edge of the crowd had formed up shoulder-to-shoulder and brandished the brooms handle-out, like a phalanx of spearmen. The anti-Nazi protesters had the Nazis outnumbered by a factor of five, but that didn't mean the red-shirts weren't dangerous. I remembered something my dad had told me as a kid: scared dogs are the ones that bite.

"This might get ugly," I said aloud, before remembering that my friends weren't within earshot. I spotted them about a hundred yards away, pushing to the front of an increasingly agitated crowd.

The speaker's words had washed over me so far, like a song whose words I couldn't make out, all howled vowels and spat consonants, but as my focus shifted to the stage I heard him say, "Here they come, hungry, greed, lazy, weak, and woke—to take what's yours. What do we do with that trash?"

"*Sweep it away!*" Roared his crowd, brandishing their brooms.

*Ugh. Total bad luck vibes,* I thought with disgust, and the tug of *the work* on my hands throbbing stronger.

A few police in riot gear had made their way between the groups, their shields and armored bodies keeping the factions apart—for now. At the speaker's provocation, the crowd around me lurched forward, almost taking me off my feet. Only by flaring charm was I able to keep my balance. I sidestepped, slipping between bodies, and managed to clamber onto a concrete planter. I stood among the mums and surveyed the scene. Handmade flags. Battles lines. Faces contorted with anger. A few rocks and bricks arcing through the air.

My hands went warm as I flared charm.

*Chill out, people. Take it easy...*

Mind control wasn't a power I possessed, but moods are mercurial, easily nudged in one direction or another. Often a single deep breath was the difference between a thrown fist and a person walking away. That's what I tried to buy now with my charm: a second of distraction, a glimmer of doubt, a moment of hesitation. And wow was my queen charm powerful. Far different from what I had as a six. As the power burned through the heart marks on my palms, I felt the entire crowd still eerily for a beat and pull back, as if they were a sea and I the moon.

Then I spotted them on the far side of the square near a corner of the stage, black clad and dour faced: Marley and his crew of Blackovers. Clubs. Bad luck gods.

"Crap. What are they doing here?" I muttered.

But it was no mystery. Their work had probably drawn them here just as my work had drawn me. The more violence, pain, and suffering they stirred up, the more their power would grow. That was how a bad luck gods' work operated, just as happy outcomes made my charm grow. That was the eternal tug-of-war our suits faced. And at the moment, even with my queen power, the scales seemed decidedly tipped in their favor. Because all these people, even the anti-fascists, had come to see blood, not to sing *Kum Bah Ya*.

The two factions were pressing into one another, fists swinging, voices rising, signs thumping down on people's heads. I flared charm harder, gritting my teeth, and it felt like I was pulling a muscle somewhere in my gut. Struggling to restrain the crowd felt like holding back a massive ship as it strained to rip free of its mooring.

Across the way, I glimpsed Deuce and Mina. They were also using charm, but I could tell they too were having trouble holding tempers in check. The Blackovers had made their way into the crowd now, their hands up, the club marks on their palms glowing with dark purplish light. The few people who noticed seemed amused by their glowing pips. Some whooped and pointed. Several reached up to high-five them. Wherever they went, those near them erupted in greater fury.

Then I spotted another familiar face in the crowd, just to the left of Marley—but it wasn't a Blackover. This man had dark skin and a spider-web tattoo around one eye. My heart leapt. It was my mom's lieutenant, Shade. A Morbus.

Oh, did I mention Mom is the Queen of Spades? It's a long story...

No one had spotted Shade since Mom got injured two months ago, and seeing him now sent my heart galloping as my eyes traced the crowd behind him, searching for Mom. I longed to see her. To hug her. To witness for myself that she was okay—even if she was a little, you know, scary these days.

But Mom wasn't there. Just Shade and Marley's crew. Which left me with questions. Were Mom's Spades working with the Blackovers now? I hadn't gotten any intelligence to that effect, but it couldn't be coincidence that they were here together, could it? My suspicion was confirmed when Shade said something to Marley, then pulled a gas mask down over his face.

Marley spotted me then. He was wearing his trademark sunglasses so I couldn't tell if our eyes met, but his smile was unmistakable. I knew what he intended to do next. It would be like throwing a lit match into a beaker of azidoazide azide.

"No!" I shouted and I flared charm again, hoping desperately to stop him, to turn his will away from what he was about to do. But no amount of luck could turn aside that glee and determination. Still grinning at me, Marley reached out a hand and touched the shoulder of a huge bald man in a red tank top. The man's eyes went wide. His face contorted with rage. Then, he went crazy. The members of Marley's crew were doing the same thing, touching members of the crowd with their darkly glowing hands.

It was the special power of the Clubs. Their endowment, *dow* for short. The Berserker's Touch.

Each person they touched instantly went wild, set off like a mad wind-up toy, attacking everyone in sight. A melee ensued. Punching, kicking, biting. Utter chaos. The madman on stage was singing *America the Beautiful* into the bullhorn offkey at a deafening volume. A thrown trashcan flew through the air. Suddenly, I felt a sting and a tingling coldness as the charm flaring in my hands guttered. If this was a tug-of-war between good luck and bad, my side was losing. Maybe we'd already lost. The responsible thing to do was to get my crew out of there, but Deuce and Mina were nowhere to be seen among the flailing bodies around me.

Instead, I caught sight of Shade. He'd made it into the middle of the fray with that gas mask down over his face. As I watched, he pulled out some sort of a cannister and tossed it casually over his shoulder. Dark smoke erupted from the cannister, and all around it people began coughing and retching. Shade continued walking through the crowd, taking out two more cannisters and tossing them, one left, one right, as he made his way to the edge of the crowed, then jogged away across Woodward Avenue.

I leapt down from the planter I stood on and gave chase.

For two months, I'd been searching for Mom and her Spades without any leads. Now that I'd spotted Shade, there was no way in hell I was going to let him go without getting some answers. So through the crowd I ran, dodging and ducking, my small frame slipping between bodies where a larger person might have gotten blocked. With my charm flared, even in its weakened state, the movement was like a ballet, with people shifting at the perfect moment to let me through. The last few rioters parted ahead of me, then I was in the open, running across the road.

Tires squealed as a black, armored vehicle slid a stop just in front of me. Police in riot gear piled out like storm troopers, but they paid no mind to the teenage girl in glasses and a hoodie as they barreled across the park toward the chaos.

I jogged around the vehicle in time to catch sight of Shade disappearing down an alley. I sprinted after him.

He was fast, but I was devious. A burst of charm and his toe caught on a curb, sending him tumbling. When he groaned and sat up, I was already standing over him, gun in one hand, dagger in the other. I expected him to run or fight. Instead he pulled back his gas mask and eyed me.

"Well. The royal daughter."

"Tell me where my mom is."

He smirked. "Or what?"

I cocked the gun. "Listen. I've done worse things to get my mom back than hurt someone like you."

He snorted. "Someone like me? Wow. That's judgy, sis."

I took a step toward him, trying to seem as menacing as possible, and flared charm. It would be good luck for me if he'd just let something slip. A hint. A clue. Anything.

"I'm not your sister," I hissed.

His eyes narrowed. "Look, maybe she doesn't want to be found."

"I just want to know she's okay," I pressed. "And make sure she's..." I wasn't sure how to finish. Mom had promised the evil shard of sentient stone inside her, the obelisk of spades, that she would serve it for a year in exchange for being set free. She still had around seven months to go. But in the meantime, I needed to make sure Mom wasn't hurting people. And I wanted to know she was still herself, that the dark work wasn't making her irretrievably into someone else. And, of course, if there was some way to set her free before that year was up, I wanted that, too.

Shade slowly stood. He wasn't a huge man, but he still loomed over me. He was muscular, and he was a Spade. I sensed the bad luck rolling off him, and even with my queen-level charm, I knew he could be dangerous. I glanced over my shoulder. We were alone in the alley together.

"She's okay," he said quietly, a hint of compassion in his voice.

"Take me to her," I pressed. "Please."

He shook his head. "Sorry. Queen's orders," then he turned to walk away.

I followed. When he glanced back at me, his expression was equally amused and annoyed.

"Yes?" he said.

"I'm following you," I said simply.

He snorted. "Then I hope you've got your running shoes on," he said, and he took off again at a sprint. I did have running shoes on. What I didn't have was Shade's long legs and his speed. Still, I couldn't lose the only possible connection to Mom I'd had in months. So I ran.

Down the alley we sprinted, then across a road filled with cars that honked and skidded as we threaded between them. Across the sidewalk, into another alley. But I was too slow. He was getting away. I'd already been using charm to nudge my leg muscles and keep them from getting fatigued. Now, I shifted its focus and imagined Shade falling again. He was far ahead now, rounding a corner and darting into another alley. As he disappeared I flared my charm harder, and I heard a splash then a curse. I redoubled my sprint, skidded around the corner of the building, and saw a large puddle, its surface quivering with ripples—but not Shade.

I walked forward cautiously, my weapons ready. A creak of metal shrieked above me, and looked up just in time to see the staircase of a fire escape swinging down. It hit me on the head, sending stars sparking across my vision. I found myself belly-down on the hard pavement, with the fire escape steps pressing down painfully on my shoulders.

"Looks like that fire escape swung down just as you ran under it. Bad luck, sis," Shade teased, and I was vaguely aware of walking down the stairs, the metal steps clanging with each footfall. The stairs pressed down on me harder, pressing the air out of my lungs. Then suddenly, the weight was gone as Shade leapt over me and took off running again.

With his weight removed, the stairs swung up again, freeing me. Snarling, I fought to my feet and looked around. But there was no sign of Shade; I didn't even know which direction he'd gone. All that remained was the faint echo of Shade's distant footfalls disappearing—and taking all hope of finding my mom with them.

❤ ♠ ◇ ♣

Once I'd caught my breath, I made my way back to the park. The sun had set, and streetlights and headlights were clicking on, filling the city with their false white light.

At the park I found a chaotic scene. Most of the protesters had scattered and the landscape they'd left behind was a wasteland of blowing debris and burning trash cans. Red and blue lights from police cars, fire trucks, and ambulances flashed, casting stark shadows and garish color across the square. An injured man sat on a gurney, wailing. A news crew filmed at the far end of the green, the correspondent gesturing emphatically as she described the drama that had unfolded. The whole place tingled with bad luck. I could feel it sizzling in the air, taste its acrid flavor on my tongue. No question, we'd lost this fight.

Then I saw two figures rushing toward me across the park's marred lawn. A small woman, leaning so heavily on a man she was almost being carried. Mina and Deuce. I ran to them, then pulled up when I saw the rictus of pain on Mina's face. Her arm hung at an unnatural angle and spider-leg trails of blood stretched down her face.

"She got trampled. I didn't have enough charm to hold them," Deuce said, his voice wobbling with emotion. "You disappeared."

I couldn't answer. I was busy counting the flashes of the police lights. *One, two, three, four...*

"Aggie?" Deuce shouted, and his anger snapped me out of my counting. Damned OCD.

"I'm sorry," I said. "Let's get her to the car,"

**2**

———

**AGGIE**

"Where did you go?" Deuce demanded. We sat in the hallway outside the medic room in the basement of the Valentine mansion along with our fellow Valentine, Dubs. Mina was inside the room, getting her arm tended to by a doctor the Hearts kept on call. The doctor was a syco—short for sycophant—a person who liked to hang out with luck gods in order to soak up a bit of their good fortune.

I turned to find Deuce's eyes brimming with anger, frustration, and hurt. In my short rise to queenhood, I'd managed to alienate or piss off half our suit. I couldn't face Deuce turning on me, too.

"I saw Shade," I began, explaining how I'd seem him

working with the Clubs, spraying something into the crowd, then running when I tried to confront him. "We've been searching for the Spades for months with zero leads. I had the chance to follow him and I took it."

"Right," Deuce said. "And when you left, we completely lost control of the crowd. Did you stop to think maybe that was their plan all along? Have Shade draw you off so we'd be overpowered?"

"I..." I began, then paused. In fact, I *hadn't* thought of that. And it was stupid of me. My predecessor, Queen Aubra, King Michael, my rival Ten, and certainly Jack—any of them would have seen a trap like that from a mile away. But while I was undeniably book smart, in the ways of inter-demigod conflicts, I was still a novitiate.

*You have no place being queen.* It was the same intrusive thought that had dogged me ever since I'd received the crown of Hearts. *You'll fail. You'll get them all killed.* To stave off the thoughts, I reflexively began counting the bricks on the wall behind Deuce's head. *One, two, three, four, five...*

He must have seen me looking spaced out and threw up his hands in frustration. I'd never seen him so mad at me. Tears welled in my eyes, though I fought them back.

"Deuce. Lay off, man," Dubs said, patting Deuce on the chest. "It's been a long night for all of you."

"You weren't there," Deuce said, shoving Dubs' hand away. "You didn't see what happened to Mina when the crowd overwhelmed her."

Dubs went silent, his eyes flicking down to the stump of his right arm. It had been bitten off by a jinni, a luck demon, during our last confrontation with my mom. One more black mark on me leadership record....

"Of course I thought it might be a trap," I knew I

shouldn't lie, but I felt desperate to save what credibility I might have left and squelch that look of anger burning in my Deuce's eyes. "I just…"

"Care about finding your mom more than you care us?" a sharp female voice finished, and I looked up to see Ten walking into the room, with her crew of loyal Hearts behind her. In order of rank they were: our nine Cobe, our five Adelie, and our three Galen.

Ten cocked a hip and glared at me. Our run-in with the Diamond Queen had left her with a golf tee-shaped scar on her bronze-colored forehead, just beneath her dark hairline, but it only made her beauty more focused, somehow. The whole incident had focused her hatred of me, too. She loved to remind everyone how I'd abandoned her to die at the Diamantes headquarters, leaving out the part where she'd tried to stab me in order to steal my queenship. Guilt had caused me to keep her in the suit when a more ruthless queen would have killed her or cast her out. I regretted the decision pretty much daily.

"You're always going on about how the Spades are our mortal enemies, Ten," I said. "I happen to think it's in our best interest to find out where they've been hiding out for the last few months."

"Sure," she said. "And you were willing to sacrifice the safety of your crew to get that information. Just like you were willing to sacrifice me at the Diamond Queen's compound."

There is was again, her old refrain.

My fists clenched. If I were the fighting type, this was the moment when Ten and I would have been nose-to-nose. But I was the type to do my fighting on vintage video game consoles and my arguing at school-sanctioned debate competitions. So I simply said, "Whatever, Ten."

She folded her arms, a dark grin curling her lips. "No, not whatever. While you've been out chasing your mother's friends, the rest of us have been trying to solve your husband's murder."

The word *husband* still made my stomach curdle. My marriage to King Michael had only lasted a few hours and had been an empty ritual, something I had done only to gain the power of queenship. That didn't make finding him bludgeoned to death in bed next to me the morning after our wedding any less traumatizing.

"Any new leads?" I asked.

Ten arched an eyebrow. "There's one person who had the motive and the opportunity. And they were found at the scene of the crime."

I forced a laugh. "You can't possibly think I killed Michael."

"Why not? Sure, you walk around every day playing this innocent nerdy teenager routine, but the fact is you abandoned Mina to a rabid crowd. You left me to die. We all know how you feel about Jack, and Jack would stop at nothing to gain more power. What better way than to get you placed as queen and then knock off the king?"

"You all agree this is absurd, right?" I looked at Ten's crew. They all avoided meeting my gaze except for Cobe, who glared ferociously at me and inched protectively closer to Ten.

She crossed her arms gave me a harsh, self-satisfied smile.

"Come on, Ten," Deuce started.

She held a hand up in his face, silencing him. "Shut it, Deuce. Everyone knows you're in Jack's pocket. If there's a number two suspect, it's you."

I was completely sick of dealing with Ten's attitude. But the reality was, I needed her, and the Valentines who were loyal to her. Mom was out there somewhere, and she was getting more powerful. I could feel it. And I knew I would need all the Valentines behind me if I stood any chance of facing her and getting her back.

"What do you want from me, Ten?" I sighed.

She smiled, as if this were the question she'd been waiting for.

"The majority of the suit doesn't trust you," Ten said. "We need leadership we can trust."

"Last I checked, this wasn't a democracy," I said.

Ten cocked her head. "True. But a split in the suit leaves us all in danger. If the Clubs were to attack us, for example, how do we know you and your crew would fight for the rest of us?"

"You know we would," Dubs countered.

Ten's eyes flicked from him to me. "And how do you know we would fight for you?"

My jaw clenched so hard my teeth hurt. But she was right, of course. A fractured suit left us all in danger.

"We propose," Ten went on, "That you build trust—by choosing a king who will unite us all. The highest ranking male heart, as tradition dictates."

She put a hand on Cobe's shoulder and pushed him forward a step.

My eyes flicked from him back to Ten. "The highest ranking male Valentine is Jack."

"Jack is gone," Ten pointed out.

"And he polluted his charm when he took the Spade mark," Cobe added. "He's an abomination now. I'm the highest ranking pure Heart."

"And I'm the queen," I shot back. "I choose my king. No one else."

"The ace might disagree on that point," Ten observed.

But we both knew the ace was out of commission. Ever since the Spades obelisk had touched ours, she'd been unconscious. No one knew if the intermingling of the magics had injured her or sapped her strength or what—but she wasn't talking to anyone, not even in dreams. I had to solve this on my own. And I needed to do it fast, before any chance of saving mom slipped away. Every day she was under the power of the Spades obelisk, she drifted further and further from herself. If I didn't find her soon, I feared there'd be no getting her back at all.

"I'll make a deal with you, Ten," I said. "I find the king's real killer. When you see it isn't one of us, you accept my choice for king—and my leadership. Then you'll help me track down the Spades—and my mom."

I held out my hand to shake her and seal the deal. She only looked down at it.

"And if you don't find the killer, you'll make Cobe your king," she said. "Of course, we'll be investigating, too. And if we find out one of you did it, the ace will have no choice but to administer the penalty for killing a member of your own suit. Death."

I knew none of my friends were killers, but it didn't make Ten's pronouncement any less chilling.

"You have a week," Ten said, turning to lead her entourage out of the room.

"*You* have a week," I called after her.

She paused, giving me a puzzled, irritated look, then departed.

"Way to take the power back," Dubs joked.

Galen had hung back, looking down at the ground with hands in his pockets.

"Mina," he said quietly, "is she—?"

"Her arm is broken, but she'll be okay," I said. "You're welcome to wait with us."

Galen hesitated. Ten had brought him into the suit, giving him all the power, wealth and status that came with being a luck god. But he had been spending a lot of time with Mina lately, and I could almost feel him being pulled in two directions.

Finally, as if unable to hold himself back any longer, he hurried to the closed door, opened it, and went inside. Mina sat reclining on a chaise, her arm in a sling. As we watched, Galen knelt beside her and touched her cheek so tenderly it made my heart ache.

Deuce and I looked at one another. He still seemed sullen, but the anger had faded from his eyes—which was a relief.

"So we're solving murders now?" he asked wryly.

His use of *we* made me feel better. It meant he wasn't abandoning me.

"So it would seem."

**3**

---

## AGGIE

Despite having a murder to solve and a suit of demigods to lead, a girl still has to keep her GPA up. So I sat in my AP Euro class, a spiral notebook splayed in front of me, doodling hearts in the margins of the blank page with my red pen. We were supposed to be brainstorming ideas for a group project on the Magna Carta, but I was letting everyone else do all talking. Being the overachieving type, I'd always found group projects insufferable. Invariably, my other group mates would try to coast and do nothing. I'd sit back for as long as possible, refusing to do their work out of protest, but eventually I'd always get mad, panic, and do everything myself. I would do a phenomenal job, of course, so our group would get an A, and my inferior group mates would make off with their ill-gotten grades like a pack of thieves.

But this time, the tables had turned. Our group was stacked. My longtime frenemy and rival for the valedictorian spot, Claudette, was here. So was Landon Hughes, a quiet basketball player who, I'd discovered, was surprisingly smart for a handsome jock. Rounding out the group was theater boy extraordinaire Keegan Kent. Keegan wasn't the biggest brainiac in the world but he was a major ham, which would certainly come in handy when it came time to present to the class. And in this group, it seemed I was the slacker, because so far I'd contributed exactly zilch to the discussion. My mind, as they say, was elsewhere.

"If we create a 3D map," Claudette was saying, "We could chronicle all the battles and travels of King John leading up to the Magna Carta's signing. We could even rig it up LED lights that we could make light up whenever we're talking about an event in a certain location. Like, red could be battles, green could be—"

"Let's just do a skit," Keegan interrupted, earning a glare from Claudette. "That's what everyone else is doing."

"Aggie, what do you think?" Landon asked in his mild, deep voice.

Actually, I was thinking we should have dusted for fingerprints in the king's bedroom after his murder. We hadn't done it, probably because we had neither a fingerprint dusting kit nor the knowledge of how to actually dust for fingerprints. Still, there was something about that open window that bothered me, and I couldn't quite pin down what it was. But I couldn't exactly say that out loud.

"Uh. Either way is fine with me," I said.

Claudette frowned. Keegan shrugged. Landon fixed a

pair of thoughtful brown eyes on me, as if I were a puzzle he was trying to solve.

The bell rang and everyone sprang from their seats, slapping notebooks closed, snatching up tablets, and heading for the door. Claudette and I were the last two to pack up our stuff and vacate the room, and I suspected she was hanging back to talk to me. The suspicion was confirmed when we got out in the hallway and she cleared her throat and said, "So what's up with you? Queen problems?"

Now that Molly was gone, Claudette was the only person in the school who knew I was a luck goddess. She was sort of my syco, which was still hard for me to believe. She's started out as the most popular girl in school, and now relied on my good luck to stay on the top of Popularity Mountain. I considered explaining that I somehow had to find King Michael's killer and asking for her help. She was smart enough that she might actually have been of use. But it was too much to get into in the five minutes between classes. And besides, Claudette had been my nemesis not too long ago, and I was still wary about sharing too much with her.

So instead I said, "I just miss Molly, I guess."

Molly was my best friend. That is, until she literally stabbed my mom in the back. It should have made me hate her, but it was more complicated than that. Mom had been coming at me with a sword at the time, so Molly might have been defending me. Plus, Mom had just injured a boy that I had sort of charmed Molly into falling in love with. Cripes, my life was complicated...

"Yeah. I miss her, too," Claudia said, sounding surprised about it. "Any word from her?"

"Not in like two months," I said. "You?"

"Just that text she sent Bianca. About visiting her mom or whatever."

It was crazy. Just a few months ago I considered my friendship with Molly and my relationship with mom the two most stable things in my life. It just showed how fast things could shift. Among luck gods especially, loyalties always seemed to be in flux. It felt like walking across an endless dune of shifting sand.

"Well, you've still got me and the girls," Claudette said with a tight smile. I was grateful I wasn't a total pariah, but she and her popular girl crew didn't exactly make me feel warm and fuzzy, either.

"Thanks," I said. "I guess—"

"Miss Van Der Graaf? A word?" I turned to find the assistant principal, Ms. Morse, standing at my elbow.

Claudette gave her one of her patented sucking up smiles, replete with white teeth and dimples, and turned with a flick of her ponytail to head down the hall.

I turned back to the assistant principal and sighed. I was probably winning another award, or getting anointed *citizen of the week* again. I had about twenty of those ribbons lining a shelf at home. Or I'd gotten a scholarship, maybe. I'd been applying to quite a few. Whatever this was about, I didn't feel like dealing with it, not with everything else on my plate.

When we reached her office, Ms. Morse shut the door, sat in her desk chair and slid a folder over to me. I opened it, expecting to see a gold-embossed certificate. Instead, the folder contained a bubbled in Scantron test sheet with my name at the top.

"Do you know what that is?" Ms. Morse asked.

At the top of the page there was a space labelled "class,"

I'd written "AP Euro." I really hated it when people asked me questions they obviously knew the answer to.

"It *appears* to be my AP Euro test from last week," I said.

"And how do you think you did on that test?" she asked.

I glanced at the top of the page. There was a *100 percent* written there which had been scratched out and replaced by a 54. But that couldn't be right.

"I... would guess I got an A, but I'm a little confused about this 54 at the top," I admitted.

"Yes. Mrs. Chen was confused by that as well. You see, when she ran the tests the first time, you got one hundred percent. Then she remembered she had updated the test, but she was using last year's answer key. When she scored your test again using updated key, you only got fifty four percent."

"Huh," I said. That was perplexing.

The assistant principal leaned over the desk toward me, her fingers steepled. "The old answer key had been sitting in Mrs. Chen's desk drawer all year, Aggie. It would have been easy for a student to steal it... make a copy..."

Her words hung in the air for a moment before her implication hit me. When it did, I gasped.

"Are you saying I cheated?" I said, my voice going up several octaves.

Mrs. Morse sighed. "I know you've always been an exemplary student, Aggie. But I also know your house burned down last year. And I heard a rumor that your mom is no longer employed at the college. That she's... disappeared."

"No," I said quickly. If Mrs. Morse found out Mom was gone and I was living with a bunch of random people who considered themselves deities in a mansion in Grosse Point Shores, she'd be duty-bound to call Child Protective Services. That was a headache I didn't need.

"No. Mom is just... on sabbatical. She's fine. Really."

Mrs. Morse watched me for a long moment, drumming her fingers on the desk. I wasn't sure if it was a move she learned in principal training or what, but that silent scrutiny almost made me crack. I wanted to cry, to let the truth gush out. To tell her Mom was hurt and had disappeared. That I hadn't seen her in months. I'd fallen down a rabbit hole into an odd, surreal world of magic and murder and power. That I had abilities that scared me and I had lives depending on me and it was way too much pressure and I was in way over my head. I couldn't say all that, but I was afraid she'd know something was wrong, anyway, that my a notoriously bad poker face would give me away.

So I focused on counting each incredibly noisy tick of the wall clock, letting the distraction soothe me.

*...Three, four, five...*

"We take academic integrity very seriously here, Aggie," Mrs. Morse said at last. "You'll need to retake the test. And I want you to think about how else I might be able to help you. You only have the two classes here; the rest are at Oak Hill. You could consider finishing your AP Euro as an online course. Or you could take the AP test early. I remember my senior year, I was so ready to be done with school I had one foot out the door. It's easy to see how someone with... a lot going on in their lives... might be tempted to cut corners. Even a good girl like you. "

A good girl... Yes, I was always a good girl. Always going the right thing, always trying my best. Fighting to keep it all together. But ironically, now that I had the power to bestow good luck, I'd punched people. Stabbed people. Shot at people. I'd schemed, deceived, manipulated. Sure, it was for survival. To keep myself and Mom and the rest of the Valentines safe. But in that moment, I suddenly realized I wasn't sure if I was a good girl anymore. Could one be a good girl and a queen at the same time?

And that test. I hadn't cheated, I knew that much. I had studied. I knew the material. But when I took it, I'd been exhausted from a long night of searching for Mom and Jack. I was dozing off. Unconsciously, I must have relied on my charm—it was happening more and more lately.

Flaring a bit of charm made my normally clumsy self coordinated during gym class. It smoothed my awkward social skills at lunch and helped me remain unnoticed as I skulked around at night, searching the unlucky and unsafe corners of Detroit for Mom. It also allowed my fixated mind to wander when I would have been distraught over Jack leaving. Habit must have caused me to flare charm during the test. I'd zoned out, letting luck do the work. And luck had caused me to bubble in the right answers. Only they hadn't been the *right* right answers. It disturbed me, the idea that I'd checked out and let luck take the wheel. It wasn't like me. And if reliance on charm was impacting my school work like that, what other parts of me was it changing?

I stood.

"Mrs. Morse, I'm not sure what happened, but I'd be happy to retake the test and clear up any confusion. And everything is fine at home, it really is, but if I need anything I promise I'll reach out."

Now, on top of everything else, I was lying... *What is happening to me?*

Mrs. Morse stood, opening the door for me to exit. "I'm glad to hear that, Aggie," she said. "That's all I ask."

**4**

---

## MOLLY

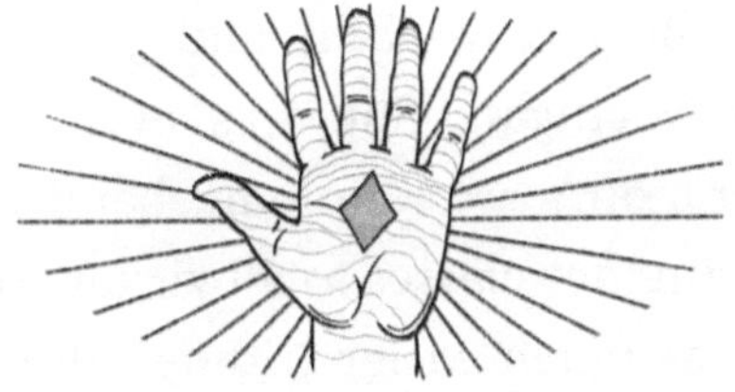

**M**olly grunted, swinging the wooden paddle with all her force. It hit the ball with a satisfying *tock* and sent it zinging between the two elderly opponents on the opposite side of the pickleball court.

"Yeah! Eat that, Flo!" Molly crowed as her vanquished opponents, Florence and Edith, slunk off the court.

Her partner, Barb, gave her a fist bump.

"Same time tomorrow?" Molly asked.

Barb shook her head, waggling her head of puffy, white hair. "Can't. Colonoscopy," she sighed as she stowed her paddle back in her gym bag and zipped it up. "Don't ever get old, Molly my dear."

Molly waved goodbye as Barb left, then sat down on a courtside bench, toweled off her face and sipped a sports drink. She didn't know what Barb was so bitter about. Sure, Barb's skin was like a mummy's and her boobs sagged down to her waist, but aside from that, the life of a retiree at Palm Vista seemed pretty sweet. Pickleball, shuffleboard and bingo were awesome. Molly even liked how all the old guys grinned appreciatively (if goonishly) whenever she went to the pool in her bikini. And not everyone here was super old. She'd noticed a few guys in their twenties hanging around the pool as well, and planned to strike up a conversation with them when the time was right.

Molly loved the blazing Palm Springs sun, especially when she thought of how chilly and gray it probably was back home in Michigan. She was even getting used to staying with her mom's two weirdo husbands.

After switching her classes to all virtual, school was now a breeze. Life was much easier without all the usual social distractions that in-person learning entailed. Before she left, Molly had made her way from being a bona fide loser to joining the pantheon of popular girls—with a little help from her former best friend Aggie. But it wasn't until she left that she realized how exhausting keeping up all those social connections had become.

*I'll never go back,* she told herself. Then she amended: *which is good, because I never* can *go back.*

Aggie had become a powerful goddess queen, which was great. Molly was happy for her, she really was. But Molly had wanted to become a demigoddess, too. So she'd started working for the other suit of good luck gods—the Diamantes. Aggie would be a Heart, Molly would be a Diamond. What could be more perfect? The catch was, to join their suit, Danusia, the Jill of Diamonds, had demanded Molly kill Aggie's mom, Rachel. Rachel had gone from being the coolest mom around to being a scary ass bad luck queen. But evil as she'd become, Molly could never have hurt Rachel—if she hadn't first hurt her crush, Lorcan.

Ah, Lorcie. What girl doesn't love a surly, tatted up leprechaun? It turned out, love plus ambition could make a girl do crazy things—including stabbing her best friend's mom.

Of course, Molly would never have been in love with Lorcan if it hadn't been for Aggie. She understood now that Aggie had used her charm power to make her fall for Lorcan. That was the only thing that could have explained how sudden and powerful her feelings for the leprechaun had been. Molly knew the signs because Aggie had charmed her into falling in love once before, with Braden from school. That had been a messed up thing to do, but this was even worse. Aggie had charmed Molly and Lorcan into falling in love just to keep Lorcan quiet about her plans during her queen trial. That made Molly nothing but a pawn. *It was sick and manipulative for Aggie to mess with our emotions like that,* Molly told herself over and over.

It justified what Molly had done to Aggie's mom. Well... Almost.

Anyway, it didn't matter now. What was done was done. Aggie was a powerful demigoddess, and she loved her mom more than anything. Friendship or no, Molly was afraid to find out what Aggie might do if Molly saw her again. So she'd hopped the first flight to Palm Springs. Molly had lost her best friend, and she could never go back to school again.

*It's fine. I'm happy. I love it here,* she told herself, for perhaps the twentieth time that day. *I don't even want to go back.*

She was bent over, stuffing her pickleball racket into her duffel bag when a voice from behind her said, "Well. You're a tricky girl to find."

She stood fast, suddenly very aware of her short tennis skirt, and wheeled to find a tall, handsome young man striding toward her. He wore a button-down shirt and a tie despite the desert heat. Her eyes traced the strong forearms revealed by his rolled up sleeves. His dark hair was meticulously styled and mischief twinkled in his almond-shaped brown eyes. She placed him immediately, even though she'd only met him once. No luck god was ever forgettable, especially not Tristaine, the Jack of Diamonds.

"Oh. Hey," she said, trying hard to sound casual.

He stopped only a foot away from her, close enough that she could smell his rich, sandalwood cologne. She would barely have had to move to stroke her fingers down his tie.

He glanced around. "You're far from home, Molly. What brings you out here to the desert? Vacation?"

Molly shrugged. "My mom moved here. I'm thinking I might stay. I like it."

Tristaine smoothly wiped a silk handkerchief across his forehead. "It's a wonderful climate—if you happen to be a lizard."

At that word—lizard—Molly's body went stiff and her hand reflexively went to her neck, where the dry, scaly skin of her *ichthyosis vulgaris* was the worst. Danusia had been giving her an expensive cream that had made it all but disappear, but she was out of it now and it had returned, worse than ever. Now, having this beautiful demigod boy staring at her, she suddenly felt very self-conscious about it.

And about her messy pony tail, and her sweaty clothes, and—

"I was concerned," Tristaine went on. "You just disappeared on us. And at such an important moment."

"Important...?" Molly frowned, confused.

Tristaine cocked his head. "Danusia made a deal with you, didn't she? Kill the Queen of Spades and you get to become one of us?"

A chill washed over Molly despite the heat. "Rachel is dead?"

Tristaine slipped the handkerchief back into his pocket. "Unfortunately, we're not sure. No one has seen her since the conflict at the Valentine house. But you did stab her. I'd say that means you fulfilled your part of the bargain."

Molly's heart leapt. "So... you'll really make me a Diamond?"

The Diamante gestured to a limousine parked at the curb. "I have a private jet waiting for us at the airport. All it needs is a passenger."

Molly's eyes lingered on the long, black car. Moments ago she'd been trying to convince herself that staying here was what she wanted. Now, that self-deception disintegrated like a sandcastle under a wave.

She wanted her fancy skin cream. She wanted money. She wanted power. She wanted to go back to her own school and be prom queen. She wanted to make out with Lorcan again. She wanted to ride on this sweet-smelling, elegant boy's private jet. She wanted it all.

"I'll just go back to the condo. Tell my mom. Get my stuff."

Tristaine smiled. "No need. I've taken the liberty of doing some shopping for you. And you can call your mom on the way. I'd be happy to talk to her. I usually have excellent luck talking to parents."

"I'm all sweaty."

The demogod's eyes roved over Molly's body in a way that made her blush. "Not to worry. There's a shower on the plane."

"If Aggie sees me again she's going to kill me," Molly said. She meant it figuratively, but hearing it spoken aloud like that made her think of how ruthless and often violent luck gods truly were. Aggie was a gentle person—normally. But she would do anything for her mom. And her queen power was no joke. Between Aggie and her mom—if Rachel was still alive—it was very possible that going back to Detroit was dangerous.

Tristaine seemed unphased. "If Aggie wants to hurt you, she'll have to go through me first," he said, offering her his arm.

Molly hesitated only an instant. Then she linked arms and let the Diamond lead her to the waiting limo—and back into the world of the luck gods.

**5**

---

**AGGIE**

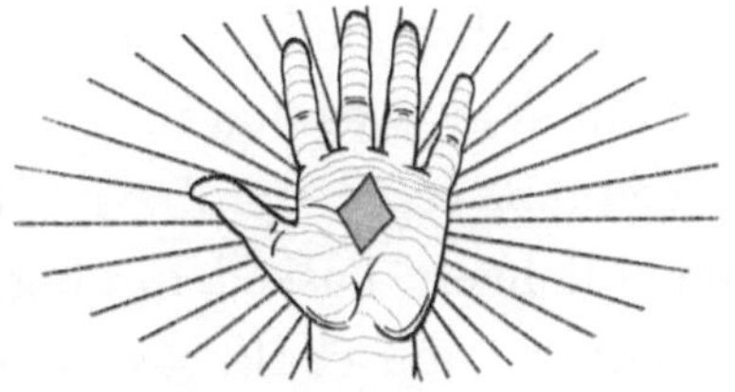

I sat cross-legged on the stone floor, eating strawberry cheesecake and staring at the elderly demigoddess who knelt at the center of the cavern-like room. Before her rose the glowing, ruby-colored obelisk of hearts, a six-foot-tall crystal tower carved with glyphs. The ace's hands were pressed to the stone, her eyes shut tight. Her body was so rigid, her breathing so shallow, and her face so wizened that someone could easily have mistaken her for a mummy. But I knew she was alive. And I suspected she was ignoring me.

"Mmm. This is some good cheesecake, Your Worship. You're missing out," I smacked my lips, taking another bite, but the old lady didn't so much as twitch.

I sighed. The ace, grand matriarch of the Valentine family, spent most of her time in a trancelike state. Normally cheesecake was enough to rouse her; she loved the stuff even more than I loved a nice honey latte. But ever since she'd tried and failed to absorb the shard of spade obelisk into our own obelisk, she'd remained unresponsive. Had fighting off the incursion of dark magic taken too much out of her? Or was she simply so busy with her work controlling good luck through the obelisk that she'd lost contact with the outside world? It was hard to know. None of the books about the metaphysical underpinnings of luck magic I'd read over the past few months shed much light on the power of aces. Their purpose, how they operated, and how the obelisk worked—all remained shrouded in mystery. It was super annoying. What I did know was that they had some psychic abilities—which could be very helpful to me at the moment.

"So, who killed Michael?" I asked, forking another bite of dessert into my mouth. "You could save a lot of time and effort by just telling me."

If there was one thing my scientist mom had taught me, it was to pursue the simplest solution first when approaching a complex problem. And the simplest solution to the problem of figuring who killed the king was to ask the ace.

If she would just answer me.

I scowled. "Listen, you're the one who made Michael choose me as queen in the first place. Don't you want me to stay queen? Because Ten and her posse are going to eat me alive if I don't prove I didn't kill Michael."

The ace said nothing.

With a groan of frustration, I boxed up the cheesecake and rose.

"Fine. I'm taking the cheesecake and I'm going," I said primly. When she didn't answer I got louder. "What if I take a hammer to that dumb obelisk of yours? Will you speak up then?"

The obelisk itself had aways creeped me out. Its unblinking crimson glow reminded me of warm, fresh blood, and its vibe was exactly like the stone monolith in *2001 a Space Odyssey.*

Thinking about that movie made me remember the day Mom had first shown it to me. I must have been twelve years old. We'd both gotten poison ivy helping Dad garden in the backyard and we'd sat watching the movie on the couch with calamine lotion all over our hands and arms, eating out of a popcorn bowl with only our mouths like dogs and laughing at one another the whole time. The memory stuck in my heart like a bur, making my mood even worse.

Mom... I needed the Valentine suit's support to find her. To get the suit's support, I needed to find the King's killer. The ace could do that for me. It would be so easy. All she had to do was open her eyes and say a name. The rest of the suit would believe her. They had to believe her; she was the ace. And yet she refused. It made me so mad my hands shook.

"Well, thanks for nothing," I said, turning to go.

A sound. A small, plaintive groan.

I spun to find the ace's head turning slowly my way, like a flower toward sunlight. Her mouth was open, her dry little tongue poking out. Without opening her eyes, she moaned again and her mouth gaped wider, like the maw of some grotesque baby bird.

I glanced down at the box in my hands.

"You want some?"

I took the cheesecake out again and forked a bite into the ace's waiting mouth. She gulped it down and opened her mouth for more. Five bites later, her eyes fluttered open.

"Mm," she grunted. "I was down deep that time."

I crossed my arms and tapped my foot, trying to look less annoyed and impatient than I felt.

"Well, sorry to disturb your beauty sleep, but I need your help. King Michael is dead."

She nodded, but neither sadness nor surprise altered the expression on her stoic, lined face.

"And I need you to tell me who killed him."

"Bite, please," the ace said.

Repressing a growl of frustration, I spooned her another bite.

"I don't know who killed him," she said when she'd gulped it down.

I threw my hands up. "I thought you were omniscient or something."

"Or something," she said with a smile.

"Well, could you use the obelisk to find out?" I nearly shouted. "Ten and her people are acting like I did it. They say they won't follow me or listen to me until I prove I'm innocent."

"Hmm. That's insubordination," the ace pointed out. "You'd be within your rights to decapitate them. Or kill one as a warning to the rest. That would be the traditional remedy."

I winced. "I'd rather not. You know. Mess. Blood. Morals."

The ace shrugged, as if it made no difference to her.

"Why don't you know?" I pressed. "Aren't you at least semi-omniscient? I mean, I get that semi-omniscient is a bit of an oxymoron since omniscient means all-knowing, and semi means, you know, *not all*, but—"

"Things are cloudy these days," the ace interrupted, squinted. "The future. The past. Even the present."

"Why?" I pressed.

Her sharp old eyes bored into me. "The future is cloudy because you haven't created it yet."

"Me?"

She nodded. "As for the rest..." she shook her head. "Perhaps that spade incursion damaged our obelisk. Or maybe I'm just getting old. Either way, the threads are too tangled for me to unravel them."

"What about my mom?" Aggie said. "And Jack? Can you see them? Where are they? Can you at least see if they're okay?"

The ace's eyes narrowed to slits again as she concentrated, then she slowly shook her head. "Jack is on his path," she said. "Perhaps that may be the problem. His gravity is warping all the other possibilities, pulling them out of alignment."

There was a lot of metaphysical stuff to unpack here and someday I wanted nothing more than to quiz the ace about it, but for now I felt like I had to cut to the chase, before she fell back into her trance again.

"You mean Jack's quest to unite the four suits?"

She nodded. "Understand the past and you'll understand the future. It's all a cycle, Aggie. Jack is the key."

I took a steadying breath as I tried to tease logic out of the nonsense. "Okay. So how do I understand the past?"

"There is a certain book... there used to be a copy in the Valentine library," the ace said. "Oh, I forget the title, but it has a reddish cover and a copper clasp. The symbol of

Uthule is on the front. Read that book, and you'll understand the path Jack is on."

"Okay..." I said. "And what about finding Jack? And finding King Michael's killer? And what about my mom?"

The ace pulled one hand off the obelisk and reached out to me. I wanted to recoil from her fingers, which were as thin as twigs and charred pitch black from the power of the obelisk—but I made myself hold still while she grasped my hand. She squeezed so hard it hurt.

"Find the book," the ace said.

❧♡♤◇♧☙

"I can fight, you know," Deuce protested, sounding deeply irritated—maybe even offended.

"I know you can fight," I said. "But who knows the library better than you?"

"She has a point," Mina said, adjusting her sling. Aside from the broken arm, she was okay—luckily.

Deuce sighed, but didn't bother arguing. Everyone knew he had read more books in that library than anyone else in the suit, except perhaps the ace.

The three of us sat in the Valentine mansion movie room. It had massively cushy, huge leather chairs that could swivel to face one another and was loaded up with a popcorn machine, an espresso machine, and tons of snacks. It was also located in the mansion's lower level, which reminded me of the basement hangout Mom and I shared in our old house before it burned down. Since becoming queen, I'd made this place my de-facto war room. Right now, one of my favorite films, *Repo! The Genetic Opera*, played in the background, creating an eerie backdrop for our conversation and also making it harder for the other Valentines to overhear.

I put a hand on Deuce's shoulder.

"The ace made it clear. We *have* to find that book."

"Fine. But what are you going to be doing?" he asked.

"Mina and I are going to scope out some of the Clubs' operations. We know the two black suits have been working together. Maybe the Clubs have been harboring the Spades while Mom recovers from her injuries."

We had sprite spies who kept an eye on the Blackovers and their activities, but they hadn't expected to find Mom at one of their hideouts. It was quite possible they'd missed signs of her presence. Checking into the Clubs was part of our investigation of King Michael's murder, too. Whenever a Valentine was killed, the Blackovers were always top suspects. By investigating them, we'd be killing two prover-bial birds with one stone.

Deuce pouted. "I still don't like it. Mina has a broken arm. And you ladies are going to be out kicking ass while I'm in the library like—like—"

"Like Giles from *Buffy the Vampire Slayer*?" I supplied. Mina gave me a confused look. "A 90's show. My Mom used to love it," I said.

Of course, I didn't have to explain to Deuce. He was the only one I knew who was as big a nerd as I was.

"Fine," he grunted. "But as soon as I find the book, I'm meeting you. Gotta protect my queen, right?"

"Right," Mina said.

I sighed. "Please don't call me that."

"Sorry, Deuce," Mina said. "I've tried looking for stuff in

that massive library. I bet we'll solve the King's murder *and* find Jack and Queen Rachel *way* before you find that book."

Deuce gave her a fiery look. "Challenge accepted," he said. Then he turned and literally sprinted out of the room in a full Naruto run, leaving Mina and me laughing in his wake.

**6**

———

**JACK**

Jack's arm quivered, his biceps and forearm burning, sweat beading on his brow. His pips burned, too—the heart on his right hand and the spade on his left. His opponent, Thad Blackover, grinned like a maniac, though he was red-faced with exertion, too. His fellow Clubs were gathered around bellowing taunts, encouragement, and threats, all while sloshing beer and rocking the table with their rowdy cheering. Jack glanced back at his only companion, Shade the Spade, as he thought of him, who watched with indifference. *Some backup. He couldn't care less if these animals tore me apart*, Jack thought. *I should never have come here.* But it was too late now, and there was little time to reflect on the mistake. Across the table,

Thad snarled and Jack's arm jolted back a few inches, pain lancing through his muscles.

*Mental note, never arm wrestle a Blackover King on his home turf.*

And yet, though Thad probably had about a hundred pounds of muscle on him, Jack could feel his pips sussing out paths to victory, ways to undermine his opponent, searching for tiny accidents of physiology and concentration that could spell bad luck for Thad—and good luck for Jack. Thad's hand could cramp. Jack could get a burst of adrenaline. Thad's elbow could slip. Jack could shift his wrist so he had perfect leverage. Thad might even suffer a brain aneurism from all that clenching.

That was probably wouldn't happen, but a guy could hope. Jack despised Thad. Walking into the Clubs Brewery, he couldn't keep his gaze from lingering on the fire pit where, a few months, before Thad had gleefully tortured Jack, nearly burning him alive. Thad had also been a cruel husband to Jack's one-time love, Carlotta Blackover, the suit's former queen. Once Thad found out about her and Jack, Carlotta had disappeared, and Jack was fairly certain he'd killed her—or had her killed. Even though Carlotta had betrayed Jack, she didn't deserve that.

There were other reasons Jack hated Thad, too. Reasons that went way, way back. But as much as he would have enjoyed humiliating Thad in this contest of brute strength in front of his entire suit, Jack wasn't ready to tip his hand and show that he had that much power. That is, if his combined charm and hex *could* deliver him a victory, which was a big *if*.

"Draw?" Jack asked through clenched teeth.

Thad huffed a breath. With his thick black beard,

massive shoulders and sharp, dark eyes, he looked like a Viking warlord in motorcycle leathers.

"I promised to tear off your arm and beat you with it," he reminded Jack. "Your arm's still attached."

Annoyance at Thad's stubbornness made Jack's charm flare. Thad's arm pulsed backward, almost causing him to tip over on his bench. The watching Blackovers gave a roar of unintelligible banter. In Thad's eyes, Jack saw the first faint glimmer of doubt. That was satisfaction enough for Jack. He let the flaring charm and hex subside, and with a mighty growl, Thad pressed harder on Jack's arm, until his knuckles thumped to the table. The Blackovers cheered wildly, some going so far as to taunt Jack. A tall blonde woman gave him a shove. Another tossed a beer bottle that narrowly missed his head and shattered on the pavers behind him.

Shade took a step forward, but Jack stayed him with a gesture.

Someone had given Thad a congratulatory bath of pilsner and he now stood, towering over Jack to wring out his beard and spit beer onto the ground.

He sat again, laughing. "Ah, Jack Valentine. Not bad, not bad. You've been hitting the gym, eh? Or maybe it's those two little marks on your hands that make you so strong. Tell me, how do you like having the powers of black and red both at your disposal?"

Jack gave a crooked smile, still rubbing the heart-marked hand Thad had just about ripped off. "It's a bit like trying to ride two horses that are running in opposite directions."

"Or two women, eh?" He banged the table with a huge fist and chuckled at his own joke. "You've had your share of women, eh Jack of Hearts?"

*Careful,* Jack thought. Thad was baiting him into asking

about Carlotta. He was probably dying to tell Jack what terrible things he'd done to her. And Jack wasn't sure he could listen to such provocations and not respond.

*Thad would love nothing more than to kill me,* Jack thought. The only reason the Blackovers had welcomed him into their headquarters at all was because he was here as official envoy of Rachel, Queen of the Morbuses, and because the Spade mark on his hand made him a fellow black suit. There were conventions going back thousands of years that required due respect between the two dark suits. If not for those factors, Jack had no doubt Thad would have tried to butcher him already.

"We're here to talk about your love life, Thad, not mine," Jack said smoothly. "My queen is still open to a union."

Thad feigned surprise. "That little thing with the strawberry hair and the glasses? Ha. I'd crush her. And she's freshly widowed, isn't she? Still mourning. Condolences on the loss of your king, by the way."

*Aggie.* The whisper of her name through his mind made him miss her, quickening the pain that had been there day and night since they'd last been together. The thought of Thad anywhere near Aggie? It made him bristle with jealous rage. But Jack swept all these emotions away in a single, slow breath and a subtle flaring of charm.

"Michael was never my king," Jack said. "And you know which queen I mean."

Thad's mocking grin widened. "Ah, the other queen. Rachel, Queen of Spades. The heart queen's mother. What a tangled web we have, eh? Rachel. Yes, a tall, scary woman, that one. But stunning. A thoroughbred, if you don't mind me borrowing your horse analogy. I'm sure you won't mind.

You never minded borrowing from me when it came to women, did you, Jack?"

Back to Carlotta again. Jack clenched his teeth. *Don't take the bait.*

Thad sipped his beer and stroked his beard thoughtfully. "I heard Queen Rachel was dead. Stabbed by some syco."

"She is very much alive," Jack said.

"More like half dead, from what I've heard," Marley said from behind Thad. Marley was one of Thad's highest lieutenants—Jack wasn't completely sure of his current rank—but he was ruthless and capable, and probably the smartest Club, now that Carlotta was gone and Gallo the Jack was dead.

"She's recovered," Jack said.

Marley snorted. "Why'd she send you, then? My guess is she wants us to think she's stronger than she is."

"Shut up, Marley," Thad said. "No one asked you."

Marley pursed his lips and took a step back. Jack noted the deep purple light glowing from within his clenched fists. It made Jack think of something his grandfather had once told him about German Shepherds. *Watch out for smart dogs,* he'd said. *Those are the ones that will bite you.* He made a mental note to learn more about Marley and his relationship with Thad. If he were disgruntled with Thad's leadership, that might be a vulnerability....

Jack went on. "Our queen has simply been planning her next move. It's going to change everything. And I think you're going to want to be part of it."

Thad raised a thick eyebrow. "You think so, eh? You think I'm dying to be second-fiddle to a woman who gives me the freaking heebie-jeebies?"

A few Blackovers chuckled nervously.

"I think you're a man who understands power," Jack said.

"I am," Thad said. "And she's a woman who'd like to take mine."

The usual chatter and tumult of the Clubs headquarters ebbed to a tense silence as everyone watched Jack and Thad. Jack forced himself to take a slow, calming breath and steepled his hands. He knew it would be impossible for Thad not to notice the strange interplay of the light from his pips, red light of charm mingling with the deep purple glow of hex within his tented fingers.

"She's a woman who'd like to share your power," Jack corrected. "And share some of hers in return. The way all great alliances in history have worked. But if you're not interested in sharing power, then yes. She'll take it."

Thad grew still, his eyes narrowing to slits, his beard quivering with the tension in his jaw. "That's big talk for a rotisserie chicken," he said. There was no mirth in the taunt, and Jack couldn't help but remember what it had been like last time he was here, being tossed over the blazing bonfire over and over again. If he shut his eyes he could still feel the pain of those burns, still smell the reek of his own burning hair and clothes.

At Thad's tough words, the surrounding Clubs shifted almost imperceptibly closer, hands drifting to weapons. Marley sidled up to stand at his boss' right shoulder. That Amazonian blonde woman with half her head shaved came up on his other side.

Thad flicked his fingers, as if shooing away a gnat.

"Off you go, Jack. And tell your queen next time she sends dogs to deliver her messages, I'm sending them back neutered."

A fire sparked in Jack's chest, but he swallowed it down.

"Don't worry," Jack said. "She won't send me. And you won't see me again, either. Not until you're handing over your crown."

Thad tried to laugh, but it turned into a quivering snarl instead. Jack rose to his feet and forced himself to walk away from the table. This was the most perilous part of the whole exchange, insulting Thad then turning his back on him. Jack's every muscle twitched with tension as he waited for the sting of a bullet, the bite of a blade. But it didn't come. All the Blackovers hurled after him was an icy silence. The Blackover escort moved in, surrounding him as he made his way toward the exit.

Shade fell in beside him. "Nice work," Shade spat under his breath. "Two months I spent building trust with these guys and you come in here and insult their king? And don't think I'm not going to tell Queen Rachel exactly what went down here. I—"

Jack spun and caught him by the neck, squeezing and flaring charm at the same time. Shade made a choking sound, his eyes going big.

"You seem to have forgotten your place, Shade, so let me remind you. I was crushing bad luck gods when you were still a two bit auto part smuggler," Jack growled. "And I outrank you."

It was his good luck hand that had caught Shade, and hurting people with good luck required some mental gymnastics. So Shade was able to flare hex and karate chop Jack in the forearm, forcing him to break his grip. Shade tried slamming Jack with a right hook but Jack stepped in, flaring hex and charm the same time. He blocked the punch with one hand while delivering a blow to Shade's solar plexus with the other. Shade stumbled back, gasping for breath, but he didn't charge in and continue his attack. Instead he stood tall, his eyes fixed on Jack, burning with anger. But Jack thought he might see something else there, too. Grudging admiration. Shade might have been a criminal in his former life, but he was a smart man. He understood power. And he respected it. In truth, Jack respected Shade, too, especially now, as he calmed himself and ran his hands down his shirt, wiping out the wrinkles.

"By all means, keep killing each other," Marley Blackover said, sidling up to them, smiling behind his ever-present dark glasses.

Shade sniffed. "Nah, that's alright. Jack and I are going to reach an understanding. First we conquer the world. Then we can fight each other over the continents. Right, Jacky boy?"

Jack nodded. "Right."

As they resumed their walk toward the exit, Jack turned his attention to the Blackover. "What about you, Marley?"

"What about me?" Marley grunted.

"You're an intelligent guy. Aren't you sick of being that meathead's punching bag?"

The blonde woman Blackover—Moira, Jack thought her name was—cut a quick glance at Marley. But as usual, Marley's poker face remained perfect, impassive. They'd reached a metal gate that led to the parking lot and Marley pushed it open on screeching hinges.

"I am but a humble servant, Mr. Valentine," he said, giving Jack and Shade a genteel *after you* gesture toward the exit.

"All I'm saying is, nothing is permanent. You should think about your options," Jack's eyes flicked to Moira and he flared a bit of charm, making her blush. "You too," he told her, his sweeping gaze taking in both Blackovers and the three syco guards who stood behind them.

Then he and Shade turned and strode out into the dark parking lot.

"Seriously, though. What are we supposed to tell the queen?" Shade asked when they were out of earshot and the gate had clanked shut behind them.

"Plan B," Jack said, opening the door of the long black Mercedes Rachel had lent them.

Shade swore under his breath and shook his head. "I'm not even gonna ask…"

Jack was about to get into the car when something caught his eye, a flicker of movement on the far end of the parking lot, where the streetlights barely reached. Then flash of red. Shade noticed Jack looking and followed his gaze, but whatever had been there had receded, leaving only shadow behind.

"What?" Shade asked.

Jack tossed Shade the car's key fob. "You go ahead. I'll catch up."

Shade seemed as if he might argue about it—he often did argue when Jack gave an order—but instead he sighed and came around to the driver's side of the car.

"I'd tell you to be careful," Shade said. "But if you die, I move up in rank. Jack of Spades. I like the sound of that."

Jack eyed Shade. A glimmer of smile had lit up the man's face, causing the spider web tattoo to crinkle at the corner of his eye. If he weren't such a power-hungry prick, Jack could almost start to like him. But then, Jack was a power-hungry prick too, wasn't he?

"Unfortunately for you, I'm surprisingly hard to kill," Jack said, and he hurried off across the dark parking lot.

7

---

## AGGIE

The plan couldn't have been simpler. Zip over to the Clubs' brewery headquarters. Capture a Blackover or one of their higher level sycos. Drag them into the back of a van, interrogate them about the whereabouts of the Spades— maybe scare them a bit—then drop them back off. Easy. The whole thing should have taken half an hour max, and it should have been a breeze with my queen-level power.

But as usual, things were not going according to plan.

The blade of my short sword clanked and screeched against a Blackover syco's metal pipe. For a moment our weapons were locked, then with a flare of charm and a grunt of fury, I shoved my attacker backwards. Two more sprang forward to take his place.

The debacle started simply enough. Mina and I had parked the van in a dimly-lit area at the back of the parking lot then crouched behind the dumpster and waited. Soon enough, the two of Clubs (Stallion was his name, if the intel reports I read were correct) emerged from the back of the brewery, tossed a trash bag in the dumpster and started puffing on his vape. A lucky opportunity if I'd had ever seen one. I give the signal to Mina and we sprung our trap—just as five more Clubs and sycos happened to emerge from the back door.

Very bad luck.

Now, what had begun as a quick grab-and-go maneuver had morphed into a pitched battle in which Mina and I were decidedly outnumbered. We stood back-to-back, ringed by six enemies. From behind I heard Mina's battle cry, which was weirdly cute, like the mew of an angry cat. But the Blackovers would be fools to underestimate her, even with one broken arm. Mina had been a Valentine much longer than I had, and I knew firsthand from sparring with her that she packed an incredible amount of ferocity in her tiny frame. As if to punctuate my thought, Mina kicked a tall syco in the face. Another one saw me distracted and lurched in with a two-by-four he'd grabbed from the dumpster. I flared charm and hit it just right, so my sword slashed through it in one swipe. Another syco reached for a revolver at his waist, but the one called Stallion stayed his hand.

"Nah, man. You got other guys in the line of fire. And she's a *queen.*"

I could still make his gun go off in his pants, however. I flared charm to do just that, except another syco and a club charged me at once from both sides—one brandishing a carving knife, the other a baseball bat. I flared more charm and ducked. The two weapons clacked together, the knife buried in the bat. Very lucky. Still crouching I spun, sweeping the legs out from the syco on my right, then kicked backwards, planting a foot in the crotch of the syco on my left. Both toppled, and for a second I felt proud of myself— until the backdoor of the Brewery banged open and more Blackovers poured out—Marley, the tall blonde they called Moira, and another female, all of them heavily armed.

"Queen Kindergarten," Marley crowed in greeting. "Our paths keep crossing."

"Unfortunately," I said.

Mina came to my side. She was flaring charm, but dimly, and I glanced over to see she wore a grimace on her face and her right arm hung limply at her side, her sling snapped. She was only supposed to be the getaway driver for this mission. Now I cursed myself for agreeing to take her at all.

"To be honest, I think it's time we stopped meeting like this. What was it Thad said?" Marley asked his lady companions. "Did he want them dead? Or alive?"

They all raised their guns toward me, but a wave of hex washed over us then so strong it made my stomach clench. But it wasn't coming from the Blackovers. The two women Clubs fell to their knees. Marley doubled over, one hand on his head, his trademark sunglasses falling off his face and into the gravel.

I turned to see a figure emerging from the shadows, and my breath hitched in my throat. Both his hands were raised palms outward, like a saint on the side of a votive candle, the glowing makers on each palm glowing ominously.

A spade. And a heart.

What's it like to be in love with a ghost?

I guess I always was in love with one in a way, because of my dad. But Dad never showed up again like Jack Valentine was now, looking beautiful and arrogant and pissed off, his enviably shiny blond hair just the right amount disheveled, his blue eyes sharp as razors as he fixed them on Marley.

"I'll take it from here, Marley," Jack said evenly.

The Blackover cocked his head. "Not this time, Jack. I have a score to settle with your little queen. And I know my king would be delighted to get his hands on her. Who knows, she might be the key we need to make our little alliance work. You'd have to play nice if we had your little queenie, wouldn't you, Jack?"

Jack's jaw clenched, his hands drifting almost imperceptibly toward his weapons. I didn't know what Marley was talking about when he mentioned an alliance, but I was pretty sure I didn't want to be Thad's pawn in whatever game he and Jack were playing. I backed toward Jack, flaring more charm, just as Jack came forward to stand shoulder-to-shoulder with me. Mina scrambled behind us, holding her injured arm.

"Marley, I'm surprised at you," Jack said. "I always took you for the smartest one in this rabble. Thad doesn't matter. He's the past."

"And you're the future?" Marley scoffed.

Jack shook his head. "No, you are. If you play your cards right."

"Wow. Excellent pun," I said under my breath.

Grim as he was, Jack let a faint smile slip.

I saw the Blackover Moira inching toward us, trying to flank me on the right and pretended not to notice.

Marley's brow lowered. "Treason? That's your proposal for me?"

Jack shrugged. "Change is inevitable, my friend. We either evolve—or we die."

Puns. Science terms. Jack was obviously trying to flirt with me.

"I'm loyal. Unlike you," Marley countered.

"Then that's too bad," Jack said. "For you."

Jack took my arm and stepped back, pulling me with him. Marley and his sycos leaned in, tense fingers on triggers.

"Jack," a voice said from behind us, and I looked back to see Shade emerging from the shadows where Jack had come from, wariness and concern in his voice. All was still and taut for a moment, then Moira lunged forward and grabbed my wrist. I swung my short sword at her and she blocked it with her dagger in a clash of steel. I could almost taste the tension as every Blackover slowly squeezed their trigger and—

"Catch!" Shade shouted behind us, and a whirling cannister lobbed over our heads, jettisoning dark smoke. It was the same sort of cannister I'd seen Shade deploying at the protest.

Reflexively, one of the sycos caught it as if it were football. When Marley saw that his eyes went wide with terror. He put his shirt over his face, stumbling backward.

"Run!" Shade shouted from behind us, and I felt his hand tugging on the back of my jacket.

Marley was also shouting, "Run!" and "Drop it!" but his syco continued to hold the smoking cannister, starting down at it dumbly.

Jack, Mina, Shade and I sprinted across the parking lot.

"Here!" Shade shouted, leading us toward a long, black German luxury sedan. We threw ourselves in and slammed the doors. Shade put the vehicle in gear and launched us into the night in a spray of gravel.

❦

I grabbed Jack's chest, pinched and twisted.

"Ouch! What the hell was that?" he winced out of my grasp, sliding as far from me as he could get in the back seat of the large sedan.

"That," I said, "was a purple nurple. And there's a lot more where that came from."

Shade, who was driving, smirked at us in the rearview mirror. "Damn. And they say her mom is the savage one."

Jack cradled his bruised pectoral, looking offended.

"You said you were going to make sure my mom was okay..." I snapped.

"I did," Jack countered. "I texted you that night. I told you she was alive and that she was going to recover."

"Yeah," I said. "And then you ghosted me for the next two months. No calls. No texts. No visits to the Valentine house."

Jack looked down at his lap, chastened, as we jostled over a pothole.

"That wasn't very nice, Jack," Shade said, needling us both.

"Shut up," Jack and I said in unison, but Shade continued to smirk at us in the rearview mirror.

A moment of heavy silence hung over us.

"You owe me like a million answers, but I don't even know where to begin asking questions," I said.

Mina looked back at us from the passenger seat.

"How about you ask him where he's been?" she suggested.

I shrugged and glared at Jack with a look that said, *well?*

He tousled his hair with a hand.

"I was with your mom," he said. "Keeping her safe while she recovered."

"Great. That doesn't explain why you couldn't answer a text," I pressed.

He shifted in his seat, antsy. "I was also training in hex," he said. "You just finished Valentine training. You know how demanding, how... *consuming* it can be. I didn't want to be around you until I knew I was able to control the bad luck work."

I supposed that was valid. Good luck work compelled us to help people. Bad luck work might have given him the urge to hurt me. But I wasn't nearly ready to let him off the hook yet.

"Okay, fine. You've been busy studying up on your bad luck power," I said. "Now you're palling around with the Blackovers?" I nodded back toward the brewery.

"That was a diplomatic mission," Jack said. "On behalf of the queen."

"I'm your queen," I reminded him.

The steel in my voice jerked Jack to attention and had everyone in the van looking at me. I even startled myself a little.

"Of course," Jack said. "Everything I've done has been—"

I held up a hand. "Do *not* say *for me.*"

Jack's eyes narrowed. "Everything I've done has been *necessary*," he finished.

Tension fairly crackled between us.

"I feel like the two of you should maybe talk in private," Mina suggested.

"Yeah," Shade said. "Get a room."

We both glared at him. Mina stifled a laugh.

"No need," I said coolly. "Just take us to my mom."

Jack crossed his arms. "We can't do that."

"Why not?"

"Because she's not awake, for one thing," Jack said.

"Not awake?" I repeated, confused.

"I originally thought the doctor treating her had put her in a medical coma or something after she was stabbed. But now I think maybe it was the obelisk. Regardless, she's been recovering. The doctor says when she wakes up, she should be fine."

"My mom has been in a coma for two months?" I said, breathless. "Take me to her. Now."

"No," Jack said again. "It's not safe. She's surrounded by a lot of firepower. And the obelisk is insanely protective of her. If you come near her, especially before she's healed, I have no doubt the shard of obelisk that controls your mom will have you killed."

His words chilled me, but I wasn't going to be deterred. "Then I'll bring my own army, then," I said.

Shade snorted. "Like you got one."

I glared at him. "Excuse me?"

"Word on the street is, even your own suit's not entirely behind you," he said. "You know. Factions. Division. Strife?"

"Yeah, thanks," I said. "If I need a thesaurus I'll be sure to look you up." I aimed my fury back at Jack, who put up his hands defensively.

"Hey, we're luck gods," Jack said. "You know everyone spies on everyone."

I bit my lip. "Okay. So maybe you're right. The whole suit isn't behind me. They're accusing me of killing the King."

Shade gave a loud laugh. "How? You're mini."

"She *is* a queen," Jack reminded him. "I've seen royals smaller than her kill Tens like you using charm alone. So I'd show some respect."

This finally caused Shade to lapse into silence. Jack's eyes met mine and lingered, both of us loathe to look away. I couldn't help but flash back to long summer afternoons spent in his bedroom. Talking. Kissing. Watching movies. Just being together. He felt so close then, the warmth of his body seeping into mine, making me feel so safe. So real. So loved. Now, he seemed as distant as the Oort cloud. But God, how I wanted to pull him close.

"So that's what you were doing tonight?" Jack asked. "Looking for evidence about who killed the King?"

I nodded and explained my conversation with Ten—how I wouldn't have the suit's full support until I found out who King Michael's real killer was.

When I'd finished, I looked at Jack sharply. "Do you know who killed him?"

He met my probing gaze and shook his head. "No. The Clubs aren't a bad place to start, though... But listen, you've never done an investigation like this before. You can't just blaze in and start interrogating random luck gods. You have to be systematic."

I was a scientist. Being systematic was in my blood—and Jack knew that.

"You don't have to mansplain investigating to me," I said. "I know how to investigate things."

"Looked more like you were about to get your ass

whooped," Shade said. Jack gave him a look and he mimed zipping his mouth shut.

"That's not all," I said. "Ten and her clique also want to pick my king."

Jack watched me intently. "Cobe?"

I nodded.

"And who do you want?"

All oxygen seemed to suddenly disappear from the car. I felt light-headed. In a big bang-like expansion, everyone and everything else seemed to fade away at near light speed, leaving Jack and I alone together at the center of our own spinning galaxy.

"I have to get Mom back," I finally managed to say. "To do that, I need my suit behind me. To get their allegiance, I have to find Michael's killer. Then I'll pick my king."

A breathless silence held us in its grasp. My whole mind was filled with Jack's azure eyes. With his face, striped by shifting shadow. With his body, finally close enough to touch after being distant for so long.

"Maybe you could use some help?" he said.

*No,* part of me silently railed. *Not after you disappeared on me. Not when I don't know if I can trust you. Not—* But without my consent, my mouth twitched with something like a smile.

"Maybe I could," I said.

8

———

## JACK

It hurt to look at Aggie, sitting there on the far side of the booth wolfing down her bagel and egg sandwich. This was the same Coney Island where he and Deuce had taken her to explain luck gods to her, where she'd first tried to use her power. That had been only a handful of months ago, but it seemed like years. How she had changed since that day. How everything had changed.

She glanced up from her plate, caught him staring, and paused her chewing. "What?" she said through a mouthful of eggs.

Jack couldn't help but laugh. "Queen Aggie," he said with a bittersweet smile.

She swallowed her bite and took a sip of coffee. Not only

did she have the power to control good luck, Aggie could also drink incredible amounts of coffee at all hours of the day and still sleep. A true superpower. Not like Jack. These days, dreams, nightmares, and premonitions kept him up all night, coffee or no.

"I'm just remembering when we were first here," he said. "And I was showing you how to use your powers. Remember? With the saltshakers?"

Back then, they'd knocked a saltshaker off the table and it had taken all Aggie's concentration to make it land on the floor upright. Now, she pointed her fork toward the ceiling, took the saltshaker and tossed it into the air. It soared high over their heads then flipped down to land miraculously on the upturned tongs of Aggie's fork. It sat there, perfectly balanced, as she took another bite of her sandwich with the other hand, the light of her flaring pip making the bagel glow red.

She gave him a smug grin, chewing again, and Jack casually took the saltshaker off the fork and dusted his eggs with it.

"Not bad," he said lightly. In truth, it was a bit scary how *not bad* Aggie was. She was young and impulsive still, but she was already far more powerful than Queen Aubra had ever been. The question was, what would she do with that power? And would she live long enough to make use of it? The lives of luck gods were often short and brutal, but Jack would do everything in his power to make sure the answer to that second question was *yes*.

"If you expect this deal to happen, you're going to need to be honest with me," Aggie said suddenly.

He paused and looked at her, a bite of eggs halfway to his mouth. "Deal?"

Her eyes narrowed. "Jack, come on," she said. "I need help finding Michael's killer. You want to be king. Let's call this what it is."

Jack lowered his fork and sighed. "Aggie…"

"Don't say you care about me. If you cared you wouldn't have disappeared for so long. If you cared—" She paused, then shook her head, negating whatever she'd been about to say. "If we're going to work together, and if I'm going to give you more power in the Valentines suit, I'm going to need you to explain it to me."

"Explain what?"

"Everything," she leveled a glare at him. "As long as I've known you you've been scheming. Every time I ask about it, you treat me like a little kid, pat me on the head and send me on my way. No more. I want to know where you've been, what you intend to do, and why you're doing it. The truth. Everything. I want to help you. But I can't do it if you leave me in the dark."

Jack recoiled a bit at the verbal barrage.

"Speak," Aggie prompted.

"Well. Now you are talking like a queen." Jack sipped his water and cleared his throat. "Okay. All cards on the table. Pun intended. Like I already said, I've been with your mom, watching over her as she got well. And I've been learning to use hex. As for what I intend, I think you already know—"

"I want to hear you to say it," Aggie said, a brittle edge to her voice. Jack understood her hostility, but it still stung.

"I intend," he said slowly. "To join all four suits, become king of all four, and then use that power to end the system of the luck gods—forever."

There. He'd finally said it out loud. It felt good, released some tension deep within him. And yet, hearing the words spoken, he couldn't help but notice how arrogant and insane they sounded.

"You want to end the luck gods," Aggie said slowly. "Because of the violence? Because they're constantly at war with one another?"

Jack knew Aggie had seen firsthand what a meat grinder the system of the four suits could be. Several luck gods she knew had already met their ultimate fate. Aubra. Ari. Gallo. Dubs had been maimed. Her Mom had nearly died, and worse than that, she was losing her moral compass, her identity.

But it wasn't just that...

"The luck gods hurt one another, yes," he said. "But they hurt others, too. Innocent people."

Aggie nodded. "The bad luck work."

"Sure," Jack agreed. "But it's not just the dark suits. Good luck work can hurt people, too. Say you shift things so that someone wins the lottery. That means someone else doesn't win. Who's to say that the person you picked is more worthy?"

Aggie tapped her chin with a forefinger, thinking. "*The work* tells us. And we assume the work comes through the obelisk," she mused. "But how do we know the obelisk is correct or moral or whatever?"

"Exactly," Jack said. "They, we, distort the fabric—the distribution—of luck. We don't know what this world would look like if we weren't tugging at its strings all the time. But we do know that luck gods regularly get killed in this never ending war of ours. Sprites and sycos do, too. Mortals suffer. Inequality is rampant. Some people are ravaged by disease, famine, war. Others live in incredible peace and luxury and abundance. Would things be like that without us luck gods shifting luck around all the time?"

Aggie shook her head. "I don't know," she said.

"I don't know either," Jack said. "Not for sure. But don't we owe it to the world to find out?"

Aggie was tapping her fingers on the table, one by one, a telltale sign she was counting. He'd made her nervous. But she'd gotten better and better at hiding her OCD these past few months, Jack thought. Her demeanor remained calm and even as she said: "And you think you can change all the bad things about the luck gods system by taking all the power for yourself?"

"I think I have to try," Jack said.

"And what happens to the luck gods?" Aggie pressed. "Do they just go out and get a real job or something? Or do you plan to kill them all?"

Jack spread strawberry jelly on his toast and tried not to think of how much it looked like blood.

"Some will have to die. Others—if we can find a way for them to relinquish their powers—will be set free to live a normal life."

Jack noticed Aggie's breathing hitch. That was always her goal: to get her mom out of the Spades' control and back to living a normal life. If he was being honest, Jack had his doubts that would ever happen. Giving up power tended to be even more difficult than gaining it. But the possibility was profound enough that Aggie's eyes now glistened with unshed tears.

"You really think that will work?" she said. "If you become king of all the suits and disband the luck gods, you really think you could set us free? Make us normal again?"

The truth was, Jack didn't know for sure. According to

legend there was a way, and if he had the power of Uthule, he was sure he could find it. So he nodded. "Yeah. If I controlled all four suits, all four obelisks, I could do it."

Aggie was counting again, pressing her thumb to her pointer finger—then her to her middle finger, then to her ring finger, then to her pinky in quick succession. It was truly remarkable, he thought, how she kept moving forward despite her compulsions. It was its own kind of strength.

She must have reached her number of completion, twenty-three, because she stopped. "Okay, then," she said, businesslike. "If you help me solve this murder *and* prove that the Spades mark on your hand hasn't turned you into some kind of evil goon—then I'll make you my king. Deal?"

Aggie stuck out a hand for him to shake. He looked down at it, then up at her eyes. There was something steely and brittle about her expression. The conversation had gone better than he expected, but her coldness and the emotional wall she'd thrown up between them, made Jack's heart ache. Of course, he understood. He deserved her derision for the things he'd done since accepting the mark of Spades. Staying away from her had been the most loving thing he could have done, and staying away forever might be more loving still. But he needed her. That was the bare truth. He was only glad that she could use him in return—it made him feel slightly less terrible.

He reached out, took her hand, and shook it. Her charm flooded through him, pure and warm and strong, like sunlight on a summer day, and he never wanted to let go. But she pulled away.

"Okay. So I guess we're partners," she airily. "Let's solve this murder."

Shoving her empty plates aside, Aggie took out a small

spiral bound notebook with an anime version of Hermoine Granger on the cover, flopped it on the table, and flipped it open. The tip of a sparkly teal pen hovered above the bare page.

"Step one: make a list of suspects."

"Whoa," Jack said. "Have you ever investigated a murder before?"

Aggie paused. "No. But—"

"Well, unfortunately I have," Jack said.

Aggie crossed her arms, irritated. "Fine. What do we do first?"

Jack's eyes met Aggie's.

"Step one," he said. "Make a list of suspects."

He'd promised himself coming into this that he'd behave. No flirting. No banter. But it seemed he couldn't help himself. He was the Jack of Hearts, after all.

Her eyes narrowed, and he reveled in the flush of color—irritation and amusement—that rushed into Aggie's cheeks. The pip on his right hand even warmed a little. Flirting fed heart charm, just like the work did, Jack had noticed.

"Fine," Aggie said, scratching *List of Suspects* at the top of the page. Underneath it she wrote the first name:

*Jack Valentine.*

**9**

---

## RACHEL

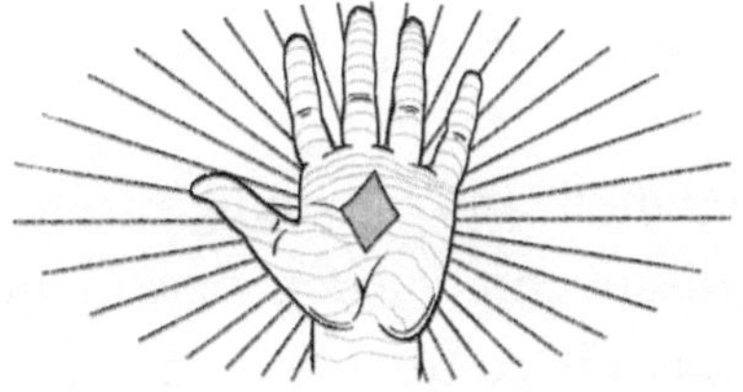

Rachel sat up with a choking gasp. The first thing she noticed were the tubes down her nose; they went all the way into her throat, gagging her, and she tore them out with a noise something between sob and a scream. They had been taped on, and ripping them free stung her skin. She coughed, sniffed, groaned. Her head throbbed and her body felt weak and tremulous. Dizziness made her head swim and she almost fell back onto—what was this? A hospital bed? She braced herself, gripping the rails on either side of the bed to stay upright, and looked around, but the world was blurred, the lights in the ceiling above stingingly bright. She was in a small room, she could tell that much, and hospital machines stood arrayed around her, sighing and beeping. With a snarl she grabbed the tube attached to the IV in her arm and wrenched it free, sending a spatter of blood across the pristine white sheets.

*How long have I been unconscious?* she wondered in a panic. Something told her it had been a long time. Her body felt leaden, her mind fuzzy as a cotton ball. *Where am I? What day is it?*

Then another thought seized her. *Am I missing class?*

She'd been teaching a full load at Oak Hill College and all her classes were supposed to have a test on Thursday. Was this Thursday? It felt like it, her bleary mind insisted. It also felt like she'd been sleeping a long, long time. And if this was Thursday, she had to get to Oak Hill. She'd just gotten her job at the college back. She couldn't, *couldn't*, lose it again.

The door opened and a young woman's face poked through, then disappeared again just as quickly. Though Rachel's vision was still coming back to normal, she was sure she didn't recognize the woman. But she heard her voice as the door swung shut.

"Doctor! Doctor Gabardine! She's awake."

*Indeed she is*, came a familiar voice from inside her mind. Her already curdled stomach turned over. The voice belonged to the shard of Spades obelisk that lived inside her. For a moment, she'd forgotten about the inanimate parasite, but at the sound of those low, strangely accented words, a tremor ran through her body, a wave of despair.

She'd forgotten she was a slave.

*You've been slumbering for awhile, my sleeping beauty*, the obelisk said. *You must have questions.*

"I'm not interested in anything you have to say," Rachel said, swinging her legs over the edge of the bed and standing. The second her weight shifted onto her feet she stumbled forward and crashed into a metal tray of medical instruments, sending them pinging all over the floor. Teeth on edge with determination, she fought to her feet again, as unsteady as *Bambi* in the opening scene of the Disney movie. Aggie had loved that movie when she was little. Where was Aggie now?

*That's fine,* the stone in her belly said. *You don't have to listen to me. You'll sort things out for yourself soon enough...*

Rachel had just gotten her feet under herself and was making her way to the door when it swung open again. For a moment, she thought she was seeing a ghost. A white doctor's coat. Disheveled brown hair. A charming smile. Her bleary eyes saw Kevin. Her husband. Aggie's father. A dead man.

But a few blinks cleared her vision, and she saw the differences. This man's eyes were blue, not brown. His skin was more olive than Kevin's. And his smile was cold.

"Well. Up and around, are we? I'm Doctor Gabardine—"

Rachel was already barreling forward, jostling past him.

"I can't be here. I have a class."

He grabbed her arm, drawing her up short, and swung her around to face him. That smile remained frozen on his face, but his grip was like an iron shackle.

"Hold on now, Your Majesty. Take it easy," his smile grew broader—and colder. "Doctor's orders."

Rachel spotted it on the table. Her obsidian sword. At the same time, the bad luck power within her seemed to stir to life. She flared hex and imagined the muscles in the doctor's hand and forearm cramping. It was so easy for a muscle to cramp; all it took was the slightest imbalance of electrolytes and—boom. The doctor winced, letting go of her arm. In a second she had her sword in her hand, its needle-sharp point pressed to the doctor's throat.

His smile faltered for only a second as he held up his hands in surrender. That's when she saw the spade marks on the palms of his hands. He was one of hers. A Morbus. Somehow, he must have been inducted while she slept...

"Of course, you can go wherever you want, my queen," the doctor said. "I was only following orders to keep you safe."

"Well now I'm ordering you to leave me alone," Rachel hissed. "I have to go..."

She backed away from him, pushed open the door and stumbled out, her legs still unsteady. She found Shade, her Ten, hurrying down a hallway toward her. She didn't know him that well and she still found that spider web tattoo around his left eye disconcerting—but he seemed to be loyal, and at least he was a familiar face.

"Queen Rachel," he said breathlessly. "You're awake."

He looked happy to see her, relieved even, but his expression changed when she brought the sword up between them.

"Car keys," she said. He hesitated. "NOW."

He dug a key fob out of his pocket and tossed it to her. She caught it and glanced around, taking in her surroundings. The room she'd woken up in had seemed to be a normal hospital room. But now, she found herself in a vast, empty office space. Here and there, wires hung from an acoustic tile drop ceiling. Fluorescent lights flickered. Half the room was filled with abandoned cubicles and desks. The other half sat vacant, a sea of short-napped beige carpeting.

"Where are we?" she asked.

"An old pharmaceutical company headquarters," Shade explained. "Your money man, Darby, sent me here with you.

When you were hurt. He said Gabardine would fix you up. That girl Molly, Aggie's friend, she stabbed you in the back, remember? We—"

"What day of the week is it?"

"What?" Shade frowned.

"What day of the week?" Rachel shouted.

"Thursday," Shade said, looking bewildered. "But—"

Rachel was already moving again, lurching unsteadily toward a glowing exit sign.

"I have to get to Oak Hill," she said, breathless.

"Your Majesty—"

Shade moved to join her but she wheeled on him and snarled. "Leave me alone."

His eyes lit on the sword in her hand and he backed away, watching as she fled.

♡ ♤ ◇ ♧

Rachel stormed into the classroom, stumbling as she made her way to the front of the room, and grasped the lectern with both hands seconds before she would have collapsed. Catching her breath, she pushed a veil of disheveled hair out of her eyes.

She looked out across the room to find her students watching her with wide-eyed expressions ranging from horror to amazement to repulsion.

"Take out your study guides, please," she said, her voice raspy with disuse. "We'll review a few things before diving into the test."

No one moved to take out their study guide. No one moved. It was like they were staring at a ghost. And for the first time, Rachel paused to look down at herself and consider her appearance. She wore a blood-spattered hospital gown with a short sleeved, fluffy black robe overtop. Her hair hung in wild tangles. Her arms were emaciated and white, and a thin line of blood drizzled down one forearm where she'd yanked the IV out. *God, I must look like something out of a nightmare...*

She felt dizzy then, whether from whatever pain meds she was on or from the shock of the situation, she couldn't tell. A disorienting feeling of déjà vu washed over her. She'd literally dreamed this before. It was a recurring nightmare from her early days of teaching: showing up for a class unprepared, confused, with the students staring at her in baffled judgement. And just like in a dream, she felt frozen in place, like a moth pinned in an entomologist's glass case, too exhausted to run or speak or even cry.

The door clicked and swung open. There stood Kimberly Dodson, Rachel's one time best friend. Kimberly had been the chair of the physics department, before she'd fallen under the sway of the dark suits and gotten injured. Apparently, she was back. But she seemed to have aged since Rachel had seen her last. She was skinnier, with dark circles under her eyes, and her lovely blonde hair had been chopped off into a shapeless coif. Still, she looked professional and dignified in her blazer and pencil skirt, especially compared to the mad queen standing at the lectern.

"Rachel?" she whispered, as if she, too, were seeing ghost. For a fraction of a second Rachel wondered if she was, in fact, a dead and disembodied spirit. But the wound in her back still hurt too much for that.

With effort, Rachel made herself stand straight. "I... we... were just about to review a few concepts before the exam. You're welcome to stay and audit, if you'd like."

One of the students muttered something. Another gave a choked laugh.

"You... haven't been here in over two months, Rachel," Dodson said. "You disappeared. I'm teaching the class now."

"I'm... fired again," Rachel breathed, and she felt her face going hot with humiliation. Devastation. And anger.

"Technically, you're on extended leave, but..." Dodson glanced to a large boy seated in the back row. "Josh, run down to the security desk. Have them send someone," she whispered—as if Rachel couldn't hear.

Rachel raised a hand, brandishing her palm toward the class. As his anger waxed, she imagined Dodson's veins constricting, imagined her choking on her own tongue, imagined her hemorrhaging in her brain, and the hex rose hungrily in response. Dodson's eyes grew wide. Her face went deathly pale.

A snarl twisted Rachel's mouth. God, how good it would feel to snuff out the light in Dodson's eyes. The bad luck work tasted sweeter than any liquor, felt better than any kiss, hit harder than any high.

Tears rolled down Dodson's eyes. Her mouth gaped as she choked and trembled.

*No. No... It's not her fault,* Rachel thought.

With great effort, she closed her hand, reining in the hex power. Dodson nearly fell forward, leaning on a desk for support as she gasped and shivered, regaining her breath and composure.

"It's okay. I'm going," Rachel said. She glanced at her students. Most were leaning back in their desks. A few had back packs hugged protectively to their chests. *Afraid of me. They're afraid of me,* she thought.

And the worst part was, they were right to be afraid.

She cleared her throat. "Remember the mnemonic for the microwave frequency bands I taught you," she told the class. "*King Xerxes can seduce lovely princesses*. And don't forget..."

Her words fell like a stone into a deep well. The silence of the students felt crushing. Their staring eyes pricked like needles.

"I... I'm sorry," Rachel whispered, stepping back from the lectern.

She drifted down the aisle, past Dodson, and out into the hallway.

Behind her, she heard the door shut and the lock click into place.

Tears rose to her eyes, bitter and hot, but before they could spill she spotted someone down the hallway, watching her. Shade. She walked toward him, willing the tears to recede with each step until she stood before him, dry-eyed.

"Your Majesty," he gave her a low nod, almost a bow. "I'm sorry for following, but I thought you might need me."

In fact, she wanted to hug him, wanted to sob into his shoulder. But who could a bad luck queen turn to for comfort? Not her ten. Not anyone.

*Teaching at this college is not your work anymore, Rachel,* the obelisk inside her said. *Your work is elsewhere.*

Nostalgia and longing—love for this college with its dusty classrooms and its polished floors—burned in her chest, its ache worse than the pain of the stab wound. And regret burned with it. How she wished to burrow through a wormhole into a different timeline, an alternate universe where she was standing behind that lectern right now instead of Dodson. Where the class would end and she'd stop by the coffee shop to grab a latte then head to her office to grade some exams, then down to her lab to work on her next big idea. Where students would look at her with admiration instead of horror. But the obelisk was right. This was not that world anymore.

Footfalls echoed behind her, and Rachel glanced back to see a member of campus security walking toward them.

"Your Majesty?" Shade prompted, offering her his arm.

Rachel leaned on him and let him lead her out of the science building and away from Oak Hill College—for the final time.

**10**

---

**AGGIE**

I followed Jack through a door labelled 504 and into the darkness that waited beyond it, a blackness so complete that for a moment it felt infinite, a starless outer space. Then a light clicked on, revealing a top-floor loft condo. It had high ceilings, exposed brick walls, and stark granite countertops with appliances so new the fridge still had a sticker on it. The place was completely devoid of furniture save for a couch and a single folding chair. There were no throw pillows, no TV, no coffee table, and no pictures on the walls. I strolled through the living room, each footstep echoing ominously. It wasn't just the emptiness of the space that made me feel uneasy. I could feel the hex from Jack's spade pip, too, a barely noticeable ambient pulsing of bad luck, like the hum of a fluorescent light bulb.

As Jack opened the refrigerator, I made my way to a set of sliding glass doors and looked out over the city. Tiger Stadium lay off to our right, it's lights blazing, although I was pretty sure baseball season was over—or hadn't yet begun.

"Wow," I said, giving the place another once-over. "This is quite the bachelor pad. No TV? No couch?"

Jack uncapped a carton of milk and brought it to his nose. Whatever he smelled made him recoil and replace the cap fast. "No need for luxuries. This is just a base for conducting surveillance—or for hiding out in if something goes down in the neighborhood."

The rift, an energy portal that led to the world of the peri (luck beings like sprites, sylph, et cetera) had appeared in Detroit almost a year earlier. Luck gods migrated along with it. The Hearts and the other suits all set up multiple hideouts like this whenever they landed in a city. It was amazing the infrastructure they were able to put in place in only a handful of months. But then, with the wealth luck gods had, renting a few apartments was nothing.

Jack was pillaging the fridge again. This time he came out with a bottle of Vodka and a carton of orange juice. He set two glasses on the counter and began uncapping the booze.

"Uh, what are you doing?" I asked as he poured.

"First on our suspect list. Lorcan," Jack said.

"The first one on the list was you," I reminded him.

He gave a beguiling half smile. "Let's skip me for now," he said, stirring the drinks.

Lorcan the leprechaun was a trusted henchman to the Diamantes, and to their Jill Danusia in particular. The

Diamonds were out to get revenge on the Hearts because I'd had to steal a shard of Spades obelisk from them during my queen trial, and their queen had been injured in the process. And Lorcan had a leprechaun key, which meant he could have easily gotten into the room and out of it again undetected. That was motive and opportunity. True, it was more likely Lorcan would have been ordered to kill me rather than Michael, since I was the one who had pissed Diamond Queen off. But killing Michael could have been a warning to me, designed to make me sweat before they took me out, too. And besides, there was no accounting for the whims of the Diamonds, especially their vengeful, superstar queen.

Jack gave me a little smile as he stirred the drinks.

I folded my arms. "Only one of us needs to get drunk to summon Lorcan," I pointed out. "Don't think I haven't figured that out since the last time."

Being intoxicated somehow allowed a person to summon a leprechaun. Don't ask me why; no one understands leprechaun power except leprechauns—and maybe not even them. But it worked.

"More people drunk makes the call louder," Jack said, finishing stirring then sucking on the spoon.

He offered me one of the drinks. But I couldn't help noticing the light from his spade mark, illuminating the cup with its dark purplish light.

"As your queen, I order you to drink alone," I said.

Jack feigned pouting. "You're no fun," he said, downing the drink in one gulp and pouring another.

I turned a circle, taking the place in once more, noticing the polished concrete floor. "Where do you sleep?" I said, stamping my foot. "On this slab?"

Jack shrugged a shoulder. "There's a mattress on the floor in one of the bedrooms."

I sipped the drink—slower this time. His sly gaze made me think of the mattress again, of the long hours we'd spent together in this room at the Valentine house kissing, watching movies—just being together. I wished I hadn't asked about sleeping arrangements. Instead, I focused on counting Jack's sips. *One, two, three, four, five...* but that was no good either. I was looking at his lips.

He nudged the other cup toward me.

"The louder the call, the faster we get Lorcan here," he said.

I eyed the cup. Mom had struggled with alcoholism, especially after dad died. I'd been through enough with her —and knew enough about the genetic components of addiction— that I had a healthy respect for alcohol. But in my time as a luck god, I'd faced enough life-threatening danger that it was impossible to be too scared of something as innocuous as a beverage, even if the person offering it was the notorious Jack of Hearts. I sidled up to the counter.

"Say please," I told him.

His smiled swelled. "Please, Your Majesty," he whispered.

I picked up the cup.

❦

Jack and I both stood at the sliding doors, looking over the balcony and across a blurred city. It might have been my hot breath on the glass or the vodka smudging my vision, but all of Detroit, all the world, seemed a kaleidoscope of alternating dark and light. Black sky, stadium lights—alley shadows, streetlights— rain-slick asphalt, police flashers. I found myself counting each stoplight. Normally I tried to stop my OCD, but not this time. I knew what I was distracting myself from. My Jack of Hearts stood so close I could feel the radiant warmth of his body, could smell that earl-grey-tea, winter-fire scent of him. Turning and looking into his eyes now was a far greater danger than counting could ever be.

"You ready?" he asked.

We'd tried calling three times already, but either the leprechaun was busy or we hadn't been buzzed enough to get through to him.

"Sure," I said, the word a bit slurred. My lips tingled slightly as if they had bees walking on them. I wondered suddenly if that's where the term *buzzed* came from, and the thought made me laugh. Jack looked at me but I refused to look back at him, preferring, instead, to watch his reflection in the glass doors.

"What?" he asked.

"Just thinking about bees."

"O-kay..."

"And wondering if it's safest to look at only your reflection," I said. "Yes, I shall promulgate that into an official rule. I shall look only at Jack's reflection and thereby be immune to his wiles."

Jack grunted a laugh. "Promulgate?"

"A vocab word. I have the SATs coming up and it's one of the words I need to memorize. If you use them in a sentence, you're much more likely to remember the definition. Promulgate means *to put into a law or formally declare*."

"Right," Jack said. "Well, I'm sure you'll pass."

"I'm not trying to *pass*," I said. "It's not even a pass-fail thing. I'm trying to get a 1570, so I'm an above-average candidate to get into MIT."

Jack folded his arms. "I thought you wanted to stay here in Detroit and go to Oak Hill?"

"Yeah. Well..."

I suddenly lost my balance a little and caught myself by laying my palm on the glass. It was cold.

"That was before..." I finished. And I knew I didn't have to specify before *what*. Before Mom changed. Before my home burned down. Before I became a demigoddess. Before my best friend stabbed my mother. Before I had my first love and my first heartbreak. I didn't have to say any of it, because Jack already knew.

That was one thing about Jack and I. All that shared trauma. I imagined dating another boy and having to explain to him what it had been like to fight my mother, sweet college professor turned bad luck goddess. Or what it was like to have the power to save someone's life burning in the palms of your hands. Or what it was like to fight to hang onto a power you barely understood, but that nevertheless had become as much a part of you as your own limbs. How would I begin to explain to anyone else the things Jack already knew?

I never could, I realized. No other boy in the world could ever understand me, could ever relate to me like Jack could.

I half turned, glancing up at him, and knew instantly that I'd made a mistake. His eyes were there, clear and azure and depthless, like staring up into a June sky.

"I'm sorry," he said quietly.

"For what?"

He looked down, long lashes veiling his eyes. "For this life. For bringing you into all this. For... everything."

He looked at me again, went to touch my face, then

seemed to realize at the last minute that it was his hand with the spade mark on it and pulled back.

It only made me want him to touch me more.

"It's okay," I breathed. "I mean, yes. Since becoming a goddess my life has become pretty ramified..."

Jack raised an eyebrow. "Ramified?"

"Split into two or more branches," I said.

Jack laughed. Not his usual guarded chuckle, but deep, full laughter let loose by his drowned inhibitions. His laugh made me laugh too, and soon we were both cracking up, laughing until I had tears in my eyes.

"Well," Jack said when he'd gotten control of himself. "I guess we'd better ramify onward and call Lorcan."

"That's not how you use it!" I said. "Don't confuse me."

I punched him in the arm. His deltoid was hard, like thumping a tree trunk, and I instantly regretted touching him. Because I wanted to do it again.

"Okay. Yes. Let's call again," I said, inching away from his body until my back was pressed against the cold of the sliding door. "One, two, three."

"Lorcan!" we shouted in unison, then we waited, listening for sounds of his approach. Leprechauns had leprechaun keys, which allowed them to travel between any two doors in the world, provided they were able to visualize their destination—or if they were being called by an intoxicated person. I knew about travelling through the leprechaun underground because I'd extorted a key from Lorcan myself. It hung around my neck now.

The silence stretched and Jack grumbled and folded his arms.

"Maybe he's busy?" I said.

"Or avoiding us," Jack growled.

That should move him up on the suspect list, I thought. But just then there came a knock at the door.

"Finally," Jack huffed, crossing to the apartment's front door and peering out he peephole.

A shiver of anxiety passed over me. It might not be Lorcan at all. Jack and I had plenty of enemies. It might be Blackover thugs. Or Mom's minions. Or— I nervously counted, tapping finger to thumb with each number in my favorite OCD tick. Unlocking doors always set me off like this. Before I became a luck god, I'd spent hours locking windows and locking doors, then checking the locks again and again in cycles of twenty-three. I was constantly using charm on myself, coaxing my brain's neurons to be more cooperative, and as a result OCD had improved somewhat, but I still hit snags like this—too often.

Jack opened the door and Lorcan stumbled through, blustering and slurring. "I might have known it was you. Always bothering a man when he's in his cups. I tell ya, a leprechaun has no privacy."

Lorcan looked around twenty years old. He was a few inches shorter than Jack, wiry and tattooed, with sparse facial hair and gold teeth. I could smell the booze on his breath as he swaggered in, but a sudden stillness arrested him as his eyes fell on me.

"Aggie..." he breathed. "Have you seen her?"

I didn't have to ask who he was talking about. I'd charmed him and my former best friend Molly to fall in love. It wasn't my finest moment, and clearly from the mournful look in his eyes the charm hadn't worn off yet—if it ever would. From what I'd read, a Cupid's Arrow could last indefinitely if the two targets came to genuinely care for one another. I might have broken poor Lorcan's heart forever. Oops.

"No. I haven't seen her since that day at the Valentines' house," I said. "You know, when she stabbed my mom?"

He straightened haughtily. "I don't know why you sound so snotty about it," he said. "Your crazy mum nearly bashed my brains in. And she was coming at you with a sword, as I recall. My sweet Molly saved your life, I'd say."

"My mom would not have hurt me," I said tightly.

Lorcan snorted. "Could have fooled me."

I tried to come up with a harsh comeback, but my mind came up blank. Probably because part of me feared Lorcan was right. I had told myself Mom wouldn't have hurt me. Over and over I'd told myself that. But I still had nightmares about her stalking toward me, an onyx longsword in hand, her eyes utterly devoid of feeling.

"So where is Molly? She won't answer my calls or my texts. I've been to her apartment, her school, the college..." he shook his head sadly. "I can't find her."

"Wow. You're throwing some real stalker vibes right now, Lorcan," Jack smirked.

Lorcan ignored him, pressing on in desperation: "Is she avoiding me? Does she not want to see me anymore?"

"Actually, I'm guessing she's avoiding Aggie," Jack said. "If I tried to kill a luck queen's mother, I'd hide out, too."

I feared Jack was right. According to our friends at school, Molly even thrown out her cell phone and gotten a new number when she fled town, apparently thinking that I, wrathful demigoddess that I was, would track her down with her phone and take my revenge. And she might not have been wrong, considering how protective I was over my mom.

"So she's gone..." Lorcan moaned.

"But I know where she is," I said.

His eyes lit up.

"First, some information," Jack cut in. "Did you kill King Michael?"

Lorcan blinked at him. "What?"

"Listen, neither of us had any love for the king," Jack said. "You might say whoever offed him did us a favor. But we need to know who it was. Tell us the truth, and we can protect you from Valentine justice."

"Plus I'll tell you where Molly is," I put in.

Lorcan looked agonized. "What the hell would I be doing killing a King of Hearts?"

"You work for Danusia Diamante," Jack said. "And the Diamonds are out for revenge on our suit. It stands to reason..."

But Lorcan was shaking his head. "The Diamonds have their assassins. I'm not one of them. I trade in information, not bullets."

"Who would the Diamonds send, then?" Jack pressed.

Lorcan shook his head. "You two are daft. The one Diamond Queen has it in for is this wee queen, not King Michael," he pointed at me. "You two were sleeping in bed together when the king died, so I hear. If it was the Diamonds, they'd have kilt you, not him."

I sighed. I'd thought the same thing.

"And how exactly did you know Aggie was in bed with the King when he died?" Jack demanded. He was a good interrogator, I thought grudgingly.

Lorcan sniffed, chuckling. "Every peri this side of the rift knows that story by now. Your sycos are a chatty bunch."

I could almost feel Jack gritting his teeth. I just hoped

whoever got fired, it wouldn't be any of the kitchen staff who made such delicious meals for everyone.

"It wasn't the Diamonds," Lorcan concluded.

But Jack wasn't finished. "Whoever it was got in and out without being detected," he pointed out. "So we're either talking about a ninja... or someone with a leprechaun key."

Lorcan took a swig from his bottle and belched. "Not too many leprechauns running around Detroit these days as far as I know. Just me and—"

"Your sister," Jack finished. "Where is she?"

Lorcan's sister Cleo had been on our list, too. Her motive was less clear, but she'd already stolen a shard of Spades obelisk from the Hearts house, and she was known as a thief without much of a moral compass. If someone had paid her enough to kill Michael, she'd probably have done it.

Lorcan leaned back against the brick wall and blinked slowly, as if struggling to keep his eyes open. "Hell if I know where she is. At her lair, probably. Playing Legos or whatever with that little whelp of hers. I haven't seen her since the heist at your place."

"Could she have killed the king?" I asked.

"Could she have? Sure. She's a badarse. She could kill any of us with those nimble daggers of hers." He eyed Jack and I again. "Well, maybe not if you two were using those luck power of yours. But a sleeping king? Sure. The question is, *why would she?*"

"For gold," Jack suggested. "You've said before your sister would slit your mother's throat for a sack of gold."

"So she would. Or my throat, for that matter. But she's no fool. She wouldn't cross you luck gods without good reason," he shrugged. "Still, she keeps an ear to the ground, and she hears things. I were you, I'd have a talk with her."

Jack glanced at me and gave a decisive nod. "We will."

I was leaning on the counter, the drink making me dizzy suddenly.

"So," Lorcan turned his attention to me. "I did my part. Where's Molly?"

"According to her friend *Bianca*," I said, trying to keep the bitterness out of my voice at the mention of Molly's cool-girl buddy—who she'd texted instead of me, "she went to Palm Springs to visit her mom."

"Palm springs..." Lorcan deflated. "Christ. I've never been to Palm Springs. I can't visualize it. How am I going to find her there?"

I put a comforting hand on his shoulder. "Maybe she'll get drunk and call you."

Lorcan took my hand, a glint in his eyes that might have been tears. "If you see her, will you tell her I miss her?"

"I will," I nodded.

When he'd left, Jack turned to me, businesslike. "Well. We'd better not let a good buzz go to waste. Next stop: Lorcan's sister."

**11**

———————

# MOLLY

olly followed Tristaine down the stark, white hallway. The Diamantes' office suite took up the top four floors of the Renaissance Center tower in downtown Detroit, and walking through the space always made Molly feel like an extra in a movie about scandals among the rich and powerful. Tristaine stopped to open a set of glass doors, behind which a meeting of high powered executive types seemed to be in full swing. A man in a finely tailored business suit spoke in an earnest monotone as he gestured up to a projector slide displaying several multi-colored pie charts, but he trailed off as Tristaine sauntered in. Chairs swiveled to face them. Molly noticed her old mentor, the

Jill, Danusia, giving them a particularly fiery glare. But Diamond Queen, the matriarch of the suit, looked bemused.

It was surreal to see her in person. Diamond Queen was a celebrated drag queen and a Grammy-winning country singer—one of the biggest stars in the world. Her face had graced everything from Times Square billboard screens to cereal boxes. She'd done a Super Bowl halftime show and hosted Saturday Night Live. Her massive, glittery blonde hairdo alone was enough to inspire awe. Molly was still wrapping her head around the revelation that she was also a luck god.

"By all means, don't let us interrupt," Tristaine said, hitching one leg up to sit on the end of the table, leaving Molly to stand awkwardly next to him.

The presenter cleared his throat. "As I was saying, the rise in interest rates makes many of our proposed real estate investments untenable. Particularly the parts of our portfolio consisting of low-income housing where the purchases were contingent on capital improvements—we're looking to get out of those deals—"

"Why?" Tristaine interrupted.

"Well," the speaker pushed his glasses up his nose, his face reddening. "The cost of interest on construction loans—"

"So we use cash," Tristaine said.

Danusia stood and leaned over the table toward Tristiane. "The original budget on these deals is out the window," she said. "They no longer make sense."

"You're looking at cash flow and the value of the assets. I'm talking about something else entirely."

"Project Aurora," Diamond Queen said in her rich,

Southern accent. At those words, some of the executives looked confused. Others nodded knowingly.

"Several of the properties in that portfolio were specifically chosen because of the... special properties of their locations," Tristaine told Danusia. "We have to keep sight of the big picture, Dani."

"I wasn't aware of that," Danusia said quietly. "Of course, Project Aurora takes precedence." Chastened, she sat.

Diamond Queen turned to the presenter and gave a decisive nod. "Tim, that's enough, thank you. We'll be in touch with instructions. Y'all have a great rest of your day. Dani, Tristaine, you stay."

The room cleared in a brief commotion of shutting laptops and hushed words. For a second, Molly wondered if she should be leaving, too. But Tristaine made no effort to shoe her out, and anyway, she hadn't flown all the way back to Michigan just to wait in a hallway. When the last person had left and the glass doors drifted shut, Diamond Queen turned her attention back to Molly and the two Diamonds. Her eyes ticked from Danusia to Tristaine—and landed on Molly.

"Well," she drawled. "Look what the kitty dragged in."

"Not a kitty. Tristaine," Danusia said with derision. "Although I can't imagine what he's playing at bringing my low-level syco into a business meeting."

Tristaine dropped himself into one of the swiveling office chairs, leaned back and kicked his feet up onto the table.

"Why not? She's great fun," he said. "On the plane ride over she was just telling me the most interesting story about how you rescued Jack Valentine from being barbecued alive by the Clubs a few months ago. It's a shame. It might have saved everyone a lot of trouble if you'd just kept well enough away and let him burn. But you've always had a soft spot for pretty boys, haven't you, Dani?"

"It might be the one thing we have in common," Danusia shot back. "And yes. When another red suit is in peril, it is tradition that we help them. Not all of us can be as heartless as you, Tris."

"No indeed," Tristaine grinned. "More's the pity."

Diamond Queen drummed her perfectly manicured nails on the table. "Boy I could just listen to you two carry on all day. I really could," she said. "Unfortunately, I've got a goddamn worldwide empire to run. So cut to the chase."

Tristaine nodded toward Molly. "We have an opening in our suit, and Danusia made a deal with Molly. I brought her here so we could make good on our word and make her a Diamond."

"She is my syco. If I wanted her inducted, I'd have brought her myself," Danusia snapped.

"And you should have," Tristaine said. "You made a deal with the poor girl."

Danusia jabbed a finger in Molly's direction. "A deal," she said, "which she did not fulfil her part of."

At last Molly found the courage to speak up. "You told me to stab Aggie's mom. I stabbed her."

"I told you to *kill* her," Danusia said. "And she's alive."

"She is?" Molly breathed, unable to hide her relief.

"Semantics," Tristaine waved a hand dismissively.

"I would think even you would be able to grasp the difference between alive and dead." Danusia said.

Diamond Queen levelled her piercing gaze on Molly. "Suppose you finish the job?"

Molly felt herself grow suddenly lightheaded. "You mean finish killing Aggie's mom?"

DQ gave a slow nod.

"I..." Molly hesitated, plumbing her soul for the will to attack Rachel Van Der Graaf again. Yes, she still wanted to become a Diamond, more than anything. But when she'd stabbed Rachel the first time, she'd been enraged that her love, Lorcan, had been injured, and she'd been sure Rachel was about her kill her best friend, Aggie. The adrenaline of the moment had fueled her. That was way, way different than sneaking up and assassinating someone in cold blood. And despite the fact that Rachel had become a hella scary woman when she received her hex power, Molly had plenty of fun memories with her. How many times had she woken up at Aggie's house after a night of sleeping over to find Rachel had made them pancakes? How many times had they sat together eating popcorn and watching sci-fi flicks in Aggie's family room? How many times had Rachel welcomed Molly popping in out of the blue and spending her entire day at the Van Der Graaf house—especially when Molly's parents were in the middle of their ugly divorce? Rachel had been like a second mom. On top of all that, Molly still considered Aggie her best friend. Sure, after Molly's betrayals it was entirely possible that Aggie would never forgive her. She might even come after her with the wrath of a demigoddess if they ever saw each other again. But that didn't mean Molly could hurt Rachel again.

"No," she said quietly. "I can't do it."

Danusia rolled her eyes gave a gesture toward Molly that said, *see?*

But DQ folded her arms, watching Molly through narrowed eyes.

"You're a bit of a complex character, aren't you, Miss Molly-Loo?" she said. "One the one hand, you're ambitious and savage enough to stab your friend's mama. But you've got some loyalty, too. Those are the sort of raw materials we can work with."

"She's smart, too," Tristaine put in. "A top ten student in her high school class."

"Please," Danusia said. "You want a list of sycos who're better prospects for induction? I have two dozen, at least."

"Maybe," Tristaine said. "But how many have stabbed a Morbus queen? How many have such close connections to the Valentines?"

"Close connections?" Danusia laughed. "If Queen Aggie sees this girl again, she's likely to chop her to bits. Her *connections* are of no use to us."

"I think there's some luck about her," Tristaine said with a shrug.

Diamond Queen was still staring at Molly, rubbing her chin. "Hmm," was all she said.

"How about this," Tristaine said. "We bring her along to the Monaco."

"Absolutely not—" Danusia began.

But Tristaine went on. "I need an assistant anyway. I'll be responsible for her, take her under my wing. If she proves useful, you consider inducting her, Your Highness. That's all I ask."

"Your Majesty, this deal is too important," Danusia said. "All of Project Aurora hinges on it. We can't risk this girl coming in and mucking it up for us."

"I assure you, she won't muck anything up," Tristaine said.

"He's only bringing her in to piss me off, you see that, right?" Danusia said, her voice rising.

Diamond Queen raised her hands, shutting everyone up,

and for a moment the red glow of her pips fell across Molly's face. The light felt amazing, like the first warm sun rays of spring, full of joy and possibility. Pure good luck. There was nothing like it. How Molly longed to have that light inside her.

DQ eyed Molly again. "Is this what you want, girl? To become one of us?"

"With all my heart," Molly nodded.

Danusia rolled her eyes, but Diamond Queen grinned. "Fine, then. Take the girl with you. She proves as useful as you say, Tristaine, I'll make her one of us. And if she screws up this deal, Dani, you have my blessing to cut her throat and drop her into the middle of the Mediterranian," she gave Molly a vicious smile. "Toodle-oo. Y'all have a plane to catch."

**12**

---

# RACHEL

In the days following her ill-fated return to Oak Hill, Rachel haunted the former pharmaceutical facility that had become her base. It was a surreal existence, and the times she peeked into doors throughout the building made it more surreal still.

One door led to a vast room full of young men with identical faces who sat in various modes of repose, playing cards, chatting, or watching TV on their phones. It was the clone army Darby had gotten her from the sylph, Bartholomew Barth. Another room was empty save for a table on which the black stone urn sat. It was the receptacle Rachel had used to gather tattered bits of the archjinni, Invidia. Even with the lid closed, it pulsed with a malevolent presence. Another room held rolls of copper wire, a crate of industrial grade mirrors, and various electrical parts. It looked to Rachel like the materials she'd need to rebuild her dark matter detection machine, DEMS. The stone inside her confirmed it by whispering, *Not yet. We'll have you rebuild it when you are stronger...* Another door was locked, with a second set of doors beyond it, like an airlock. Through both layers of thick glass she saw people in hazmat suits working with petri dishes and beakers.

*My life has become a David Lynch movie,* she thought. And she wondered if she'd ever shown Aggie any David Lynch movies. She couldn't remember, but the thought of sitting on the couch next to her daughter made her ache with longing.

After that she gave up on exploring her new home, preferring instead to walk laps around the big, empty office space. She'd rest every so often in a swiveling office chair to snack from the trays of food Shade and Dr. Gabardine would set out for her. Sliced fruit. Veggies and dip. Lunch meat, cheese, and crackers. High-protein meal replacement drinks.

During her laps, the obelisk in her belly would occasionally pipe up with encouragement.

*Push yourself, my queen. We have much work to do.*

*Just a bit more, then you can rest.*

*Feel that hunger in your hands? That's the work, calling to you. You must get strong enough to answer it.*

"Isn't there some rehabilitation facility you could send me to?" she griped once.

*None that will care for you the way Dr. Gabardine and I do,* the stone said.

"Why did you bring Gabardine into the suit, anyway?"

she asked. The doctor's resemblance to her dead husband never failed to unnerve her. Their mannerisms were even similar. But Gabardine was like a photo negative of Kevin, cold where Kevin was warm. The glint in his eyes cruel and cunning where Kevin's had been mirthful and kind.

*He brings special talents to our suit*, the obelisk said. *And the time has come to rebuild our ranks. Not to mention, he did save your life.*

Rachel supposed it was a valid point. Still, something about Gabardine bothered her. From being married to a doctor for fifteen years, she knew enough about medical care to understand that a stab wound, even a serious one, should not have necessitated putting her into an induced coma for months. She suspected that particular treatment had more to do with her mind than her body. What tinkering had the stone inside her done with her psyche while she was asleep, she wondered? What horrible nothings had it whispered in her ear as she slumbered?

Now as she completed her lap of the abandoned office area, the doctor stood at the snack station, waiting, as if her thoughts had manifested him. The cubicle had a TV in it, which was always tuned to one of the more obnoxious cable news stations. Rachel had tried to change the channel once, but the obelisk had told her that leaving the station on would increase her bad luck power—which Rachel didn't doubt, since just watching it made her feel nauseated.

Gabardine was watching the TV now. Footage of a protest showed on screen, and Rachel recognized one of the parks downtown. Someone held cardboard sign with a swastika on it. Another group of people stood rallied around a rainbow flag, and the two groups looked as if they were about to go to fisticuffs. Then a projectile about the size of a pop can zinged across the screen, smoke billowing from it. Where it landed, protesters turned away, coughing violently.

"...seemed to be normal teargas," the newscaster was saying. "But now, eleven people who were present at the protest have been hospitalized—not for injuries from the rioting or lung damage from the pepper spray, but from a never-before-seen virus. Three of those infected have already died. And all of them were near the spot where these cannisters released. Anti-terrorism experts are saying—"

Rachel lunged forward, though the sudden motion made the wound in her back scream. She grabbed the remote off the desk, pausing the newscast on a grainy image of the person launching a second cannister. He wore a gas mask, but something about his proportions and the way he moved reminded her disturbingly of... Shade? She felt a burning, tingling sensation and looked down at her hands. At the mere thought of sickness and suffering caused by her suit, her pips burned with a gleeful, grim light. The feeling was intoxicating as a drug and her eyes fluttered shut, savoring it.

"You know what they say," Dr. Gabardine said, "No such thing as bad press."

Rachel looked and saw a giddy, hungry expression on his handsome face.

They were in a medical research facility. Gabardine was a doctor with "special skills." And now, Shade was out infecting people with some terrible virus—which was already making her power swell. It didn't take a master detective to deduce that something awful was happening.

"Eat something. You'll need your strength," Gabardine urged. Then, registering the sharp look she gave him, he quickly added, "my queen."

"What have you and Shade done?" she demanded with a nod toward the TV.

"We've been busy while you were recovering, and I'll be delighted to update you. But first, I have a fellow patient I'd like you to meet. Come." He turned with a swoosh of his white coat. That was another thing. Why did he wear a white coat with no on here to impress but her and Shade? she wondered. But she followed.

The facility was huge. Rachel had spent most of her time inside this large office area and in the smaller office that had served as her hospital room. Gabardine and Shade each had a room in the same hallway as Rachel's, and so did the nurse who sometimes appeared to take Rachel's blood pressure or place a few pills on her tongue. Rachel had also seen bathrooms, a copy room, a storage space, more offices—all pretty boring stuff, aside from the lab, the barracks, and the room that housed Invidia.

But there was a set of double doors at the far end of the empty offices had always been locked. That was where Gabardine led her now, taking a key card out of his pocket and swiped it in front of a keypad. It beeped and the doors yielded, revealing a hallway. The floors were of polished concrete, the walls unadorned, the décor more industrial than in the office area. Rachel heard voices echoing ahead— quite a few voices, from the sound of it—but Gabardine led her down a side hall, through a metal door, and down a set of stairs, and to another metal door.

The doctor gave a cursory knock, then turned the knob and pushed the door open. The room was dimly lit with only the shifting glow of a lava lamp to illuminate it, but Rachel could see it was set up as a hospital room, very similar to her own. Someone lay in the bed, asleep. It was a man, broad-shouldered, with shoulder-length black hair. He was shirtless, and his body looked like something an ancient master might have chiseled out of granite, all muscle and tendon and veins, each striated angle set into relief by the shadow and light.

Rachel was no artist, but she longed to paint him, sculpt him, photograph him—something. To leave such carnal beauty undocumented seemed like a sin.

The slumbering man gave a low groan, stirred, and opened his eyes. Or, his eye. One looked green in the eerie light of the lamp. The other was covered by a patch. The good eye fixed on Rachel and she felt a shiver cut through her. The man's face was model-beautiful, but it wasn't just his looks that roiled her insides. Hex rolled off him in powerful waves.

"Sorry to disturb your nap," Gabardine said. "But I wanted to introduce you to another patient of ours. This is Rachel, Queen of Spades."

The man in the bed did not reply. With the slow majesty of a Clydesdale, he swung his legs over the edge of the bed and stood. He had to be at least six-foot-four. And he wore nothing but a pair of clinging boxers.

Rachel made a great effort not to let her jaw drop.

The man's hand went up in greeting, and she saw the Clubs pip emblazoned on his palm, glowing with its dark light.

"This poor fellow was in worse shape than you when I received him," Gabardine said. "It has taken months to restore his health, but as you can see, he's doing much better now. Which is good luck for us, since he is our ally. And very bad luck for those who tried to kill him in the first place.

Rachel wanted to speak, but between the man's godly handsomeness and his palpable power, she was struck dumb.

"Your Highness," Gabardine said, "meet Gallo, Jack of Clubs."

# 13

## CLEO

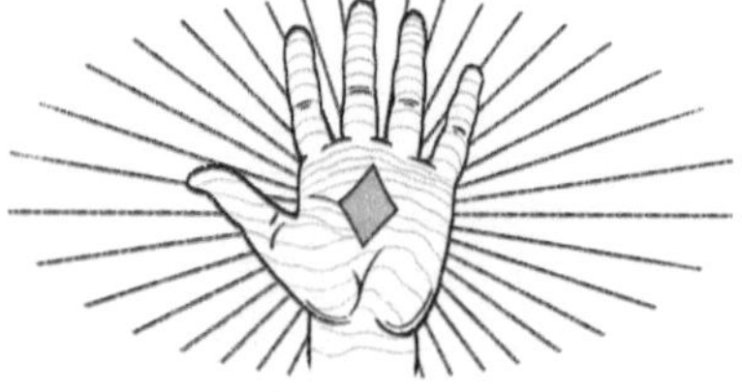

The boy was a brat, but damned if Cleo hadn't grown to love him.

She watched him as he sat cross-legged, looking small on the oversize couch in the middle of Cleo's underground lair and playing a handheld video game he'd swiped from a big box store. In the beginning, Cleo had needed to coach the boy on the finer points of thievery— how to redirect a cashier's attention, schmooze a security guard into complacency, or pick a mark's pocket by bumping him. The boy had taken to it like a minnow to swimming, and as he'd grown more comfortable with his Spade power, the addition of bad luck to his arsenal had made the little arsehole an unstoppable thieving machine. Truth be told,

Cleo was in awe of the kid. And worried about him. And sometimes, a little afraid of him.

Now, Cleo glanced over and saw the pips on the boy's hands glowing with deep purplish light as he bit his lip and clicked video game buttons furiously.

"I told ya," Cleo sighed. "You can't hex a video game. There's nothing to push against. Bad luck has to be bad luck *for someone.*"

"It'll be bad luck for his zombie when I cut his head off," the boy said, clicking the buttons harder.

"Right," Cleo said. "But he's not a real person, is he? So hex won't work."

Cleo had learned a bit about the powers of the luck gods during her lessons as a girl growing up on the far side of the rift. And she'd read up on them more lately, in part for her own safety. It was dangerous having a boy with hex powers running around, and even worse if he didn't know how to use them. He might easily get annoyed and make a brick fall from a building and land on Cleo's head, or cause a fire, or a car accident. To make matters worse, luck gods had something they called *the work*, a need to do things that furthered their powers. In the case of a dark luck god like Junior, it meant he had a constant urge to make bad things happen.

Cleo understood. It wasn't so different from the leprechaun drive to gather up gold. Except that bad luck work often involved maiming and killing and, from what Cleo had read, didn't always spare those the bad luck god was closest to.

The boy died in his game, grunted in frustration and tossed the game system. It clattered across the rug and onto the concrete floor.

"Junior!" Cleo snapped. "We don't do that. Are you trying

to break your game?"

"Yes," he crossed his arms sullenly.

"Well you'll be boo-hooin' if you do," she said. "You play that damn thing all day long."

He shrugged. "Who cares? I can just steal another one."

The leprechaun girl walked over and squatted down to his level. Once again, she was impressed with the boy's beauty, his dark hair, pale skin, fine eyelashes. But no matter how cute he was, she wasn't going to go soft on him and let him grow up to be a little shite.

"We don't steal lightly," Cleo said. "Every time we do, we run the risk of being caught. You may be clever and tough, but even a wee god can get nicked and put in jail."

The boy looked down at the Spade mark on his hand. "So? I could just make the cop bleed out of his eyeballs."

Cleo scowled. "So you could. But don't say stuff like that, alright? Just because you're bad luck god doesn't mean you have to be a spooky little arsehole."

The boy sighed. "I'm just bored. Let's get out of here. I want to go to a park. Or to the movies."

They both glanced around. Cleo's lair was a cold-war era bomb shelter deep under the California desert. It was a perfect place because it was secluded and safe. She'd done what she could over the years to make it comfortable, plastering the barren walls with posters and covering the cold concrete floors with rugs. She'd replaced the fluorescent lights with warmer LED ones and had brought in a nice TV, a good stereo, and comfortable furniture. And of course, gold was everywhere—coins and necklaces, bars and nuggets, bangles and broaches—all spilled from chests, glittered on shelves, and sat in shiny drifts in the room's corners. The lair's two exits could be barred, creating a highly defensible stronghold, yet she could use her leprechaun key and be anywhere in the world in seconds. It really was the perfect lair for a leprechaun. But it wasn't until the boy showed up that the place had begun to feel like a home to Cleo. It hurt her feelings that he might feel restless here, that he might want to get out, although she understood. He was a human boy, not a leprechaun, after all. She should have known he'd need fresh air and sunshine once in a while.

"I'm bored," he said again, more petulantly this time.

"We—" she started to answer, then stopped, interrupted by a sudden feeling. A restless stirring inside her chest. An inner tug.

She ignored it.

"We could go back up to the surface," she said. "Kick the soccer ball around again."

"Nah," Junior picked at the Spade mark on the palm of his left hand. "My hands are itchy again."

That would be *the work*, calling him...

A sick feeling made Cleo's stomach clench. She was worried for the lad. Jesus, was this what being a mother was like? It was terrible.

"You'll get used to it," she said gently. "All luck gods have feelings like that."

"It makes me feel like I can't sit still," he complained. "Like I have to go somewhere. Do something."

"Well—" Cleo started to speak, but was interrupted by that feeling again. An uncomfortable tug. And she heard something, too. Voices calling her name from afar. Someone was drunk summoning her. But Christ, who on earth would be doing it now? The few friends she had knew better than to bother her like that. Her mind went to that rotter of an ex-boyfriend of hers, Varsmith. He worked for Bartholomew

Barth, and had been hunting for her ever since she'd swiped the boy from that piss-wicked sylph. It was probably him, luring her into a trap.

And yet, Cleo knew it was almost impossible for a leprechaun to resist a drunk summoning. It was like the compulsion to gather gold—an imperative. Insistent. Consuming. And it was getting louder, stronger with every second.

Gritting her teeth, she said. "Listen. I'm going to have to run out."

"I want to come!"

"No," she said quickly. "It might be dangerous."

"*I'm* dangerous," he said, flashing his Spade pips.

Lord, she should never have told him that—even though it was true. Cleo scooped the video game system up off the floor and put it back in the boy's hands.

"I'll just be gone a few minutes."

"But if it's dangerous you might need me."

"No," she said firmly. "I'll be right back. You don't open the door, and you don't go anywhere. Promise me. And get your jammies on. It's past your bedtime."

The boy sighed, looking adorably sad. Part of her wanted to hug him. But she was always reminding herself not to get too attached. He was a cute little boy now, sure. But he was a bad luck god. It was like having a lion cub for a pet. He was adorable today, but tomorrow he'd be tearing out throats.

She couldn't help herself. She hugged him anyway, kneeling so they were cheek to cheek.

"Bring me French fries?" the boy asked as they pulled apart, fixing those sweet, eager eyes on her. She mussed his hair.

"You got it, Gallo Jr.," she said.

**14**

———

## AGGIE

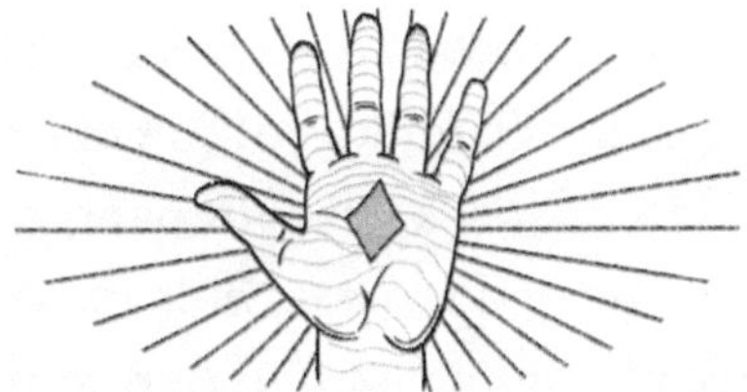

I jerked awake. The first thing I noticed was the smell, like warm Earl Gray tea with honey, with a hint of woodsmoke in the background. A smell of warmth in winter. And there was real warmth, too. Jack's body. He reclined next to me on the couch, and I was snuggled up to him. I sat up fast, my cheeks going hot. I must have fallen asleep momentarily with my head on his shoulder. A mistake.

The alcohol made me so groggy and I wanted nothing more than to drift back against him and fall back asleep, but there was no way I'd let that happen, even if I had to down a gallon of coffee.

Jack watched me with a look of familiar amusement.

"Don't worry, Your Highness, you didn't snore. Much."

I would have whacked him in the arm, but I didn't trust myself to touch him again. Instead, I scooted backward across the couch until my back rested against the far armrest, gaining some distance. My head swam, and for half a second I thought I might puke. Or try to kiss Jack. I wasn't sure which.

A crunching sound crackled through the quiet and I looked toward the kitchen. A young woman in a green jumper stood there. A wild mane of curly blonde hair circled her head like a nimbus and a pair of curved daggers hung at her hips. She held a box of breakfast cereal and was eating a handful. As she chewed, she made a face.

"Captain Crunch? More like Captain Stale," she said. "You summon a girl in the middle of the night, you should at least have some decent snacks in your pantry."

I saw that the pantry door was, indeed, ajar. It must have been the entrance the leprechaun underground had brought her through. There was no accounting for the weird quirks of leprechaun magic. And Lorcan's sister was quirkier than most.

Despite her griping, I was glad to see Cleo. I hadn't talked to her since my queen trial months before, and although that heist did not go particularly well, I'd still developed a fondness for the feisty leprechaun thief.

"Hello, Cleo," Jack said.

She crunched another handful of cereal and took a seat on the barstool at the kitchen counter.

"So, what's up?" she said through a mouthful.

"We're investigating King Michael's death," I said, over-enunciating to compensate for my boozed speech.

"Ah, your dearly departed husband," Cleo gave a laugh.

"I assumed you killed him. And I wouldn't blame you, either. Who would want to be hitched to that old crustacean?"

"It wasn't Aggie," Jack said. "But whoever did it was able to get in and out of the Valentines house undetected. There were no witnesses, and nothing on the security cameras, either."

I wanted to mention the shimmer I'd seen at the open window, but Jack had coached me not to bring up those points. If someone mentioned an open window or a peri shimmer without our telling them, it might be an indication of guilt. Of course, leprechauns couldn't turn invisible like sprites or goblins could, but that didn't mean Cleo or Lorcan couldn't have done it with a peri accomplice. They may have opened the door and sent the assassin in, then let them escape through the open window.

But Cleo didn't look guilty now, just bored. And a little restless, I thought, as she glanced back toward the pantry door.

"So...?" she prompted.

"Several items were found missing from the Valentines house after your little friend was there," Jack said.

"Sure," Cleo said. "The boy steals everywhere he goes. A regular leprechaun in training, he is. The apple of my eye."

"Maybe you were interested in stealing from Michael," Jack pressed. "Maybe that's why he ended up dead."

Cleo's eyes narrowed. "Was anything missing from his body? Or from the room where you found him?"

"You tell me." Jack said.

Cleo snorted. "Listen, you two. I came when you called and I'm trying to be polite, but don't try to play bad cop / drunk cop with me."

Jack crossed his arms. "Fine," he said. "Nothing was

missing. Except, of course, for the chunk of Spades obelisk that disappeared the night before his death. But I'm sure you know nothing about that, right?"

"No, I don't," Cleo sniffed. "And even if I did, it's a far cry from thief to murderer."

"Sometimes not so far, in my experience," Jack countered.

"Your experience, yes," Cleo scoffed. "How many have you killed in your time as a luck god, Jack of Hearts? For that matter, rumor has it the king had it out for you. And weren't you sweet on this one, too? His new wife?" she nodded to me. "Now the king is dead, Aggie is the queen, she's single, and you're next in line for the throne. If you're making a list of suspects, I'd say you should be at the top, Jacky boy."

"Oh, he is," I said, holding up my list of suspects.

"I don't disagree," Jack said evenly. "Except we're investigating you at the moment. And you're deflecting. What are you hiding, Cleo?"

Cleo was looking at her phone now. Checking the time? She was half off the stool, one foot tapping on the floor. Jack was right. She looked nervous. Eager to be gone.

"What am I hiding?" she repeated. "Where to begin? I'm a mysterious girl, and I don't trust luck gods a bit. But I'll tell you this, I never killed your king. If I did, you'd can be sure he'd be missing his crown, his rings, even the gold fillings out of his damned teeth."

I glanced at Jack. The resignation on his face told me he was thinking the same thing I was; nothing was missing from the room where the king died. And Cleo was a thief above all else. She was telling the truth.

"Any other information you can give us?" I said. "Have you heard any rumors? Seen any unusual peri activity?"

She was on her feet now, checking her phone again.

"The only unusual peri I can tell you about is one who came over from the other side a few months ago. Varsmith, his name is. He's a goblin, one of the worst—and they're all bad. If you're looking for a peri who's up to no good, look for him."

She backed toward the kitchen, pulling the leprechaun key on its golden chain from out of the top of her shirt. As she did, another neckless came with it. This one was silver; it had a pendant on it that I recognized, a strange sort of star, but I couldn't place where I'd seen it before.

"Now if you'll excuse me," Cleo said, "I need to go back. I've got a child to care for, after all, and I wouldn't want him getting in trouble while auntie Cleo is away."

Jack snorted. "If he gets into the same sort of trouble he did at the Valentines' mansion, he'll already have the place burned down by the time you get back."

Cleo jabbed a finger toward Jack. "Watch what you say about my boy, now. I said I didn't kill any Valentine royals. I didn't say I *wouldn't*."

Then she took her glowing leprechaun key through the pantry door and was gone.

Jack's gaze swung slowly back toward me. "Well, that might have been mildly helpful. That Varsmith character seems—"

But I had drifted in until my face was inches from his. The world swam deliciously around me, and all I could see was Jack's eyes, bright and vivid and blue. His gaze drifted down to my lips.

"Aggie..." he whispered. It was the beginning of a warning. A denial. But I didn't care. I was drunk beyond reason. Beyond fear. Beyond pride. Beyond counting. He held me at arm's length, keeping me back, but I flared charm and shrugged off his hands, moving forward until my body was pressed against his. I collided with him, my lips finding his, our teeth banging together, our tongues meeting. The world spun and I spun with it, ready to collapse into him in a delicious frenzy of heat and light, like two stars meeting and imploding together.

**15**

---

## CLEO

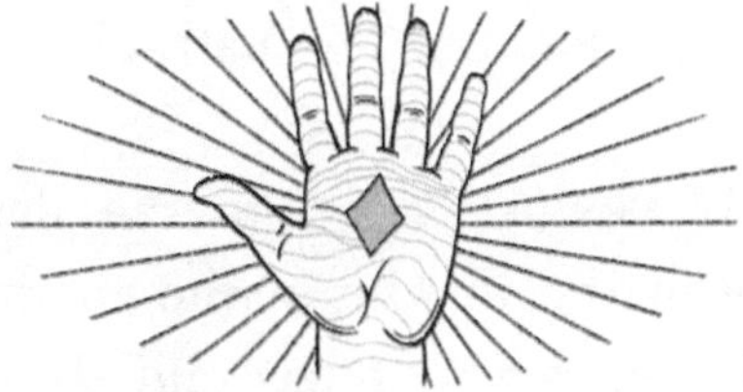

Cleo grumbled as she emerged from the leprechaun underground into her dim, cavern-like lair. She hated dealing with luck gods. They were always trying draw the rest of the peri into their bickering and battling. Then they had the nerve to act offended when Cleo made it clear she wanted no part of their squabbles, as if she owed them something. Absently, she fingered charm that hung from her necklace, symbol of the secret order.

Yes, the only way to deal with the luck gods was to undermine them. Marginalize them. Keep them as weak as possible. And most of all, keep them on this side of the rift.

Cleo had a pretty good idea who might have killed the Valentines' precious king, but she wasn't going to use that information to curry favor with the Valentines the way her boot-licking brother Lorcan would have. Dead luck gods were nothing to her. Hell, she'd have been happy to smoke that dour sot King Michael herself.

Flopping down on the couch, she gave a heavy sigh, grateful, as always, for the peace and security of her lair.

Then it hit her. Something was off. The silence…

She sat up fast, listening. The boy's dumb video game was always humming and chiming with its infernal music. Now, it was quiet. Cleo went to the sleeping area expecting to find the boy curled up in her bed, adorably slumbering. But no. His tangled covers lay empty.

"Junior?" she called, striding fast to the bathroom, craning her neck to look in. The bathtub was empty. Ditto the toilet.

Cleo cursed, moving back into the living space and turning a circle in the middle of the room. "Junior!" she shouted. But the lair wasn't huge, and she could see at a glance the boy wasn't here.

Hands on the hilts of her daggers, she walked with purpose toward the exit, then hesitated, detouring to the black chest that sat against one wall. The clasps were open, and Cleo would have cursed again if it weren't for the lump in her throat. She kicked the lid of the chest open. It was empty. The shard of Spades obelisk that had sat inside was gone.

"Damn it," Cleo snarled, wheeling, bursting out the door, sprinting up the metal steps. Each footfall rang ominously, like the tolling of a bell. Up and up and up. "I should have gotten rid of that thing… I should have smashed it with a hammer… I should have…"

Hell, she could have given it back to that spooky old

Spade queen, for all Cleo cared. But she should never have kept the thing in her house. Especially with the boy there. Objects like that could call to people. Warp them. Especially with those marks on his hands. Cleo had known better. She'd been stupid. So stupid. And greedy. She'd been angling to sell the stone chunk to the Diamonds or the sylph for maximum profit. Now, look what her greed had wrought.

She reached the metal door at the top of the stairwell, unbarred and unlocked it and pushed it open, revealing empty, moonlit desert.

"Gallo Junior!" she screamed.

The only answer was the faint pinging of bats, churning against the black sky. She took a few erratic steps one way and then the other, but there was nowhere for the boy to hide. The only feature on the landscape aside from low scrub and a few stones was the cinder-block hut that housed the entrance to Cleo's realm—and the boy wasn't hiding behind it. That left one possibility.

Cleo jogged down the rutted dirt trail to the main road, some five hundred feet away. She reached it and stood on the gravel shoulder catching her breath, looking first left then right up the two-lane road. A couple of cars whooshed past, raking her with their cold, blue headlights.

*Gone. Junior is gone.*

The words stung her like a cold wind, and only then, as tears welled in her eyes, as her lips quivered, as the thought of going back down to her lair alone fell upon her with smothering force—only then did she realize how much she'd come to love the boy.

*Junior is gone. He's gone. He's gone,* she thought in despair.

And another part of her answered: *So go and get him back.*

**16**

———

**AGGIE**

I woke with a thumping headache and a mouth dry as cat litter. With great effort I peeled my eyes open and found I was lying alone on the bed in Jack's crash pad although I had no memory of getting there.

*Oh, God. What did I do last night? What did* we *do?*

I plumbed my memory for any hint of what might have happened, but I could find no clues. Still, I could imagine all the beautifully naughty things I might have attempted with Jack, alone at night with him, all fears and inhibitions quashed by alcohol, at it made me blush. *Four, five, six...* I counted the beats of my speeding heart until it slowed down again.

I already knew Jack wasn't in the condo. Something

about the depth of the silence tipped me off, and the bed was way colder than it would have been if he had been with me recently. Still, I rose and shuffled to the living room, shivering as my bare feet crossed the polished concrete floor. Sure enough, on the kitchen counter lay a hastily scrawled note:

*Had to take care of a few things.*
*Left the car.*
*Meet you back at*
*the Hearts house later.*
*-J*

*Disappearing again. Typical Jack.*

A paper bag next to the note yielded a bagel with cream cheese, and a cup next to it sloshed with a still-lukewarm latte. Thoughtful touches. But I still felt lonely and annoyed Jack had left me. *Disconsolate*, I thought, trying out another SAT vocab word, although it was perhaps a bit too strong for what I was actually feeling.

Having a belly full of bagel and coffee improved my mood and my headache immensely. I took the car keys Jack had left, found a red muscle car down in the apartment complex parking garage—such a *Jack* vehicle—and drove off to the Valentine house through a sunny, frosty morning.

When I arrived, my first impulse was to go looking for Jack, but I resisted. Instead, I headed to the Valentine library. The place was a bibliophile's wonderland, two-stories tall with lovely carved wood bookshelves, a spiral staircase, Tiffany lamps, and a collection of big, perfectly broken-in leather chairs. It was one of my favorite parts of the house, a place I could easily lose myself in for hours.

I found Deuce slouched at one of the tables, morning sunlight spilling onto him from one of the tall windows, poring over a stack of books.

"Whatcha doing, book nerd?" I greeted him.

He looked up and I noticed his messy hair and wrinkled clothes, not to mention his eyes, which looked like those of a bear emerging from hibernation, all squinty and blinky.

"This book the ace has us looking for is a serious needle in a haystack," he said. "And do you know bad the organization in this place is? It's like the Dewey Decimal system on crack. So I'm redoing the whole thing. Top to bottom."

"Wow," my eyes ranged around the room, taking in the haphazard stacks of books, old pizza boxes, and empty coffee cups. "How long have you been in here?"

Deuce blinked at me. "Since you left," he said. "You asked me to find the book, I'm finding it."

"Have you slept?"

"I might have bonked out for a few minutes last night. There was a pretty good drool puddle on this table about four AM or so."

I laughed.

"But hey, when my queen gives an order and I get hyper-focused on it..." he shrugged, punctuating the sentence with a colossal yawn. "I'm going to find you that book. It just might take me a while."

I smiled. "Thanks, Deuce. You're the best."

He returned my smile, looking oddly cute in his wan, rumpled state. "Yeah. Old reliable," his eyes drifted shut in what started out a blink but might have become a nano-nap. "How was your night with Jack?" he said when his eyes popped open again. There was a certain bitter twist to the words that set off alarm bells for me. The night of my marriage—the night Michael died—Jack and Deuce had gotten into a fight. I'd never questioned either of them as to what it was about, but I suspected it had something to do with me.

"It was uneventful," I said pointedly, lest Deuce think we hooked up. "We talked to Lorcan and Cleo. And I think we can pretty much cross both of them off the suspect list."

Deuce rubbed his eyes. "About Jack," he said. "I've been meaning to talk to you..."

But the mention of Cleo had me thinking. "Oh, hey," I interrupted, grabbing a piece of scratch paper and a pencil from the table and sketching the necklace Cleo had been wearing, then shoving the paper over to Deuce.

"Have you seen this symbol? I know I saw it in one of these books, but I can't remember which one, or what the symbol meant. Cleo was wearing a charm with this symbol on it. It's probably nothing, but..."

Deuce looked at my sketch and rubbed his chin. "Yeah. This does seem familiar. Looks like a seven pointed star inside a crescent moon."

"Or a horse shoe," I said. "I'm a bad artist."

Deuce nodded to himself, rising and drifting to another table. His fingers walked down the spines of a stack of books, then he pulled one out and flipped it open, flipping through the pages. I peered over his shoulder and saw a title at the top: *Peri Wars and Factions: 1895-1995.*

At last, he stopped and tapped his finger on a page. "There."

The pen-and-ink illustration was very similar to what I'd drawn. I read the caption.

"Symbol of the Shastaryan," I glanced at Deuce. "Who's that?"

"If I remember right, it was a group of jokers from the other side of the rift who wanted to wipe out all luck gods or something back in the early 1980's."

I bit my lip, pondering. Could the group still exist? Could Cleo be part of it? Or was it a dead end? The necklace might just be a meaningless bangle, of course. But my gut told me otherwise. Leprechauns always decked themselves out in gold. This necklace was silver. Why would Cleo be wearing it, if it didn't have some significance?

"Could I borrow that book, Mr. Librarian?" I asked.

Deuce marked the page with a piece scratch paper, clapped the book shut and handed it to me. "Just make sure when you're done you don't just chuck it on some shelf, like the rest of these heathens. A mess, I tell you. A mess!" he shook his head ruefully.

I backed toward the door. "Alright. Well..."

"Where are you off to now?" he asked, wilting a little as he added, "More sleuthing with Jack?"

There it was again. That jealous tone.

"No," I said. "He's... busy this morning."

Deuce blinked nervously. "Has he talked to you about the two of you? How you... got together?"

I shook my head, confused. Obviously, I knew how Jack and I got together. I was there. "No," I said warily. "Why?"

Deuce looked at his shoes and cleared his throat. "Well. He should tell you. It's not my place."

"Tell me what?"

He seemed about to answer, then shook his head. "You should ask him."

He looked at me again, as if willing me to understand his meaning. Except I didn't. And frankly, I didn't have time to wonder about it.

"Alright. I'm off to school now," I said, forcing a smile. "You keep looking for that book for me, alright?"

He gave a grand bow. "Your wish is my command, my queen."

I groaned. "Please don't call me that."

"Sorry," he said, that mournful look in his eyes again. "Your wish is my command—Aggie."

# 17

# JUNIOR

The door dinged as Junior stepped into the convenience store. There was a long line at the counter, but almost no one glanced at him as he made his way down the aisle toward the bathrooms, picking up whatever looked good to him as he went. A king size Rice Krispie Treat. A granola bar. A baggie of peanuts. A banana. A bright blue Powerade from the cooler. Probably nobody would have noticed him, but he flared a little bad luck anyway, willing the clerk and any nosy customers to be distracted. It was easy. Adults with phones were always distracted.

He didn't like the bathroom. The walls were covered in old-fashioned wood paneling, there were rust stains in the sink and the floor was slimy under his sneakers. Still, he peed, washed his hands, splashed water on his face, rinsed his mouth out and spat in the sink. All night he'd been walking through the desert. The wind had stirred up dust until his mouth was filled with grit and his eyes ached. It felt good now to be clean, though his feet still hurt from walking all night, his eyes were rimmed with pink and his blinks were long and slow with sleepiness.

*No time for rest yet,* the voice said to him. *She'll be searching for you. She'll be coming.*

The voice, Junior knew, came from the chunk of dark crystal in his backpack. It had led him all night, telling him which direction to go, urging him onward. How it was able to speak inside his mind he wasn't sure, but then he'd given up on questioning the line between make-believe and reality months ago, the day that alien looking man had kidnapped him. Since then, he'd been sold to another alien guy (sylphs, they were called.) He'd been held captive in a place that was like a freaky *Ripley's Believe it or Not* full of lucky and unlucky creatures and artifacts. He'd met a cruel, purplish skinned goblin. He'd seen luck gods do battle and glimpsed a bad luck dragon made out of smoke (a jinni, Cleo had called it). He'd lived with a pretty leprechaun who had the power to move between any two doors in the world. And of course, he'd touched the chunk of crystal that now sat in his backpack and it had made him into a demigod.

But before all this, he'd lived with his mean single mom and her string of weird, abusive boyfriends. Life had been bad. To Junior, being bossed around by a chunk of stone rather than by his mother was an improvement.

*You'll need to hitch a ride here,* the stone was saying in its deep, strangely accented voice. It sounded to Junior like a cartoon bad guy—except he knew it was very real. *We'll have to choose the driver carefully. Pick someone too responsible and they'll call the police, someone too disreputable and they're liable to hurt you.*

"I know, I know," Junior muttered, taking a bite of the Rice Krispie treat and shoving the rest of the snacks in his pockets. Someone banged on the locked door.

"Just a minute!" Junior shouted.

Cleo had taught him that harsh responses tended to surprise people and get them to back down. No luck this time. The knocking came again.

"There's no merchandise allowed in the bathroom. Open up."

The cash register guy. Junior huffed a frustrated sigh, glancing around the room and settling his attention on the paper towel dispenser.

"Just a sec," he shouted, waving his hands under the dispenser and ripping off towels as fast as he could. When he had two handfuls, he crushed them up and poured hex into them.

The stone's voice in the back of his mind chuckled as he dropped the wads into the toilet and flushed. The water spun and gulped, then started rising. Junior munched his Rice Krispie Treat and watched with morbid fascination as the water rose, then overtopped the bowl and began drizzling onto the tile. The clerk was banging on the door again. This time, Junior opened it.

"Uh, I think the toilet is clogged," he said in his littlest voice. The man's eyes went to the toilet. He hurried forward, cursing, while Junior slipped past him.

The doors slid open and Junior stepped out of the convenience store into the cool, early morning air, scanning the cars fueling up. His gaze settled on a white pickup truck, the owner of which wore a red baseball cap and a cowboy-style plaid shirt with pearl buttons. The man got the gas going then headed toward the convenience store, taking an empty cigarette packet from his shirt pocket and chucking it into the trash as he went, without a so much as a glance at the boy standing on the curb, watching him. When he was inside, Junior jogged to the man's pickup truck.

*Perfect,* the stone whispered in his mind.

Junior put a foot on the truck's back bumper and vaulted over the tailgate—only to find himself inches from a snarling mouth, sharp white teeth, and icy blue eyes. A wolf.

For a second, Junior started to use the spade marks on his hands, to pour out bad luck on the wolf before it could bite him. But he stopped himself. The thing was only scared. Junior had probably startled him. And hitting the poor thing with bad luck would only make the fear worse.

*Calm yourself. Dogs can smell fear. Be brave,* Junior told himself. That inner voice, half encouraging, half admonishing, sounded like more Cleo's than the stone's. Thinking of her made Junior want to run back to her cozy hideout, to eat some microwave pizza with her and curl up on the couch to play video games.

But the stone in his backpack chastised him, *Remember what I told you, boy. Go back and you'll be endangering her. You see that snarling dog? You're far more dangerous than that. You're a bad luck god now. Spades don't have mommies.*

The beast snarled again, its body rigid, its hackles up. Junior reached out to it and the wolf snapped.

*The marks. They're scaring him. He can feel the bad luck,* Junior thought, and he turned his hand over, offering the back to the wolf. The beast crouched, eyes narrowed. Then it inched forward to sniff Junior's hand. It stopped snarling, blinked, and gave his knuckles a lick.

"See? I'm not that scary, am I?" Junior said, stroked the creature's silky head. It wasn't a wolf after all, Junior thought. More of a big, tough looking husky.

He heard footsteps behind him and glanced back to see the man coming toward the truck, looking down at his phone. Just in time, Junior dropped to lie flat on the truck bed.

The dog looked at him quizzically, nudging him with a wet nose, then looking up at his master.

"Shh," Junior put a finger to his lips, willing the dog to stay quiet. For a second, he thought the dog was going to bark and rat him out. He gritted his teeth, held his breath. But the dog just watched the man pass.

Junior let a bit of bad luck out of his hands. *Don't notice me. Look at your phone. Be distracted.*

The man replaced the gasoline nozzle, shut the fuel door, then climbed into the truck's cab, eyes still on his phone screen. Too easy. The engine fired, and the vehicle started to roll forward.

"Thanks," Junior whispered, stroking the downy fur on the husky's flank. The dog looked at him for a moment, then sighed and lay down, nuzzling into Junior. The truck picked up speed, wind rushing past. The air was cold, but the husky's body and fur were warm against Junior's cheek, and the sound of the truck's tires on pavement made a pleasant hum. Before long, Junior's eyes drifted shut.

# 18

# AGGIE

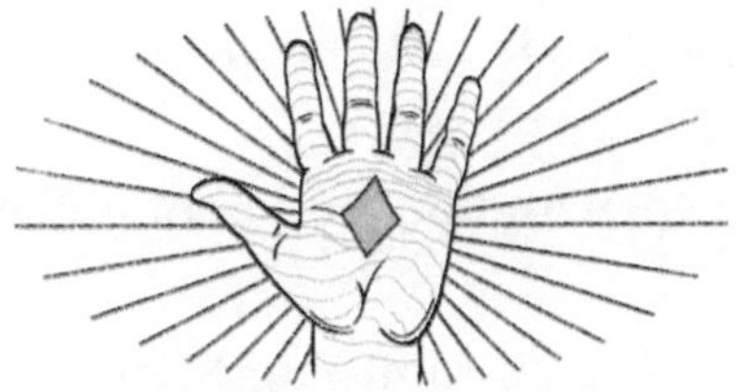

I sat in Mr. Kleinman's French class, gazing out the window as few snowflakes drifted listlessly from a cast iron sky. The leaves had fallen, leaving the patch of forest that bounded the school looking skeletal.

Kleinman was regaling us for about the fortieth time with the story of his third visit to Paris and the waitress he'd met in the coffee shop who'd been kind enough to show him around. It would have been a sweet story in a romance movie, but coming from a teacher it had some *ick* vibes. I was doodling a baguette on the margin of my long-forgotten handout as Kleinman said:

"So there I was, sitting on the back of her Vespa as we

zoomed around the Arc de Triomphe and holding on to her for dear life, when—"

I glanced outside the window again. There, at the edge of the woods, a figure shimmered into existence. A peri. Whoever it was wore a hoodie and their face was covered, but I recognized them. It was the same person who'd cornered me in a rest area on my way down to Tennessee for my queen trial. I thought they were going to try to kill me, then. Instead, they'd told me I was walking into a trap— which had turned out to be true. They'd also told me to "watch out for my husband." I'd thought at the time they meant Michael might be plotting against me. In retrospect, though, the meaning became clear. This person knew someone was going to kill Michael. That meant they probably knew who did it.

I dropped my pen and bolted out of my seat, heading for the door.

"Miss Van Der Graff?" Monsieur Kleinman said.

"Little girls' room," I called back without slowing, then added: "Tampons and stuff," just to ensure I wouldn't be questioned. Kleinman didn't say another word, but I did curse myself at the ripple of laughter and "ews" that went around the room. So, becoming a goddess hadn't completely cured me of being socially awkward. Oh well. I flared a little charm on the way out, urging everyone to forget about my dumb joke fast. And indeed, as I hurried down the hall, I could hear Kleinman already diving back into his story.

I pushed out a side door to find myself in the small forest that bordered the east side of the school and immediately wrapped my arms around myself. I wore no jacket, and the November wind seemed to slice through my thin cotton shirt. The door drifted shut behind me and I heard it click. I was locked out here with whoever it was. And I was unarmed. Not the world's smartest choice, even for a someone with queen power...

But there was no going back.

When I'd awakened to find Michael dead, the first thing I saw was a shimmer near the open window, the telltale sign of an invisible(ish) peri. I'd nearly convinced myself I imaged that shimmer, but it was too much of a coincidence. This peri had told me Michael was in danger. And a peri had been there when Michael died. Now, they were following me. I'd teased Jack by putting him at the top of my list, but as far as I was concerned, this was my number one suspect.

Except there was no sign of them.

I strode ahead, moving past the strip of mowed lawn that bordered the school and passing into the forest. I tried to move in stealthy silence, but even flaring charm it was impossible. Dead leaves crunched under my feet. Twigs snagged and cracked around me. I stepped over a fallen log, sidestepped a small boulder, circled around the trunk of a massive, ancient Mulberry tree—and there my stalker stood.

I glanced around for a weapon. A stick, a stone, anything —but I found nothing.

The peri stepped forward. I noted a pair of silver-hilted daggers at their belt, but no weapon in their hands. That was a good sign, maybe.

"It's interesting to find you here again," the intruder said evenly. "Most demigod queens don't do high school."

"Yeah. Well. Most demigod queens aren't trying to get a full ride to MIT," I said. "Who are you and why are you following me?"

The figure hesitated for a moment before reaching up for their hood. As they did, I noticed their hands, just as I had months ago at the rest stop. There were glowing marks there —but not hearts, diamonds, clubs, or spades. These were many-pointed stars, and their glow was teal rather than red or dark purple.

Those glowing hands grasped the hood and pulled it back.

The first thing I noticed was the man's shaved head. No, not a man. The lips were too full. The eyes too large and sensitive. The cheeks too soft looking. It was a woman. Beautiful.

And familiar, though I couldn't place her.

She gave a small smile, apparently amused by my expression. "You don't remember me. That's okay. There was a lot going on, and so much has happened since then. It was almost another life..."

She eyed me, waiting, then crossed her arms. "Last time we met, Jack was jumping over the candle stick."

That sounded like a nonsensical riddle, but I knew what she was talking about. The day Jack and I got captured by the clubs and they forced him to jump over the bonfire over and over again. My OCD had gotten in my way. I'd failed to help Jack and he nearly was nearly cooked alive. It was a shameful memory, one I'd never forget. Just thinking of it made me want to count the tattered leaves still clinging to the branch above the intruder's head.

The woman snorted a laugh at my confusion. "Wow. They told me jokers were basically ghosts, but I didn't believe them."

Joker. That's when it clicked.

"You're Carlotta Blackover."

Her eyebrows went up. "Not Blackover anymore," she said, brandishing her starry palms. "But yes."

Looking at her again, it seemed obvious.

Her beauty, her height, her regal power—all were still there. The only thing missing from the last time I'd seen her was the mane dark hair. *Great,* the petty girl in me said, *another of Jack's exes, back in the mix.* But the ramifications of this revelation went far beyond my love life, and I frowned, trying to make sense of them.

"So... you're a joker?"

Jokers were outcasts, luck gods who, one way or another, had ended up exiled from their suit. Everything I'd heard about them was pretty bleak. Jokers were loners, usually banished to the world beyond the rift, a place filled with dangerous, luck gobbling monsters. There they lived, short, lonely lives before dying some horrible death. But Carlotta seemed pretty alive to me.

She gave a nod. "Yes. I'm a joker."

"You've been beyond the rift?"

Again she nodded.

"What's it like?" I asked.

My scientific curiosity about the world beyond the rift had been burning ever since I first heard about it. But I'd never gotten that chance to talk to anyone who'd actually travelled there. Even most of the sprites who served our suit were second or third generation immigrants. Their parents or grandparents might have come from beyond the rift, but they'd never been there themselves. And they were generally evasive and dismissive when asked about—well, anything.

"Our order holds certain knowledge secret," Carlotta said now.

"What order? You mean the Blackovers?"

She shook her head and gave me a crooked grin. "That's one of the things that's secret," she said. "Before we share knowledge, we must confirm you are worthy by asking you three questions."

Another riddle. I shrugged with a nervous glance over my shoulder. Class would be getting out soon, but we weren't within view of the school's windows, and nobody seemed to have noticed I was gone. "Okay. Three questions," I said. "Shoot."

"First, what is the source of luck?" she asked.

I pushed my glasses up my nose, thinking. "Well, that's not exactly clear, but the best theory I've heard is it's connected to sub-atomic particles called luckeons. It's basically a poorly understood natural phenomenon."

I couldn't tell if this answer pleased her or not, but she asked a second question. "What's the purpose of luck?"

I frowned, thinking harder. After a moment I noticed myself flaring a little luck to help my mind land on the right answer; I hadn't even been aware I was doing it. "Like I said, it's a natural phenomenon. It doesn't have a purpose on its own. It all depends on how we use it. On intention."

Carlotta nodded. "And who should control luck?"

Finally, an easy question. "Us. The luck gods," I said.

But the pleased look on Carlotta's face hardened.

"I'm sorry," she said, backing away.

"Wait!" I said quickly. "Are you the one who killed Michael?"

But she was already gone, disappearing into the underbrush and flickering out of existence.

"Please! I have to know!" I shouted after her.

But my voice echoed into silence.

**19**

---

## RACHEL

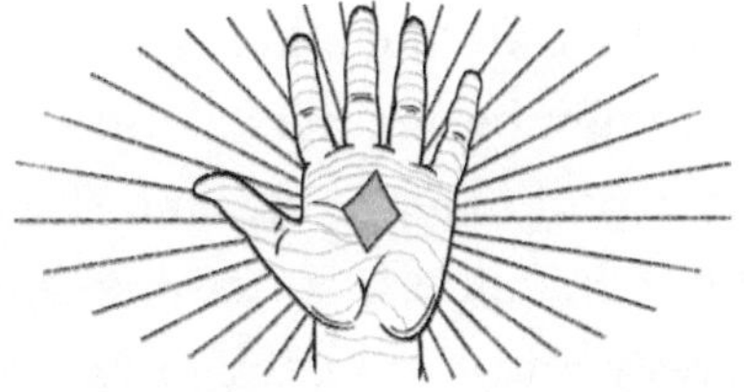

Rachel knew Gallo Blackover by reputation. He'd figured prominently in some of the stories the obelisk shard had told her, as its whispered rants about the history of the suits kept her awake at nights. According to the stories, Gallo was powerful. Ruthless. Ambitious. And dead.

He'd been spurned by his suit, in part because he'd formed an alliance with the Morbus when they had secretly backed Rachel's work on the dark matter machine. He had quarreled with King Thad during the battle near Oak Hill. And then Jack Valentine had shot him in the eye.

And yet he stood before her, two-hundred and fifty pounds of grunting, quivering man in a sweat-soaked tank top, performing bicep curls with a pair of dumbbells, each of which was nearly as heavy as Rachel herself.

They were in the basement of Gabardine's facility, where a workout room had been set up. It featured treadmills, elliptical machines, rowing machines, and punching bags. A rack of weights gleamed along one mirrored wall, and an array of stretchy weight bands, jump ropes, and other workout accoutrements hung on hooks above a large swath of pristine training mats. There were loads of other machines, too, most of which Rachel had no idea what to do with.

All of it was clearly brand new, no doubt procured by Darby. *I finally have endless money and several man-servants to get me whatever I want,* Rachel reflected. Who would have thought she could have all that and take no joy from it?

She blinked, remembering herself. She'd been staring at Gallo for the better part of a minute, and she realized he was looking back at her, his mouth curled into a dark smile. She quickly looked away and went back to her own workout. It was a chest press machine—one of the few contraptions that she'd immediately understood—and she shoved the handles upward, her arms trembling despite the low weight. She continued until she couldn't anymore, then let the handles fall back to their resting position with a bang. Her heart thumped fast and her head swirled with dizziness, making her shut her eyes for a moment. *Easy. Gabardine warned me to take it easy.* But she knew the obelisk had big plans and wanted her strong. The pips on her hands also burned with a need for her to return to her former health—so she could inflict bad luck on others. And of course, it was hard to be casual with muscle man over there lifting enough weight to shift tides.

When she opened her eyes, he was looming over her.

"Oh, God," she said, still catching her breath. "Look at you. Sneaky as a cat." The luck god didn't answer, of course. Dr. Gabardine had explained that the bullet which entered his brain, while not deadly, had taken away his power of speech, although Rachel imaged him as the quiet, brooding type anyway.

Gallo reached out a hand to her. She hesitated, then took it, her hand feeling like a child's in his much larger one. He helped her to her feet, placed a hand on the small of her back, and led her toward the large mats.

"Okay. Where are we going?"

He took one of the stretchy weight bands down from the hooks and approached her with it. The mischievous glint in his eye made her wonder what he intended to do with it, and her own imagination made her blush.

"Okay, that... see, I don't even know what to do with that," she said.

"I've usually done most of my workouts to vintage VHS tapes. It kind of takes the sting out of working out if you're doing it ironically. Step aerobics. Dance aerobics. You know. Sweat bands and leg warmers. Jane Fonda..."

She trailed off as he held each end of the band liked a jump rope then stepped on the center of it with both feet, pinning to the floor, and demonstrated a few slow bicep curls. Her gaze lingered on his arms, all hard, straining muscle and delicate, bulging veins. Then he stepped off it and offered it to her.

"Me? Oh, okay."

She did as he had done, holding the ends, stepping onto the center, and pulling upward. She trembled even more than she had on the machine, but she managed to do a few reps.

"Feel the burn," she quipped. The black Jack looked at her with the calm expectancy of a wolf, but there was intelligence in those deep-set brown eyes. Well, the one eye. And there was amusement there too, though he did not laugh.

"You know, in the future I think all women will have their very own mute man-friend. You can keep a secret, I bet." Her smile faded. "I bet we both have plenty of secrets."

She wondered suddenly why Gallo was here. The obelisk shard had brought him, no doubt, and Gabardine had healed him. But why?

That blasted chuck of stone orchestrated everything in its manipulative way, playing some long game Rachel hardly understood. It had been working with Gallo back in Siberia. But why was he here now?

Slowly he came around behind her, looming close, and she tensed. His hands went to her shoulders, standing her up straighter, then drifted down to her hands, one finger brushing her forearm as they did, making her shiver. Hands on her wrists, he guided her arms up again, with better form this time. Her arms burned and trembled, but all she was aware of was him, his body against hers, the dark pulse of his hex as palpable as the warmth radiating from his body. So close. Too close. She wanted bolt, to shrug away. But the one thing he'd learned over her months as the rock's prisoner was that there was no escape. The only way out of the black tunnel she was in was to plow forward until she came out the other side. To enjoy what she could and endure the rest. And so she shut her eyes, clenched her teeth and forced her muscles to work as the man they called the Heart Slayer guided her every motion.

**20**

---

**AGGIE**

"**A**ggie!"

School had just let out, and I walked in the throng of students exiting the school. My mind had been awhirl, lost in a maze of speculation about the peri and Michael's murder, but the sound of my name startled me out of my thoughts. It took me only a moment to pick out the tall, perfectly put-together blonde girl hurrying up to me.

Claudette. My former nemesis turned friend.

After everything that had gone down with Molly, she was perhaps the *best* friend I had left outside of the Valentines—a scary thought.

She jogged up and fell in beside me.

"Everything okay?"

"Hmm?" I responded absently.

"I heard you bolted out of French and didn't come back."

"Oh. I'm fine. Just lady stuff, you know. Period and whatnot."

"Ah," she was giving me her *not buying it* look. "I thought it might have something to do with Danforth calling you into her office the other day."

Nothing made it past Claudette unnoticed.

I certainly wasn't going to tell her about the cheating thing. It was too mortifying. "She may have noticed that my mom isn't exactly in the picture right now."

"Ah," Claudette said.

It was awkward having my former rival as a confidant. But she had been there on the day I battled Mom at Oak Hill. She'd witnessed the surreal supernatural powers of the luck gods firsthand, and her mom had been hurt in the battle. Though Professor Dodson had mostly recovered, she was still dealing with the aftereffects of the head injury. We'd both lost our moms that day, or nearly lost them, and Claudette and I had shared a strange comradery ever since.

"Whatcha reading?" she asked.

I glanced down at the book in my hand. It was the one Deuce had given me that morning from the Valentine's library. I still hadn't gotten a chance to read it and was hustling to the car to do just that—before Claudette had snagged me.

"Just a little extracurricular reading," I said, reflexively clutching the book to my chest.

Claudette craned her neck to read the title.

"Is it a luck gods book?"

"Uh, yep," I said, glancing longingly toward my car, then

scanning the lot for any tell-tale shimmers. Carlotta might be out there now. Watching me. Stalking me. I really didn't have time for chit chat.

"Can I borrow it sometime?" Claudette said. "Or any of the luck gods books? Molly said they have tons. I just find that stuff so fascinating."

I wanted to come back with a snarky remark, something about how the Hearts house wasn't just some normal library she could check books out of. But I preferred to extricate myself from the conversation, not start an argument, so I said, "Not sure I'm supposed to share them. I've gotta—"

"I've been wondering: what do you think about the website?" she asked.

I'd been turning away, but I pivoted back now. "What website?"

"Oh, you haven't seen it?"

She unlocked her phone and offered it to me. On the screen was a website with a border of hearts, clubs, diamonds, and spades at the top. Below it was a photo of Danusia Diamante, the Jill of Diamonds, with a headline that read, *Rich Heiress, or Blessed Goddess?* I saw that the web address for the site was LuckGodSightings.com. I scrolled down to find a picture of Marley Blackover walking down the street and of Adelie sitting at a café with some boy I'd never seen before, making flirty eyes.

"What the...?" I muttered, looking back at Claudette. "Where did you find this?"

"Just Googled Luck Gods," she shrugged. "It was the only thing that came up. It looks like the site has been up for a couple of months."

I stared at the phone, my heart racing. I wasn't sure what this meant, but having some paparazzi type following luck gods around and trying to expose them seemed like a bad thing.

"Any mention of who runs the site or what their agenda is?" I asked, scrolling down the website.

She shook her head. "I can look into it, though, if you want. By the way, any leads on who killed King—oh..."

She trailed off and I followed her gaze down to the parking lot. A glistening red luxury car sat idling on the curb, which could only mean one thing.

Sure enough, the driver's side door opened and Jack emerged. In his sunglasses and with the collar of his winter coat popped, he looked like the poster boy for some fashion designer's winter collection.

"Oh, my," Claudette said. "You didn't tell me Jack was back."

*There are a lot of things I don't tell you,* I wanted to say. Instead, I forced a smile and handed the phone back.

"Let me know what you find out about the website," I said, and hurried toward Jack.

❦

Wordlessly, I got in the car and thumped the door shut. Jack surged us away from the curb, his aggressive driving momentarily pinning me to my seat.

I was determined not to break the silence first, but I wasn't the silent type. After about twenty seconds I cracked and said, "So..."

"So..." he echoed playfully.

*What happened between us last night?* I wanted to blurt. Had we made out? Had we done more? I desperately wanted to know, and I'd wracked my brain all day in trying to remember, but it was no use. And given Mom's history with alcohol, I felt too guilty and ashamed to admit I'd blacked out. I also wanted to know why Jack had disappeared and where he had been, but I wanted him to volunteer that information. I didn't want to interrogate him. So all my questions and turmoil and hurt feelings came out in passive aggression.

"I didn't ask you to pick me up," I said. "So why are you here?"

"I missed you," he said, unfazed. "Isn't that enough?"

Was he implying something? About last night? I couldn't tell. I didn't know. Ugh, this was going to drive me crazy.

Intent on changing the subject, I flipped open Deuce's book. I explained about the Shastaryan, about noticing Cleo's necklace and about Deuce finding the book. I was about to tell Jack about seeing Carlotta Blackover, too, but something stopped me.

I'd like to say I was being cautious, withholding information until I knew I could trust Jack completely again. But to be honest, I was afraid of look I might see on his face when I told him Carlotta was alive. They'd been in love once, before she betrayed him, ambushed him, and got his best friend William killed. He professed to have no feelings about her now. But if she suddenly turned up alive—no longer a Blackover but a joker—who knew how me might feel?

So instead of getting into any of that, I flipped through the book, looking for a passage that might illuminate the symbol I'd seen. It didn't take long to find the pen-and-ink illustration of the many-pointed-star and moon, and I read aloud:

*"The Opela has been in use for over a millennium as a symbol of the Shastaryan. In the sixth century, following the downfall of*

*Uthule and the rise of the four suits, there arose a faction of castoff luck deities driven from the dimworld by their former suitmasters. These exiles gathered together in the hills outside the capital city Loroplom. They believed the luck deities had become as tyrannical as Uthule before them, and formed a blood pact to rid the world of all controls on luck, both charm and hex."*

I looked up, rubbing my eyes with one hand. "Ugh. This thing reads like the Silmarillion."

"The silly what?" Jack asked.

I rolled my eyes. "You are so un-nerdy. It's a real turnoff," I said. "You honestly need to work on that."

"Anyway..." Jack grunted.

I read on. *"In the ensuing centuries, the Shastaryan has remained active. Three times its numbers swelled into the hundreds and the group made attempts to overthrow the luck gods through force. Each time, their rebellions were thwarted, their ranks decimated and their members scattered. But each time, the survivors banded together again and a period of rebuilding ensued. During these times the Shastaryan continued to operate in a clandestine fashion, building networks of peri spies, sewing division among the luck gods, and carrying out assassinations."*

I looked up from the book to Jack.

"Assassinations!" I said.

"And peri spies."

"I told you, I saw a shimmer in the room just after I found Michael dead."

Jack nodded.

"What do you know about the Shastaryan?" I asked.

He drummed his fingers on the steering wheel. "My dream meetings with the ace are always a bit hazy, but I'm pretty sure she's mentioned them. I don't remember a lot of detail, just that she said they're on the rise again. Aubra and

Michael mentioned them occasionally, too, but they always were always dismissive. They called them jokers and acted like they were banished beyond the rift and would never come back."

I'd been weighing how much I should tell Jack, but given this new information I decided I had to put my cards on the table—pun intended.

"Soooo... That person I saw in the rest stop during my queen trial visited me today, at school. I feel like they might be Shastaryan, too."

Jack looked at me sharply. "Really? What happened?"

"I... nothing happened, really. But the star on the joker's hand, it glowed like our pips, but it reminded me of the symbol Cleo wore. A star. And they mentioned a secret order."

"Who was it?" Jack pressed. "Did they give their name?"

I knew I should tell him. We were investigating this stuff together. And if the Shastaryan were known for carrying out assassinations, and they could turn invisible, that really did vault them to the top of our suspect list. Still, my jealousy got the better of me. I just couldn't bring myself to say the name Carlotta Blackover to Jack. Not yet. "I... don't know," I lied.

"What did they say?"

I shook my head. "Nothing really. Or... it didn't make sense. She asked me a few questions. Like, quizzing me or something."

"It was a she?" Jack said, and I cursed myself for revealing too much.

"Yes," I breathed.

I was looking ahead out the windshield, but in my peripheral vision I saw Jack's watching me intently. "Can you describe her?"

"I didn't get a good look. She had a hood on. I just saw that her head was shaved."

Jack watched me for long enough that I became worried he'd crash the car. Reflexively, I flared charm to keep us safe.

"Watch where we're going, please," I said at last.

Just out of spite, he kept his eyes on me for a moment longer before looking forward.

"There's something you aren't telling me," he said.

"Yeah. Well. There were plenty of things you didn't tell me when you disappeared for months, weren't there?" I huffed.

He sighed. "I explained that. I—"

"Or how about where you went last night."

"Aggie, I was—"

I held up a hand, shutting him up. "It's fine. We both have our secrets."

That made me think of what Deuce had said, to ask Jack about how we got together. What was Deuce getting at with that comment? I wasn't even sure I wanted to know. Especially not now, when I was so confused about what was happening between Jack and me.

"If we're going to be working together," Jack said tightly, "I need to know what you know."

I knew I was about to start a fight, but I couldn't help myself. My head hurt. And I was feeling bratty. "Great. Let's tell each other everything we know, then. Starting with where my mom is."

Jack sat back, simmering. "You know I can't tell you that right now. It isn't safe."

"You know, sometimes it's hard to tell whose side you're on. Mine, or my Mom's."

"Wow. Fine. Be that way," Jack growled.

"I will. Because I am that way."

"Yeah, you sure are," he said.

I could tell he was genuinely irritated, just like I was. But when I exchanged a glance with him, I saw we were both holding back smiles from the absurdity of the exchange. Damned Jack. Why was he so hard to hate?

A sudden buzzing sound made me jump. On the car's screen, Mina's name popped up. Jack pressed a button to answer and the call connected.

"Mina. What's—" he started, but she wailed, interrupting him. The sound sent a shiver through me.

"Galen," she said, her words broken by sobs. "Galen is dead."

**21**

---

# MOLLY

*I am literally on a private jet,* Molly thought, gazing out the window as they banked and descended. For a moment, clouds obscured everything in a slippery white vapor. Then they gave way, revealing the sparkling Mediterranean and a coastal city of white and terracotta towers nestled between green mountains and teal sea.

"Beautiful, isn't it?" Tristaine said in his magical accent, leaning over Molly to peer out. But before Molly could respond, he was turned away again, and she realized he'd been talking to Ten. Tristaine had been chatting her up all flight and had actually managed to wring a few cold smiles out of the famously fickle Heart. Why the Valentine was on a plane full of Diamantes was a question Molly hadn't asked yet, but she intended to find out.

Ten shrugged a shoulder. "You've seen one paradise, you've seen them all."

"I don't know about that," Tristaine said. "I've experienced any number of paradises, and I must say, each was exquisite in its own unique way."

Danusia approached up the aisle. "Before you get your snorkel wet, brother," she said pointedly, "how about we brief our young guest Molly on her task. That is, if you still insist on including her."

Tristaine's attention settled on Molly for the first time in several hours. "Of course. She's come all this way, hasn't she? I think she'll excel."

Danusia sized Molly up, as if considering a questionable dress from the discount rack. "She is unassuming," she conceded.

Tristaine reached for Molly. "Here, my dear. Give me your hand."

Molly hesitated, feeling heat rise to her cheeks.

"Go on," Danusia snapped. "He doesn't bite."

"Actually," Tristaine gave a sidelong glance to Ten, who crossed her arms sternly—though Molly saw a blush creeping into her cheeks.

Tentatively, Molly let Tristaine take her hand. He reached into the interior pocket of his red sport coat. His hand emerged with a pretty silver bracelet which sparkled with what could only be real diamonds, and he fastened it on her wrist.

She traced a finger over the gems. "Wow. It's beautiful."

"It's a tool," Danusia corrected her.

Tristaine sat in a captain's chair across from Molly and

leaned towards her, elbows on his knees. "We'll be visiting a man by the name of Roland Klepper. Of Klep Industries. Have you—?"

Molly shook her head. She'd never heard of them before.

Tristaine waved a hand. "Doesn't matter. The point is, we're looking to close a very important business deal with them. Danusia will be..." he glanced at her, then put special emphasis on the next word. "...interfacing with Mr. Klepper. I will be delving into some business concerns with Mr. Klepper's associates, discussing details of our possible merger. Your job will be to go downstairs, find a black laptop with a sticker that looks like this on it."

Tristaine showed Molly an image on his phone of a logo, the letters K and I interwoven.

"When you find the laptop," he went on, "go as near to it as you can and hold the bracelet right next to it for at least three seconds."

"What's that going to do?" Molly asked.

"It will copy the contents of the computer's hard drive so we can have a look at it later."

So that was what they wanted her for, Molly thought. Espionage. She was basically a spy. Freaking girl boss stuff, right there.

"So everything you're doing is basically a distraction," she said, "so that I can...?"

"Don't flatter yourself," Danusia said. "The merger is the important thing, and Tristaine, Ten and myself will be cementing it."

"However, before we go through with the merger," Traistaine said, "it's essential that we have this information to confirm that Klepper's company actually has the... *technology* he claims."

"And if I succeed, then—"

"Then we won't dump you in the middle of the Mediterranean Sea," Danusia said.

Tristaine placed a hand on Molly's knee. It sent a shiver through her, and she thought immediately of Lorcan. Would he be jealous if he saw Tristaine do that? She sort of hoped so.

"If you succeed," Tristaine went on, "then the entire Diamond suit will be very grateful to you indeed. I have no doubt our queen will reward you as promised."

"But you can't be noticed," Danusia cautioned. "You must not be seen poking around, or caught stealing the data we need. Yes, we will be appreciative if you succeed in your task. But if you fail, you will be jeopardizing years of work, billions of dollars, and the balance of luck worldwide for generations to come. Our gratitude is vast. But our vengeance—"

Before she could finish, a thud jerked the plane and its tires squawked on the tarmac. They had arrived in Monaco.

❦

Sipping a latte on the limo ride to a five-star waterfront hotel. Showering and dressing in one of the most opulent hotel rooms Molly had ever seen. Taking another limo down to a palm-tree-ringed helicopter pad. Riding the helicopter over the flashing, sapphire sea. Finally touching down on the deck of a yacht the size of a battleship; all these experiences passed by Molly as if they were happening to some girl in a TV show she was watching. They didn't seem remotely real.

And it didn't help the surreal feeling that throughout the

process, no one spoke to her. Ostensibly they were going to party on a yacht, but the Diamantes went about their preparations with what Molly imagined was the grim efficiency of a military unit prepping for a mission.

It wasn't until her newly gifted Gucci boat shoes hit the ship's deck that reality smacked her back into focus. A row of crisply uniformed, white-clad servants lined up to greet them as they stepped off the chopper.

Every surface of the ship shone, polished and pristine. As the helicopter's rotors wound down, their thunderous sound replaced with the hush of the ocean and the wind, Tristaine took Molly's hand and helped her down the steps of the aircraft like a gentleman.

For an instant, Molly thought of the kids at school, what they must be doing right now—laboring through some dull physics lecture or choking down another hot lunch in the cafeteria. How tragic for them. She thought of her mother. Molly had told her she was heading back to visit her friends in Detroit and would be staying with Aggie. Lying was easy when your parents were too self-obsessed to care. What would Mummy say if she knew Molly was jet-setting with the rich and famous? Well, she'd be jealous, of course. So Molly vowed brag about it after the fact, even if it did get her in trouble.

One of the servants snapped her out of her daydream. It was a white gloved butler—no kidding, a real butler—offering everyone what appeared to be orange juice with crushed mint leaves and little umbrellas poking out of the top. Molly accepted one gratefully and discovered at the first sip that it had champagne in it. Tristaine startled her by placing a hand on her back as another butler escorted the group through an airy living space and out another door, onto a sun deck.

Mournful musical tones wailed against the sea breeze, and Molly saw their source. A man lay reclining on a teak chaise, playing a saxophone. He wore a pair of baggy linen pants and a white robe that flapped open to reveal a sunburned physique surprisingly fit for a man his age. His hair was dark and shot through with silver, and he had a face that could have gotten him cast as the love interest in one of those holiday movies Molly's mom so adored. This had to be Roland Klepper. When he saw them approaching, the billionaire stopped playing and stood.

"There they are!" he said, swooping and planting a kiss on Danusia's lips that made Molly glance away. *I guess I know how Danusia will be keeping Klepper occupied,* she thought.

"Haven't seen me for a week and already you're playing the blues?" Danusia teased, poking his sax.

"Ha. Right. My New Year's resolution last year was to brush up on my playing. I hadn't picked one of these things up since middle school band, but I'm getting back into it." The man brandished his instrument and played a few warbling notes. "This bad boy used to belong to Clarence Clemons."

When no one responded, he added: "Sax player for Bruce Springsteen's E Street band?" Again there was no response, so at last the handsome man frowned. "No Boss fans here, eh?"

Danusia shook her head, but Molly spoke up. "Mom was pretty into him. I learned to play *Dancing in the Dark* on piano for her birthday a few years ago."

The billionaire lit up. "Ah, hell yeah. We gotta do a duet later, right? What's your name?"

"Molly."

"And how are you connected to this rabble, Molly?" he asked, sidling up to her. "You seem too young be one of their corporate shills."

"I'm—" Molly glanced at Tristaine.

"My cousin," Danusia said, stepping forward. "She'd never been out of the States and I told her she could tag along. Hope you don't mind."

"Not at all. Always glad to meet a fellow musician." He glanced over to one of the servants. "Christian, find us a piano or keyboard or something."

The white-clad man tilted his head in a tiny bow. "Right away, sir."

From the cabin, several men and women in business attire had appeared, bearing laptop computers or briefcases. The billionaire handed his saxophone off to another servant and made introductions.

There was too much going on for Molly to catch most of the names, but after some discussion it was decided that Tristaine would go with Klepper's employees to talk business while Danusia, Molly and Ten (she'd introduced herself as "Tina," which Molly for some reason found amusing) would head to the foredeck for a swim.

Molly had expected to find a little lap pool, but nope. This mega yacht boasted a pool nearly as large as the one at her high school, complete with a fake rock formation and waterfalls. Klepper shed his bathrobe and climbed to the top of the faux cliff with the exuberance of a little boy as Molly, Danusia and "Tina" stood lined up on the pool deck below, watching him.

"Woooo!" he howled when he'd reached the top.

"What a complete asshat," Danusia muttered drily.

"But he's your asshat," Ten pointed out.

"He will be," Danusia agreed. "And his whole empire with him."

Klepper gave another battle cry and dove off the fake rocks, hitting the water below with a wince-inducing smack.

The party proceeded from there. Molly felt super self-conscious as she shed the gauzy wrap the Diamonds had gifted her, revealing the swimsuit beneath. Though everything she wore was expensive designer stuff that fit her perfectly, she knew how her body must look compared to the sculpted goddesses Ten and Danusia. Not only did her tummy and thighs jiggle disconcertingly with every movement, she was also hyper aware of the patch of red, scaly skin creeping from her left clavicle up her neck.

*Lizard girl. Snake face.* Taunts from middle school echoed through her mind. Suddenly she wished she were back on the helicopter. Or that Aggie were here. Molly's former best friend always had a way of disarming her insecurities, of twisting her self-hatred into self-love. Or at least of making her feel less alone. But Aggie wasn't here. It was hard to imagine how they might ever be friends again.

So Molly did her best to forget her lost friend and her insecurities. She downed her drink. Then, she got another.

She imagined if Tristaine were there he'd be keeping an eye on her, perhaps giving her a subtle frown that would cause her to put that second drink down. But he was off conducting business. And everyone else was in the pool, Danusia riding on Klepper's shoulders while Ten playfully splashed at them. Amazing how well those two were playing the role of flirty water nymphs. Laughing. Teasing.

*But they're more like sirens,* Molly thought. *Watch out, Klepper.*

For a second, as her head started to buzz, Molly thought she might warn him, just to see the pissed off looks on the faces of those two bitchy goddesses. But Klepper was a billionaire. He should be savvy enough to protect himself from a pair of flirtatious women—goddesses or no. So she sat back on the chaise and gulped back her drink. Like magic, the servant appeared at her side and placed another in her hand.

*I could get used to this life,* Molly thought. *This is how I was meant to live.* At that thought, her mind snapped back into focus. She could live this way. But she had a task to complete first. And she'd better focus.

She set her glass down and stood, one hand drifting to the bracelet to make sure it was still there.

"Uh, I have to use the restroom," she called down to the pool. Then added: "Sir."

"Hey, don't call me sir," Klepper said, pointing at her. "We're supposed to be band mates, remember?"

Molly returned his smile with a tepid grin of her own as he gestured to the far side of the rocks.

"There's a restroom over there," he said. "Right past the—"

His words were lost as Danusia jumped on him playfully, dunking him under the water.

Molly went in the direction he'd pointed, skirting the outside of the fake rock formation to find a door just beyond it. She cursed to herself. Of course, there was a locker room right by the pool. That gave her no excuse to go down below. She'd just have to sneak.

One glance over her shoulder told her nobody was watching. Splashes and laughter still came from the pool, and there were no servants in sight. Moving swiftly on silent, bare feet, Molly hurried down the wooden walkway between the cabin and the ship's edge. Before long she came upon a sliding glass door. Unlocked. She slipped into the cabin, closing the door behind her. Immediately, she saw the challenge she faced. Tristaine had talked as if finding the laptop would be easy—but this was no little fishing boat. The cabin was far larger than the townhouse Molly and her mom had shared, and that was just the part of it Molly could see. The yacht was at least a hundred and fifty feet long. It would take a ton of luck—and time—to find a laptop in here.

She made quick and lap of the living space. Nothing. By then her morning coffee had run through her and she needed a moment to pause and strategize, so she found a bathroom and slipped inside. She peed, wiped, flushed, and washed. By then, the panic that had been starting to set in had subsided.

She was overthinking this. With Klepper out there occupied, the servants busy, and Tristaine making business plans with all the executive types, nobody would care what Molly did. She could scour the whole boat for the laptop. Hell, she could do cartwheels through the cabin naked and no one would probably care. She looked at herself in the mirror. *This will be simple,* she thought. *All you have to do is be invisible. It should be easy. You've been invisible your whole life. But not any more. Not after this.* Steeled with a mix determination and self-pity, she opened the door—and gasped.

A boy about her age leaned against the back of a couch, staring at her. He had tattoos running up both arms and on one side of his face—a wild mishmash of dragons and guitars and mermaids and god knew what else. His hair rose to a spiky bluish faux-hawk, and his face, though sprinkled with acne, was handsome in a shrewd, mischievous sort of way.

"Uh, hi," Molly said.

"You have a nice voice," he said.

She blinked. "Um. Thanks?"

He nodded toward the bathroom door. "I heard you humming."

Molly crossed her arms. "Do you usually listen at the door when girls are peeing?"

"Sure, when they're cute," the boy shrugged. "I saw you when you came in."

Molly had no idea what to do with that statement, but she felt her cheeks warm spite of herself.

"You one of them?" the boy asked, nodding toward the pool.

"Them? Oh. Sort of," Molly said.

He held up his hand as if waving to her. "Let's see it," he said.

Molly frowned, confused. "See what?"

"What have you got? A diamond?" the boy pointed to the palm of his hand. "I heard they brought one of the heart ones with them this time."

He laughed at the look of surprise on Molly's face.

"Yeah. I know about them. I make it my business to know about everything that has to do with my company."

Molly arched an eyebrow. "*Your* company?"

The boy gave a harsh chuckle. "My uncle runs the company, but little-known fact—guess who's the number one shareholder?" He thumbed toward his chest.

Molly didn't know much about stocks, but she thought that meant this punk kid actually controlled the company.

"I inherited it from my dad. He founded the company,

got crazy rich, then got his dumb ass killed in a skydiving accident."

"Bad luck," Molly said, half to herself.

"You said it." The boy sipped a beer then took a hit off a vape. The smoke smelled to Molly like grape juice. He shrugged. "I didn't know Daddio that well, but everyone says he was a prick. Anyway, he left me with a company and a butt ton of money. My uncle thinks he's a genius because he runs a fortune 500 company, but I spend my days skateboarding, playing in my ska band and getting baked. I'm richer than him and I don't do shit. So who do you think is the smart one?"

Molly laughed. She was starting to like this guy, despite her better judgment.

She glanced away from him, and saw a window that looked out onto the pool. As she watched, Ten gestured toward Danusia and Klepper. It was the same motion she'd seen Aggie use when she charmed two boys at school into falling in love: Cupid's Arrow. And just like that, Klepper took Danusia into his arms, gazed into her eyes, and kissed her, like something straight out of rom-com climax scene. Ten smiled in satisfaction. Too easy.

Molly wondered how people allowed themselves to be sucked in to such transparent manipulations. Love wasn't instant and perfect like that. It was messy. Like between her and Lorcan.

Or between her and anyone...

"You never answered me," the boy said, getting her attention again. He stepped toward her, took her hand and turned it over. Seeing no mark there, he snorted. "Huh. I figured for sure you had to be a goddess."

"Oh, stop," Molly pulled her hand away, her heart suddenly racing.

But he leaned closer. "Why? We're all here discussing a merger, right? Let's merge."

"I can't," she said, feeling her cheeks burn—and other parts, too. "I mean, not right now."

The glimmer of hope she'd given him elicited a smile. "Why's that?"

This was her moment. The boy wanted her. That meant she could get him to help her. She thought fast.

"I... need to check my email," she waggled her phone. "And cell reception out here sucks."

"I can give you our wifi password," he offered.

"A computer would be better," she said, then added, "I have to review some marketing materials. For the company. I need a bigger screen."

She felt proud of the smooth lie, then alarmed when he hesitated, taking a hit of his vape. Then he looked around, spied something and crossed the room.

"Here. My uncle's laptop." He retrieved it from a table and tossed it onto the couch. That was it. It had the sticker on it and everything.

Molly's heart thumped faster with excitement as she sat, picked up the computer and opened it, making sure her bracelet was close to it the whole time.

*Dude, I am a damn good spy,* she thought. *Danusia can suck it.*

The boy was watching her, slugging his beer. God, he was a weirdo, this one. But she liked his eyes on her. She made a show of sitting up straight and acting prim as she opened her email account.

"What's your name, anyway?" the boy asked.

"Molly."

"I'm Seth," he answered. "Hey, mind if I rub your feet while you check your email? I like feet. And I like your pink toe nails."

*An absolute weirdo,* Molly thought, breathing a little laugh. But the weirder this guy got, the more she liked him, somehow.

And this was an interesting situation. While Danusia was out there courting Klepper, she was in here, getting to know the person who really controlled the company. Theoretically she'd accomplished her mission and should be welcomed into the suit. But did she trust the Diamantes? Hell no. And anyway, a little insurance never hurt.

*Sorry, Lorcie. A girl's gotta do what a girl's gotta do,* Molly thought, thumping her feet onto the coffee table.

"Sure, Seth," she wiggled her toes. "Knock yourself out."

**22**

---

**AGGIE**

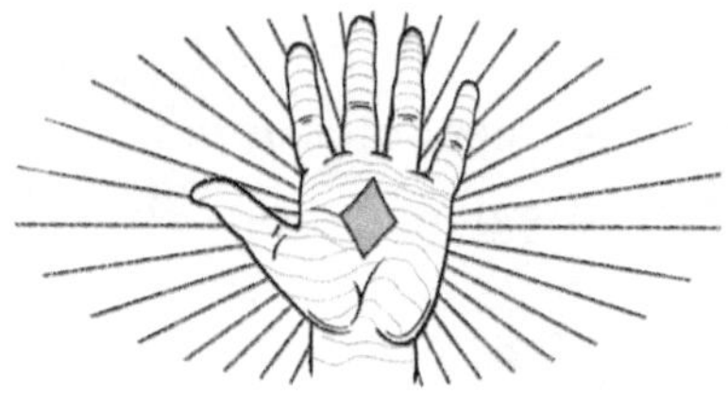

**G**alen's body lay on the floor.

He might have only been sleeping, except for the unnatural angle of his left arm, and his blood, which made a dark stain on the carpet, shaped vaguely like a butterfly wing.

"He was only twenty," I whispered, unable to take my eyes off his still face. In death, he his handsomeness was more pronounced than it had been in life. Or maybe it just seemed that way because it was okay to stare. My eyes traced the fine structure of his cheek bones, the silky nap of his dark hair. It was easy to see why Mina found him so attractive. My OCD tugged at me and I began counting his eyelashes, reaching twenty-three before I stopped myself.

Splayed out like this, his height had turned into length, but big though he was, his smooth face reminded me he was a boy, really. A boy with everything to live for.

My attention drifted to the bloody gashes in his body. Four of them. Stab wounds, according to Jack's assessment. But who had done it? So far, we had no clue.

I pulled my eyes from the grizzly sight and took in my surroundings. We were in vacant office space on the second floor of a strip mall in Dearborn, a suburb of Detroit. The front of the office featured floor to ceiling windows, which had been covered by taped-on brown paper, as if the place were under renovation. But there was no sign any work had been done. Bare cubicles and empty desk chairs still filled the space, all of it beige and banal. Judging by a few old flyers still sitting on one of the desks, this had previously been an insurance broker's office. It wasn't a place where one was likely to find anything interesting—certainly not a dead demigod.

Jack and Seemor stood over near the papered-up windows, conversing in low voices. Seemor was a sprite, and with his backward-bending legs, his squinched up pug-dog face, his antlers, and his height—he was only about four feet tall—seeing him was always surreal. But he possessed the peri trick of turning invisible, and he was Jack's most trusted spy, in charge of all the suit's espionage. With Jack absent, he had been reporting to me. Or, he was supposed to be.

"So what's the story?" I demanded, approaching the two. They went suspiciously silent as I drew near, and I noticed Seemor giving Jack a sidelong glance.

"Seemor was just telling me that he had Galen watching an office across the street."

I noticed a tear in the paper and approached the window,

peering out. Across the street stood a one-story office building with a sign that read Pathos Wealth Management.

"The man who runs it is named Darby," Jack said. "He's been the Morbus' money man for years."

Morbus. *Mom.*

"You've been spying on my mom's accountant," I wheeled to glare at Seemor. "And you didn't tell me?"

The sprite gave Jack a pointed look. "I asked him to do it," Jack said.

The charm reflexively flared in my palms, rising with my anger.

"You know where my mom is. You were with her," I pointed out. "But you needed to get *even more* information about her that you weren't going to share with me? And you decided to endanger my Valentines in the process?"

"I never said I wouldn't share the information," Jack said. "And they're my Valentines too. I've been with them a lot longer than you have."

"Right. But I'm their queen now. It's my job to protect them. Not to let you get them killed." I jabbed a finger toward Galen.

"Let's just take it easy—" Seemor crooned.

Jack and I snapped in unison: "Shut up."

The sprite did as he was told, shrinking back a step.

"While I was with the Spades, I learned about Darby," Jack said, the slowness of his words betraying his irritation. "The Valentines knew the Morbuses had someone keeping track of their finances, but we never learned his identity before. Getting access to his records could give us a huge amount of information about Morbus operations. Plans they're making. Sycos they pay. Properties they own—not just in Detroit, but worldwide. Remember, that the shard of obelisk is the one really directing their suit. Darby probably has tons of information that even your mom doesn't know. Learning what they're spending money on might give us an indication of what that damned rock has planned. It might help us save your mom."

Fine. I had to admit there were good reasons to spy on this Darby guy. But...

"Why did you keep it a secret from me?" I demanded.

Jack sighed. "If you knew I was still in communication with Seemor, you'd have demanded to see me. If you saw me, you wouldn't have been safe—not until I learned to control my hex power."

I crossed my arms. "So instead, you directed my people behind my back, without my consent, and got Galen killed by the Morbuses."

Jack gave a rueful glance at the dead college boy.

"I don't know about that..." Seemor said.

"What? You think he's alive?" I shouted, pointing at the body.

"No. I mean I don't think it was the Morbus who did it," Seemor said. "Darby came into the office today, same as usual. The bugs we put in his office are still in place and the spyware on his computer is functioning normally."

Jack and I looked at each other. We both knew Seemor had a point. If Galen's cover was blown, they'd be scrubbing the offices down. An army of Morbus sycos would be swarming on us right now, and that Darby fellow would probably be on the first plane out of town.

"So who do you think killed him, then?" I asked.

Again, Seemor glanced at Jack.

"I asked you the question," I said sharply.

"I don't know," Seemor grunted. "But I intend to find out. That Galen kid was alright."

"He was more than alright," I snapped. "And he should still be alive. Who knew he was here?"

Seemor shook his head. "I didn't tell anyone except Abraham. The two of them were alternating shifts here at the stakeout location."

Abraham. He was one of the only Valentines who hadn't come out strongly as a member of Ten's faction or mine. Interesting.

"I told them both to keep it a secret, but who knows who either of them might have told," Seemor said.

"Obviously Mina knew," Jack pointed out.

That was true. She'd been the one to tell us Galen was dead. She was standing outside the office now, trying to get herself together.

"She said she and Galen allowed one another to track their phones—just in case something ever happened," I said. "When he didn't answer her calls or texts for ten hours, she went to look for him and tracked him here."

It surprised me that the two were so serious already in their budding relationship—but then, Hearts were known for moving fast in romance.

Jack was looking at me expectantly.

"Mina is not a suspect," I said.

He nodded grudgingly. We'd both seen her tear-streaked, blotchy face when she arrived. No actress could be that good. She was truly devastated that Galen was gone. And besides, I trusted Mina more than just about anyone else in the suit.

"It could have been Abraham," Jack said.

"Or Galen may have told another Valentine about his surveillance duty."

"A Valentine..." Seemor mused. "And are we thinking whoever killed Galen is the same one who killed Michael?"

Jack nodded. "It seems likely. A Valentine wouldn't have needed any special power to gain access to the mansion on the night of Michael's death," he pointed out. And plenty of them would have wanted the King dead."

Jack was right. In terms of motive, the death of a high ranking suit-mate caused everyone else to move up, thereby gaining more power. Plenty of times in the history of the luck gods, assassinations had taken place for that very reason.

"We need to come up with a Venn Diagram," I said. "Where the Valentines who wanted Michael dead and the Valentines who would want Galen dead overlap, that's our suspect."

"The problem is, we don't know who wanted Galen dead. And everyone wanted Michael dead," Seemor pointed out.

He was right. It felt like we were back to square one, but at least we'd narrowed our suspect list down. Unless Galen had told someone outside the suit about his surveillance duties, our suspect was a Heart. It didn't make me feel any better that we had a killer in our midst, but at least we were closer to solving the mystery.

"So I guess we'd better go back and interview our top suspects," I said.

"To the Hearts house," Jack agreed grimly.

# 23

## JUNIOR

The boy awoke with his face nuzzled in fur. The air rushing past around him was cold, and his arms were wrapped around himself for warmth. Even before he was fully conscious, he knew from the jostling and the drone of the engine that he was in a vehicle on the road, but it wasn't until the wolf shifted and stretched and nudged his cheek with a wet nose that the facts of his situation returned to him. He'd jumped into a truck. Run away. Run away from Cleo. The thought of her gave him a stab of loneliness.

*Don't worry, my boy.* The voice belonged to the chunk of crystal in his backpack, whispering in his mind. *You're doing the right thing. Just keep going. But be careful. It's starting to get dangerous now.*

The big dog looked at him almost as if it heard the voice. It gave a low growl. Then, as if unable to stay mad at the boy, it licked his hand, making him laugh.

The laugh made him think of Cleo again. She'd been one of the only people who had made him laugh in a long time, and he'd run away from her. He missed her already. Missed the way she doted and fussed over him—while pretending not to care. Missed the way she tousled his hair. Missed the earthy smell of her underground lair. He missed the old couch she'd let him sleep on and the feel of the knitted blanket she always threw over him when he fell asleep without covers. He'd never missed someone before. He was surprised how much it hurt, ached like a wiggly tooth.

But it was too late now. He'd left her and she was probably mad. Even if he went back, she'd probably hate him.

*You did well leaving her,* the obelisk assured him. *Your path lies ahead, my boy. Great things await you. All staying with that leprechaun would do is put her in danger.*

He wanted to ask the stone for clarification. What did it mean, he'd put Cleo in danger? But as he thought about it, he realized he had thought of hurting her. Putting a plastic bag over her head while she slept. Making the boiling water from the spaghetti spill on her. Making her fall down, or get hit by a car, or all sorts of other terrible things. He knew intuitively that these thoughts weren't his own, that they'd been put in his head by the spades marks on his hands and by the stone obelisk that gave those marks power. He knew that he liked Cleo. Even loved her. He would never want to hurt her. And yet... maybe the stone was right. Maybe she was in danger around him.

*She'd only have held you back, my boy,* the stone said soothingly. *Suffering awaits anyone who stands in the way of your destiny.*

Junior liked that sort of talk. *Destiny.* It made him feel like the chosen one from a storybook, and who wouldn't like feeling that way? But he had questions. What was his destiny? And what would he have to do to fulfill it? But there was no time to get answers from the obelisk now. The truck was exiting the highway.

His heart thumping faster, Junior crouched lower in the truck bed, crunching himself into a ball in hopes that the driver wouldn't see him. They slowed, the tires grinding and hissing on stones before coming to a halt. The engine sighed and went silent. Junior held his breath, waiting to see what the man would do, and whether he would be discovered. From inside the cab of the truck, he heard the crinkle of a plastic bag, then a distinctive crunch. The truck window slid down and the man spit out of it.

The man was eating sunflower seeds, Junior realized. He recognized the sound of it from one of his mom's jerk ex-boyfriends, a minor league baseball player. His stomach gurgled at the thought of the seeds, and he realized he was hungry again. But before he could reach for one of the snacks in his bag, the truck door swung open. The man stood and stretched with a heavy groan, then walked around the front of the truck. Junior heard his boots crunching on the pavement then swishing through grass. The was the zip of a zipper, the sound of the man sighing, and the pitter of pee hitting the ground. The wolf had sat up and looked out of the truck bed, and Junior steeled himself, then poked his head up, too.

They'd parked in a deserted rest area. A squat brown

building stood about fifty feet away—bathrooms. But the man had chosen to pee here. That wasn't good, Junior thought. A man who would do that must be either lazy or a rule-breaker.

Suddenly, the man whistled and turned toward the truck and Junior crouched down again, his heartbeat galloping.

The dog next to him tensed, but didn't move.

The man whistled again, then shouted. "Zak. Come on, you worthless mut. Come."

The dog flinched at the man's words, then finally obeyed, leaping out of the trunk and loping out into the lawn. It sniffed around where the man had peed and followed suit, peeing in the same spot. The man watched him, sticking another sunflower seed in his mouth, crunching it, then spitting out the broken halves of the shell.

A feeling stirred in Junior, then, the same feeling he'd felt toward Cleo a few times. A desire to hurt the man. He closed his eyes and shook off the feeling, the way a dog shakes off water.

*We don't hurt people,* he told himself—only the words in his mind came out in Cleo's voice.

"Hey, off," the man said, and Junior saw the dog was jumping on the man. "I know you're hungry, but don't have any food, dimwit. And I ain't playing fetch with you. Get off. *Off.*"

Junior watched the dog crouch, wagging playfully then jumping up on the man again. The man shoved it down.

"Dammit, off!" he shouted, then leveled a kick at the dog's face. It caught him in the muzzle, making his teeth clack together. The beast snarled for a second and Junior thought—even hoped—it might attack the man. He deserved it. But the man kicked again, this blow landing in the dog's ribs. It whined, dropping onto its belly and slinking away from its abuser. But the man wasn't done. "Damn dog," he said, positioning himself for another kick.

The word came out of Junior's mouth before he had a chance to think. "No!"

The man had just cocked back his leg for another strike, but at the sound of Junior's voice he paused and looked back at the truck.

"What in the hell?" he muttered, shading his eyes. "What are you doing in my truck, kid?"

Junior's heart raced. His body went cold and shaky, his mouth dry. "N-nothing," he stammered, grabbing his backpack out of the truck bed and quickly shouldering it. "I was just hitching a ride. I'll go."

"No you don't." The man took a menacing step toward him. "What's in the bag?"

Junior shook his head. "Nothing."

"Bull. Don't you lie to me, kid. It's in my truck, it's my property. What are you, a runaway? Or has somebody got you moving drugs for them?"

"Drugs? No," Junior said.

The man's eyes were squinty and dark, his face narrow and cruel. His stubbled jaw held a twisted smile. His hair was buzzed and bristly. His muscled arms writhed with sloppy tattoos. Junior knew men like this. His mom had dated plenty of them over the years. Men like this had blacked Mom's eyes. Dislocated Junior's elbow. Men like this had taken their money. Broken his toys. Shouted in the middle of the night, keeping him awake. Men like this had made him get them beers from the fridge, mocked him when he played imagining games, and called his mom names like dumb and bitch and whore. The man was nothing but a grown up bully. He'd never met this man before, but Junior knew him. He knew him very well.

The man held his hand out. "Give me the gooddamn bag, kid, before I bust your teeth."

Junior held the bag to his chest, feeling the dark throb of the stone shard's power within, and backed to the far side of the truck.

The man gave a mocking laugh. "Ooh, what? You gonna run away? Good luck. We're in the middle of nowhere, New Mexico. Ain't no amount of running or screaming that's going to get you any help out here."

With a slow hand, the man took a sunflower seed and slipped it into his mouth.

Junior glanced at his friend the dog, hoping for help, but the poor thing still cowered in the dirt.

Junior felt something, then. A twinge in the palm of his hands. An itching, burning, wanting feeling.

*Go ahead,* the stone whispered in Junior's mind. *Do it.*

"That bag of yours and whatever's inside is mine, kid," the man said, his feet crunching over the gravel as he rounded toward the tailgate of the trunk. "And so are you."

He spat the shell of the seed out and slipped another in his mouth, then tossed the seed bag over his shoulder and opened the tailgate. And Junior let the power that built up in his hands go.

He watched the man's mouth as his bared teeth pressed down on the seed, snapping its shell, then the seed disappeared behind his lips. The man started to climb up on the tailgate—then stopped. His eyes went wide, his face red. His hands went to his throat and his mouth opened, gaping in a silent cough. He blinked, looking around in a panic, as if searching for help, and his eyes fell on the boy.

Junior was holding up his hands, the spade marks on his palms burning with a dark light. It felt so good to let it go, that bad luck power. It was better than eating Halloween candy. Better than slipping into a hot bath. Better than anything.

He watched as the man spun in a circle, panicked and red-faced, then took off running toward the restrooms. He only made it halfway before he fell, landing face-first in the long, dry grass. He rolled for what seemed like a long time, convulsing, his face redder than ever, his feet kicking, then he lay still. Finally, Junior lowered his hands, closing them into fists. The marks on his hands felt good now, like a sunburn that had been soothed with lotion.

The dog loped over and licked the tears from the dead man's face.

Junior watched the scene for a moment, then went to the driver's side of the truck. The truck's key fob sat in a cup holder, and the engine was still running. He'd played enough video games that he thought he could figure out how to drive the truck. The problem was, his feet wouldn't reach the pedals. After a little searching, he found a couple of soda cans under one of the seats. He took the laces out of his shoes and lashed the cans to the pedals, running the laces through the tabs on top of each can then tying them tight so they wouldn't fall.

*Hurry,* the stone whispered as he worked.

Just as he was about to shut the door and take off, he heard a whimper at his elbow and saw the dog there, watching him with eyes so big and expressive they seemed almost human.

Junior stroked the dog's head. "Don't be sad, boy. He was

a bad man. You deserve a good owner. One who won't kick you."

The dog placed a front paw on Junior's lap and tensed, ready to vault over him and into the passenger seat. Junior shook his head.

"No," The dog tried to nose his way in anyway, but Junior push him back. "No," he said again.

Fending the dog off with one hand, he reached with the other into his backpack and took out the Rice Krispie treat. He got out of the car, unwrapping it. The dog sat, eyes locked on the treat, licking its chops.

"You want this? You want it?" He cocked back his arm and threw the treat out into the grass as far as he could. The dog tore off after it, and Junior watched him go with an ache in his chest. But it didn't compare to the ache that rose in his hand again at the thought of making the dog fall and break its leg.

"Sorry, boy," Junior said quietly. "You're not safe with me."

By the time the dog returned to the parking lot with the Rice Krispie Treat clenched in its jaws, Junior was already pulling away, the truck accelerating onto an endless, windswept highway.

# 24

# AGGIE

Strong nuclear force, weak nuclear force, electromagnetic force, and gravity. The four fundamental forces of physics. Except it now seemed we had discovered a fifth force of nature. No, I don't mean luck power. I mean the visceral awkwardness that permeated the room as Jack and I sat at the dining table with the other Valentines.

At my direction, the sprites and sycos of the kitchen staff had whipped up a fantastic meal of pasta bolognaise, chicken parmesan, and a delicious salad sprinkled with goat cheese. They'd baked beet flecks into the bread to give it a red tint and the vegetables were reddish carrots mingled with succulent roasted Brussels sprouts. It all smelled amazing. The problem was, news had already spread about Galen's death, and nobody had an appetite. So the food sat there, mocking us.

The appointed meeting time had passed twenty minutes ago, but Ten hadn't arrived yet and I didn't want to have to recap when she got there. So, we waited, the tension in the room rising with each minute that ticked past.

There were a few forays into small talk.

Jack to Dubs: "How's your arm?"

Dubs, brandishing his stump: "Gone, mate. Ha. No, it's better. Thank you."

Mina to me: "Hey, did you get that video I sent you?"

Me, managing a smile as I remembered the video of the flash mob at the Seoul Grand Park Zoo she'd sent me: "Yeah. That was amazing."

Despite her puffy eyes and blotchy cheeks she smiled back and I squeezed her hand under the table, impressed by her courageousness—and by the strength in the hand that squeezed mine back. I couldn't imagine what it would be like to lose the person you were falling in love with.

Well. I sort of could…

"You see the game last night?" Cobe asked Abraham, who nodded.

"Yeah, that was a crazy one."

I had no idea who had played or what the game was, and nobody asked. But I did note that Abraham's eyes looked a bit red. Had he cried when he got the news of Galen's death? That would imply he wasn't the killer. Or that he was a killer consumed with guilt—which meant he might come clean when interrogated.

So it went for another fifteen minutes. Each attempt at

conversation only left us to fall back into another even tenser silence.

Finally, I dropped the fork I'd been scraping around my plate.

"Where is Ten?" I demanded of Cobe.

He crunched into an apple. "Oh. I meant to mention—she's not here."

"Obviously," Jack said. "The queen asked where she is."

Cobe glared sidelong at Jack, but he directed his response to me.

"She's out of town," he said. "Helping the Diamantes out with something."

"Helping the Diamantes?" I repeated. "The ones who have basically been at war with us ever since my Queen Trial?"

"What exactly is she helping them with?" Jack demanded.

"With all respect, I don't have to share information with a Spade," Cobe said.

"With very little respect, I was defending this suit when you were still carrying a lunch box. Answer the question."

Cobe gave a lazy shrug. "Don't know," he said.

"And let me guess, you don't know where she is, either?" I pressed.

"No," Cobe said. "Sorry."

Jack and I exchanged a look. I could guess what he was thinking. Ten's absence should have upped her on our list of suspects. Except that Galen was one of hers. He was defi-nitely sympathetic to her, if not absolutely loyal. She had no motive to kill him. Except....

Galen had been getting closer with Mina. Perhaps Mina had been swaying him over to her way of thinking, to our side. Perhaps Ten decided to end him before he tipped the balance of power in my favor. It would have been a horrible thing to do. But after everything I'd seen from Ten, I wouldn't put it past her.

"What about you, Jack?" Cobe said. "Where have you been?"

"None of your—" Jack began.

But Deuce spoke up for the first time all night. "It's a fair question."

Jack gave Deuce a long, hard look, then folded his arms. "The past couple days I've been helping Aggie. Before that, I was with the Spades. Keeping an eye on Aggie's mother. Learning to control bad luck. Watching our enemies."

"Where?" Adelie asked. "In a mirror?"

"Ha! Sick burn," Cobe muttered before a glance from me silenced him.

Abraham chuckled, too—which I noted.

"Jack is no danger to us," I said. "But there's still someone out there who is. Whoever killed King Michael and Galen."

"And how's that investigation coming?" Cobe asked.

Jack and I exchanged a glance.

Abraham asked, "Any suspects?"

Jack met his stare. "Every person at this table."

His words seemed to suck the air out of the room. Even Deuce paused his chewing.

"You're joking, right?" Adelie said in her French accent.

Jack leaned forward. "The people in this room were all in the mansion the night Michael died. Every one of you has a motive—to move up in rank and gain power. And let's be honest. Did any of you really love Michael?"

"Just because someone isn't your favorite doesn't mean you're going to kill them, Jack," Mina said.

"True," Cobe added. "With Michael gone, we're left with a highly inexperienced queen and a Jack who's already corrupted by bad luck power. Chaos. Why would any of us have wanted that? There are plenty of outsiders who might have wanted Michael dead in order to weaken our suit. It could have been the Blackovers, the sylphs. I wouldn't even put it past the Diamantes."

"I agree," I said. "We're investigating all those groups." And more, I thought, my mind returning to the Shastaryan. But I wasn't ready to tell everyone about them. Not yet.

"Even if a lot of us had reasons to kill Michael, who had a motive to kill Galen?" Dubs asked. "We all liked him," his lip quivered for a moment as if he would cry.

"We're not accusing anyone here," I said. "We're just trying to look at every possibility."

"Oh, no," Cobe said. "I think you're on to something, for sure. The most likely suspect is sitting at this table. An enemy agent. The person who could gain the most power—a kingship—by ending Michael. A person loyal to Queen Aubra, who Michael killed. A person ruthless enough to kill a two just to balance the loyalties of the suit in his favor. Our very own Jack of Hearts."

Jack sat up straighter and took a slow sip of water.

"Whoa, whoa, whoa," Deuce said. "Jack would never kill a Valentine. Plus, Michael only killed Aubra to *stop* her from killing Jack. That's not a motive."

"Still, nobody hated Michael like Jack did," Cobe said. "We all know that."

Abraham and Adelie nodded. This wasn't going according to plan. I felt the urge to rein things in, to get control back. Queen Aubra would have known the perfect thing to say to get everyone off one another's throats, but I found myself pinioned by the tension around me, counting the mushrooms in my plate of pasta. Stupid OCD. And I counted only twenty-two mushrooms, not the twenty-three I needed to feel a sense of completion. I started counting again.

"And nobody loved Michael like Ten did," Jack growled to Cobe. "Oh yes. Aggie told me she caught the two of them kissing. He kisses her, then marries another. I'd say that's a pretty good motive for murder, wouldn't you?"

"She didn't—" Cobe started, then he went pale. "Look, she told me about that. He kissed her. She didn't kiss him back."

"Regardless, he picked Aggie for his Queen," Jack concluded. "Maybe she killed him for it. Maybe that's why she isn't here now, eh, Cobe?"

Cobe rose from the table, and Adelie rose with him. Deuce and Dubs stood too, in a squawk of pushed-back chairs, ready to keep the peace.

Twenty-two mushrooms again. I stole one off Jack's plate and tossed it onto mine. Twenty-three. Completion. I sighed with relief as the compulsion ebbed.

"Do you have proof Ten did it?" Cobe demanded.

"Do you have proof she didn't?" Jack countered with teasing calm.

"Innocent until proven guilty," Cobe snarled.

"We're Gods," Jack said. "We are the law."

I slammed a hand on the table.

"Listen. I will not brook such inconsonance!" I shouted.

"Two SAT words. Nice," Deuce muttered.

Cobe looked at me then at Jack, his eyes afire. Then he spat a curse, turned, and stalked out of the room. Adelie and Abraham exchanged a glance and followed.

"We'll be questioning everyone in the mansion," Jack called after them. "Don't go anywhere."

The door swung shut, leaving behind a tension so thick I felt like I could swim through it. Deuce broke the silence first.

"That went well," he said.

❦

We set up shop in the library and spent the rest of the evening interviewing Valentines one by one about Michael and Galen's deaths. I let Jack do most of the talking while I sat off to one side, making notes in a composition book.

*Deuce: Keeps cracking jokes, talking in a cheesy New York accent like an old time movie gangster and calling Jack a "gumshoe." Went for a long walk the night of the wedding, then returned to his room alone, watched movies and slept. Was in the Valentine library at the time Galen was killed. No, there were no witnesses to prove he was there.*

*Adelie: Continuously vaping, rolling her eyes at us and sarcastically saying, "sure, I killed them. Why not?" Finally snapped that she was in her room alone all night when both murders took place. Generally uncooperative and unpleasant. We dismissed her. She is rotten and annoying, but seems too apathetic to kill anybody.*

*Dubs: Was at the hospital the night of the wedding with his arm bitten off by a jinni. Not a suspect. Last night, when Galen died, he was out on a date at a salsa club with an undisclosed lady. Despite ample teasing, he would not reveal her identity, except that she is not a luck god. "Hearts will be hearts," Jack said. Not a likely suspect.*

*Abraham: Was at the hospital with Dubs the night of the*

*wedding and did not come back to the Hearts house until the next day. Last night when Galen died, he went to the gym, then to bed. (House surveillance video confirms this.) His demeanor is quiet and direct. Seems honest enough—but where do his loyalties lie? Hard to peg. Still, he has alibis for both nights. Not a likely suspect.*

*Mina: Her words are halting and tearful. The night Michael died, she dropped Dubs and Abraham at the hospital, stayed until late into the night, then came home and slept. She was the first to come running in the morning when I found Michael's body and woke up screaming. Possible motive for killing Michael: she was my friend and didn't want to see me married to him. During Galen's murder, she was baking in the Hearts house kitchen, then went to bed early. And she was falling for Galen. Let's be honest, she's not a suspect.*

*Cobe: Surprisingly cooperative. The night of the wedding he was with Ten until late into the night in the game room—says they were talking, drinking, and playing pool. Then he went to bed alone. Claims he had no animosity toward Michael. When asked again if he knew Michael and Ten's kiss his face does go noticeably red. But when asked if he's involved with Ten romantically, he says he isn't. Jack points out Cobe is the highest ranking male except for Jack and should therefore be in line for the throne, but Cobe shrugs off this motive. Claims he was content with being a nine and is interested in kingship only to serve the suit, now that Jack is part Morbus. When asked about Galen he seemed a bit more cagey. He only says he stayed in last night and was alone, but has no one to corroborate. No security footage shows him going in or out of the house, but none confirms that he was here, either. Could he have been avoiding the cameras?*

*Ten: She is gone, location unknown. Didn't show up for the interview, despite texts from Jack and me demanding she do so.*

*Cobe only said she's helping the Diamonds but would not confirm her location or what she is doing. Although the King and Galen were both allies of hers, she remains a suspect.*

When the last interviewee had left, I read these notes back to Jack, then flipped the notebook shut.

"And that's it," I finished with a sigh.

"Not quite. There's us," Jack said with his little mischievous grin. "I'm your number one suspect, right?"

I looked at him for a long moment trying to hold back a smile. Of course, it was impossible. That's the effect the Jack of Hearts had on me. "Fine," I said. "Where were you that night after the wedding, Toby?"

Using his given name usually elicited squirm and a dirty look from him. This time, he just held my gaze. "We started to take your mom to the hospital. But she was muttering, half unconscious, telling us her to take her someplace else. The voice, though. It wasn't really her voice. It was male. Creepy. The voice of the obelisk inside her, I guess. Anyway, she kept repeating an address. We took here there, Shade and I. It was some abandoned office building..."

My heartbeat sped up. Was Jack finally going to tell me where to find Mom?

"There was a doctor there," Jack went on, "and he seemed to know your mom or to know of her, at least. We took her in and he started working on her and sent us out. I spent most of my night in the parking lot of that place, just pacing and watching the sky."

"The sky?"

He shrugged. "Something about clouds at night... I like it watch them. It calms me."

My eyebrows went up. "You needed calming down?"

"Well, we had just fought a battle. I'd seen your mom get stabbed. And…"

"And?" I pressed, playful but earnest, too.

Jack watched me. "And my girlfriend had just married someone else."

This wrang a sound from me, half laugh, half sigh. "I was your girlfriend? Funny, I didn't know that."

"Why not?"

"You never said I was."

"You never asked."

He gave a hint of a grin. The smile I returned held a lot in it. Reproach. Pain. Regret. Frustration. Longing. Still, so much longing. But I felt like there was something he wasn't telling me.

"And what did you do then," I asked. "After you got done looking at the sky?" I poised my pen over my notebook, half teasing.

He raked a hand through his hair. "Really? You honestly don't trust me? After everything I've done for you?"

"Yes. Jack Valentine, always loyal to his queen."

"Always loyal to you," he said.

Somehow, I found the courage to take his hand and turn it over. I studied that black mark there. Even now I could feel its energy pulsing through the room.

"And yet more loyal to your quest," I said thoughtfully. "To gain power."

"To bring peace," he corrected.

I studied him. "And to you, those two things are the same."

His hand squeezed mine, the chill of the hex sending a thrill through me. "We have to take the power from those who are bad and put it in the hands of those who are good, don't we? Take it from the reckless and give it to the responsible. Take it from those who are violent and give it to the—the gentle? It's the only way."

"You are a gentleman," I teased. "Most of the time."

But he stayed serious.

"You're smart, Aggie. If there's another way to end this violence, this endless war, then tell me. I beg you. Because I never asked for this. The burden. The darkness. I don't want all the power of the suits, especially the bad ones. It's terrible. But—" his eyes shone with emotion for a moment. "I don't know any other way."

I took his charmed hand so that I held both of them.

"I don't either," I whispered. We were close. I felt the warmth of his body, could almost feel the beating of his heart as he tilted my face up to his, the spade-marked hand cold on my cheek. His lips drifted down and touched mine. Just the barest whisper of a touch was enough the send a tremor down to my toes.

The warmth of his hand in mine, the cold of his fingers on my cheek... was he charming me?

"Then make me your King," he whispered. And his lips were on mine again. I felt breathless, dizzy, drunk with wanting. His fingers tracked down my neck, across my collarbone, making my skin alive with gooseflesh.

A creak. We both looked to find Deuce in the doorway, looking as startled an wild-eyed.

"Sorry," he said quickly, ducking out again.

"Deuce. Hey, Deuce," I called after him, but I heard his footfalls as he departed—nearly running—down the hall.

I looked back to Jack. My body still quivered from his kiss, but the moment was ended. I gathered my notebook and pen from the table.

"Aggie—" he started, but I interrupted him.

"I'd better do some SAT prep," I muttered, backing toward the door. "Only two days until the test. But hey, good news. I've crossed you off my suspect list."

And I hurried out of the room.

**25**

---

**AGGIE**

After leaving Jack, I went to the royal bedchamber, intending on flopping down on the massive bed and zoning out for a while. But once I got into the room, I felt like leaving. The bed had been replaced since Michael had died in it, but there was still something about it that made me uneasy. I didn't believe in ghosts, of course, but that didn't stop this place from feeling haunted. I couldn't relax here. So instead, I wandered the room, looking for clues. The Valentines had been through it a hundred times after Michael first died, searching for hairs, blood stains or other evidence. We had even had a syco in a lab in Washington DC who analyzed any samples we found. But nothing helpful or conclusive had been discovered.

I finished a lap of the room, pausing at the far side of the bed to examine the window that had been left open the night of the murder. It was shut and locked now, but I opened it again, scanning the window frame for scuffs, scratches or caught fibers of clothing, eyeing the glass for fingerprints. The night of the murder I'd seen a shimmer of a peri in front of the window. Afterward, we discovered the screen had been removed. We'd found it lying in the lawn, heavily implying that the peri killer had entered and escaped through this way.

Something about this window had always bothered me, but I couldn't quite put my finger on what it was.

I wasn't going to come up with any Holmsian insights now, either, I realized. Not with thoughts of Jack still pinging around my brain.

So I went back to my room. Not the massive royal bed chamber I'd inherited when I became queen, the much smaller room I'd gotten when I first joined the Valentines as a six. It suited me much better.

I knew I should be working on SAT prep. Instead, I just sat on the bed, staring at the door.

The door... It didn't have a lock on it, which at first had been hard. My OCD always compelled me to lock doors, and the lack of a lock had been maddening. But I'd forced myself to get used to it. Now, I wished again that it had a lock. That I could click it in place twenty-three times and scare away the nagging anxiety haunting me. But there was no lock. No safety. No relief. Not for a person with OCD, and certainly not for a Valentine queen.

The knock at the door made me gasp. *Jack.*

Which Jack of Hearts would I get this time? Would he be apologetic? Dismissive of my feelings? Would he be so charming and seductive that my brain circuits would just fry and I'd melt for him? Better to just send him away.

I whipped the door open.

"Jack, I—" I started. But it wasn't Jack on the doorstep.

Deuce blinked at me, a plate of pasta in one hand and a book in the other.

"Sorry," he said. "Am I bothering you?"

I smiled in spite of how I felt. "Never," I said.

He brandished a tray of food. "You didn't get dinner with all the interrogations you were doing, but chef made your favorite. I thought you might like some. And I found a book. I think it might be the one you've been looking for."

❦

While I shoveled pasta and garlic bread into my face, Deuce read to me from the book on Uthule he'd found. There was an urgency to his cadence and he looked up from the page at me regularly, as if to make sure that whatever message he was trying to get across was landing. In truth, my mind was somewhere in deep space, my thoughts so distant and remote I barely heard his words.

"...And in the twentieth year," he read, "the nobles of his house gathered in the chambers of Uthule's most favored consort, a young woman of common birth whom the Luck Lord had plucked from a small village. Despite her obscure parentage, the girl was known for her intellect. As the story went, following the second jinn war, Uthule was travelling home and stopped in her village for the night. The innkeeper who hosted Uthule bragged of his daughter, whose intelligence, he boasted, could match Uthule's luck. Intrigued, Uthule had called for the girl and the two had played a game of Omo that lasted far into the night. In the end, Uthule bested the girl through considerable exertion of his powers of luck, but he was so impressed with her that he declared his love and invited her back to his palace. Though he had many consorts, Uthule said the beauty of her mind surpassed the beauty of every face in the land, and he placed her above all the women in his harem."

"How romantic," I snarked.

"He gave her a name meaning *prism of light*," Deuce went on, "Shastaryan."

At this, I looked up from my plate. "She's the one who organized the rebellion against Uthule?" I said. "And the rebels today are named after her..."

Deuce flipped pages now, scanning ahead.

"Shastaryan came to believe Uthule was a dangerous tyrant... she formed alliances with other powerful nobles... they tried to kill him one night and failed... A civil war ensued... Everyone turned against Uthule except his elite force of goblin warriors, but they were still formidable enough that the war went on for another ten years... blah, blah, blah. Finally, Shastaryan's forces caught up with Uthule at a rocky peninsula known as Chessemy, and there the god was drawn and quartered. Shastaryan by now had become quite the sorceress and had figured out a way to capture the dead god's power in crystal. The four obelisks were made, and she had the four remaining generals who had defeated Uthule take them away, travelling in opposite directions, three by land, one by sea. The remnant of the goblin horde went into hiding, continued to worship Uthule, and built a religion around the idea that he'd someday return... The four generals and their companions cared for the obelisks and soon realized that the stone monuments conferred power upon them—hence the modern luck gods were born... Hmm. What else?"

My plate was clear now—and so was my head.

"What happened to Shastaryan?" I asked.

"She formed a secret group dedicated to making sure the four luck powers stayed separated. Beyond that, no one knows," Deuce said. "She died, I guess. It was like two thousand years ago."

He clapped the books shut.

I regarded my empty plate and sipped my coffee—which Deuce had also brought me, bless his heart. I couldn't help but think how much drinking it this late at night would have irritated Mom. Even after everything, the thought of her still felt like a thorn in my chest.

"Look," Deuce said. "About Jack... Did you ask him what I said to ask him? About how the two of you got together?"

"No," I said. "I've been a little bit busy. Whatever it is, can you just tell me?"

He picked up a piece of garlic bread, then put it back down. He picked up a spoon and drummed it on the table. I counted the beats.

"Right. Just spit it out. Tear off the Band-aid," he muttered to himself, then cleared his throat. "When you and Jack fell for one another, it didn't... you know... happen organically. You were charmed. With Cupid's Arrow."

The world seemed to fall away so that only Deuce was in focus. His words reverberated like a gong.

"What?" I shook my head. "That's ridiculous."

Even as I protested, another part of me was turning the idea over in my mind. Jack was gorgeous, but he wasn't exactly my type—as far as I had one. And I certainly wasn't his normal type, either, not a perfect goddess like Ten or

Danusia or Carlotta. My falling for him hadn't exactly been insta-love—it had grown on me gradually. But it *had* grown fast, and it had taken me by surprise.

The plausibility of Deuce's words only made them hurt worse.

"Is it that incomprehensible to you that Jack would actually like me because of who I am?" I asked. "Am I that repugnant to you? Am I that ugly? That annoying?"

"No," Deuce said. "Of course not."

"Why, then?" I demanded. "Why are you so sure he was charmed into loving me?"

He tore his gaze from his folded hands and looked up at me. "Because I know who did it. It was Ari. At the Coney Island. The day we were teaching you to use charm with the saltshaker." He shook his head. "I suspected, so I started asking around. Before he died, Ari told Abraham. It was supposed to be a secret, but I got Abraham to tell me. The night before it happened, the ace had gone to Ari in a dream and told him to—"

I put up my hand, stopping him. "I don't believe you."

"Aggie—"

"How long have you known?"

Deuce sighed. "A couple months, I guess."

My voice rose to a shout. "And you're just telling me now?"

"I wanted to give you time to—"

"I can't. I can't do this." My heart was racing and I couldn't stop counting the beats. *One-two-three-four—*

"Aggie."

*Five-six-seven-eight.*

"Aggie?"

"Leave!" I shouted.

Deuce slumped as if deflate completely. "I just want you to know—"

"Leave me alone," I said more forcefully. "That's an order."

He looked at me one more time, hurt and frustration brimming in his brown eyes. Then he stood.

"Your Majesty," he gave small bow, then he turned and left.

I wished I could lock the door behind him.

# 26

# JACK

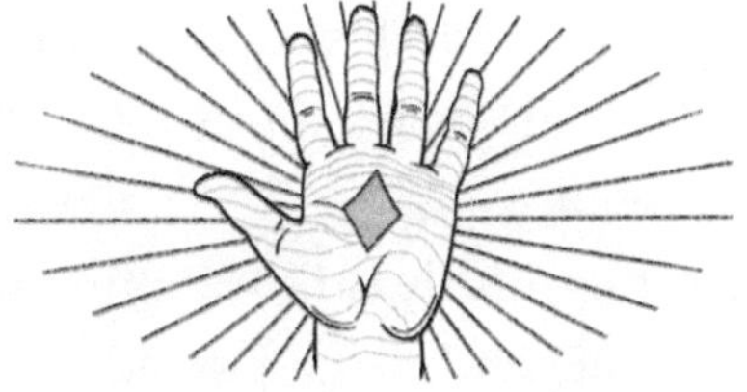

Jack felt numb as he merged off the freeway and turned toward the abandoned pharmaceutical Research & Development facility where the Spades queen held court. There had been only one response he'd expected when he suggested Aggie choose him as king: *of course.* He had just assumed she would pick him. That all the feelings they shared, not to mention his rank and experience, would make him the obvious choice. The fact that she had reservations stung like a slap. And yet he should have known it wouldn't be easy. Nothing with Aggie was. She was cerebral, a classic overthinker. He just had to hope that all her reasoning would lead her back to him.

In the meantime, he'd do what he'd always done for the women in his life: prove himself useful.

He found Shade in the parking lot of the Spades hideout, talking with a couple members of his former gang—who had now become his sycos. As Jack got out of the car, Shade was holding a red gas can and pouring hex into it, the palm of his hand pulsing. When he was finished, he placed the gas can in the trunk of his friends' black Impala and gave the driver a fist bump. The other crew members gave Jack the side-eye as they got into their vehicle, but no one said anything. As they pulled out of the lot, Jack approached Shade and they stood together, watching the vehicle pull away.

"The work," Shade said, flexing and unflexing his hand, looking down at the dark mark on its palm. "It's better than any dope I've ever seen, man."

Jack nodded thoughtfully, still watching the black car as it rounded a corner and disappeared. Ever since he'd become a Spade, Shade had been conducting a crusade of arson against the multi-national chain stores, restaurants and real estate operations that had been springing up in his old neighborhood, their competition driving up rents and driving out local businesses. One by one, the interlopers had gone up in flames.

It was a savage way to defeat gentrification, but Jack had to respect Shade's initiative. He was not only defending his neighborhood and its people, he was also building up hex power in the process. Jack could feel the strength rolling off him, a hex considerably greater than would be normal in a luck god of his rank.

"Where you been?" Shade asked, his tone more curious than probing.

Jack saw no reason to lie. "With the Hearts," he said.

"Is her Majesty's daughter okay?"

"Yes," Jack said.

Shade nodded. "She'll be glad to hear that."

That was another thing about Shade. He seemed truly grateful for the power Queen Rachel had bestowed on him, and from what Jack could tell, he was completely loyal. It was a code of the streets, Shade had told him once. When you join a gang, you have their backs all the way to the grave.

Jack knew Shade was leery of him, though. The idea of being in two gangs at once was antithetical to Shade's world view.

*Everywhere I go they're suspicious of me,* Jack thought glumly. Of course, most of them had good reason.

"Speaking of the Queen's daughter, I have a favor to ask."

"What's that?" Shade asked.

"I need you to confess to killing the King of Hearts."

Shade gave Jack a double-take. "Hold up. What?"

Jack glanced around the parking lot to ensure no one else was listening.

"Queen Aggie's suit doesn't trust her because they think she killed Michael. Or at least, they're using it as an excuse to question her leadership."

"Sure. But I didn't kill his ass."

"I know," Jack agreed. "But if they have someone to pin the blame on, then they can quit fighting among themselves and support Aggie. Until then, Aggie is in danger, just like Michael was."

Before Shade could dissent, Jack went on.

"You know Queen Rachel loves her daughter. She'll want you to do what you can to protect her."

"Right," Shade said. "So why isn't this order coming from her?"

Jack made a show of glancing around again, then whispered. "She's still recovering. I'm trying not to worry her. If she thinks her daughter's in danger, she's going to feel compelled to go in and take out the Hearts who are threatening Aggie. I don't think she's strong enough to do that yet, do you?"

Shade shook his head bitterly. "Right. So instead, I'm gonna have a whole suit of luck gods gunning for me for something I didn't even do."

Jack put a hand on Shade's shoulder. "I know it's a lot to ask. I just don't see any other way."

Shade raised an eyebrow. "How about you find the real killer?"

Jack snorted. "We've tried. We don't know who did it yet."

Shade folded his harms. "Sure you don't," he sighed. "Fine. I'll be your damned scapegoat. But I'm doing it for the queen. Not for you."

It only took a few minutes for Jack to film the video he needed, holding his phone as if it were a hidden camera and prompting Shade to make a false confession through a series of seemingly casual questions.

Would their acting be good enough to fool the Hearts? Jack hoped so. The investigation was dragging on too long, and every day his sense of urgency grew, like the screw of a vice turning, tightening. The investigation had been a good opportunity to spend time with Aggie again. But every day it dragged on, the danger increased.

Aggie was astute. Jack had no doubt she'd find the true killer soon enough. But in the meantime, her crown would be secure. And, Jack hoped, she'd be grateful enough for his help to make him king.

"Thanks, man," he said, clapping Shade in a quick hug.

When they pulled apart, Jack froze. A figure had emerged from the doorway of the hideout. Tall. Broad. With long dark hair and a beard and one glinting, cunning eye. A ghost.

Jack drew his dagger.

"I killed you," Jack whispered. Gallo, the Heart Slayer, only grinned.

The queen emerged from the doorway behind him. She came to Gallo's side and nudged his ribs with her elbow. There was a familiarity in that gesture that made Jack's blood run cold.

He'd been counting on becoming the Spade king. His entire plan hinged on it. But he was only a Jack of Spades now. And if Gallo were to insert himself, to convince Rachel to give him the power of both black suits... well, Jack had killed Gallo once. He wasn't sure all the luck in the world would allow him to do it again.

"Oh. Jack," Queen Rachel said easily as she caught sight of him. "We've been wondering about you. Where have you—?"

But Jack was already stalking away, adrenaline thumping through him like fire.

*This changes everything. Everything,* he thought as he slammed the card door, hit the accelerator, and peeled off into the night.

**27**

---

# MARLEY

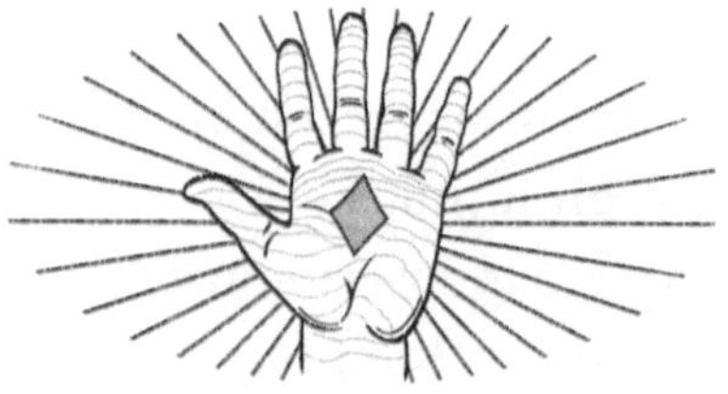

**M**arley approached the steel door as cautiously, as if it were rat trap, ready to snap. The freshly heated microwave meals burned his trembling hands as he paused and listened for sounds from behind the door, but the groans and sobs he'd heard earlier were mercifully absent. All he heard now was his own breath rasping inside his N95 mask and the shuffle of his feet on the concrete. This dungeon, one of many special features the Blackovers had included in their brewery when it was built, sat two levels beneath the bar itself, and the thick layers of concrete choked the raucous sounds of drinkers above.

Marley leaned closer to the door, listening again. Were

his patients dead? He could hear labored, raspy breathing. Good.

He knelt, tipped up the metal flap on the bottom of the door, and slid the food through. Then he took a water bottle from each of his pockets and rolled those through as well, then hastily turned to go.

The heavy breathing behind the door hitched.

"Marley?" a hoarse voice said from behind the steel, and Marley cursed to himself and knelt next to the food flap.

"Yes?"

The response was a fit of coughing that lasted nearly two minutes. Another voice chimed in, this one female.

"You need to get us to the hospital. We—" her words, too, broke off into coughs and groans.

"Help us," the man's voice came again.

"Please," the woman said.

"Please," the man rejoined.

Then they were both coughing again.

Marley backed away, his teeth bared with frustration and anger as he turned and ascended the steps, taking them two at a time.

He found Thad in his office, hunt-and-pecking into his laptop. He seemed like a normal business owner, Marley thought, until you spied the black .45 sitting on the desk, the spiked mace hanging on the wall behind him, and the gut-roiling feeling of dread his hex exuded. A stripper from the gentleman's club next to the casino—a newly acquired syco —lay napping on Thad's couch, faintly snoring.

"They any better?" the king rumbled without looking up from his work.

"They're worse," Marley said.

Thad rubbed his chin and pointed at the computer

screen. "That payment from the distributor is almost two weeks late. Have you check with Mike to see what the holdup is?"

"No. I will," Marley said. "Listen, your highness, we need to get them to the hospital."

Thad snorted and crossed his arms. "Do we?"

"They sound like they're dying," he said.

"So they die," Thad shrugged. "So what? They're sycos."

"They're people. Derrick and Liza. They've been with us since before we came to Detroit."

Thad rubbed his hands together then showed the palms to Marley. The club marks there glowed with a sinister light.

"So we help them along. Put them out of their misery, nice and slow. That bit of work has been calling to me. It's been calling to you, too, I bet."

Marley winced, because Thad was right. Thoughts of going down to that basement dungeon and pressing his hands to the door and been intruding in Marley's mind more and more often. When he was running errands. When he was restocking the bar. When he was about to drop off to sleep at night. Someone that sick, just a nudge of bad luck might end them. Make them choke on their phlegm. Knock their immune systems down just a bit. They die. Then the sweet hex would come flowing like sap from an amputated tree limb, delicious power.

But it was wrong. Even a bad luck god should be able to tell right from wrong. Even with all the nasty shit he'd done in his time as a Club, Marley still believed that to be true.

He closed his hands into fists, dousing their unlucky light.

"Liza has a son. He's two years old," he said.

"So?" Thad growled. "My mother left when I was three. I made it."

"Yes. You're extremely well adjusted," Marley said.

Thad glared at Marley from beneath his heavy brow, a look that had presaged death for more people than Marley could count. He had held his tongue for years in the face of Thad's needless cruelty. His callous barbarism. But it was getting harder and harder to keep silent. Marley was aware he'd been skating closer to the edge with Thad lately, that his mouth was going to get him into trouble eventually. But this time, the King gave a laugh.

"I'm a psychopath, my friend. And you're a psychopath's lackey. So which one of us is worse? Eh?"

Marley didn't answer. No response he could give at that moment was civil enough to keep him from getting his head bashed in. Instead, he bit his lip until he tasted blood.

"Hey, chicky," Thad barked to the girl on the couch. When she didn't respond he picked up an empty coffee cup and tossed it at her. It hit her in the breast and she sat up fast.

"Ow!"

"Look alive!" Thad bellowed, laughing. "Get your ass in the kitchen and bring me some nachos and a pint of amber. You want anything, Mar?"

He looked to Marley, who shook his head.

The girl sat up, looking disgruntled. "You could say please," she pouted.

"And you could get a fat lip," Thad boomed. "Now scoot."

She slipped from the room, moving fast despite her high heels.

Thad watched her shapely butt until it was out of sight

then looked back to Marley, rubbing his chin. "We better kill them quick."

"What?" Marley said.

"Derrick and Tina or whatever their names are. They have whatever disease that Morbus, Shade, gave them. That means the Spades are farming the hex off them. The longer they suffer, the stronger that bitch queen of theirs and her Heart boy get. We're better off taking them out fast and harvesting that hex for ourselves."

Marley's jaw clenched so hard he thought his teeth might break. He remembered the day Liza had brought her little daughter to visit the brewery. The girl had sat on Marley's lap and played with his sunglasses. She was tiny. And beautiful. And sweet. And Thad wanted to make her an orphan. Marley knew what it was to be an orphan. And it was hell.

And yet the pips on his hands sizzled with wanting at the thought of doing *the work* on Derrick and Liza. That was the worst part: knowing how much pleasure he'd get from ending them—and how much power.

"What do you say," Thad pressed. "You snuff the guy, I'll do the girl, eh? Just like old times."

*Thad always preferred killing girls. How have I put up with this monster for so long?* Marley asked himself. But he already knew the answer. It was because Thad would kill him just as readily as he'd kill Liza—or anyone else. Kill or be killed, that was life as a Club. And whatever else Marley might be, however he might hate his life sometimes, he was not suicidal. He did not want to die. But he couldn't kill Derrick or Liza, either.

So he met Thad's gaze. "That's okay. You go ahead. More power for the king means more power for all of us. Your Highness."

Thad rose to his full, towering height. "That's right," he agreed, coming around the desk to loom over Marley, poking him in the chest with one thick finger. "But I think you're getting soft in your old age, Mar. There's no room for mercy in the suit of berserkers, my friend. Remember that."

He plucked the N95 mask out of Marley's hand then shouldered past him. Marley closed his eyes, steadying himself and listening to the King's heavy footfalls receding as he made his way down the stairs.

When the footsteps gave way to silence, he took out his phone and made a call.

It rang, rang again. Then he heard a click as the connection went live. No one said *hello*, but Marley knew they were there, listening. He hesitated, knowing what a pivotal moment this might be. What a dangerous moment. It was a threshold, a doorway into another life. And once he crossed it, there would be no turning back. And yet he couldn't go on like this anymore. And he wouldn't.

"Okay," Marley said to the silence at the other end of the phone line. "I'm ready to talk."

**28**

---

# MOLLY

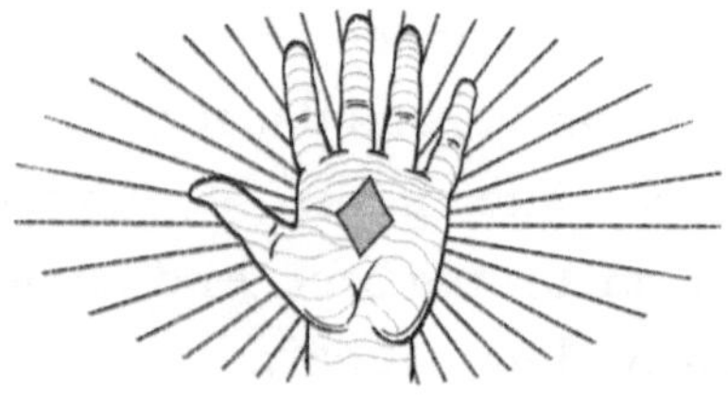

After a long day on the yacht, Klepper sent the Diamantes, Ten and Molly back to the mainland on a helicopter. The afternoon had passed like a sunny dream—eating a lavish lunch, swimming, and playing shuffleboard. Of course, the luck gods had won every time, the fiercest competition being between Danusia and Ten, the Valentine. Molly hadn't talked to Seth again once she'd come back on deck, but she'd seen him watching them out the cabin windows, creeper-style, like a goblin peering out from a keyhole in some fairytale. He was clearly obsessed, Molly thought, with a little, private smile that made her cheeks ache.

How would Lorcan feel about her hooking up with this

odd rich boy? He seemed like the jealous type, but if cheating on him would allow her to become a luck god, she was pretty sure he'd understand.

The helicopter's rumble set her whole body humming, made her heart feel like it was skipping beats. Below, the water flashed like a dark jewel in the setting sun. Lights spread out on a hillside ahead and they flew toward them, like a starship bound for a constellation.

*What the hell is this life?* Molly thought, glancing around at the beautiful faces around her in the half-light. Tristaine. Danusia. Ten. *How did I even get here?*

Of course, how she got there wasn't the important part. The important part was how she would stay.

They touched on a rooftop helipad overlooking the city. A cadre of hotel staff loaded their bags into carts while another led them down an elevator, which let out directly in the two-story suite where they'd be staying. Klepper had several times invited them to stay the night with him on the yacht, but each time the Diamonds had politely refused, explaining they already had hotel reservations in the city, but promising to meet up at Klepper's estate, after cleaning up and changing, for a late dinner.

Once the staff had departed and the door to their suite clapped shut, all attention was on Molly. They hadn't asked her anything about her mission while on the boat or on the helicopter. Both were owned by Klepper and she guessed they were worried about listening devices or something. But now they interrogation began.

"Did you get it?" Tristaine asked.

"Of course," Molly said.

Danusia snorted, already dabbing lotion on her sun-reddened face. "We'll see."

Tristaine took the bracelet off Molly's wrist and set it on the coffee table next to a tablet computer. For a second, the tablet's screen said *uploading*. After a moment, a folder appeared.

"There's something here," Tristaine said.

Tristaine clicked into it and gave an exuberant clap. "She did it." He levelled a smug smile at Danusia. "I told you."

"Calm down. She was my syco in the first place," Danusia said. Still, she approached to look over Tristaine's shoulder. "There. Project Portal," she pointed.

Tristaine clicked on it and I held my breath as the files loaded.

Then documents appeared. Hundreds of them.

"It's here. It's all here," Tristiane whispered excitedly.

"Click on that one," Danusia gestured, and Tristaine opened a file.

"The seventy-second test, completed this morning, presented us with a stable boundary and safe energy levels," Danusia read breathlessly. "Test team sigma passed through and returned safely, bringing back several artifacts as proof of contact…"

A hush fell over the room. Danusia was pale with wonder. Tristaine was flushed, giddy.

"Okay," Ten said. The Heart had been uncharacteristically quiet all day except when playing the role of water nymph, but now, her one word commanded the room. "I've come this far with you. It's time to come clean. What is this?"

Tristaine beamed. "It's Christopher Columbus' route to the new world, my dear. It's Neil Armstrong stepping foot on the moon. It's—"

"So dramatic," Danusia rolled her eyes. "It's a rift. A door to the world of luck beings. Klepper's company has developed the ability to generate them synthetically."

Ten's hand went to her mouth. "That's impossible. There's only one rift."

"Not once this technology is fully developed," Danusia said. "There'll be as many rifts as we want. And the Diamonds—*and our allies*—will control them all."

"You'll finally break the control of the Sylph Council," Ten said, and for a moment all three luck gods seemed struck silent as they considered the implications of—whatever the hell was happening.

Molly waited for someone to explain it to her. When no one did, she finally piped up.

"I'm sorry, what does all this mean?" she said. At Danusia's annoyed look she said, "I did get you this information."

"There's something called a rift," Tristaine explained. "A portal between our world and the world of the peri—the luck beings. Everything that goes between the two worlds has to pass through that one door. Every creature, every object."

Molly nodded. Aggie had explained that much to her before.

"But the door is controlled by the sylph," Ten added.

"They're rotten peri," Tristaine said. "Slave traders, black market antiquities dealers, and purveyors of mercenaries. But they're very powerful, very rich, and very dangerous."

"They guard the other side of the rift with an army," Ten went on. "No one gets through without their say so."

"They have a complete monopoly on trade and travel between the two worlds," Danusia agreed. "And they've grown grotesquely rich because of it. Both in money and in luck. Almost as rich as us."

"So you get this technology, you break their monopoly," Molly concluded.

"And reap unimaginable profits," Tristaine said.

"And unimaginable power," Ten added, thinking it through. "The luck gods have been cut off from that world for centuries. Supposedly there are vast numbers of beings there who still worship us."

"Yes. And others who are hostile to us, as well," Tristaine said.

"Both have the potential to completely destabilize the balance of power between the suits," Ten said. "If someone were to bring an army through one of those portals…"

"Yes, well, it's a good thing we'll be the ones controlling them," Danusia said.

"And it's a good thing you're friends with us, Ten," Tristaine added.

"Wait," Molly said. "Didn't Aggie's mom already do this? She created a portal. And what came through it was a bunch of scary, luck-eating shadow monsters."

"Different kind of portal, my dear," Tristaine said. "There are many layers and facets to the paranjama, the veil between worlds. Hers, I daresay, pierced a bit too deep. But that is a danger of this sort of technology. And it's part of why it's imperative that we control it rather than the dark suits—or some clueless corporate bureaucrat like Klepper."

A silence settled then, Tristaine clicking on more files on the computer, Danusia watching over his shoulder. Ten went to the window, staring out at the deepening night, probably pondering the implications of the day's revelations.

"As expected, nothing technical on here," Tristaine said.

Danusia tutted. "Well, of course they're not going to keep all their trade secrets on their CEO's unencrypted laptop.

We'll just have to complete the merger, as planned. Then the keys to the kingdom, quite literally, will be ours."

"The key's on your finger now, actually," Tristaine said, taking Danusia's hand and inspecting the ring there. "That's quite a rock. If an asteroid that size hit Earth, we'd be sunk."

Klepper had proposed to Danusia sometime between the mimosas and the lunchtime taco bar. She'd said yes, but the Diamonds seemed to take the idea of a marriage with the same practical stoicism as the idea of the merger. Clearly, it was not a union born of love—for Danusia, at least. In fact, Molly got the feeling the Jill would as easily kill Klepper as marry him if it meant she got what she wanted. It reminded her of what a dangerous game she was playing, seeking a place among these heartless demigods.

Danusia regarded the massive diamond on her finger.

"Pretty. But not nearly as impressive as the rocks inside that fool Klepper's head," Danusia huffed. "But I will gladly suffer his company for a chance to *win* his company."

"What about the nephew?" Molly said. "Seth?"

Danusia grunted an *ugh*. "What about him? The boy is about as pleasant as a piss-drunk sprite—and twice as ugly."

Tristaine put a hand on Molly's shoulder. "You did well keeping him out of our hair."

Did they not know Seth's real importance as the heir of the company's founder—and its largest stockholder? Or had he lied about those things to impress her? The latter was entirely possible—but somehow, Molly felt he was telling the truth. The sort of odd entitlement Seth exhibited seemed hard to fake.

"Right. I did my part," Molly said. "So you'll make me a Diamante now?" Tristaine and Danusia both looked at her.

Tristaine barely spared her a glance before returning his attention to the files.

"All in time," he muttered.

"Demanding sycos," Danusia rolled her eyes, turning back to Tristaine.

A fiery mixture of anger and hurt burned in Molly's chest. *You better not break your deal with me,* she wanted to say. But she had no basis to threaten these demigods. All she could do was keep her mouth shut, keep playing nice, and hope they'd do the right thing when the time came.

"Let's just get all this completed as quickly as possible," Danusia was saying. "The wedding, the merger. All of it. Then the door will open, and the prize will be ours."

Tristaine eyed the Rolex on his wrist. "Speaking of hurrying up, we'd better get dressed. Klepper will be expecting us for dinner."

**29**

---

## RACHEL

Rachel shifted into sun pose on her yoga mat. The stone in her belly seemed intent on rehabilitating her and getting her back into fighting shape, which was concerning. What was it prepping her for? Part of her aimed to find out. Another part preferred not to know.

But what concerned her most was remembering the look on Jack Valentine's face when he saw Gallo. They were sworn enemies, she knew, the animosity between them so potent that Jack had nearly killed Gallo the last time they met. It seemed he would have preferred to kill him again, and no doubt the feeling was mutual. That would spell trouble in the future, Rachel had no doubt. But the stone had made it clear in its whisperings to her: both Jacks were integral to their plans. She'd have to keep them both around no matter how volatile their combination might be.

*Just focus on yourself. On getting strong,* the stone inside her advised. *Concentrate on the yoga. On your breathing. In, out...*

Though she'd woken from the drug-induced coma Gabardine had placed her in only a few days ago, she felt much stronger already. Perhaps the bad luck was healing her. Her enemies wished her to be weak and injured. Using that ill-will as something to push against, her hex could make her well. Unluckily for them.

But, she thought, perhaps it was something else. Ever since she'd swallowed that ghastly stone, she'd felt subtly ill, like—well, like she had a rock in her stomach. But ever since she'd awakened from the coma her creepy doctor placed her in, that feeling seemed to be less prominent, replaced instead with a radiating, pleasant coldness. It was more than just the normal sensation of her power. It was energy, invigoration, excitement. *Maybe that quack doctor operated while I was out and took that stone out of me,* she thought fleetingly. But there were no scars. That couldn't be it. *Maybe I absorbed it into myself,* she thought next. That possibility scared her, and she pushed the thought away.

Downward dog, into *Bhujangasana.*

The yoga instructor on the TV screen prattled a string of encouraging new-age platitudes underscored with music comprised of droning strings and oooing voices. Her underlings had almost balked when she told them she preferred working out to videos. Darby was ready to shell out for an expensive personal trainer. Dr. Gabardine favored hiring a full time in-house rehabilitation expert. Gallo, judging from his grunts, seemed happy to train her himself. But Rachel had overruled them all. She liked her videos. Besides, what fun was being a dark queen if you didn't get to overrule people once in a while?

Now she felt the prickly sensation of eyes on her and rolled onto her side to find Gallo watching her. Hungrily. Again.

She wanted to feel offended. Annoyed. But part of her, naughty, dark queen that she was, enjoyed his gaze.

"Can I help you?" she asked.

He quirked an eyebrow and continued shoulder-pressing a colossal barbell.

"Take a picture, it'll last longer," she said.

At this, he paused mid-stroke and lowered the bar, then dropped the weights to the ground with a thud that shook Rachel to her taut, freshly worked-out core. He reached into the pocket of his workout shorts, took out his phone, pointed it toward her, and took a picture.

Rachel couldn't repress a smile, and Gallo gave one right back to her.

"Brute," she said. It came out sounding more flirty than she'd intended.

Huffing a sigh of pleased frustration, she went back to her exercise, catching up with her instructor and going into warrior pose. She'd only just settled into it when a cramp shot through her hamstring. With a cry she toppled sideways, grabbing at her burning leg. For a moment, all she could feel was the searing pain; the entire world condensed like a black hole down, narrowing to a single searing point at the back of her thigh. Her face froze in a mask of agony. Breath came in tiny gasps.

Then she felt the pain easing. The muscle releasing. It was a moment before she realized Gallo's strong hands were kneading her muscle, each stroke pressing away the pain and tension... with his hands uncomfortably close to her butt.

"Um—" she tried to protest, to roll away from him, but at her first movement pain zinged back and she sank back to the mat with a hiss. She gave in then, lying still with her eyes closed as Gallo massaged her. She lost track of time for a moment, but when she came back to herself the pain was gone, and the Club sat watching her, as still and huge, self-satisfied and dangerous as a jungle cat. His hands were still on her thigh.

She rolled away from him and sat up. "Thanks. I guess."

His only response was a shadow of a smile.

"What's your deal, anyway?" Rachel said. "I mean, Rocky told me the basics—"

*I've told you, do not call me Rocky.* The voice in her gut said. She ignored it.

"The Valentine, Jack, shot you in the head. Gabardine healed you. I heard you hate King Thad so maybe you don't want to go back to the Clubs—but why are you still here?"

The big, sweaty luck god watched her for a moment longer with those predator's eyes. Then he took out his phone, typed something into it, and offered it to her. She looked at the word on the screen.

*You,* it read.

"Me?" she demanded. "You're here for *me*."

Gallo nodded, a lock of his long, dark hair falling across his eyes. They were a luminous hazel, she noticed, like the clay of some alien planet. He was the most handsome man she'd ever seen in person, bar none, and she reflexively touched the ring finger of her left hand, where the wedding ring Kevin gave her had rested for nearly twenty years. At some point during the ravages of her life as a dark queen—months ago, now—she'd lost the ring. She'd simply woken up after a night of bad luck work to find it gone. And instead of crying or turning the world upside down to find it, she'd surprised herself by simply sighing. A cold, empty feeling had settled in her stomach then, ominous as a lone raven. *What does it matter anyway? Kevin's dead.* She'd thought. Or the stone insider her had thought it. It was difficult to tell the difference sometimes.

Was the stone dissolving into her? Is that why she didn't feel it anymore?

Or was she dissolving into the stone?

Nine months. She'd promised herself to the stone for nine months, then it had sworn to let her go. But what if the stone had chosen nine months for a reason. What if it knew at the end of nine months, there would be nothing left of Rachel to let go of anyway?

The thought should have terrified her but the truth was she felt nothing.

*What does it matter?*

Those words now hung like a banner over so much of life that had once caused her anxiety and angst.

*My house—gone. What does it matter? I have a roof over my head.*

*My job—gone. What does it matter? I have all the money I need.*

*Aggie—gone. What does it matter? She's almost eighteen anyway. And I was bound to let her down eventually. Better to let her go now, before she learns how disappointing I really am. Before I drive her away. Before I hurt her.*

Part of her knew these thoughts weren't hers. She could never truly feel ambivalent toward Aggie. Or could she?

The man-specimen in front of her was typing again. When he finished and turned his phone around it read: *It's all part of the plan. I become your king. You become my queen. We rule the dark suits together, Morbus and Blackovers. United, no one can defeat us.*

Rachel found herself frowning at the words. In truth, she'd imagined marriage was in her future. Not the sort of marriage she'd had with Kevin, but the sort a queen was expected to endure. Not a love match, but an alliance. She'd assumed her stone was setting her up to elevate Aggie's flame Jack to the kinghood, to stitch up their control of the Valentine suit and destroy it from within. But in Gallo's words, she glimpsed new possibilities. A new way. A darker way. At least this wouldn't require a union—symbolic or otherwise—with her daughter's beau.

But this union raised other worries. Other dangers. Marrying Aggie's Jack would have been an emotionally safe partnership. He was a boy, and she could easily have held him at arm's length. But she could already tell that a marriage with Gallo would be more complicated than a simple political arrangement. He was force of nature. A hurricane.

She turned her head to the side and whispered to the stone in her belly: "Is this what you have in mind for me?"

A response came, but not in words. It came in a feeling. A flaring of need as strong as any she'd ever felt in her life. But it had nothing to do with the hunk looming over her. This feeling throbbed in her hands. It was *the work*, calling her. It jerked her like a dog with a choke collar. She looked down at the Spade pips then closed her hands into fists, baring her teeth with the pain of her wanting.

Rachel noticed Gallo was looking at his hands, too.

"You feel it?" she asked.

He gave a single nod.

For an instant she felt the impulse to resist. To shy away from the urge boiling in her blood. But what was the point of that? The work always won. And for six more months, she belonged to the stone. Resistance, as the saying went, was futile. So might as well enjoy the ride.

So she grinned, letting the Jack of Clubs take her hands and haul her to her feet.

♡ ♤ ◇ ♧

Dr. Gabardine and Shade were waiting when they emerged from the workout room.

"Your majesty," Shade said with a nod, sweeping a long, dark coat over her shoulders. It was new, beautifully made, and dark as the underside of a raven's wing, with a pattern of spades subtly stitched into the silk lining. She nestled into it, luxuriating in the black fur collar. These days, wearing black felt like slipping into a hot bath.

"I've got the car pulled around back," Shade said, his voice a low rumble.

Dr. Gabardine stepped forward then and offered what Rachel at first took for a black gun. But the barrel, she saw, was too wide. Next, Gabardine slung a bandolier over her shoulder. Instead of bullets, it held perhaps a dozen cylindrical cannisters. She felt a creeping feeling, then. Foreboding, like spiders tickling up her spine.

"What is this?" she asked.

She glanced over to see Gallo had donned a weathered black cloak and he, too, held the strange cannister gun. But of course, he couldn't answer her.

Shade, instead of answering, glanced at Gabardine, but his only response was a sickly smile that reminded her again of a strange, carnival-mirror version of her dead husband. She realized they were all waiting for something. For the obelisk to answer her, perhaps. But it did not. It had been more quiet lately. What did that mean?

It seemed an important question, but she had no time to answer it. Shade was holding the door open and Gabardine gestured toward it, that unnerving smile plastered across his face.

Rachel and Gallo got into the back of a long, black sedan and Shade took the wheel. As they pulled out of the parking lot, Rachel's hand fell on something rubbery. A gas mask sat on the seat. It repulsed her. Those creepy round eye holes and the respirator cannister nose reminded her of apocalyptic movies, watched late at night in her youth. She felt like yelling at Shade to stop, felt like getting out of the car and running away. But the hunger in her hands was too strong. And with every yard the car travelled, the delicious wanting became stronger.

"What are we going to do?" she asked. It took effort to grind out the words.

Shade glanced at her in the rearview mirror. "Same thing the stone has had me doing for a while, Your Highness," he said. "You're going to love it. It tops up the hex like no other."

"Yes, but *what*—?"

Shade chuckled. "You haven't been watching the news, eh?" he said, then caught himself and added, "your Majesty."

Gallo typed into his phone then turned it to show her what she'd written.

*We're doing what Morbus do best, beautiful. Using the most ancient bad luck weapon of all. Pestilence.*

The winter festival was in full swing by the time they arrived. The city had set up a ice skating pond in the square. Vendor booths sold winter-themed drinks—boozy cocoa, eggnog and hot toddies. Couples with scarves around their necks milled about, holding hands and looking like extras in some romantic Christmas movie. On the far side of the square, a few hot air balloon teams had set up their baskets, sans balloons, and were firing geysers of fire up into the night sky, eliciting hoots and applause from the crowd. One went off nearby, the sudden burst of heat and light making Rachel blink and recoil. It felt good, that warmth, but it was nothing compared to the fire pulsing in the palms of her hands, the burning, churning desire for *the work*. She felt it trying to claw its way out of her, to burst forth like a handful of squirming maggots from a carcass. The teargas launcher hung from its strap beneath her coat, heavy on her shoulder.

She stopped at the edge of the revelry, watching as a group of teens surged past, exchanging raucous shouts and laughter. Gallo and Shade formed up on either side of her.

"Should we mask up?" Shade asked. "Wind's coming from the west. We fire from here, we should be able to arc them over that ice rink. The wind will blow the smoke back toward us—but we'll be hell and gone before it gets here."

Gallo grunted and nodded his approval.

"Has Gabardine told you what's in these things?" she asked, her fingers drifting to the bandolier under her coat. "Some sort of virus, I take it?"

The question was directed half at Shade, half at the

obelisk shard inside her. Both answered at once, making a strange cacophony.

Shade: "Yeah, a virus, Gabardine says."

The obelisk: *It is suffering, my dear. Sweet pain and debilitation.*

"Does it kill?" Rachel pressed, steeling herself for the answer.

Shade shrugged. "Gabardine won't say much about what it does to people long-term."

*It makes for a rich harvest,* the stone said, not quite answering her question.

Rachel couldn't repress a shiver.

"It's not pretty," Shade was saying, oblivious of the stone's words. "But we're soldiers, right? We do what we do for the cause."

*And what is the cause?* Rachel wanted to ask. She knew what the cause was for Shade. It was power, and the things he could do with it. Not for himself, but for others. Degentrification, he called it. Shade's cause was helping the people from his neighborhood. But what was Rachel's cause? What was her excuse? Just to live long enough to be free. But could her own survival justify the suffering she caused others?

"Does it kill?" Rachel whispered again through teeth on edge. This time, the obelisk answered.

*It is a deposit into a bank,* the voice within her said. *We'll be able to draw hex from for years.*

"Meaning it doesn't kill—not right away. It just makes people suffer," she said. "And we reap hex from it the entire time."

The obelisk's voice modulated lower. *For some, it is worse luck to live than to die. And yet we do what the work demands of us.*

*Just get it over with,* Rachel told herself, her hand finding the grip of her gun before she could think any more about it. And her pips hummed pleasurably in anticipation. But just at that moment, Rachel's eyes fell upon a little girl, her cheeks rosy with cold, frolicking down the sidewalk. The glasses she wore made her think of a little Aggie. She froze, watching the girl.

*Rachel,* the stone said. A warning.

"And what if we don't do what the work demands of us?" she asked. "What if we refuse?"

Shade seemed to understand she wasn't talking to him and stayed silent.

After a second, the stone replied, its voice low and menacing, but amused, too. *What if lungs refuse to take in air? What if a heart refuses to beat? All things that refuse their function meet the same fate, Rachel.*

Shade gave Rachel a nudge with his elbow. She followed his eyes to a pair of police in bullet proof vests, making their way through the crowd.

"We best get this done," Shade said. "As soon as they get to the far side of that rink."

The trio watched in silence—black-clad, still, unsmiling, like wraiths among the living—as the cops made their way through the crowd. When they were distant enough, Shade freed his launcher from inside his coat. Gallo reached into his cloak, following suit.

"On your call, Highness," Shade said.

Rachel's gaze remained fixed on that little girl. A light dusting of snow had begun to sift down from the dark heavens, and the girl, so like a little Aggie, skipped along, her face upturned, mouth open, hoping to catch a snowflake on her tongue.

Rachel's itching, burning palm found the grip of her gun and closed on it. But she did not take it out.

"Highness?" Shade repeated.

Rachel remained frozen. Fixed. Rigid. The girl was twirling now, arms outstretched. The crowd parted for her— as if she, not Rachel were the demigod. Maybe she was.

*How I've taken everything for granted my whole life,* Rachel thought. *How divine, to be normal. To live a normal life.*

"Your Highness?" Shade pressed.

"No," Rachel shook her head. "I won't."

*A heart that will not beat...* the stone whispered inside her.

"No," she said again, backing away.

It hit her then, worse than ever before. Agony. The stone twisted something inside her, like a hot fork stirring her guts. Pain and nausea struck with the force of birth-contraction, causing her to jackknife at the waist, buckling her knees.

Shade caught her, or she'd have gone down face-first on the pavement.

Somewhere within the chrysalis of her agony she heard a hollow *shup* sound, then the whistle of a projectile. Her eyes rolled to see Gallo had fired one of his cannisters. She glimpsed it flying a high arc over the crowd. Shade fired, too. Then both men were grabbing her arms, helping her through a chaos of churning, running bodies. The black pips on Gallo's hands hummed with a dark glow, seeming to cast them in a halo of blackness, an envelope into which the streetlight could barely reach. And in that protective sheath of darkness, they made their way all the way back to the car before the sirens started.

With gentle hands the two men placed her in the back of the car. She was vaguely aware of the shifting motions of the vehicle as they pulled away, speeding away through the city.

"You alright? Your Highness? You okay?" Shade was asking.

Gallo watched her too, his gaze surprisingly gentle for the eyes of a killer.

"You okay? You alright?"

But she couldn't answer. Her hands were on fire, and the stone inside was ripping her in two.

"Just kill me," she grated through bared teeth.

Neither man answered, but the stone inside her did, *As you wish, my queen,* it said.

# 30

# AGGIE

He found me in the heart mansion fitness room, jumping rope. I'd been there for over an hour, exercising and watching online test prep videos. I was trying to get my mind off queen drama and back on prepping for my SAT, which was coming up fast. But I couldn't process anything the videos were saying. My thoughts kept returning to Deuce's words. *When you and Jack fell for one another, it didn't happen organically. You were charmed with Cupid's Arrow.* I didn't want to think about it. I didn't want to believe him. And yet it was impossible not to rewind my thoughts, not to think about every single interaction Jack and I shared and ask myself: *was it genuine? Or was charm nudging our emotions, pushing us together?* I'd quickly realized there was no way to differentiate between genuine feelings of love and magicked ones. Both were irrational, capricious, and frightening. But that didn't stop me from examining each moment, each word, each thought, like turning over a stone to see what bugs might be crawling underneath.

Working out and thinking about Jack probably wasn't the best use of my time given that a killer was still on the loose. But I'd done a lot of investigating earlier.

First, I'd scoured the surveillance camera footage of the mansion grounds again, looking for evidence. If our killer was a peri, they were probably invisible as they approached the house, but if I looked closely enough, I should be able to see the telltale shimmers. Yet despite watching hours of video, I'd found nothing. No one going in, no one coming out.

If we couldn't see them going in or out on the cameras, did that mean our killer had a leprechaun key? Maybe. But it was hard to know for sure.

There was one secret entrance, a tunnel from the basement that came out in a camouflaged hatch beyond the edge of the property. The passage wasn't monitored by cameras, and it was possible the assassin might have entered that way. But the tunnel was rarely used, and it was locked. Not even every Heart knew about it, so it seemed unlikely that our enemies did.

Something else bothered me. Michael had been killed in the bed right next to me, yet I hadn't woken up. Sure, I'd been exhausted, and I was a pretty deep sleeper, but not that deep. The killer had been lucky I didn't wake up and see them. Or I'd been unlucky. That pointed to the use of charm or hex—a luck god. But there were other possible explanations, too. Maybe I'd been drugged. Maybe someone had hit me with a tranquilizer dart. Maybe I just didn't wake up.

Next, I'd gone into the mansion office and dug out the report our syco doctor had done on Michael's body. Jack had already looked it over and said it contained nothing of interest. But I did what all good test takers do: I went back to check our work. And I found something interesting. Michael had been killed by a single blow to the head from a blunt object. To kill a person with only one blow was noteworthy. It meant that the killer was either very big and strong, very lucky, or both.

That seemed to point away from Lorcan or Cleo. Carlotta the Joker still had some luck and was probably fairly strong, but she wasn't very big. And while Jokers did have some luck power, it wasn't the queen-level hex Carlotta had once possessed. It seemed unlikely she'd made it past our cameras undetected *and* had the power to assassinate Michael with a single blow—all without waking me up. Again, the information I had was inconclusive.

Finally, I'd gone into Galen's room. I didn't expect to find much there, but I thought there might be a clue as to why the assassin targeted him as opposed to one of the other Hearts.

Clearly, no one had touched the room since he died. There were balled up socks on the floor, a button up shirt draped over a chair, and empty Mountain Dew cans on the dresser. It felt very wrong to be in there among his things. A fog of sadness and loss seemed to hang over it all, almost as bad as the feeling I got in hexed places. But I made myself push through and poke around.

For the bedroom of a demigod, it was incredibly ordinary. There was a laptop and an iPad—both password locked. Clothes. A strip of pictures from one of those photo booths of Galen and Mina together, looking cute and flirty— I looked away from that one fast, before I teared up.

I was about to give up when at last I found something. Under the bathroom sink, in a basket wrapped a towel, was a pile of money. Like, a lot of money. I counted it and found $490,000 in neat little packets like the ones I'd won at the casino downtown, once upon a time.

*Why would Galen have so much cash?* The Valentine suit had plenty of money and we all had access to it, so it wasn't that he couldn't get a hold of this much cash if he wanted to. The question was, why would did he need so much? What was it for? Dubs kept track of the Valentine's finances, and I made a mental note to have him check and see when Galen withdrew the money, and what reason he gave for needing it. Mina might know, too, although I wasn't going to start grilling her about Galen for at least a couple of days.

I'd taken one more lap of the room, then left—even more confused than I'd been when I arrived.

I'd texted Jack hoping to talk things through with him but, surprise surprise, he didn't answer. I would have liked to talk to Deuce, but was I still mad at him. Mina was asleep, grieving for Galen, and there was no way I was going to wake her up and stress her out with my theories.

So where did that leave me? Confused. Alone. And jumping rope.

It felt good, my heartbeat pounding in my head, my spiraling thoughts distilled to animal simplicity. *Jump, jump, jump, jump.* Occasionally that mantra would become *one, two, three, four,* until I reached a set of twenty-three. A little indulgence. A little comfort, that dollop of OCD.

As I jumped, I watched myself in the mirror.

I was never a sports girl, never worked out much before becoming a demigoddess, but I'd grown to love it. My legs, which would have been aching mush in the past, felt strong as steel springs beneath me. My breathing was strong and rhythmic, and I wasn't dizzy with hyperventilation as I'd been before becoming a Valentine the few times I'd actually exerted myself in gym class.

Of course, in the past I would never have been coordinated enough to jump rope. The old Aggie would have been a frustrated tangle of feet and rope, and I'd probably have fallen on my face and broken my glasses. But now I cruised along, each hop perfectly timed to the metronomic tick of the rope whirling around me. *I'm pretty good,* I thought. Then I felt the warmth flowing from my hands and realized why. Each jump was a lucky jump. I was charming without realizing it again.

With a shout of alarm I released the rope, letting it whip into the mirror in front of me. I stared at my reflection, illuminated by the red glow of my hands as I caught my breath. Even sweaty and disheveled, I looked pretty. Not awkward. Not geeky. No acne. I'd even taken my glasses off to jump rope. I looked nothing like myself, I realized.

*So who am I? Who am I becoming?*

"Wow. What did that rope ever do to you?"

I looked up to find Deuce watching me from the doorway.

"I came to apologize," he said, leaning on the doorframe, arms crossed, exuding a surprising amount of swagger. I wondered if luck was making him look better, too. But I was mad at him, I reminded myself.

"I'm sorry I didn't tell you sooner about you and Jack," he went on. "I suspected for a while, but I didn't want to interfere with your relationship. Then when I found out for sure, I was afraid to tell you."

I frowned. "Why?"

He shook his head. "I guess was afraid you'd think I was just... you know... jealous of Jack. But I'll never keep anything secret from you again. I promise."

I wanted stay mad at him. I really did. But he looked so cute and contrite with his disheveled hair falling into his brown eyes that I relented.

"It's fine," I said, wiping my face with a workout towel. Of course, everything was far from fine—and Deuce seemed to know.

He opened his arms and I hesitated only for a second before letting him pull me into a hug. Deuce always gave the best hugs, all warm and big and tight. It made me want to shut my eyes and go to sleep. *I should push him away,* I reminded myself.

Instead, I held him tighter and felt the anger draining out of me. It took a second to realize I was crying.

"I'm sorry," he whispered again.

I shook my head against his chest. "It's not just that," I said. "Lately I've found myself using charm for everything. I used charm to cheat on a test. I was just using charm to jump rope. The other day I caught myself using charm when I was got out of the shower to give myself a good hair day. I never used to care about my hair. I barely used to wash it."

"Ew. You're also very sweaty now," he said. "But go on."

I pulled away from him but kept hold of his forearms.

"I just feel like the more I use charm, the further away I drift from... myself."

He gave a slow, knowing nod.

"When Jack first recruited me, I was a senior in high school," he said. "I was on the football team."

"You? Football?"

"Shut up," he smiled. "I'd been a bench warmer—"

"You? A bench warmer?" I teased.

This time he laughed out loud.

"Do you want to hear my super wise story or not? Yes, I was a bench warmer. My dad always wanted me to be the starter. When I was playing video games or reading comics or whatever, he was always trying to get me into the back-yard to practice. And I did sometimes, but I wasn't that great. So anyway, after I got my pips I came back for one last game. I was the backup tailback, and I didn't usually play that much. But it was Senior Night. My dad was in the stands and I was flaring charm the whole time, willing myself to get in the game. Halfway through the first quarter, the starting tail-back sprains his ankle. Coach would have normally put the second string guy in, but on a whim, he decides to put me, the third stringer, in instead. Very lucky, right?"

"And it was a disaster?" I surmised.

Deuce's smile was sad. "Nope. I rushed for a hundred and fifty-six yards and three touchdowns. I won the game for us. The guys carried me off the field on their shoulders. Everyone in the stands was going wild. My dad literally cried he was so happy. And I felt... nothing."

"Because it wasn't real," I said. "Because it wasn't you, it was just the charm."

"I mean—it was me, sort of," Deuce said. "I had the sweat and the bruises and the sore legs. But it was me from the luckiest timeline, you know? One where everything goes right. But... this isn't supposed to be that timeline. This is a timeline where a lot of times, things are pretty messed up.

So, to glimpse that other world, just felt... I don't know... wrong."

Deuce shook his head.

"I turned my jersey in and quit the next day," he said, pensive for a moment. Then his eyes found mine. "You learn to live with the power. You learn how to use it. You might even enjoy it most of the time. But you never really get used to it. Otherwise, you really would lose yourself. You'd become... I don't know..."

"Am I interrupting?"

Deuce and I both looked up to find Jack leaning in the doorway.

I was suddenly aware of how close the two of us were standing and stepped back. "No, you're not interrupting," I said. "We were just talking about the lovely gift of charm you gave us by bringing us into the Valentines."

Jack's expression didn't change, but I could see the wheels behind his eyes turning as he tried to parse whether I was joking or criticizing or what. He entered, brandishing his notebook.

"Good news. I solved the murders," he said.

The nonchalant way he said it made Deuce and I glance at one another. Was he joking? He took out his phone, pulled up a video, and played it for us. The image was grainy with low light, but I recognized the dark skin and spider-web eye tattoo of Shade, my mom's right hand man. He stood against a brick wall, illuminated by a streetlight.

"Yeah, I took out the Heart King," he was saying. "And their two."

"Why?" an off-screen voice that I recognized as Jack's said.

Shade shrugged, looking away. "Following orders."

"Whose orders?"

"From the queen. Or from that stone inside her, I guess. Look, I do what I'm told, alright."

"How did you kill them?"

Shade hesitated. "Uh… the king I hit over the head with a club. No guns, you know. The queen told me it had to be silent."

"Because you were doing it in the Hearts house with the queen sleeping in the same bed," Jack said.

"Right," Shade agreed.

"And the kid?"

Shade shrugged, gave a small shake of his head. "Him I just… snuck up on him with a knife and—*bow, bow, bow.*"

He mimed stabbing.

"You know the Valentines are going to be pissed, right? They're going to come after you when they find out."

Shade snorted. "They can bring it on. Spades for life."

Jack ended the video and looked at us. When neither Deuce nor I responded, he said, "Case closed."

I pursed my lips. "No. He's lying."

Jack gaped at me. "What do you mean he's lying? I filmed him with a hidden camera. He thinks he can trust me."

I shook my head. "Play the video again without sound."

I could tell Jack was irritated, but he took his phone out again and did as I asked, playing the video again. I pointed to the screen.

"He looks away from you here… this is where he's scuffing his foot nervously. Here, he gestures with both hands after he's done talking. There, he purses his lips… And now he's rubbing his eyebrow. All classic signs of lying," I concluded.

Both guys were looking at me, Jack with barely concealed annoyance, and Deuce with an admiring grin.

"What? I've done some research," I said. "You think I'd become a detective without doing my homework?"

"She does love doing homework," Deuce confirmed.

Jack had his arms crossed.

"This body language, for example, shows you're closed off and angry," I told Jack. "Which is understandable. You thought you had solved the case, so this must be disappointing for you. But I promise, he is lying."

Jack took a calming breath. "Okay. Let's say you're right and he is lying. This video still solves our problem. You show it to Cobe and Ten, it proves our innocence. They'll have to fall in line."

"Lying might solve our problem with Cobe and Ten," Deuce pointed out. "But we still have to figure out who the real killer is. You know, before they kill again."

"Fine," Jack huffed, flipping open his notebook and tracing his finger down the line of suspect names. "Then let's review... Lorcan."

"Had access with his leprechaun key, but his motive seems weak," I said.

"Cleo."

"Same as Lorcan. Except we know she was associated with the—"

"Unknown peri," Jack read, tapping the paper with his finger.

*Carlotta Blackover*, I thought, and I almost said the name aloud, but again something held me back. Now that she was Shastaryan she could go invisible somehow—and she certainly had the chops to sneak into the Hearts mansion, judging from her ability to stalk me at school. But there was the question of whether she could have killed Michael in one blow. And her motive remained unclear, too. If the Shastaryan wanted to weaken and destroy the system of luck gods, that was a solid motive for killing a king. But why start with Michael? Our intelligence had told us that she'd been exiled from the Blackovers after King Thad found out the full extent of her affair with Jack. If anything, she'd be more likely to go after Thad first to get revenge.

Carlotta might have killed Michael in order to elevate Jack, I thought suddenly. That motive would have made sense, if she was still hung up on Jack and wanted to make up to him for her betrayal. But Jack had told me he used his Cupid's Arrow in reverse to make Carlotta fall out of love with him, and I believed Jack. About that, anyway.

"Given what I uncovered about the Shastaryan, the motive is there," Deuce said. "Kill a king, destabilize our suit, and the power of the luck gods weakens."

"Sure," Jack said. "But if they're starting a war on luck gods, how come there have been no killings in other suits?"

We all fell silent, pondering the question.

"Warrants further investigation," I concluded.

Jack's finger traced down the list.

"Everyone in the Valentines," he said with a dark smile.

"We all did hate Michael," Deuce said. "He was very hateable."

"But we all liked Galen," I pointed out.

"I hoped we might gain some insights from our interrogations," Jack mused, rubbing his chin. "But I didn't learn much. What about you?"

I shook my head. "Not really," I snorted. "Motive-wise, the ones with the most to gain from killing Michael are the three of us."

Deuce's hand went to the knife on his belt. "I might be a badass assassin," he said. "You never know. It's always the person you least expect."

Jack gave him a bemused look then went back to the list. "Bartholomew Barth, the sylph."

"The sylph are always trying to gain power over the luck gods," Deuce conceded.

"But Barth hated Jack more than Michael," I pointed out.

Jack shrugged. "Maybe. But sylph live over nine-hundred years. They play the long game. Disarray in our suit might elevate me temporarily, but it could benefit Barth long-term."

"He could definitely access peri assassins," Deuce mused.

"Which brings us to the last one on our list who is also associated with Barth. One we haven't investigated yet," I said. "That goblin cutthroat Cleo told us about, Varsmith."

Deuce nodded. "Goblins are nasty. Made for killing. They're dangerous. Even sylph are wary of them, normally. If Barth brought one through the rift and is risking having him around, that almost puts Barth and this Varsmith at the top of the list."

"My thoughts exactly," I said, taking the notebook from Jack and clapping it shut. "That's why I made an appointment with Barth's assistant, Lura. Get ready. We're meeting her in an hour."

# 31

# AGGIE

"I don't like this," Jack said as he drove. "I mean, last time I saw Barth I almost killed him. I seem to remember him screaming something about vengeance."

"You've seen him since then. When he kidnapped you and sold you to someone he thought was going to kill you, remember?"

"Thanks for reminding me. I feel much better now," Jack said with a grudging laugh.

"That's why we're talking to Lura and not Barth," I said.

Jack winced. "That's not great, either. Lura and I have a history."

I grimaced. "Of course you do."

Jack glared at me sidelong. "What's that supposed to mean?"

There was plenty I had to say on the topic of Jack's many, many past relationships, trysts, flings, hookups, et cetera. And dumping all that on him probably would have felt great, like popping a zit. But it certainly wouldn't have helped us solve Michael's murder. I also wanted to ask if he knew about Deuce Cupid's Arrowing us, but that was a question I couldn't bring myself to ask. Would it be better if he knew, if he was part of tricking me into loving him? Or would it be better if he didn't know—and I'd have to watch him realize in real time that he never actually loved me. Either revelation wasn't something I could take right now.

I wished Deuce was there. He'd wanted to join us, but I'd given him other important duties: to stay and comfort Mina and to protect the suit in case our killer showed up again. He hated staying behind. It was written clearly in his eyes as we departed. But I reminded him that I needed him, that he was one of the only people in the world I trusted completely. And as always, he followed my orders. Ol' reliable Deuce.

"That's it," I said, pointing out the windshield to a grand but abandoned building. The white marble façade had turned to gray and was streaked with dark lines. The dome above was the green of burnished copper and looked like a giant closed eye.

"Grayling Observatory," Jack said.

I had let Lura pick the meeting place with the stipulation that it had to be in neutral territory—but although this wasn't a full-fledged bad luck place, I could sense a faint, metallic tingle of hex in the air. This could be a trap. It wouldn't be the first time one of Jack's exes lured him into an ambush, either. But we had to solve these murders before another Valentine died. This was a risk we'd have to take.

We parked on the street, got out of the car, and checked our weapons.

"Do me a favor and let me do the talking this time, would you?" Jack said.

"Don't I always?" I batted my eyelashes at him.

His eye roll was ferocious.

We made our way warily toward the observatory. The front doors were chained and padlocked, covered with a patina of dust. We went around to the back, passed through what once seemed to have been a Japanese garden—now wildly overgrown—and found the back door which, as Lura had promised, stood ajar.

"Ladies first," Jack gestured to the ominous blackness beyond the doorway. When I glared at him, he laughed, but when I stepped forward, he stepped in front of me. "Kidding, my Queen," he said.

"Don't call me that," I muttered.

"Why?" he said as we stepped into the darkness. "You are my Queen."

"Because it sounds like something else," I said, walking forward in the gloom. "It sounds like you're flirting or... What's that?"

A sound came from the darkness around us. A slow mechanical grinding and clicking. I heard Jack's blade ring as he drew his short sword from its scabbard. I drew mine, too, along with my pistol.

Then, lights flared above us, a million pin-pricks of light, slowly revolving. A night sky.

"Whoa," I said, unable to conceal my wonder.

"Lovely, isn't it?" a voice said.

I looked down from the ceiling and saw, in the newly kindled light, that risers of seating stretched out on either side of us to ring the room. In the center of the round space Lura the sylph stood, looking like a pretty, lavender-skinned movie alien. She gazed at the dome above.

"Stars are sacred to the sylph. That's why we get them tattooed on us," she said, running a hand over her bald head and its inked constellations. "We meditate for three weeks before our naming day and choose which portion of sky to have placed upon us. The choice dictates what sort of luck we will have for the rest of our lives."

"I hope you picked lucky stars," Jack said.

Lura's eyes flicked back to the display arching above us, but she didn't answer. Jack moved slowly toward the center of the room, his eyes darting left then right before he finally sheathed his sword. I followed suit, a step behind as we made our way to Lura.

Jack glanced up. "It is beautiful," he conceded.

Lura's too-small mouth frowned. "This rift location is problematic because of its lack of stars. Too many clouds. Too much light pollution." She shook her head. "It was better when it was in Siberia."

Jack snorted. "In Siberia it was cold enough to freeze vodka. Well, almost."

The sylph's large eyes shifted their focus from the dome for the first time and settled on me. "You asked about Varsmith."

"We'd like to set up a meeting with him," Jack put in before I could answer.

"We're investigating King Michael's death," I added. Jack glared at me.

The sylph's tiny mouth quirked in a half smile. "He hasn't

mentioned killing any Valentine royalty to me. But then, Varsmith and I don't chat much."

"Not a big fan of his?" Jack asked.

Lura shrugged. "I'm not a fan of any goblins. Most sylph are not. They have their uses, to be sure, but most are not to be trusted."

"But sylph are super trustworthy," I said. "Like that time your boss tried to lock me up and sell me for my luck."

The sylph's gaze shifted with unnerving slowness to fall on me. "Your Highness, we sylph have an old saying. *Czhtyl ézôchotlum ozozek.* It means the fish that swims into your net is yours."

"Yeah, well I'm not a fish. I'm a Queen," I said, sounding more like petulant child than a deity.

"Barth would never have deigned to bring a goblin to this side of the rift, even one as distinguished as Varsmith, if not for the incident between the two of you," Lura told Jack. "You really rattled him, Jack of Hearts."

"Well, he deserved to be rattled," Jack said. "You say this Varsmith is distinguished? How?"

"He is Kandluza."

"What's that?" I asked.

"A head warrior priest of his order, the Uthmura."

"Priest?" Jack scoffed. "I thought the only things goblins worshipped were violence and yunqi."

"Oh, no," Lura said. "They are very devout. But I find religious fanaticism to be far more corrupting than greed. I don't trust Varsmith. I'd like to see us rid of him. And so, I would be glad to give you access to him. If you decide he's your killer and you choose to punish him, I'll even turn my head. For a price."

Jack grinned. "A price, eh? Name it."

"There is a shipment coming through the rift, being brought in by a rival sylph. We'd like to intercept the boat while it's still on the water and get our hands on the cargo. Do that, and I'll give you Varsmith."

Jack's smile faded. "Piracy? We'll pass."

"We'll do it," I said, my words overlapping with his.

"Aggie…" he took me by the arm and pulled me a few steps away, then leaned in, speaking low in my ear. "Let me remind you, Barth has his own army. If this mission is too dangerous for them, it's sure as hell too dangerous for us. But more likely there is no cargo and this whole thing is a trap."

Jack was trying to keep us safe and it was sweet. But we're already burned through nearly all of our suspect list and had yet to find the King's killer. And we'd lost Galen. I wasn't going to sit by while we lost another Valentine. We'd been careful so far, but we were out of time.

"We'll do it," I said again, putting all my queenly authority into the words. I turned back to Lura. "When is this shipment supposed to come in, exactly?"

The sylph's unnaturally large eyes narrowed. "Tonight."

**32**

---

# JUNIOR

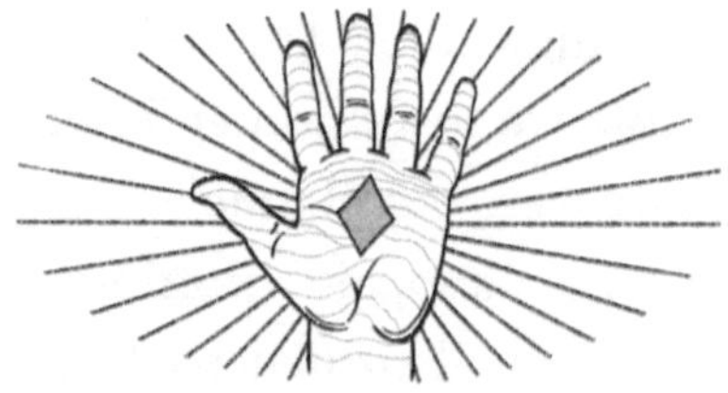

Junior sat at the booth in the truck stop Subway, watching out the plate glass window as people pulled in to fueled up their cars or walked into the convenience store to grab snacks. His stomach ached with nerves and hunger. He worried about the truck he'd stolen. It had become so low on gas its engine had been coughing as he pulled into the station, but he had no money to fill up the gas tank or his stomach.

*Just do it,* the voice of the stone said from inside his mind. *Hurry up.*

The more Junior tried to ignore the voice, the more belligerent the stone got.

But exhaustion tugged at Junior's eyelids. Stress left his

hands jittery. He needed just a moment to sit, rest, think.

*Think while you drive,* the stone hissed. *She's coming. And you have an appointment to keep.*

Junior knew who *she* was. It was Cleo. And part of him wanted her to catch him, to take him back to her safe, underground home for more video games and Hot Pockets, more quiet and peace and safety.

*Don't be stupid. She'll hate you for running away,* the stone hissed in his ear.

Junior didn't want to believe that was true. But his mom flashed through his mind, memories of the things she did to him when she was mad. Pulling his hair. Breaking his toys. Pinching him until his arms bruised. Cleo wasn't like that. She'd never hurt him. Still, the stone's words gave him pause.

As for this *appointment* the stone was talking about, Junior didn't know what it meant—but it scared him.

He rubbed his hands with his forehead, as if doing so would scrub the obelisk's voice from his mind. But nothing could keep the stone out of his thoughts. He'd tried.

"Are you okay?" a voice asked, and Junior looked up.

A woman with curly hair and a teal windbreaker stood looking down at him with concern. She looked like she'd have patted him on the back or hugged him or something if her hands hadn't been full of a bag of sandwiches, two drinks, and her purse.

"Oh. Fine." Junior muttered.

The woman glanced around. "Is someone here with you?"

"My mom," Junior lied. "She's in the bathroom."

The woman peered toward the restrooms. "Yeah? You've been here by yourself for a while. Should I go check on her?"

"No," Junior said. "She has irritable bowel syndrome, also known as IBS. Sometimes she takes a long time."

Junior remembered seeing ads for IBS medicine on an online video and asking Cleo about it. Whenever Junior had asked his mom about things like that she usually told him *how the hell should I know?* or *stop bugging me.* But Cleo had answered his questions. Remembering made him miss her even more. She'd be proud of his lie, too, because it was working. The woman spared one last glance at the bathroom door, then backed away.

"Okay," she said hesitantly, turning to go. "Bye."

*Do it. Now,* the stone urged.

As the stone spoke, pain spiked through the palms of Junior's hands. It was as if he were cupping scalding water, and he needed to throw that water away in order to make the pain stop. That's what he did now—he threw the power, released it, sending it toward the woman along with a vision, a wish, a word.

*Fall.*

It happened almost immediately. The pain in Junior's hands released in a rush of pleasure and the woman tripped, going down belly-first on the tile floor. Both paper drink cups flattened beneath her, their contents flooding out. The purse biffed, coughing up its contents, a debris field of makeup stuff and tampons, a phone, a pack of gum, a prescription bottle—and a wallet.

Junior rushed to kneel next to the woman, taking her arm as she rose unsteadily to her knees.

"You okay?" he asked.

"Yeah. I think so." She said breathlessly, looking down at the messy floor in bafflement. "Whew. I don't even know what I tripped on."

Junior handed the woman her pack of gum as she reloaded her purse. By the time her things were cleaned up, a teenage employee had arrived bearing a mop.

"Thank you," the woman said, patting Junior on the shoulder.

Then she was gone, exiting hastily in embarrassment.

Junior's hand snaked into his pocket and felt the wallet there. Too bad he'd had to steal from such a nice woman, he thought. But Cleo would have been proud.

Although the sandwiches smelled good, Cleo had warned him never to linger at the scene of a theft. So he crossed over to the convenience store side of the building and bought a big hot dog and a bunch of other snacks and drinks—enough, he hoped, to last him the rest of the trip.

Then he pulled the car up to a gas pump. After some fumbling, he managed get the gas door open on the side of the car and figured out how to use the gas pump. When he swiped the card, the pump asked him to enter a pin number and he paused, stumped.

*It would be awfully bad luck for that woman if you were to guess the pin number, wouldn't it?* the voice of the stone said.

Junior shut his eyes and reached a finger out toward the keypad, feeling the strange, tingly cold-hot feeling in the palms of his hands once more. He punched four buttons without even knowing which ones he was pressing, then hit enter. The screen blinked PROCCESSING for so long that Junior's heart started beating fast. But a second later a word blinked the screen: APPROVED. Then: BEGIN FUELING.

"Sorry, nice lady," he muttered, squeezing the handle and listening to the whoosh of the gas filling the tank.

He stood watching the numbers climb when a screech of tires drew his attention, and an emerald green Mustang skidded to a stop in one of the handicap spots in front of the convenience store.

Out jumped a character that drew glances from everyone at the gas station. That wild blonde hair. The green jumper. The twin daggers at her waist. The swaggery, bouncy steps. It was Cleo. Looking for him.

At the sight of her, Junior's heart lurched in his chest. He thought of all the times he'd run away from his own mother. Ten times, at least. She'd never come looking for him. As far as he knew, she'd never even noticed he was gone. He'd just run out of food or gotten cold or bored or lonely and come slinking back. Until that last time, when he hadn't.

But here Cleo was, storming the convenience store, as fierce as a Navy Seal. He wanted to run to her.

But before he could so much as take a step toward, the stone spoke in his mind.

"She sees you, she dies."

"But—" Junior started.

*You are bad luck, boy. When I'm done with you, you'll be the worst luck in the world. You'll be poison. Toxic waste. You'll be a trap. A prison. A bullet. A nuclear bomb. She sees you again, and she's dead. That is a vow. Do you believe me, boy?*

That voice, low, grating, strange, like a ghost out of hell itself. Of course Junior believed. He more than believed. He knew what the obelisk said was true.

If he loved Cleo, she could never find him. If he loved her, he had to run.

So he got into the car and started it. Scrubbing a tear from his cheek with the back of his hand, he pulled out of the gas station and screeched off into the desert once more.

He didn't even look in the rearview mirror to see Cleo run out of the gas station, staring after him.

# 33

# MOLLY

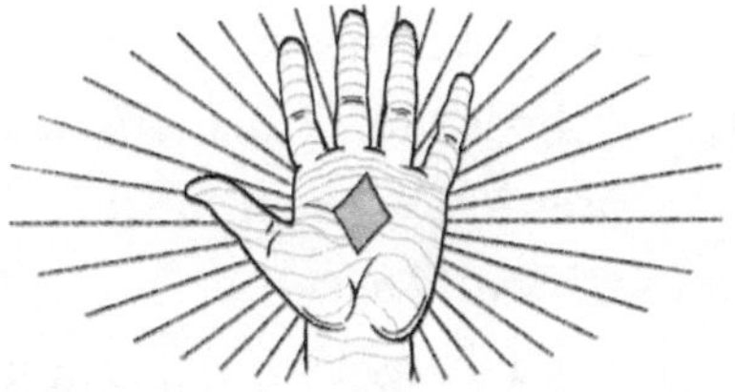

The Klepper estate lay a few miles northwest of Monaco. According to Tristaine, it was near Roquebrune-Cap-Martin—whatever that was. They took the helicopter there, then disembarked and took a van along a narrow road cut into the side of the mountains that ran along the sea.

They passed through a gated checkpoint and emerged into what looked to Molly like the fanciest resort in the world. The main building sprawled easily as large as the condos in the complex where her Mom lived in Palm Springs, but this place boasted clay tennis courts, bronze sculptures of Greek deities, glittering pools and trickling waterfalls. Immaculate landscape offered up flowers of varieties Molly had never even imagined, all lit with twinkling lights and flickering gas lamps. Molly gulped to prevent herself from whispering *wow*.

From a quick internet search of Monaco, she'd learned it was a place where even one-bedroom apartments cost a fortune. If the Kleppers could score a spread like this nearby, they had to have Diamond level money. It explained Seth's behavior, Molly thought. A person could act as weird as they wanted when they were this rich.

"Right. This is it," Danusia said. "Tristaine will clean up any details with Klepper's attorneys and make sure the merger documents get sent to our team. Ten will provide general charm and bat her eyelashes at any Klepper employees who appear hostile to our venture, and I will once again drive our host out of his wits with my feminine wiles. This is it, my pretties. We seal the deal."

"What about me?" Molly asked.

Tristaine glanced back, as if noticing her in the van for the first time. "Uh. Chat with Klepper's nephew if he's around—what's his name?

"Seth," Molly said.

"Right," Tristaine agreed. "From what I've seen he can be a bit of a pest, but the two of you seem to have hit it off. Keep him busy so he doesn't bother Klepper and Danusia."

"And stay out of our way," Danusia added.

❦ ♡ ♤ ◇ ♧ ❦

The vehicle pulled to a halt next to a gurgling fountain. Again, an array of servants stood ready to greet them. But instead of Klepper presiding over them, Seth was there. He wore a dress shirt buttoned all the way up and his green-dyed hair was slicked back. He'd made an effort to look nice, Molly thought, and she was glad the Diamantes stylists, almost as an afterthought, had given her a short, white dress to wear and had done her makeup so well she almost felt cute.

As everyone stepped out of the van, Seth nodded politely.

"Hey. Welcome," he said. "My uncle is inside busting the cook's balls for messing up the *fois gras*. He'll be out in a second."

His eyes settled on Molly.

"Join me for a ride?"

He offered his arm and Molly took it, blushing in spite of herself as he led her away from the others, down a path lined with lush plants and flowers. It had been unseasonably warm earlier in the day, but now that evening had settled in Molly was glad she had a sweater.

"This place is gorgeous," she said, taking in the immaculate grounds.

Seth gave an awkward chuckle. "I like our place in Connecticut better," he said. "Or the ranch in Montana. But this is okay."

"What kind of horses do you have?"

He side-eyed her. "In Montana?"

"Here. You said we were going riding."

He snorted. "Yeah, but I never said it would be on a horse."

They emerged from the thick foliage to find a motocross dirt bike standing atop a rise. Next to it, several beers sat on ice in a silver bucket. A butler in a white sport coat stood by, holding two helmets, which he now offered to Molly and Seth.

The one she took was white with pink decorations and had her name, "Molly," airbrushed on the back.

"What?" she squealed. "You had this made for me?"

Seth shrugged one shoulder. "What's the point in being rich if you can't do dumb crap to impress cute girls?"

Molly did her best to look coy as she pulled on the helmet. "Well, I'm impressed." The truth was, she was more than impressed. It was probably the nicest thing a boy had ever done for her.

"You ever ride a dirt bike before?"

"No," Molly said, looking at the big hill they sat at the top of. "Do I have to now? Or can I just wear my helmet and sit here and look pretty?"

Seth put on his own helmet on and winked at her.

"You don't have to ride," he said. "But you'd be a lot cooler if you did."

He threw a leg over the bike, fired it up and revved it. It sounded to Molly like a man-sized hornet, and the buzz made her heart beat faster.

In front of Seth, the black dirt trail snaked across the landscape, first dropping precipitously then running up and down ridges, balancing on rocky peaks and tracing the edge of cliffs. A person would have to be a maniac to ride a motor- cycle along that trail.

Seth revved the bike again and patted the seat behind him.

A maniac. That's what she'd have to be to go with him, too. And yet if she didn't go, she knew that her entire life she'd look back at her cowardice in this moment and feel disgusted with herself. Better to be a maniac than a coward. Better a broken neck than a slowly dying heart.

And so, with a nervous squeal, Molly ran to the bike,

hiked up her dress nearly to her waist, threw her leg over the bike, and wrapped her arms around Seth's body.

"Any advice?" she shouted over the bike's grumbling engine.

"Hold on," Seth said. He twisted the accelerator and they were off like a gunshot.

❦

Thirty minutes later, Molly reclined with Seth in an open-air cabana overlooking the ocean, her once pristine white dress spattered with mud. At Molly's request, they'd skipped the beer in favor of Capri-suns, and they both sipped juice and listened to the sound of the ocean. Molly had also opted out of pot, but Seth was smoking a massive joint with barely a cough. Both their bare feet kicked lazily as they rocking the hammock. Occasionally their feet would brush, sending a naughty little frisson through Molly's body.

*Eek. Sorry, Lorcan,* she thought, then pushed his image away. What was the saying? Out of sight, out of mind.

Seth took another hit off the joint and took Molly's hand, interlacing his fingers with hers.

"They want the portal system, eh?" Seth said out of the blue.

Molly half sat up in surprise. She found she was a little dizzy with the second-hand smoke.

Seth shrugged. "Half the reason we developed it was to entice the Diamantes to merge so we could cash in. What the hell were we going to do with a door to another world?"

"Good point," Molly said, sipping her juice. "The Diamonds plan to import stuff, I guess."

Seth nodded approvingly. "That's cool. I'd totally buy

some other world shit. By the way, I found a pic of you online."

"Ah, stalking me?" Molly teased.

"Yep," he said, turning his phone toward her. On it glowed an image of Molly and Aggie walking across the Oak Hill College campus. Aggie had her hand raised, as if waving to someone, and the heart mark stood out clearly on her palm. The caption read *The Valentine Queen and One of her Sycos*.

"What the frick?" Molly snatched the phone from Seth's hand, examining it more closely. "Where did you find this?"

Seth flopped back in the hammock.

"Just some weird fan site. Don't worry, it's the only one like it, and it gets barely any traffic. I checked."

With relief, Molly saw Seth was right. The site didn't belong to a major news organization. It looked like a simple Wordpress template with some thrown-together text and photos. A quick scroll revealed images of Danusia, Tristaine, Mina, Deuce, and even several Blackovers at their brewery.

Questions flitted through her mind. Who made this site? What was their intention? Was it the hobby of some weirdo in the know? A blackmail tool? Or a true journalistic attempt to out the Luck Gods? And who knew about it, anyway? Her first impulse was to tell Aggie. It made her heartsick to remember they weren't friends anymore.

Instead, she merely said, "Wow," and handed Seth's phone back.

"So if you're the heart queen's syco, how come you're here with the Diamantes?"

"I'm not her syco, I'm her best friend. Or... I was." Molly sighed, lying back, too. "It's a long story. Aggie and I had a falling out. And I've been sort of working with Danusia for a while."

"Why? They pay you?"

She glanced over to find him watching her, sly amusement in his otherwise unremarkable brown eyes.

"You're trying to get them to make you one of them?" he guessed.

"Um... yep," she said with a laugh.

Seth grunted a laugh, too. "I don't blame you. I'd do the same thing."

"Reallly," Molly said. "You'd want to be a luck god?"

"Hell yeah," Seth said. "Come on. Haven't you read any of those vampire books where someone gets a chance to become immortal and they're like, *nah, that's okay.* And you're like, *are you kidding me? Become immortal, dumbass.*"

Molly laughed.

"Hell yes I'd become a luck god," Seth concluded.

"Luck gods aren't exactly immortal, though," Molly said. "In fact, they seem to kill each other pretty regularly."

"Yeah," Seth conceded, "but they have everything else. Powers. Good looks. Mojo."

"Mojo?" Molly giggled.

"Yeah. You're a luck god, you get any girl you want."

"You could probably get any girl you want anyway," she flirted.

He rolled his eyes, but leaned closer to her. "Right. Because I'm rich."

"Not just that. You also jump motorcycles, which is pretty dope. And you have weird hair. Girls love weird hair. Or so I hear."

He drifted nearer to her now, only inches away. It gave her a weightless, tingly feeling in her tummy. She thought of

Lorcan fleetingly, but her feels for him felt distant now. Like a pinecone in a stream, flowing away.

"Do you think they'll do it? Make you one of them?" he asked. He was looking at her lips now.

"I'm trying to get them to," she whispered. "I think I'm close."

"If you become a Luck God, will you promise to make me one, too?"

"Sure," she breathed.

His gaze drifted from her eyes down to her lips again. "Cool. It's a deal. You want to make out?"

Instead of answering, she grabbed his shirt front and pulled him down until their breathless mouths met.

# 34

# AGGIE

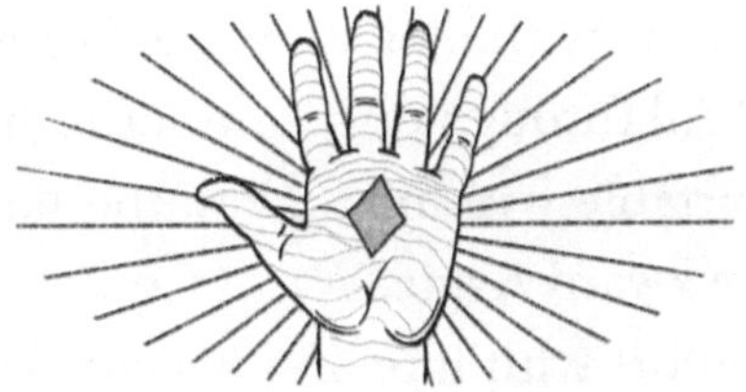

A frigid wind ripped across the water and I tried to fold into myself for warmth. The full moon didn't help; its cold white light made Lake St. Clair's waves look tipped with frost, and the black sky made me think of the brutal coldness of outer space.

Jack killed the engine and the speedboat Lura had loaned us whooshed to a near-halt, waves slapping the hull. The rift loomed a good hundred yards off the starboard side, a wall of greenish illumination which wavered and undulated like the Northern Lights.

"Did you know outer space is negative two-hundred-and seventy degrees Celsius?" I asked.

Jack turned his attention from the rift to glance at me. "What?"

I repeated my fun fact and he frowned.

"Sounds preferable to a Michigan winter night," he grumbled, stuffing his hands in his pockets and scanning the horizon.

"Well, it's the equivalent of negative four hundred and fifty-five degrees Fahrenheit, so, you know—even colder than the D." I knew I was rambling, but couldn't quite stop myself. "By w-w-which I mean Detroit. Have you ever heard that song? *It's s-s-so cold in the D...*" I sang—off key.

"Aggie," Jack interrupted. "We're on a mission. Sound travels over water, remember?"

What was wrong with me? Why was I so nervous around Jack right now? All through our summer romance I'd gotten to feel so comfortable with him. Now, the nerves were back —and so was Awkward Aggie. Was it Cupid's Arrow wearing off? Was my comfort with him and his comfort with me just an illusion all along?

And was he party to the ace's plan to trick me into loving him? Or was he duped, just like I was? I'd already mostly forgiven Deuce for keeping the truth about the Arrow from me. He was a hard person to stay mad at. But Jack... whether he knew or not mattered. Only right now, I was just too scared to ask him. And anyway, it didn't seem like the time, judging from his sour mood.

"Did I mention this is probably a trap?" he muttered now, crossing his arms.

"Only about twenty times," I whispered through chattering teeth.

He eyed me for a long moment, until he apparently couldn't stand to watch me shiver any longer.

"Come here," he said, opening his arms. I started to say no. *No thank you, I'm fine.* But my lips felt almost too numb to form the words. I'd brought a casual winter jacket, not the parka I needed to block this wind. And who knew how long we'd have to wait out here? It would be wise to stay warm, I told myself.

So I approached and leaned against Jack's chest, let him wrap his arms around me. The resulting temperature still felt just a few degrees higher than the background radiation of deep space. But it was better than nothing.

For a long time he held me and we remained there in silence, still except for our breathing and the rocking of the boat on the waves. With my ear pressed to his chest, I listened to Jack's heartbeat as we both took in the rift. I'd never been so close to it before, and it rose before us, a quivering, shifting, multi-colored aurora borealis. The idea that we could go through it and wind up in another world filled me with wonder.

"You've never wanted to go through the rift and see what's on the other side?" I asked him.

"I've thought about it," Jack said. "I'm sure every luck god has. But even without considering the sylph army that supposedly guards the gate, I've heard the world on the other side it's a brutally dangerous place, especially for Luck Gods."

"Why?"

Jack shrugged, his body shifting against me. "Apparently they still haven't forgiven us for the brutal wars that happened around the time Uthule was killed. Peri have long memories."

I digested that information.

"They haven't forgiven us... does that mean they want us

dead?" I asked, wondering if our list of suspects in Michael's death should be even longer.

"Sure. Who doesn't love a nice, dead god?" Silence came on the heels of his sour joke. The minutes stretched long. Clouds swept in, dousing the moon and deepening the darkness around us. The rocking of the boat lulled me, and as I released myself, leaning on Jack, I nearly fell asleep.

I awoke with a jerk, disoriented, and tried to take a step. But the shifting boat deck moved and I lost my footing. Jack caught me and eased my fall, and I found myself lying over a boat seat, Jack on top of me. My heart pounded, the cold in my body replaced with a rushing, yearning heat. Impulsively, I put a hand on the back of Jack's neck and pulled him down to me, our lips meeting as another wave surged beneath the boat, pressing us even closer. A sound escaped from somewhere inside my chest, a moan of pent-up longing. I pulled Jack even closer still, felt his body against me, felt that he wanted me as much as I wanted him.

Thunder rumbled in the night, matching the longing that growled inside my core. I pulled Jack closer still. Kissed him harder.

Then, he was gone. Swiping a hand through is hair and pacing deck. Cold returned in his place, knife-sharp and painful. And anger came with it.

I stood, wiping my lips with the back of my hand.

"You know, I understand a lot of things," I said, fighting back tears. "Nuclear fusion. Quantum physics. Computer engineering. But I don't understand you, Jack Valentine."

He rolled his head in frustration.

"It's simple. You should stay away from me," he growled, leaning on the edge of the boat as if he might puke.

"Ooh, I'm Jack," I mocked. "I'm so dangerous. So mysterious. No one could possibly get me."

"Stop," Jack chided wearily.

"No!" I shouted. "You stop. You claim to care about me, but all you do is push me away. You claim to care about the Valentines, then you betray us by becoming a Spade. I know you're good, Jack. Despite everything you do to show me otherwise. So just explain it to me. Why? Make me understand."

Jack turned to face me, the light of the rift playing over his face, making it seem to shift like a kaleidoscope. I felt a tug of energy and saw both Jack's hands glowing, charm and hex at once. But whether he was trying to influence me or just flaring it out of stress, I couldn't tell. But red light poured from my hands as well—again, without me even trying.

How lucky would I have to be to get Jack Valentine to tell me the truth?

I decided to find out and flared my charm harder. Jack's eyes flicked to my hands, then back to me. Whatever my charm was doing, he felt it.

For a long moment he stood watching me in the changing light. Then a breath hissed between his teeth. "Fine. You want to understand me? I told you about my parents. How they died in a meth lab explosion when I was a teenager. How I was the only one to survive."

I nodded.

"What I didn't tell you," he went on, "Is that they weren't just making those drugs for themselves. They were working for the Spades. I found out later they were sycos. And it wasn't just them and me, either. I... had a little sister."

My mouth fell open and I covered it with a hand. "No..."

"Her name was Gracie," Jack said through clenched

teeth. "We were a normal family, before my parents met those Spades. My dad worked at a shoe store. My mom was a waitress. We were poor, but happy. And Gracie... I loved her so much. She followed me everywhere. I taught her to climb trees. She... she loved horses. That's why my parents started working for the Spades at first. To afford her riding lessons."

Jack rubbed a trembling hand over his brow. "If we'd just had normal luck without meddling, she'd be alive. They'd all be alive. That's why the suits have to end, Aggie. No matter what good things the red suits do, it'll never outweigh the bad. It'll never..." his voice faltered.

"It'll never bring Gracie back," I finished in a whisper.

I opened my mouth, tried to find the breath to speak to say more. But before I could, the buzz of a boat engine cut through the stillness, coming from the rift.

Jack's head snapped in that direction, hand going to the grip of his gun.

"They're coming," he said.

❧♡♤◇♧☙

The craft that emerged from the gauzy glow of the rift looked like a rusty old ferry boat, but it moved with eerie speed, cutting through the choppy water like a diamond across glass. By the time Jack had our boat's engine fired up, they'd already zipped past our starboard side. Jack slammed down the throttle and cranked the wheel, and soon we were bounding along in our quarry's wake.

We were about a hundred yards back and I could make out dark figures moving around on the deck—lots of them— but I couldn't tell if they were human, sylph, or something else entirely. We blazed along like that for a few minutes, staying a constant distant from one another like a pair of bonded particles. Then, despite our boat's speed, they began pulling ahead.

"We have to go faster!" I shouted.

Jack bared his teeth and pressed down on the throttle again, but there was nowhere for it to go. We were at full speed, and they were still becoming more distant.

"They're getting away!" I shouted.

"I can see that," Jack snarled. "Take the wheel."

I did—reluctantly. "I've never driven a boat before," I protested as I perched on the edge of the captain's chair.

"Just keep yourself pointed at the other boat—and don't slow down."

"What are you going to do?" I demanded, but Jack didn't answer as he stumbled to the boat's bow.

*All this for a chance to interrogate a goblin,* I thought, wondering if it would be worth it. But the time to back out had long since passed. So I held the wheel straight and watched as Jack braced one foot on the bench seat at the boat's bow and raised both his hands into the cutting wind.

I knew what he was charming—I was doing it, too. Envisioning the other boat's engine going out, envisioning the wind gusting to slow them down. Even envisioning them hitting a rock, though I doubted there were any rocks out here in the middle of the lake. My efforts, even with queen power behind them, seemed to do nothing. Jack's didn't seem to be working either. That is, until I noticed the sky.

Ahead, banks of dark cloud scudded toward us at unnatural speed. Even through the darkness of night I saw them, writhing, swirling, tearing and recombining, billowing up before us like a cobra poised to strike. Greenish lightning crackled and shivered among the storm heads, illuminating their dark flanks like camera flashes.

*This is bad,* I thought. My hands trembled against the steering wheel, from fear as well as cold. My mind started counting the waves slamming the hull as we pounded over them.

*One, two, three...*

Then, *bad* became *worse*. Off to our right, I caught sight of a trio of long speedboats blazing toward us from shore. What had Jack said about this being a trap?

"Jack!" I shouted, pointing at the oncoming boats. But he just kept his hands raised to the sky. They glowed now brighter than I'd ever seen them, the red and the dark purplish light from his warring pips mingling into a new and strange color so vibrant it seemed to make my eyes vibrate in my head.

In all my training, all my reading, I'd never heard of a luck god being able to control the weather. A small gust of wind, sure, but a real, true storm? Too many variables stood in the way; from wind currents to water and air temperatures to atmospheric pressure—the complexity of the problem was too much. Yet here Jack stood, summoning a tempest.

Thunder heads built and whorled, a deeper shade of angry black against the night sky. The first gust pushed me back in my chair. Then I saw it coming, a wall of water and wind. It slammed the strange ferry boat in front of us first, the wave dashing it sideways, the wind making it list so far it nearly flipped.

But whoever steered it was smart. Instead of continuing into the teeth of the storm they turned around—now barreling toward us. And the other pursuers were still coming, too. Four deadly vectors and us, the point of inter-section.

"Hang on," Jack said, coming back to the helm and wrenching the steering wheel to the right. We came about, dashing over waves, until we were flying straight toward the center speed boat. Closer. Closer they came.

"Jack..." I warned.

"They'll turn," he said.

Only they weren't turning. They continued speeding toward us, unwavering in their trajectory.

"They'll turn," he said again, his voice barely audible over the boat engine and the rushing water.

The storm hit before the others boats did, a stronger blast of wind and a stinging spatter of cold rain.

I huddled lower behind the boat's windshield, flaring charm so hard my hands burned, counting the waves we pounded over. *Eight, nine, ten...*

At the last second, Jack must have realized the other boats weren't turning, because he cranked the wheel again to the starboard. Too late. Two of the boats pursuing us met, their bows colliding in an explosion of fiberglass. We were lucky they didn't slam into us and sink our boat. But they did clip our back end with a jarring force that made me made me bang my face into the windshield's aluminum frame. I felt spreading heat and touched my forehead. My fingers came away bloody.

The two boats that had collided were now melded together into a roughly heart-shaped wreckage—and sinking fast. Dark figures leapt from it like fleas from a drowning rat. The third boat had managed to avoid ruin and buzzed past us, circling for another pass.

"Let's go!" I shouted to Jack. When he pushed the throttle

forward, the engine grumbled and gurgled, but we didn't move. Jack's eyes met mine. I knew what the look in them meant, a feral, brutal expression that set my heart racing. *Get ready to fight.* I drew my weapons. But Jack surged across the rocking deck, catching me in his arms.

"You're hurt," he called over the sounds of storm and surf, leaning close to my forehead.

"It's just a bump," I said, though I did feel a bit dizzy as I shook my head.

Jack's fingers pushed my hair back as he examined the gash on my head. Satisfied, he turned away, drawing his weapons.

"Stay close to me," he said—just as the third cigarette boat stuck us broadside.

The *boom* of the impact seemed to shudder the world, a sound straight from the plains of Alamogordo. I tumbled to the deck and clung desperately onto a boat seat to avoid being pitched into the water. When I opened my eyes, I found black water roiling just inches from my feet.

The impact had sheared our boat in half. I was on the stern. Perhaps twenty yards away, Jack stood unsteadily on what remained of our bow. Rift light shimmered over us, casting an eerie, tremulous glow on the scene. All around bobbed the flotsam of our attackers' broken vessels. And among them, the darks shapes of swimmers. Dozens of them. Some swimming toward Jack, others toward me.

My trembling hand reached down, first touching my gun holster then my sword's scabbard. Both were empty. I reached for the trusty knife at my belt. It was gone too. Very unlucky.

"Ugh. Really?" I bellowed into the storm, feeling for a

moment like a teenage Ahab. But there was no time for literary allusions.

The first attacker clambered onto the boat. With the rain and spray in my eyes, I couldn't tell if he was human or peri. All I could tell was he was big, as his fist flew at my face.

I flared charm and the boat deck shifted, making him stumble as I blocked his punch and countered with a kick to the inside of his knee. His leg buckled and he tumbled back into the dark water.

But two more were already climbing onto the deck, both holding long, wickedly-curved knives. My queen charm flared, spilling blood-red light over the pair. The first one slipped on the slick decking, slowing him slightly. The second one reached me first and stabbed at me, but I managed to step aside. The tip of his knife stuck into the side of the boat behind me. I kicked upward at the same time, striking him in the elbow. It gave a satisfying *crack*, and a stomp-kick to the gut sent him tumbling backward, taking out his companion on the way. They both hit the water in an explosion of foam, but the shout of triumph died on my lips. Four more were already grasping the boat's broken edge, trying to clamber up. My half of the boat was riding lower in the water, now. Sinking. My whole body shook with cold. And across the water— fifty yards away, now, I saw at least six bad guys swarming over Jack's half of the boat. We wouldn't last long like this.

Steeling myself, I flared my charm harder, making it more difficult for my enemies to climb aboard. At the same time, the wind picked up again, howling and gusting so fiercely I nearly stumbled down the slanted deck and into the water.

Lightning flashed in the sky, and the sight it revealed

made the breath catch in my throat. At least twenty attackers swarmed around my boat, ready to claw their way up to me. Even more surrounded Jack, but instead of fighting he stood on the bow, both hands raised skyward, the strange light of those opposing pips burning through the night like beacons.

Then, lightning struck again, a jagged bolt, crackling down from the heavens and striking the water directly between our two boats. The boom of its coming rattled my chest and made drop to my knees. Its power illuminated the water for a second, making it pulse with deadly electricity. In that moment of illumination, all those figures in the water, stark, flailing silhouettes.

Then, it was over. The thunder boomed so loud it felt like the world was cracking in two. Steam rose off the waves. I held my breath, waiting for what would come next—a renewed attack.

The wind continued. The rain battered and the waves swelled. But no more attackers clambered on to my deck. I counted the seconds, hitting twenty-three five times before willing myself to lean over the edge of the boat and shine my red pip light down on the water. I'd already guessed what I'd find, but seeing it sent a sickening spasm through my stomach.

Our attackers were still in the water, but they were no longer coming for us. They floated, their steaming bodies dark as the night above, still as driftwood.

Jack's bad luck power had summoned the storm, brought the lightning—and killed them all.

Bile rose in my throat but I gulped it back, pulling my eyes from the bobbing dead bodies to Jack. His half of our boat had drifted and was now a football field distant. He still had his hands raised to the storm, and I felt the wind shift and gust. A wave swelled with it, and it seemed to lift both our broken crafts, pushing them toward the shore.

The third large speed boat was still out there but it circled us from a distance, its driver no doubt wary after what had happened to the other two boats. The mad ferry that had come from the rift had already made it to shore and looked from here to have tied up to one of the docks.

Like a director zooming in with a movie camera, I watched dilapidated wharves rise before me. A concrete sea wall's scars and cracks betrayed veins of rebar bleeding rust-colored streaks. Several dozen docks jutted into the water, each tilted and warped as a fun-house image. The rift ferry was tied to one of them, but it seemed deserted. I felt the prickle of bad luck and I wondered if this was the place Jack and his friends had been ambushed by Carlotta Blackover before they met me—and if we were about to be ambushed again.

Regardless, when my broken boat thumped into the pylon I clambered onto the dock, grateful to be off the storm-wracked water. I lay splayed on the rotting boards for a moment and allowed myself a few breaths to steady my nerves. I counted the raindrops striking my face, and when I hit twenty-three, I rose. The gray boards of the dock groaned and shifted with my weight as I grabbed a pylon to steady myself and took stock of the situation.

Jack was about to make landfall, too, but he was even further away now, at least two hundred yards distant. And from the warehouses between us, more creeping figures were emerging, set in relief by another flash of lightning.

Did I even want to get back to Jack? After what he'd done out on the water, did I ever want to be near him again? All that hex power... All that killing... it repulsed me. I didn't know if I'd ever be able to look at him the same after what just happened.

Regardless, I couldn't stay here. Some of those figures from the warehouses were creeping closer. And out on the water, the third pursuit boat buzzed toward shore with alarming speed.

I ran. Up the dock, onto a gravel lot that ran between the docks and the warehouses, then between two warehouses. *Bam.* A door burst open ahead of me and a hooded figure stepped out, grabbing my wrist. I wrenched my arm and twisted, trying to get free, but the grip was fierce. Then a flash of lightning illuminated the features of my attacker, revealing a familiar face, one I'd seen hundreds of times on hundreds of different people, though the dark curly hair was flattened by rain. One of Bartholomew Barth's clones.

I yelled, flared charm, and send a wild kick that—luckily—caught my attacker solidly between the legs. I twisted my arm again and yanked, and this time the slick rain allowed me to free myself. I sprinted back toward the water, then cut down an alleyway between warehouses. All around me, more attackers were emerging from the shadows. Behind me. In front of me. Everywhere. *It was a trap. Jack was right. God, how could I have been so stupid?* I flew blindly down alleys, scrambled around corners, cut down narrow passages, a doomed rat in a maze.

I heard Jack calling my name and responded reflexively.

"Aggie!"

"Jack!"

"Aggie!"

I followed the sound of his voice and burst free of the warren of alleys onto a gravel roadway that led along the edge of the marina—and there he was, coming toward me.

"Aggie!" he shouted once more, in relief this time.

But I was no longer running toward him.

"Come on," he said, the jerk of his head indicating that I should follow him.

But I remained rooted in place. "No."

He looked puzzled. "Come on. Hurry."

"No," I said again. "What you did out there on the water..." I shook my head.

He gave a furtive glance down one of the alleyways. Footsteps were coming toward us. When he turned back to me, his bafflement had become anger.

"On the water. You mean saving us?"

"I mean killing all those people," I said.

"Barth's clones?" Jack scoffed. "They were coming for us. They still are."

Just then one of the assassins burst from the warehouse to Jack's left, swinging a cudgel. Deftly, Jack grabbed his wrist and hurled him into the water. Seeing the attacker's slashing, flailing form, the image of those smoldering bodies flashed through my mind once more. *Jack killed them. Slaughtered them all.*

I'd been warned he was ruthless. That he was dangerous. Over and over, I'd been warned, but I'd ignored the warnings.

But if he could kill so many in an instant without remorse, what had made me think he wouldn't hurt anyone else who stood in his way? Even me?

The thought gave me a feeling in my stomach like I was falling. Not falling in love; falling off a building. He was as beautiful as ever, there watching me through the storm. But for the first time, looking at him made me feel not longing, but fear.

Impulsively, I stumbled backward, away from him.

"Aggie!" he called, hurrying to close the distance between us, but I wheeled and darted down the passage between two buildings.

I ran blindly, tears blurring my vision, breath hitching and heaving in my chest.

Finally, I rounded a corner and found at least two dozen enemies waiting. They shouted and surged forward at the sight of me and I spun and charged down a different alleyway, only to find even more attackers. I froze, my heart pounding against my ribs, and raised my fists to fight. Closer, closer they came. I steeled myself to weather the onrushing wave of bodies, braced for pain.

Then, I felt myself jerked roughly to the side, into an alcove.

I tried to shout, but a hand clapped over my mouth. An arm encircled me, holding me still. But when I looked down to see the arm and try to pry it off me, I saw nothing. No arm. No *me*. Just a shimmer of peri magic.

Every instinct told me to fight, to get free. Especially when I heard Jack's voice calling me over the wind and the rain, distant now and hoarse with desperation.

What if he was hurt? What if he needed me?

"Aggie! Aggie!"

But I forced myself to flare charm and stay still as, just a few feet away, my pursuers growled and jostled, looking left then right in agitation. They weren't speaking English, I realized. Their low words were in some unknown, savage sounding language. And this crew wasn't clad in the puffy parkas of the clones, either. They wore thick, dark robes over glinting armor, with hoods hiding their faces. Were these the intruders from the rift ferry? I didn't know. But whoever they were there were a lot of them, and they were heavily armed.

I forced myself to stay still until they skulked off, the blades of their strange weapons glinting in the lightning.

I forced myself to stay still as the rain slowed and my abductor's grip on me loosened.

I forced myself to stay still—until the moment I heard Jack scream.

**35**

---

## JACK

"Aggie!"

It was like a nightmare. Running through a maze of dark alleys. Pursued by mysterious attackers. Searching for Aggie, calling for her, unable to find her. It began to take on the endless feeling a dream, too. Each corner Jack slid around revealed only another narrow, weedy, gravel path between the slanted walls of falling-in warehouses. No matter how fast he ran, footsteps haunted him. Behind. Ahead. Everywhere.

"Aggie!"

He flared both charm and hex until his hands stung and trembled, but to no avail. Here in this bad luck place his charm barely functioned. His hex worked well enough to keep him out of range of blades, clubs and grasping hands, but not well enough to find—

"Aggie!"

Where was she? Was she really running from him?

Then, suddenly, Jack burst into the open—into a large, overgrown gravel parking lot. Beyond it, a dirt track led through some trees to where a road awaited. The exit to this sprawling, crumbling industrial complex. He could sprint across the lot now, outpace his attackers, and escape. Be free.

But Aggie might still be here. He couldn't leave until he knew she was safe. So, he turned back, swiped his wet hair out of his face, and plunged back into the nightmare.

He'd only gone a short distance before a mob appeared out of the darkness ahead, their feet pounding toward him. He veered right, between a pair of warehouses so run-down their walls nearly slumped against one another, like the shoulders of a pair of drunken friends. The gap between them narrowed and narrowed until Jack had to crouch to keep going. Still, the sounds of his pursuers' footfalls came, thumping closer. Behind. Ahead. He was trapped. Then a gap opened up in the wall to his left. Jack hesitated only a second before plunging through it, into the darkness that waited beyond.

His first instinct was to whip out his phone and turn on the flashlight, but that would give away his position. And the phone was probably destroyed from the water anyway. So he stumbled ahead into the darkness, hands outstretched in front of him like a B-movie sleepwalker. Rain beat upon the roof of the warehouse, pouring in through the broken places to pitter on the concrete floor.

Jack heard a sound in the dark and froze. Another sound followed. The scuff of a foot. A sigh of breath. A sniff. A low laugh. Slowly, Jack turned a circle, staring into the blackness. And he saw something. Faintly glowing yellow spots, like an ominous constellation of stars. In pairs.

Eyes. Yellow eyes.

With a hiss of breath Jack brought up his hands, charming, hexing, ready to block, punch, fight, though he could already tell the odds were madness.

Then with the heavy clunk of a breaker, overhead lights turned on. Jack winced, half blinded, but when his vision returned, he saw who surrounded him. *What* surrounded him.

Gaunt, human-like faces. Lavender-tinted skin. Sharp teeth. They were peri, all right. Hundreds of them. But they weren't just any peri. These were the most savage, most reviled ones of all. The worst of the worst.

They'd asked Lura to bring them Varsmith. She, in turn, had sent them to intercept a shipment. Here, Jack guessed, was the cargo of that otherworldly ferryboat, its forbidden passengers—an army.

They'd asked Lura for a single goblin.

They'd gotten a thousand.

❦

For an instant, everything froze, as if all the world balanced on the tip of a blade. Jack braced himself for blood and pain. Then, the doors at the far end of the warehouse banged open, revealing several dozen armed figures in hooded coats. The foremost of these whipped back his hood, and Jack saw the face of those who had been chasing him on the boats. He'd seen that face a thousand times—and that puffy hair, too. It was Barth's clone army.

The young man pointed the short sword he wielded at Jack.

"I claim the prisoner in the name of Bartholomew Barth," he shouted. "Get him!"

The clone strode toward Jack, shoving through the goblins, and his copies followed.

Jack glanced over his shoulder, ready to flee, but hundreds of goblins stood between him and any exit, and they showed no sign of letting him through.

He waited with growing alarm as the clones surged toward him. The goblins stood aside, letting the clones pass until the foremost one was only a few paces away. Jack bit his lip and raised his fists, cursing the ill luck that caused his weapons to be lost in the lake. Still, he'd be damned if he let himself get dragged back to Barth's lair. He'd rather die here than in some menagerie cage.

But just as the nearest clone was about to grab him, a goblin stepped forward and thrust a wavy-bladed dagger into the charging man's gut. The clone took one more step then fell to his knees, wide-eyed. As one, the goblins set upon the other clones. They gave no word of command, no battle cry. They just hacked and stabbed, punched and bit, in eerie silence. In less than a minute, the entire host of clones lay in a blood-soaked heap on the warehouse floor. The sight sickened Jack. He'd seen a lot of bloodshed in his life, but never butchery like this.

As one, the goblins turned their yellowish, human-like eyes directly on him.

Icy terror stole over Jack, a return of that prickly, out-of-body, nightmare feeling. His mind, so accustomed to searching for escape, could see absolutely none. *They'll kill me now. There's nothing I can do,* he thought. And so he stood in numb with dread, waiting for the goblins to do what goblins do. Stab. Rend. Tear. End.

The first goblin stepped forward, and Jack didn't even bother with charm or hex. He let his hands hang loose at his sides, and he forced himself to meet the eye of his attacker. But the goblin didn't strike. Instead, he raised both his hands as if in blessing. Jack hesitated, puzzled, followed suit, raising both his hands. The charm and hex responded instinctually, flooding the room with their unholy glow.

Still, Jack waited for the surge of attack, the death blow.

Instead, a hiss of awe went through the goblin throng. One by one, they fell to their knees, kneeling before him.

# 36

## AGGIE

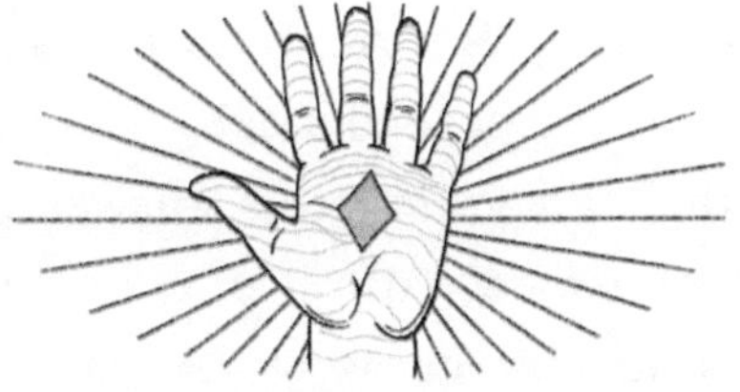

We waited breathlessly still until my pursuers were gone. Then, my cloaked protector took my hand and towed me across the alleyway, through a shifted parallelogram of a dilapidated doorway, and down a set of rickety steel steps. Alarm bells rang in my mind, naturally, but outside I could still hear shouts and footfalls of my pursuers echoing in the night. Being out of sight seemed like a good thing. And whoever this was hadn't harmed me or given me up to Barth's thugs—so far.

At the bottom of the stairs, we found ourselves in a small, wood-paneled room. An electric lantern sat on a table and my rescuer turned it on then spun to face me. I'd already guessed who it would be.

"Carlotta Blackover," I said.

"Again, not Blackover anymore," she said, pulling her hood down.

"No," I said. "You're Shastaryan."

A faint smile crossed her lips. "You've been doing your homework. They said you were smart. And have you been thinking about the questions I asked?"

In fact, I had been thinking about her questions. I just wasn't sure I had answers she wanted. But it seemed I would have to come up with some, because her hand went to the hilt of the short sword at her belt as she asked:

"What is the source of luck?"

Last time I'd tried to offer a physics-based explanation. But I had a simpler answer now. "Nature," I said.

"And what is the purpose of luck?"

I wasn't sure if I'd gotten this answer right or wrong before. But if luck was a natural phenomenon, then there could be only one answer as to its purpose. "It has no purpose unless someone directs it," I said.

Carlotta's eyes narrowed. "And who should control luck?"

I opened my mouth to answer, then stopped myself. Last time I'd said *the luck gods* should control luck. But I knew now the Shastaryan opposed the luck gods. And if luck was a force of nature, then...

"No one," I said, the words feeling like a revelation. "No one should control luck."

Carlotta hesitated for an instant, then gave a single nod, her hand releasing its grip on her sword.

I realized I'd been holding my breath and exhaled.

"Good," Carlotta said. "We have a saying. Knowledge is the beginning of wisdom. Wisdom is the beginning of righteousness. And righteousness is the beginning of life. You have the knowledge now. Are you ready to take the next step?"

"Next step?" I parroted, confused.

"Give up your Valentine mark and your queen power."

Automatically, I clutched my hands to my chest, as if the pips there were things she could snatch away.

"There is a place on the other side of the rift," Carlotta said, "Where the curse of Uthule can be washed away. I can take you there. You can become one of us."

"I..." I tried to respond, but the words wouldn't come. Thoughts were pinging through my mind like excited particles in an enclosed space, too fast and too erratic to capture. If there was a way to wash the marks away, that meant I might be able to take away Mom's Spade marks. I might be able to free her. We might be able to return to our normal lives. It was exactly the hope I'd been dreaming of. But...

"Are you ready?" she pressed.

Of course, I couldn't give up my queen power. Not now. I'd need it to face Mom. To capture her, if need be, and bring her to this place Carlotta spoke of. If it really existed, that is. It was always possible Carlotta was just trying to tell me what I wanted to hear in order to make me let my guard down and follow her.

Seeming to sense my hesitation, she stepped forward and put a gentle hand on my shoulder. I could still feel the luck power within her, though not as strongly as I could feel it in the other luck gods.

"Aggie," she whispered. "I was a queen too, remember. I know what I'm asking of you. I know how hard it is to set that kind of power aside. But I also know the burden power can be. The responsibility. I can see it when I look at you. The stress. The pressure. It's constant. It's crushing. Isn't it?"

Tears rose and I squeezed my eyes shut.

"Yes," I whispered. "The pressure is a lot. But..."

Carlotta's hand drifted back to her sword hilt. "But?" she prompted.

"But I need you to answer my question now," I said. "Truthfully. Did you or your people kill Michael? Or our two, Galen?"

Carlotta stiffened, making herself taller—and she'd already been looking down on me.

"All the scions of Uthule must either relinquish their power or die," she said.

That wasn't an admission, exactly. But it certainly wasn't a denial.

"That doesn't answer my question," I pressed. "Did you—"

I heard it then—footsteps in the warehouse above.

"It doesn't matter who held the blade," Carlotta whispered. "Michael and all the other luck gods make their choice and reap the consequences."

"It matters to me," I shouted. "I didn't love Michael. I didn't even like him. But he was my husband. He was a fellow Valentine. And he was in the same bed as me, for Cripe's sake. And Galen—Galen was just a kid. He'd barely become a luck god. And he was *good*."

"Everyone gets a chance to relinquish their place as hoarders of fortune. There is a choice, Aggie. Michael and Galen could have joined us and received our protection. You could do the same. And as a token of my goodwill, I have a gift."

She took something out of a pocket and I tensed to defend myself, but what she offered me was only a folded up piece of paper.

"What is this?" I asked, unfolding it. On the paper was a hand-written address.

*Chemiceutical Ventures, 2115 N. Trace Rd., Dearborn.*

"You've been looking for your mother, haven't you? This is where she's been hiding out."

My hand holding the address trembled. Not just from fear and cold, but from excitement. It had been so long since I'd seen Mom. As this point I didn't care how dangerous it was, I wanted to find her. To hug her. To capture her and keep her and find some way to drive the darkness out of her. When I saw her this time, I'd never let her out of my sight again, I vowed it.

But even now that I knew where she was, that was only half the battle. The Spades wouldn't let her go without a fight. I'd need the Valentines to get her back.

"We can help her," Carlotta said. "We can help you both escape your suits. You can leave this life behind—and join us."

The footsteps above were louder. Closer. I should be quiet, I knew. But I couldn't help myself.

"Why would we join a pack of murderers?"

"You're already the leader of a pack of murderers," Carlotta pointed out.

"Tell me the truth!" I shouted. "Did you kill Michael?"

The footsteps above stopped. Whoever it was, they were listening.

"The truth," Carlotta said fiercely, "is being a luck god is deadly. The same thing that happened to him will happen to you if you don't give up the mark of Hearts."

I opened my hands, charming in self-defense. "First you save me, then you threaten me. I think I've heard enough."

"I'm not threatening you, Aggie. I want to help you. But if you don't make the right choice, I can't."

"Well, I can't give up my queen power. Not until my mom gives up hers," I said.

"I'm sorry to hear that."

Carlotta's hand went to the hilt of her sword, her eyes locking on mine. I flared my charm. And behind me, I heard the clangor of footfalls on the metal steps.

Our enemies were coming.

My pursuers swept in, a maelstrom of figures clad in black parkas. Carlotta spun and struck one in the head, knocking his hood back, and I saw a face I'd seen far too many times. Barth's clones. The sylph had bred his army of identical young men for their genetic predilection for good luck. My luck should far exceed theirs, I reminded myself, but numbers were not in our favor.

More and more of the sylph's thugs poured down the steps and I fought the urge to count them. There had to be two sets of twenty-three at least, with more coming. Carlotta didn't hesitate. She attacked, quickly finding a rhythm among the chaos, her sword blade swishing and snicking, dropping enemies at every turn. She was not as graceful as Aubra had been in battle, nor as brutal as Gallo Blackover, nor as powerful as Jack. But she was eerily fast, ruthless, and deadly in her efficiency, and I watched her dismantle five enemies before I shook myself out of my daze and stepped forward to help.

I wasn't sure I could do much. My body still shivered beneath my wet clothes. My muscles were tight, my mind scattered. But as the first clone stepped up to me, a double-bladed dagger in his fist, I let my charm go, and it felt like my hands ignited. As the clone lunged, I stepped right, slapping his hand and causing him to drop his blade. I followed through with an elbow that caught him in the temple, and he stumbled forward and fell. I ducked under a sword swing from the next attacker, and as he followed through I stepped behind him and stomp-kicked him in the back of the knee.

I flared charm harder, savoring the delicious power flowing through my hands.

Two clones came at me at once, but they made opposing swings at the same time and their weapons clacked together —lucky for me—as I dodged out of range.

Carlotta had made her way to the foot of the stairs by then, and side-by-side we fought our way up, one enemy at a time. I knew from my training that this bottleneck would work to our advantage, nullifying our enemy's numbers because only one or two of them could attack us at once. But they had the high ground and were blocking our way. To get by, we had to either fling them past us down the stairs or knock them down and clamber over them. And I was unarmed, at least until I snatched a tactical tomahawk out of a clone's hand, then threw him down the stairs to bowl over the clones who were charging up to attack us from behind.

Somehow, step by bloody step, we fought our way up. At the top, dozens more clones crowded in on us. The blade of my 'hawk made wide arc, nipping fingers from grasping hands. I felt Carlotta grabbing the back of my coat, trying to pull me along with her, but I shrugged roughly out of her grasp and slipped between two clones, then two more, putting distance between myself and Carlotta.

She tried to get back to me, but she was bigger and taller than I was, and the gaps I'd slipped through closed behind me.

"Aggie!" she called. It seemed an echo of Jack's voice

earlier. A voice I didn't hear now. Was Jack okay? Where was he?

I spied an exit and fought my way toward it, listening for Jack's voice, counting the seconds I didn't hear it. Guilt hit me like a gut punch. What if Jack he was dead? Or captured? I shouldn't have run from him, shouldn't have left him to face so many enemies alone...

At last, I managed to battle my way out the door, into the frigid night air. Here, clones were few and I had a second to take a breath, ready to call Jack's name, just as he'd called mine.

But an image blinked into my mind. The storm. That flash. Lightning on the water. Smoking, waterlogged bodies. The dozens Jack had killed in a single instant. And I stopped myself from shouting his name.

In silence, I buried the tomahawk in the shoulder of one last clone, slipped past him, and ran.

---

# 37

# JACK

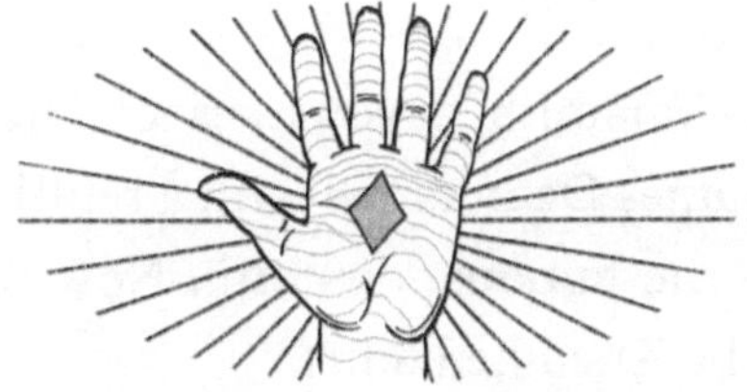

Jack stared out at a sea of bowed heads, lean faces, eerie, purplish eyes. Hundreds of goblins, kneeling for him. *This is the strangest dream,* he thought. Only he knew full well it wasn't a dream. For better or worse, this was real.

One of the goblins rose and stepped forward. He was tall—a few inches taller than Jack, and he wore a sleeveless leather vest despite the chill. The garment exposed oddly long, muscular arms. The nails on his fingers were longer than a male's typically were and looked sharp, and Jack remembered learning that goblins had retractable claws, like a cat's. The goblin's teeth were a bit jagged, too, giving his smile a sinister aspect Jack found disturbing.

Without warning, the goblin whipped a sword from his sheath and swung it at Jack's throat. Jack was unarmed, but did the only thing he could, flaring charm and hex at once and flailing out desperately with one hand, slapping the flat of the blade. The weapon broke, pieces of glinting metal flying across the room. In a fluid motion, Jack countered, stepping forward and clotheslining the powerful goblin, taking him off his feet and causing him to land on his back with bone-rattling force.

Polite applause rose from the goblins, and Jack looked down to find the goblin who'd attacked him smiling again.

With predatory grace, the goblin kicked his legs back over his head and rolled smoothly to his feet, then swept into a low bow.

"My name is Varsmith, at your service," he said in a voice that wedded a James Dean drawl with a reptilian hiss.

So this was the famous Varsmith. Now that he'd found him, Jack sort of wished he hadn't.

"Forgive me, Lord," Varsmith said. "But we had to ensure you were the indeed the foretold one."

"The foretold one?"

The goblin's grin widened, his eyes lighting up with creepy fervency. "Uthule," he breathed.

"Uthule," the others repeated, the whispered word sizzling through the crowd, causing them all to kneel and bow their heads again.

"And you're here to stop me?" Jack asked. "To capture me? To kill me?"

Varsmith shook his head. "Oh no, my Lord. The opposite. We have come to serve you."

Varsmith approached Jack, but this time it wasn't an attack. His movement was slow and deferential. Jack noticed he was clad differently than the rest, in contemporary human clothes rather than the vaguely medieval garb and ragged pieced-together armor the others wore—clothing, no doubt, from the other side of the rift. Varsmith was taller than Jack, muscular and humanlike—but his proportions were off. His arms a smidge too long for a human's, his cheekbones a little too prominent. As he drew near, Jack saw him reached into a pouch at his belt and draw something out. Jack tensed, but it wasn't a weapon the goblin pulled free. It was some sort of jewelry. Clinking metal disks strung on a fine chain. The goblin stopped a few paces away from Jack, holding the chain out like an offering.

"We have waited a long time for you, my liege," he said.

"For me...?" Jack repeated numbly.

"For the return of Uthule," the goblin explained. "As I said, I am Varsmith, chief priest of the Uthmura. For centuries we have worked in dusk and shadow, making straight paths for the day you would return."

Jack's hand went to his chest. "I'm not..." he started, but seeing all those purple-irised eyes burning into him, all the strange beyond-rift weapons clutched in their fists, the words choked off in his throat. What would he rather be right now—a heretical impostor, or their god? Jack had always hated cults. But being the head of one, and having an army of ruthless, fanatical goblins at his disposal? That could be useful...

But first he had questions.

"You all were on the boat? The one that came through the rift?"

Varsmith nodded. "Yes, they were. I was already here, of course. We heard rumors you had emerged, and I knew I had to come over and meet you for myself. When one of the more prominent sylph, Bartholomew Barth, put out a call for a new bodyguard, I sent him a letter. It wasn't hard to get the job. You don't become high priest of the Uthmura without knowing how to fight and lead. Barth knew that. So, he brought me through. After that, all it took were some threats, bribery, and a bit of sneaking to get my brothers and sisters through, too. I guess Barth got wind of their arrival and thought he might be clever and have two threats to power butcher one another. He had Lura send you to intercept us. But even the machinations of the sylph can't stop the destiny of a god."

"So... what do you want?" Jack asked.

"To serve you," Varsmith said again.

"To serve," the other goblins agreed in eerie unison.

"Then you'll help me," Jack said.

Varsmith nodded. "In all things."

"Fight for me?"

"To the last drop of our blood."

Jack tried to hold back a grin. "You'll be loyal? Follow my orders without question?"

"It is what we have waited for all these long, long generations," Varsmith said.

Jack's eyes narrowed. "You'd stand with me even against other luck gods? Of both suits?"

"All suits must be united in you," Varsmith said. "In thy being resides all power. So it is written."

"So it is written," the other goblins echoed, as if it were an *amen*.

Jack noticed other figures creeping in at the periphery of the crowd. The newcomers were shorter in stature, green-skinned and ugly. Hobgoblins. *Really? Are these monsters going to be my people now?* Jack asked himself. And yet, as they looked at Jack the same fervency shone in the hobs' eyes as in the eyes of their taller brothers. The idea of having loyal followers, whoever they might be, gave Jack a feeling of rising pride.

Jack looked back to Varsmith and nodded to the chain of coins in the goblin's hand. "What's that?"

"Our holiest, most treasured relic," Varsmith said. "Made from the coinmail robe of Uthule himself. It has been held by the Uthmura since the day of dismemberment so that the high priest of our order could present it to the scion of the Great One on the day of his ascension. And so, I present it to you."

For a second, Jack felt dizzy. All of this felt so surreal, he was having trouble wrapping his head around it. A moment ago he'd been friendless and hunted. Now, he was being regaled as a god and had a literal army kneeling at his feet. And they'd already proven they would kill for him. The butchered bodies of the clones who'd come after him still lay in the middle of the floor, heaped and bloody. Jack looked away from the grizzly sight back to Varsmith, who stepped forward, offering the ancient necklace to Jack.

He nearly dropped it. The second the metal touched his fingers, an uncomfortable buzzing, vibrating sensation pinged through his hands. It was dully painful, like a mild electric shock. He held the jangling chain up and saw that it was indeed a loop. A necklace of coins. So, he slipped is over his head. It was surprisingly heavy, and its weight seemed to ground him, pressing his feet to the floor. The rest of him felt hot and shaky, the way he imagined it would feel to stick his head in a running microwave. But he sensed power, too, charm and hex rising into his pips and making them glow like never before.

*No. You can't do this,* he told himself. *You have to tell them you're not Uthule. That you have no intention of being Uthule.* After all, how many times had he sworn to Michael and Aubra that his quest to unify the suits had nothing to do with himself, that he didn't want the power, had no intention of being a tyrant, a ruler, a new Uthule.

And yet, Aubra and Michael were dead, weren't they?

And if Jack wanted to remain alive—and complete his quest—he'd need a lot of help. Right now, he was far from ruling all the suits. The Clubs and Diamonds hated him. The Spades barely tolerated him. The Hearts distrusted him. Aggie hadn't yet made him her king.

After years of deluding himself, he now allowed himself to see the truth. He could not unite the suits with a charming smile, or wise words, or cunning plans, or any amount of luck. He needed an army. Now, he had one.

And so, he raised both hands over his head and let the strange, two-tone light fall upon his priests and priestesses. His servants. His warriors. Heads bowed. Mouths whispered prayers.

"What is your command, your worship?" Varsmith asked.

Jack took in the sight one more time, all those fanatical goblins kneeling before him. All that power. What to do with them? Where to begin?

He thought of something he had heard once. Maybe the ace had said to him in a dream. *Before going to save the world, put your house in order.* It seemed good advice. And order, in the house of Hearts, was long overdue.

"I came here with a girl queen, Aggie," he said. "Find her."

# 38

## AGGIE

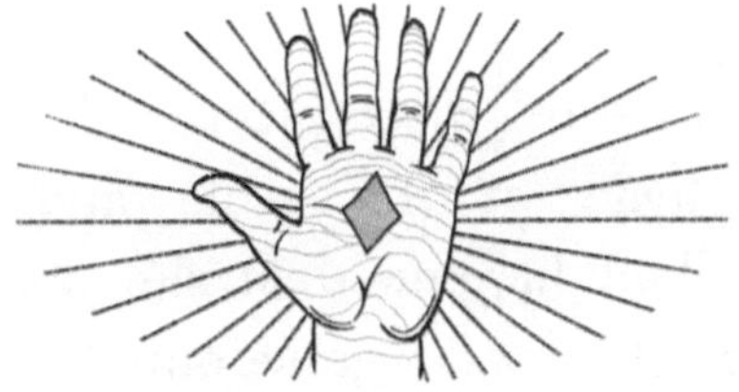

I rushed into the kitchen of the Hearts' mansion, soaked with rain, my heart still pounding, and announced, "I know who killed Michael."

My fellow Valentines paused in the middle of their dinner, forkfuls of jambalaya halfway to lips, glasses of wine sloshing onto the tablecloth. I took in the milieu at a glance. Mina sat at the head of the table, setting her fork down as she looked up at me. Cobe was on his phone. Dubs and Abraham were playing chess at their own small table in the corner. Deuce, who had already graduated from dinner to dessert, sat forking his pie and talking with Adelie, who leaned in, watching him with a rapt look that seemed almost flirtatious.

Out of everything in the room, that jumped out at me the most. I wanted to blurt out to Deuce, *really? Adelie?* But I had far more important business than who my suit members hooked up with—even if the pairing did leave an uncomfortable, tight feeling in my chest.

I scanned the room again. "Ten's still not here?"

"No," Cobe said, a challenge in his voice. "Whatever you want to say to her you can say to me."

Deuce had risen and gotten a blanket from a chair in the corner. He wrapped it around my shoulders.

"You're shivering," he said, then seemed to catch himself and added, "Your Majesty."

"Where's Jack?" Mina asked. "Didn't you leave with him?"

"Well..." I sat—or more accurately fell into—the chair at the head of the table and explained to everyone what had happened at the docks. How we'd met with Lura. How we'd gone out on the water and Jack had killed all those clones with lightning. How I'd met Carlotta and she'd all but admitted to killing Michael.

When I'd finished, Cobe sat leaning back in his chair, arms crossed over his chest. "But you still don't really *know* who killed Michael," he concluded.

I gave him a pointed frown. "Sure I do. Carlotta basically confessed. It was the Shastaryan."

"*Basically* confessing isn't the same as actually confessing," Cobe said. "Even if the Jokers are responsible, which one of them actually carried out the assassination? How did they infiltrate the mansion? How many of them were part of the conspiracy? For all we know, their agent is still here somewhere."

Cobe was doing his best impression of Ten, being belligerent, cynical—and making annoyingly decent points.

"I'm guessing they went out through the open window," I snarked back. "And I'm also guessing it was Carlotta, since she's the only Joker I've seen."

"That's a lot of guessing," Cobe said. "And it doesn't make sense. Why would Carlotta, who's not even a Blackover anymore, want King Michael dead?"

"It's their ideology," Deuce said. "The Shastaryan want the free flow of luck. No more luck gods."

"That would be convenient for them," Dubs pointed out. "With us gone, the Jokers would be the only ones with the power to control luck this side of the rift."

"Right," Deuce said. "Although their luck powers are less than they were when they had the pips of their suit, they can still control luck—good or bad—usually at a power level about half of what it would have been when they were luck gods. At least, that's what the books say."

"Even at half the power she had as Queen of Clubs, Carlotta would be formidable," Abraham mused. "She has the capability and the motive... I'd say an open window counts for opportunity as well."

"And you think she killed Galen, too?" Adelie asked, her voice dripping with skepticism.

At the mention of his name, I looked at Mina to make sure she wouldn't burst into tears, but she seemed to be holding it together.

"It would make sense," Deuce said. "When you're attacking a suit, it's good strategy to take out the strongest and the weakest ones first."

Cobe huffed and rolled his eyes. "This is all conjecture. It isn't proof."

I glared, but before I could respond, Dubs said: "So what about Jack, eh? What did he say when he saw Carlotta?"

I bit my lip. "He didn't see her," I said. "We... parted ways."

For just a second, I felt like I could cry, thinking of Jack at that wharf, calling for me. But overlaid on that, like a double exposure of film, was the image of lightning, burning the sky and the water white—then all those floating bodies.

"He's a Spade now," I said quietly. "He's gone."

My words brought the room to silence.

"If Jack is out of the running..." Cobe began.

"I'm not choosing my king yet, Cobe," I snapped, the queenly ire in my voice bringing about another silence.

"So... what now?" Mina asked.

*Save Jack*, I wanted to say. It still hurt my heart that I'd left him there, alone among enemies. But I highly doubted he needed saving. Jack had more lives than a cat.

"According to my test prep guide, I should be getting a good night's sleep ahead of my SATs tomorrow morning," I sighed, then I whipped out a scrap of paper Carlotta had given me—the one with the address on it. "But what I'm actually going to do is get some dry clothes and some weapons, then go find my mom. Who's with me?"

My usual allies looked eager, though no one threw up a fist and shouted *hurrah*. But Cobe crossed his arms and huffed.

"No way. This wasn't the deal."

"Yes it is," I said through gritted teeth. "I find the King's killers, you follow me. That was the deal. And I found them. Carlotta and her Shastaryan are the assassins. Now, you're going to help me find my mom."

Cobe wasn't the tallest luck god, but I still usually felt

like he towered over me. Now, though, he seemed to slump as he said, "or what?"

The charm was flaring in my hands, I realized, boiling out of me like a slow volcanic eruption. I pointed all of it at Cobe's mind. If I was lucky, he'd see things my way. And I was so lucky the room trembled.

"Or—" I said pointedly. "You'll face the wrath of a queen. And as you know, the penalty for disobedience is death."

I couldn't believe those words came out of my mouth. It was such an un-Aggie-like thing to say. And the power behind the words felt foreign, too. I wanted to follow up with an *oops, sorry. Just kidding.* But the truth was, I needed Cobe. I needed all the help I could get.

For an instant Cobe remained still and silent, his psyche teetering on some invisible fulcrum. *He's going to attack me,* I thought. *Or run away.*

Instead, he bowed his head. "Yes, Your Highness," he said.

# 39

# RACHEL

It had been like a nightmare. Rachel had lain on the concrete, doubled over pain as the obelisk shard in her stomach twisted her insides. She'd heard with preternatural clarity the sounds of Shade opening the truck of the long black sedan, getting something out, walking back to Rachel, whispering "I'm sorry," and then setting the *something* on the ground. With effort, she'd craned her neck and forced her eyes open. On the road next to her sat a familiar black stone urn.

Before her injury, Rachel had spent hours carrying that urn around the unluckiest haunts in Detroit, gathering up flittering bits of shadow—the scattered pieces of dissipated jinn. They were Lovecraftian monsters from some other dimension that fed on luck, and the greatest of them was Invidia, who had once possessed Rachel and who seemed disposed to cooperate with the Spades obelisk for reasons Rachel hardly dared think about.

As she watched, Shade had taken the lid off and stepped back. Out poured Invidia, her body of smoke black as oblivion, her face terrible in its feminine, inhuman beauty. In form she looked something like a dragon mated with an insect, a grotesque being made of matter belched from a smokestack.

The agony in her gut relented, but before Rachel could so much as take a breath, Invidia had snatched her up in her claws and began winging straight up into the sky.

Rachel felt like a rocket reaching escape velocity as the jinn bore her up, up, up in her talons of pure, roiling, smokey hex. Higher and higher she went, until the world below seemed a miniature of itself. The temperature dropped with each beat of the demon's fearsome wings. At first Rachel shivered, then she became so petrified with cold she couldn't shiver any longer.

Then, all at once, the ascent stopped. The smoke creature opened her wings and they paused, hanging in the sky like some dreadful constellation.

From Rachel's belly came the voice of the obelisk. *My dear Rachel, we need to talk.*

"W-what's there to talk about?" she said, her jaw quivering as she shivered again. "You want me to spread a plague and kill people."

*Many will not die,* the stone said. *Only suffer. Think of yourself as a farmer, Rachel. You will sow suffering, and reap power.*

"Yeah. N-no thank you," Rachel said.

*You may recall, we have an agreement,* the stone said. *I believe I demonstrated once before how your refusal to cooperate could impact others. Like Aggie.*

"Aggie is a queen," Rachel said. "She's too powerful for you to hurt her now." Even as she said it she knew it was a bluff. Wishful thinking.

In response, Invidia's talon clamped down tighter on Rachel. The air left her lungs, stars swam before her eyes, and pain lanced through her body as she felt her ribs bow, on the verge of snapping.

*Oh, I can't hurt a queen?* the stone crooned from within her. *You're a scientist, Rachel. I think you'd better reexamine your premise.*

Invidia gave her one more strong squeeze, sending a shock of pain down her back, then loosened its grip enough that she could at least take a half a breath.

She felt tears squeeze from her eyes and roll down her cheeks.

"Why don't you just let me go?" she begged. "Pick someone else to do your dirty work. There has to be someone else."

*This is a rather inopportune time to talk about letting go, don't you think, Queen?* the stone asked, causing Rachel to look down once again. The city looked miniature below her.

*Just a little longer, dear Rachel. A few more months and your work for me will be done. Then, I'll let you go. I swear it.*

Rachel hissed a breath through her teeth. "I can't do it anymore. I won't. You can't make me."

*I think I've demonstrated that I can.*

"Fine. Then I'll... I'll k-kill myself."

*Oh,* the stone feigned surprise. *You want to die? Why didn't you tell me? All you had to do is ask.*

The jinni let her go, and Rachel plummeted into the night.

**40**

---

## JUNIOR

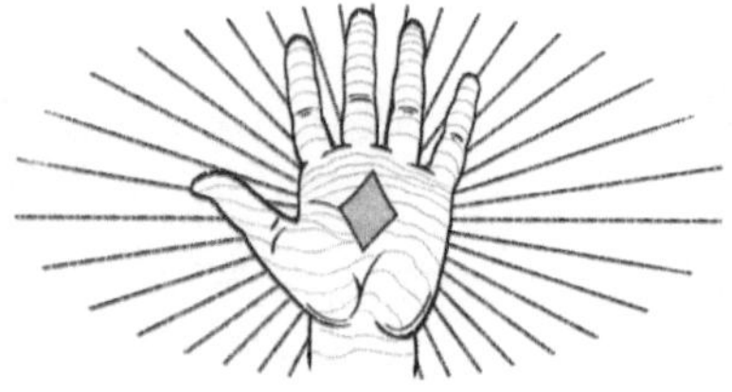

**M**oonlight frosted the desert with a sheen of pale white. A stillness had settled over the landscape, as if the earth were a thing huddled in fear. And yet the wind had picked up, making the faint outlines of clouds above, black on black, shoot past at an unnerving speed. It also shoved the car around on the road. Three times, wind actually pushed the pickup truck *off* the road, and Junior had to wrestle the steering wheel to get it back in its lane. Blowing sand and gravel peppered the windshield and ticked against the truck's body.

This was West Texas, and it seemed to Junior like a wasteland from a storybook, someplace where a dragon might slumber under a mountain or where an evil overlord might hold court in a black castle. The place was forbidding. Creepy. He had seen this landscape in dreams, he realized. Every night over the past few weeks, he'd been driving this empty, windswept road. It felt familiar. As wrong as the place was, coming here felt right. Several times, he heard the stone in the bag on the passenger seat whispering in his mind:

*Yes, closer, yes.*

The marks on his hands drew him onward, too. He could never have described the feeling, but the Spade pips tingled and pulsed more and more with each mile, until they almost seemed to sing.

The sameness of the straight, two lane road had almost lulled Junior to sleep when something suddenly loomed out of the dark ahead, a red spot on the black landscape. A stop sign. Junior mashed the brake pedal—too hard. His head whipped forward and the car fishtailed, left, right, left. The tires screeched, and for a second Junior felt the center of the car's gravity lift, as if it were considering whether or not to roll. Then, mercifully, it settled back into place. A rush of dust ticked and whooshed across the windshield as the truck shuddered to a halt, then all went still except the distant, plaintive howl of the wind and the pounding of Junior's own heart.

His hands burned stronger than ever now, the pleasure and the pain of the feeling almost unbearable.

The truck sat at a crossroads. *Left,* the shard of stone in the backpack said.

Junior gulped more air, catching his breath, slowing his heart, then he slowly removed his foot from the brake pedal, moved it to the accelerator, and turned the wheel. The tires hissed and crackled as they left the blacktop and passed onto a dirt road. The wind seemed to grow wilder, dust devils swirling up around him, actual tumble weeds bounding past, as if excited about their journey from desolation to desolation.

Junior didn't know how long he travelled down that dirt road, but his mind began to wander. He thought about gas and whether he'd have enough to get back. He wondered why the stone was taking him way out here in the middle of absolute nowhere. Was it trying to get him lost? To kill him and lose the body? Was it making him take it home—to what Junior imagined as a black mineshaft, infinitely deep and dark, a vein worming all the way to the core of the earth?

But what emerged from the night into the car's headlights was no mining elevator, no gaping hole. It was a town. A trailer half fallen off its blocks. A tiny house stripped of paint by the gritty wind, left bare as gray bones. A church with a toppled steeple. A ramshackle downtown, stores lining both sides of the street for half a normal city block, their black windows staring, glassless and lightless, into the barren desert night.

*Here*, the stone said, and Junior slowed the truck until it came to a stop. He killed the engine, which seemed to turn up the wind, a sound like the never-ending sigh of God.

The pips on Junior's hands ached and quivered strangely, and he rubbed his palms together, trying to get rid of the feeling. A single shutter on a storefront hinged back and forth in the wind. All else remained excruciatingly silent.

"Is this a ghost town?" Junior asked. He'd learned about ghost towns back in Miami—when he was still in school, still living with his stupid mom—in what seemed now like a totally different life. He'd been fascinated by ghost towns then. Once prosperous palaces which, wracked with bad luck, got abandoned. He'd wanted to visit one. Now that he was here, he wished he were anyplace else. And yet, there was no place else he could be. This was his destination. He could feel it in his hands.

*Open the glove box*, the stone said.

Junior obeyed. Inside, he found papers. Receipts. And beneath them, a small pistol left behind by the truck's dead owner.

*Take it*, the stone said.

"But—" Junior had never shot a gun before. Never held one, even.

*Take it*, the stone demanded. *Time is short.*

Junior picked up the little gun—so heavy for its size. Then he picked up the backpack with the stone inside, opened the truck door, and climbed out. Immediately the wind buffeted him so hard it nearly lifted him off his feet, but he managed to steady himself, put on the backpack, and stuff the gun in the waistband of his pants.

He started up the street. The black windows on either side seemed to watch him. Dead eyes, staring.

"What is this? Why are we here?" Junior whispered.

*Careful*, the stone answered.

A figure emerged from one of the stores on the right side of the street, silhouetted by moonlight. Then another appeared from a store on his left. And another.

They were tall—unnaturally tall—and slender. Recognition sliced into Junior, and with it a dread that set his whole body quivering. Those tall, strange bodies were the same as the creatures who'd first kidnapped him. The ones he thought of as aliens—even though Cleo later told him what they really were. Sylphs.

Into his mind flooded memories of that enchanted prison full of horrors Bartholomew Barth kept at the top of his Detroit office tower. The Menagerie. The sadistic clones who'd been his jailors, the creepy artifacts and chained-up animals, and cruel, otherworldly Barth himself—these were all components of Junior's nightmares now. They combined and rearranged themselves in his mind each night in a never-ending array of ghastly variations that caused him to wake gasping.

For a while at Cleo's, he'd almost convinced himself that none of it had been real. But here the sylphs were again, here in the place where the broken obelisk had led him.

*Run*, he thought, but just as in a real dream, his legs refused to respond. His body quaked. His bladder felt about to give way with fear.

*Steady,* came the voice of the stone. *They're here to do business, not steal little boys. And remember what you've become. The sylph are powerful—but you are a Morbus god.*

The three sylph stopped perhaps ten yards away and stood shoulder-to-shoulder, regarding Junior. The one on the left held a large plastic storage bin, which he set down on the dusty road with a thud.

"Well met, young luck god," the center sylph said.

"Well met," Junior forced himself to say, but his voice came out small, and was nearly gobbled up by the wind.

"You may call me Saddam," the center sylph said. "This is Maybelline and this is Ford."

*Weird names,* Junior thought. *They sound fake.* Cleo had told him sylph came from some strange world beyond a doorway called the rift, and Junior guessed these sylph's real names were probably strange and unpronounceable—in some language humans could never understand.

The sylphs nodded their large, bald, star-tattooed heads in greeting.

"We were told you have a something interesting in your possession," the one who called himself Saddam said.

*Show them the stone,* the obelisk said in Junior's mind. The boy hesitated for a second, then unslung his backpack from his shoulders, unzipped it, and took out the chunk of rock, cradling it like a child. Almost instantly, his hand and arms began feeling tingly and numb, like limbs that were asleep, and he knelt and set the crystal chunk on the ground.

The big, dark eyes of the lead sylph widened.

*Ask them to show you what they have,* the stone told Junior. He repeated the command, and the sylph called Ford peeled the lid off the plastic bin and dumped out the contents—dozens of chunks of black crystal, the same as the piece Junior had brought, but smaller.

"We purchased these pieces from a wholesaler out of Belarus," the sylph called Saddam explained. "We weren't entirely sure they were authentic, but... perhaps we'll take yours, try to fit them together, and who knows?"

*Tell them your piece is not for sale,* the stone said.

"It's not for sale," Junior repeated.

The sylph's unnaturally small mouth shifted into a grin.

"I didn't say buy, I said *take*," he said, and nodded to the other sylphs, who both stepped forward menacingly.

Reflexively Junior opened his hands and held their palms toward the sylph, washing them in the purple glow of his pips. At the sight of them, they paused.

Saddam rubbed his chin with eerily long fingers. "It is

strange to see one so young with the power of the gods. But there is a saying among the sylph. A cub is not a lion."

Saddam nodded, and his henchmen advanced again, until Junior jerked the gun out of his waistband and aimed it at the sylph on his right. Both henchmen hesitated, looking to their leader. Junior flared hex and the wind gusted, sending sand skittering across the landscape.

"We'll do it the hard way, then," the Saddam said, snapping his long fingers. More figures began emerging from the stores on either side of the street—more sylphs, Junior thought, his heart lurching with fear. But the proportions of these new figures were wrong for a sylph. They were human. As the figures began to step into the open, he saw they were women, dozens of them, all with identical faces.

*Clones,* the stone explained in Junior's mind. *Don't be afraid.*

But Junior was afraid. The women were tall, and mean-looking. They reminded him of his mom. And there were fifty of them and one of him.

He flared hex harder, and far above, heat lightning lit up the menacing black clouds.

*Tell them all the shards are yours, and you're taking them,* the stone commanded.

"Those shards are mine and I'm taking them," Junior said, echoing the conviction in the stone's voice.

"They belong to your suit," the sylph leader conceded. "But what if I were to own a restored obelisk of Spades? Perhaps that would give me the power the Spades possess, eh?"

Junior frowned. He wasn't sure if that was how luck gods' power worked or not. And he suspected the sylph didn't know, either.

"And if not," Saddam went on, "I imagine I could sell an obelisk and a little prince of their suit back to your Morbus brethren for a pretty penny. I heard your new queen is quite canny. I'm sure she'd make a deal. Probably one that would make us as rich as Bartholomew Barth. So what do you say, boy? Let's drop that gun." The sylph's eyes narrowed. "Before we drop you."

Junior was about to shout, *never*, when he felt himself hit from behind. Strong arms wrapped around his body. His arm holding the gun was wrested upward. *Crack*, the gun let off a single shot, which went wild into the desert sky before the gun was snatched out of his grasp. A hand tried to clamp over his mouth. Junior bit it until he tasted blood, but a fist hit him in the gut, making him cough and let go with his teeth. The clones had him. One shoved him to the ground and knelt on his chest while two more put bags of shiny gold foil over his hands.

"Sorry, boy. It's just business, eh? No hard... feelings..." Saddam's voice trailed off, and Junior glanced over to see the shard of obelisk from his back pack shifting. No hands touched it, but it moved anyway, first wiggling, then sliding across the desert floor. The sylph's shards were moving too, skittering across the dirt road and coming together, fitting themselves into place. Rebuilding. Saddam backed away. Junior watched in awe as a tower of stone began to take shape.

A sudden flare of light burst across the roadway and Junior turned his head to see a pair of headlights whooshing toward him, then coming to a skidding halt. A figure stepped out of a car.

The sylphs and clones all glared into the blinding headlights.

"Whoever you are, go back the way you came," the sylph named Saddam barked. "This is not your business."

"Oh, but it is my business," came the reply. At that sound of that voice, with its faintly Irish accent, tears almost rose in Junior's eyes. Cleo had found him at last.

**41**

---

# RACHEL

The Queen of Spades screamed toward the earth. Icy wind tore back her hair and ruffled her shirt. Death flew up to greet her, streets and buildings, cars and telephone poles whooshing toward her, all the world a weapon meant to destroy.

*Bad luck queen.*

*Bad luck has finally caught up with me...*

She saw her life. Cozy Christmases. Pastel Easters. Raucous nights on the town. She saw her childhood. The family farm where her grandfather taught her to ride horses. Her first two-wheel bike with the sparkly ribbons coming out of the handlebars that fluttered in the wind as she rode.

Like her hair, fluttering in the wind now.

As she plummeted.

To her death.

She thought of Aggie.

Aggie the baby, a little swaddled unit, a nugget of cuteness.

Aggie the precocious toddler, sitting in the bathtub and pretending to conduct experiments with cups of water.

Aggie the pre-teen, a ribbon in her hair, so sweet and so clever. Always doing everything right. What had poor Aggie done to deserve a mother like Rachel? If she had it all to do over again, Rachel would do so much more. Be so much better.

And Kevin. She thought of him. Her husband. Her beau. She remembered their first date. It had been a blind date, and he'd met her at a coffee shop. It had been open mic night, and a string of performers had come up one by one, most of them terrible. Rachel had had a few drinks beforehand and suggested she and Kevin get up and sing. They did an acapella rendition of "I Got You Babe," by Sonny and Cher. Neither of them knew the words and neither could sing, so the act had devolved into laughter, the onlookers watching in puzzlement, Rachel and Kevin cracking one another up, falling into one another's arms, ending the performance with a kiss. Then she'd taken him back to her apartment. The rest, as they say, was history.

Death, flying up to greet her on the wings of gravity.

Maybe death was only a glitch in time, a crafty wormhole. She'd pop back into existence on her wedding night. She'd have a chance to be a better wife. A better mother. She'd never touch booze. She'd never let Kevin get into the car on that fateful morning of the accident that had killed him. She'd be there for Aggie. She'd smash her damned dark matter machine with a baseball bat before it had a chance to rip a hole in reality and fill her with bad luck. Before it made her who she was. A menace. A fairy tale villain.

Death. A glitch in time. Nice thought. No evidence to support it, though.

More likely death was oblivion. No second chances. No do-overs. Nothing.

A final dispersal of matter and energy. A supernova of blood and guts. Impact on the pavement. A red period. Ending.

*I don't want to die.*

The thought lanced through the chaos of her mind, clarion, blazing and true. Echoing and growing louder, stronger with each repetition.

*I don't want to die.*

*I don't want to die.*

*I want to live.*

*Good or evil.*

*Happy or miserable.*

*Myself or some grotesque demigod.*

*Just let me exist.*

*Let me eat ice cream.*

*Make love.*

*See Aggie again. Even from afar. Even if she hates me. Even as her enemy. Even if I'm such a horror she has to kill me. Let me see her one more time.*

*I want to live.*

All these thoughts washed over her in a handful of heartbeats, then the ground was there, a manhole whooshing up to smack the existence out of her. She saw it growing larger, larger, larger.

*I. Want. To. Live.*

Eyes shut, teeth clamped, braced for pain, then—then —then—

Nothing.

Rachel opened her eyes to find herself floating perhaps five feet over the ground. She was in the middle of an inter-section, above the street. A handful of cars were lined up at the stop signs. Somewhere, someone screamed. A car horn blared. Rachel looked up and saw Invidia held her aloft, one smokey claw wrapped around her abdomen. Then, it gently set her on her feet. When she looked back at it, the jinni was already evaporating, wisping upward in a column of swirling smoke and disappearing into the sky.

Rachel felt weightless, her face numb with cold and shock, her hands trembling. She fell to her knees, almost taking the clichéd step to bow down and kiss the ground.

She barely noticed when a black car pulled up alongside her.

Shade was there, opening the door for her, helping her into the back of the vehicle, closing the door when she was inside. Dr. Gabardine sat in the passenger seat, a gas mask shoved back on his head. He gave her a nod as the car started moving, snaking through the backstreets, toward downtown.

*So, we have an understanding*, the stone inside Rachel said.

Rachel didn't have to ask what the stone meant. It was part of her. Inside her belly, inside her mind. It knew her and she knew it.

Before, she'd been sleepwalking through her days. She had allowed herself to believe that she didn't care if she died, that she only cared about Aggie. And if Aggie was powerful, safe, out of the stone's reach, then the stone had no leverage over her. Now, she saw that wasn't true. Rachel wanted to live. And if she wanted to live, she would have to do exactly what the stone said, no matter how terrible it was. Aggie wasn't the obelisk's hostage. Rachel was.

The car lurched to a stop, and Rachel blinked out of her reverie. Gabardine was handing her a gas mask and something else, a metal cannister.

"Just pull the pin and walk away," the doctor said in that eerily calm voice of his.

Shade opened the car door for her and she emerged, pulling the gas mask down over her face. They were at the back entrance of a brick building, and two bouncers in black outfits stood at either side of a metal door. As she approached, they opened it for her. She entered and found herself in the backstage area of a theater. To her right stood lineup of ropes and pulleys for theatrical rigging. Ahead, she was able to peer between a set of side curtains and onto a stage, where a black-clad rock band was playing in a hail of drumbeats and a howling storm of electric guitar.

A small man with a clipboard hurried up to Rachel and Shade.

"Go ahead, you're on," he said, taking her elbow and leading her toward the stage.

Rachel came out from the wing and into the bright lights of the auditorium. A crowd of hundreds or thousands filled the room, and they cheered wildly as Rachel made her way to the center of the stage, adjusting her gas mask self-consciously. The guitar had cut out but the drums and bass continued, throbbing in time with Rachel's heartbeat. She glanced back at Shade, who stood waiting in the wings. He gave her a nod, and she turned her attention back to the audience. That crowd. All those people. Their faces were made indistinct by the glare of the lights, but she knew every one had a family. A lover. A dream.

*As I once did. As I could have again.*

She looked down at the cannister clutched in her hands. God, how this felt like a strange, strange nightmare. *But it's real,* she reminded herself. *As real as dirt. Real as bone. Real as hell...*

*You can't do this,* some faint voice inside her pleaded—not the stone's voice. A different voice. One from deeper inside her. *Do this and it's over. Do this and you've lost. Lost Aggie. And lost yourself.*

Her fingers caressed the cannister, drifted to the pin. The pips on her hands throbbed with an almost sensual longing.

*It's very simple, really,* the stone inside her said. *Either you die a good girl. Or you live as a queen.*

A microphone squealed as the guitarist set a mic stand front of her. Rachel looked at it through the foggy, round holes of the gas mask.

For a moment, even the bass and drums hushed. The crowd went silent as death. The mic squealed again as Rachel leaned into it.

"I want to live," she said.

The crowd erupted in cheers as she pulled the pin and dropped the cannister into the stage. Black vapor boiled out of it. Pestilence. Suffering. The crowd screamed with adulation. Rachel felt the pips on her hands sizzle as the power of the work rushed into her, more glorious than any drug could ever be. She raised both hands in the air, exhalant, shrouded in roiling smoke. Then she dove from the stage. Hands caught her, dozens of hands, passing her along, raising her up, even as she killed them. The music kicked back in, guitar sharp as razors, drums like cannon-fire. The crowd screamed with joy and excitement, sounding like people wounded and dying. A few started to cough. And Rachel crowd-surfed atop them, feeling more alive than she had ever felt, queen of it all.

**42**

———

**CLEO**

She'd found her boy at last.

Lorcan was always grousing about her toxic lack of trust in people, but this time it had paid off. She'd given the backpack to the boy as a gift, and slipped a digital tracking device inside—just in case he decided to flee. She'd done it when she first brought him home, as a way of protecting her investment. He was far more than a mere commodity to her now, but she was glad she'd had the tracker as she followed that flashing circle on her phone app across a thousand miles of American desert. And because she was heading into unknown territory, she'd had to travel the human way, driving in a sun-bleached old Dodge Challenger she'd stolen a few years back, rather than using the faster and more elegant mode of travel, the leprechaun key.

She knew what had happened. That damned stone had the boy in its sway. And that was bad news. More than once, she'd nearly turned back, given the kid up as a lost cause. She'd be a fool to try to wrestle Junior away from the gods. But she couldn't quite bring herself to abandon him, either. If it had been the red suits that had their sights on him it might have been different, but the thought of him growing up a Spade was something she just couldn't accept. After all, it was her fault he'd gotten those black marks on his hands. If she hadn't gotten greedy, hadn't made the kid steal that bit of obelisk in the first place, none of this would have happened. The kid would be safe. Under the radar. He would be hers.

She would not stop, would not give up, until she got him back.

And so here they were. In the middle of nowhere. Endangered and outnumbered. Facing a trio of notorious sylphs and a battalion of clones in a midnight showdown at the OK corral.

Junior wriggled and squealed in his captor's grasp, sending a pang through Cleo's heart. Her hands went to her sides and she drew her curved daggers. They were paltry weapons given how outnumbered she was. She needed a pair of golden machine guns. But as always, their weight seemed to ground her, to connect her to the world.

"Let the boy go. You'll not get any profit out of him," Cleo shouted.

The lead sylph—Saddam—stepped forward. Cleo knew him by reputation. He was the foremost sylph lord of the American West and had a trading monopoly that ran all the way from Mexico to Saskatchewan, administered a base outside Las Vegas. His corps of female clones were among the best trained and luckiest in the world—and Cleo could see at least a dozen of them now, illuminated by the moon and the disquieting, throbbing light of the re-formed obelisk.

Certainly, Cleo would have no chance against so many. But for the boy, she would try her damnedest.

"Find a door and go, leprechaun," Saddam barked. "You won't get any gold out of us."

Cleo stiffened at his words. Everyone always assumed leprechauns cared about nothing but gold. And that was true, generally. But not today.

Cleo nodded toward the crystal monolith.

"You've got the completed obelisk. Sell that to the dark queen and you'll get a fortune. You don't need the boy, too."

The sylph's too-big eyes narrowed. "Don't tell me what I need, greenie. I'd take you, too, if I thought anyone would pay for a mouthy, trouble-making leprechaun."

In her periphery, Cleo watched the clones moving in behind her. Flanking. Encircling.

"Actually," Saddam rubbed his chin. "The more I look at you with that pretty blonde hair of yours... maybe I can think of a few customers who'd pay for you."

The sylph gave a nod, and his clones lunged at Cleo. She raised both her hands and did the only magic she could— turning her enemies guns to solid gold. A few triggers clicked, hammers clacking down dully, but no bullets fired from the now-golden guns.

The first two clones reached Cleo and she buried a kick in the gut of one and a dagger in the neck of the other.

"Bring her down!" Saddam barked.

A shriek brought Cleo's attention back to Junior. The clone who'd been holding him was now cradling a bloody, bitten hand. Junior stepped away from her and raised his hands, a flash of eerie anti-light emanating from the Spade marks on his palms.

A clone who'd been charging Cleo stopped and looked down at herself. A dark stain was spreading on the crotch of her pants, and from the smell Cleo judged she'd shat herself, too.

"My, that's very bad luck," Cleo said, before smashing the clone's nose with the pommel of a dagger.

The air fairly quivered with the force of the boy's hex.

A second clone went down with a twisted ankle.

A third fell on her own knife.

A sign above a shuttered hardware store fell, crushing a clone beneath it.

The remaining women paused their attack, retreating back to the shadows of the buildings.

*Damn, the boy is strong,* Cleo thought. He was far more powerful than she'd imagined—more powerful than a two-ranked luck god had any right to be.

*I can't bring him back to my lair. Sooner or later his bad luck will do me in,* she thought. It would be like having a rabid wolf for a pet. And yet, she'd knew she'd rather be done in by him than to lose him, crazy as it seemed.

"Get them both!" Saddam snarled. "The last one to battle gets a slit throat!"

This spurred the clones once again—and even more of them seemed to have emerged from the buildings, falling on Cleo like a wave. There was no art to her fighting now. She thrashed and flailed in mad haze of limbs and teeth, weapons and fists, punctuated here and there by bright shocks of pain. All the while she trudged her way forward, toward Junior. She glimpsed him, too. Both his dark hands were still raised defensively, their black light keeping his attackers at bay as he backed toward the obelisk. Saddam and one of the other sylphs emerged from behind the stone tower and grabbed Junior by the collar, trying to drag him away.

"Fight, boy! Figh—" Cleo stared to say, before a set of knuckles banged into her teeth, silencing her. Hands clamped onto her arms. Several clones jumped onto her back. She took another staggering step, then fell to the ground in a bone-rattling heap.

A hand grasped her hair, pulled her head back. A cold line of a knife pressed against her throat.

"Boy!" Saddam shouted. "Surrender. Lower your hands and put those gold gloves back on—and we'll let your friend here live."

Junior froze, looking wild-eyed and feral. He glanced from Cleo to the obelisk, and Cleo knew the damned stone tower must be whispering in the boy's mind.

Would love for Cleo be enough to wrest him from its dark sway?

She doubted it. And it didn't make her feel better that he still hadn't lowered his hands, still hadn't run toward her. He had, if anything, shuffled a step closer to the obelisk, as if pulled by an invisible cord.

The blade pressed harder against her throat, and she shut her eyes against the coming pain.

Then—a hot wind washed over her face. Dust filled her mouth. She opened her eyes to see something impossible: a massive beast made of what appeared to be black smoke swooped down from the sky and alighted on the ground between her and Junior.

It roared, but when it turned its neck toward her, Cleo saw it had the face not of a beast, but of a woman. The sight sent a shiver through Cleo.

With one swipe of a vaporous claw, the creature sent half the clones flying. Two of the sylphs tried to run, but the monster snatched one of them up and brought it to her face. It inhaled, its nostrils flaring, and as it did the sylph screamed and went limp. The smoke beast dropped it to the ground and it landed in a lifeless heap.

The creature had sucked all the luck from the sylph's body, Cleo realized. This was a jinni. A mythological monster from the nether realms, the sort that appeared in bedtime stories to scare wayward leprechaun kids into behaving. Well, it wasn't a myth anymore.

Saddam had already let her go and fled down the road, with the other sylph a few steps behind. The clones that had been holding her followed suit, releasing her and running.

Cleo stood on unsteady legs.

The Jinni was holding a clone in each set of foreclaws. As Cleo watched it sniffed each of them, sucking their luck dry, then dropped their dead husks to the street with a pair of thuds that made Cleo wince. It shifted then, looking for its next prey, and as it did it moved aside, revealing Junior. He stood next to the obelisk now, close enough to touch it.

"Junior!" Cleo called, and he turned back. Their eyes met. The boy's lips parted; he was about to speak. Even from this distance, Cleo could see the emotion in his eyes.

On aching legs, she stumbled forward, arms outstretched to embrace him.

"Junior. Come here!" she called.

He took one step, then stopped, cocked his head as if

listening to a voice only he could hear. He looked at her once more, apology in his eyes. Then he reached out and touched his hand to the black crystal tower. In a blink, both boy and obelisk were gone.

Cleo stopped dead, the breath stolen from her lungs, her heart pounding, her eyes scanning the street in vain as her brain struggled to process the impossibility of what she'd just seen. Her dear boy there one instant, then the next —gone.

There was really and truly no sign of him. The clones had all fled, too. All that remained in that ghost town beneath the feckless moon was Cleo and the massive shadow monster.

The leprechaun looked up at the jinni. The jinni looked down at the leprechaun. Slowly, it lowered its massive head until they were eye to eye, but Cleo forced herself to stand firm. Running would do no good, anyway. Not in the face of this beast. She stared into those eyes of smoke, ancient and demonic, and she felt not a single wisp of fear. Only anger burned within her now.

"Go ahead, ya ninny," Cleo growled, blinking back tears. "Do it. I have no luck left anyway."

The jinni's black eyes narrowed. Then slowly it spread its storm cloud wings and shot up into the sky, leaving the snarling, trembling leprechaun alone in the night.

**43**

---

# MOLLY

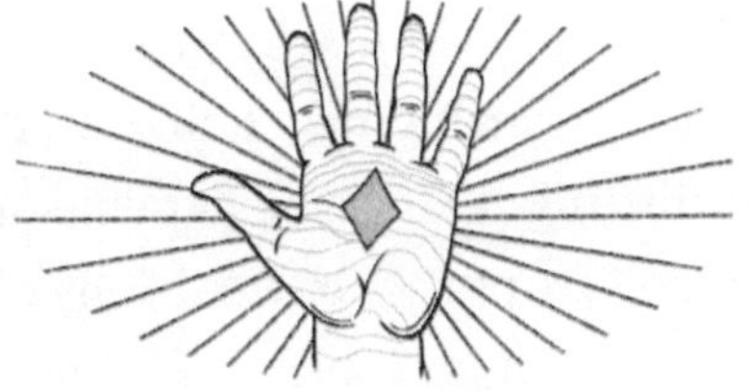

Molly lay in bed, staring at her phone. The sheets in this hotel were smooth as cream, the pillows soft as puffs of dandelion fluff. God, she could get used to this Diamante lifestyle. But her old life always seemed to butt in. Currently, that came in the form of highly dramatic texts from her mom. Though Molly had texted her and explained, in detail, that she was going back to Northville to meet up with her friends, Mommy dearest had flown off the handle. She'd gotten a hold of Bianca's mom, who Molly said she was staying with, and found out Molly wasn't there, that they had never heard about Molly coming at all. When Molly pivoted and said she was actually staying with Aggie, Mom came back again, saying that she couldn't get a hold of Aggie's mom, either.

*That's because I stabbed her,* Molly thought miserably. *She's probably dead. Or if she's not, she and Aggie must both hate me.*

But they wouldn't hate her forever. When she became a Diamond, she'd be useful. They'd need her as an ally, Molly told herself. She'd be too valuable to hate.

The door burst open, banging against the wall and Molly gasped, dropping her phone onto the bed spread.

Danusia was there, her pretty nostrils flared, her blue eyes fiery.

*Jesus, she's even prettier than me when she's pissed,* Molly thought forlornly. *I want to be just like her.*

"What in the ever-loving hell is this?" Danusia demanded, brandishing a stack of papers—almost a whole ream's worth—and dropping it on Molly's stomach with enough force to make her go "oof."

She looked down at the papers. At the top of the first page she read *Merger Agreement,* followed by a bunch of dense-looking numbered paragraphs.

She looked back up at Danusia, confused, as Tristaine and Ten crammed through the doorway behind her. She felt hopeful for a moment at the sight of Tristaine, but he only watched, wide-eyed. Whatever Danusia was about to do to her, it didn't appear he was going to intercede.

"I don't understand," Molly said.

Danusia jammed a finger toward the contract. "Turn to the flagged section."

Molly saw a little red marker poking out the side of the paper stack. She lifted the papers that sat above the flag and set them aside, revealing the marked page.

"This is the latest version of the merger agreement," Tristaine explained as Molly scanned the page. "A courier just dropped it off this morning."

Under a heading titled *Officers and Executives*, a highlighted sentence read: *CEO of the newly created entity shall be Molly L. Carpenter.*

"Is this a joke?" Danusia demanded.

Molly shook her head, her mouth hanging open in wonderment. "Maybe?" she said. "I mean, have no idea..."

Then she did have an idea. And she smiled.

"What is so funny?" Danusia asked through bared teeth.

"I asked their attorneys about this," Tristaine frowned. "They told me the company's largest shareholder insisted on it. The problem is, the largest shareholder is a trust. So far, we haven't been able to figure out who's behind it."

"Seth," Molly said, catching her breath from the laughter. "It's Seth."

"Who the hell is Seth?" Danusia demanded.

"The pimple-faced kid Molly was palling around with," Ten said.

"What did you do, you little—? Did you seduce him?" Danusia demanded with such force Molly scrambled backward on the bed.

"Nothing. I didn't do anything. I was just nice to him, that's all."

Danusia glared at her, one hand on the hilt of her dagger.

"Look, just make me a Diamond," Molly pleaded. "And I'll be the CEO. I'll do whatever you want."

"I don't want you to be the CEO, you little scab," Danusia shouted.

"She may have a point," Tristaine said.

"No!" Danusia wheeled on him. "She's been playing us from the beginning."

"And she's done an impressive job of it, wouldn't you say?" Tristaine said. "While we were off wooing the uncle, she found the real power broker. She beat us at our own game, I'd say. That takes guts. And smarts. Not to mention luck."

"Luck?" Danusia shrilled. "I've been working on this deal for over two years. Then you drag her into it and she mucks it up in two days. She'll be *lucky* if I let her live."

"The point is—" Tristaine started, but Danusia was beyond hearing. She lunged at Molly, flaring charm and grabbing her by the hair.

"Ow!" Molly wailed as Danusia yanked her to her feet and dragged her through the suite's living room to the front door. She opened it and shoved Molly out.

"Take her somewhere and drop her off," Danusia told a pair of syco guards standing outside. "I don't care where. Just be sure she doesn't come back."

And the door slammed.

Tears blinded Molly as the men gently took both her arms and led her to a waiting limo. The world remained a blurry kaleidoscope as the car kicked into gear and they wove through the streets. Molly's chest heaved with sobs. Her face ached from being contorted. She thought of how ugly she looked when she cried, and what the sycos must think of her and her hysteria, but she couldn't stop crying.

She'd been so close. Why did Danusia hate her so much? Why did everyone hate her so much? She and Aggie had been together when they first encountered the luck gods. How had Aggie wound up a demigoddess while Molly was rejected at every turn?

*Because I'm worthless,* Molly thought. *Worthless and ugly with lizard skin and dumb hair and— And even when someone likes me—Lorcan or Seth—it's just another disaster. I have such bad luck.*

If one of those dark suits had been there at that moment and offered her their black mark, she'd have taken it. But after she'd stabbed Aggie's mom, even they would hate her, wouldn't they? And sure, Seth had put her into the business agreement, but he'd probably just done it to screw with his uncle, or as a poison pill to mess up the deal. He didn't really want her to be CEO. He didn't really like her. No one did. Even her mom was livid with her.

She had no one. Nothing. And no place to go.

Her tears had just about stopped when the limo glided to a halt. The door opened and one of the men took her under the armpits like a toddler, hauled her out of the car, and unceremoniously dropped her onto her butt on the sidewalk. The doors slammed shut and, without a word, the Diamantes' thugs pulled away, leaving Molly alone.

She sat on the curb, feeling too numb to cry, and people-watched, her eyes tracking every person who passed— mostly couples going to dinner. From what she could tell, the people in Monaco all seemed to be as rich as Diamonds themselves, the women tall and perfectly done up in colorful designer dresses, the men in fancy suits or half-unbuttoned shirts or weird polos that she assumed had to be expensive. The women were all lovely no matter their age. The men glowed with good health and sophistication as they strode past in gleaming leather shoes.

It made her feel self-conscious, and she scratched at the dead skin on her neck. She'd been so close. Seth had tried to make them accept her. And yet here she was, spurned by the gods and left to wander among the angels, an outcast and penniless in the richest country in the world. Being in hell would have been better.

And how was she supposed get home? She'd be trapped here forever, the only homeless person in this immaculate city.

With a sigh she rose and started walking. Maybe she could find Klepper's yacht and plead her case to Seth. Get him to intercede with Danusia, or at least give her a good meal and a place to crash. But as she walked the docks, all the yachts looked the same. And then she remembered Klepper's yacht had been anchored in the bay anyway; it was probably still out there. She made her way to the end of a dock and squinted out across the water. In the darkness, there were plenty of lights hovering over the black water, illuminating the spots where boats lay at anchor. But there was no telling which one was Klepper's, and she certainly would not have tried to swim out to it at night anyway.

"Mademoiselle?" She turned to find a dock attendant. He attempted to interrogate her in French, and when she became flustered he kindly but firmly escorted her off the dock.

She left the marina feeling more desolate than ever.

This was an infuriating analogy for her whole life, she thought, as she hiked up a hillside path that ran along the water. Surrounded by people wealthier and prettier, just wanting to be accepted. But she never would be accepted, would she? She'd always be haunting the periphery, a moth fluttering around a flame, trying to reach a light she could never touch. She'd done everything to get accepted by the cool people. She'd acted fake. She'd spied on her best friend. She'd helped close an international business deal. She'd even stabbed someone. If they hadn't accepted her by now, they never would. It was futile. Stupid. She'd might as well stop trying.

She found herself on the outskirts of the city, in a tiny park, on path perhaps fifty feet above the water. A stone wall ran in front of her and she approached it and leaned over, looking down. Far below, waves tinged with moonlight crashed into jagged black rocks. She stared, mesmerized by the crashing surf.

Then, slowly, she lifted one foot up and set it atop the wall. She lay her hands flat on the rough stone and pushed herself up, until she atop the wall. She was afraid to look down, but she could imagine the surf crashing against jagged rocks far below. Even gazing out toward the horizon was bad; it gave her a weightless, fluttery feeling.

Klepper's yacht was out there somewhere. Somewhere out there movie stars were enjoying cocktails. Starlets were laughing. Heiresses were sipping champagne. While Molly stood here, alone in the dark.

She shut her eyes. Gulped. Held her breath. Spread both her arms, like wings, like a bird preparing to fly—for the last time.

"Molly."

The sudden voice startled her, and Molly windmilled her arms, almost pitching head-first over the edge. But she caught her balance at the last second—luckily—and fell into a crouch, her heart pounding.

She looked back to see the path illuminated with a faint red light, cast from a pair of glowing, diamond-shaped pips. For a second, she thought it was Danusia here to finish her off, and fear shot through her. But as the figure moved closer, she realized it wasn't Danusia. This woman was taller and older, though still lovely. She wore her long, platinum hair in ringlets pinned up to the top of her head, and her lips were as red as a blood moon.

"Not thinking of taking a swim, are you?" the woman asked, her voice as warm and sweet and Southern as honey on biscuits. She sidled to the stone wall next to Molly and peered down. "Cause that water looks cold as hell to me."

"Diamond Queen," Molly said, feeling a bit star-struck and nervous despite everything.

"And you're the famous Molly Carpenter," the goddess said. "You pissed my Dani off good. You ask me, I think she's just jealous."

Molly blurted a laugh. "Danusia? Jealous of me? That's hilarious."

The Diamond Queen tilted her head. "Well, I don't know about that. She's been trying to close that deal with Klepper for a long time now. You blew into town and it got done faster than a cat can say meow."

"That was just..." Molly trailed off.

"Just luck?" the Diamond Queen supplied. "But luck is everything, sweetie. Everything."

The music star gazed out over the black, moon-gilded waves.

"You know, I grew up poor. In southern Georgia. My daddy owned a car dealership. All he cared about was selling cheap used cars. All my momma cared about was wearing flowery dresses and making dishes for church potlucks. And me? I had the worst thing in the world."

"A... disease?" Molly guessed.

The Diamond Queen gave her a sideways glance. "A penis, honey. Daddy wanted me playing ball games. I wanted to wear ball gowns. Momma wanted me to date the prom queen, I wanted to *be* the prom queen. You want to talk about feeling left out? Try being a boy who loves to sing and dance and wear sequins living in the Bible belt. I got in so many fights my gramma started calling me Black-Eyed Pea."

"So how did you get out?" Molly said. "How did you become a luck god?"

Diamond Queen gave a sly smile. "That's a story for another time," she said. "But listen to my albums, honey. It's all in my music. Suffice to say, I had what you have. Moxy. Fire. Desire. And I did something else you've done, too."

"Stabbed your best friend's mom?" Molly asked wryly.

Diamond Queen laughed and they paused as well dressed couple strolled past down the path, then Diamond Queen leaned in to Molly and said, with a conspiratorial wink, "I made myself indispensable."

Molly felt her spirit lift. "Indispensable. You mean...?"

"I mean, we need the technology the Kleppers have. I'm not going to lose that deal. And I've looked into that boy, Seth. He really is the kingmaker in this whole thing. And I think his little ass is just crazy enough to scuttle the whole deal unless you're in it."

"So..." Molly began, but she couldn't finish. It felt like her heart was about to burst.

"It appears you're going to be the CEO of a new multinational corporation," Diamond Queen said. "What are your salary demands? How much is it going to cost me?"

"Uh... a hundred thousand," Molly said, throwing out the first number that came to mind. "Per year."

Diamond Queen snorted. "Are you trying to be the lowest paid CEO in the Fortune 500? Think millions, honey."

"Okay..." Molly paused, thinking. "Twenty million?"

"That's more like it," Diamond Queen said.

Molly repressed a squeal, then made herself get serious.

"And..." she hesitated, then forced herself to sound authoritative. "And make me the two of Diamonds."

One corner of Diamond Queen's red lips rose in a half smile.

"That's what I figured," she said with a sigh. "I'm going to warn you, girl. Being a luck god comes with a lot of headaches and a lot of danger. But if your heart is set on it..."

"It is," Molly said quickly.

Diamond Queen nodded. "So be it, then. Don't say I didn't warn you."

She shifted, and Molly saw a tower of crystal had appeared in the pathway behind her. It was clear like quartz and had facets like a diamond, but it was shaped like an obelisk. A core inside it glowed red, an essence that trembled like flame.

"Alright then, my little black-eyed pea," the Diamond Queen said. "Let's make you a goddess."

---

# 44

# AGGIE

We sat in an SUV outside a large, non-descript commercial building. It had beige aluminum siding and, in one upper corner, I could see the discolored rectangle where a sign had been removed. The part fronting the road had windows and seemed to be an office, but the back looked like industrial or warehouse space, a long blank rectangle with a few loading docks near the back. We'd been sitting across the street watching for ten minutes, but no one had come in or gone out. There were lights on inside, but there was no movement.

"Are you sure it's the right address?" Deuce asked.

I flapped the paper Carlotta had given me. "Yep."

We all watched the building again. Nothing happened. Nothing moved.

"If Seemor were here we could send him to scout it out," I griped. But Jack's favorite spy wasn't answering texts—not from me, anyway. I shook my head in frustration. "The place is totally untenanted."

"Nice SAT word, love," Dubs said, but his usual bubbly good humor was absent. He sounded as uneasy as I felt.

"You're right. There aren't even any cars in the lot." Deuce said doubtfully. "It doesn't look like anyone's home."

"That's because they're not," Mina said excitedly, leaning up between the seats and showing me her phone.

On its screen was a video of a woman on a stage wearing all black. The image on the screen was grainy with low light, but though it was hard to make out her features, I would have known her mannerisms anywhere.

"Mom," I whispered. "What is this?"

I could see the video was from a social media site.

"Someone sent this link to me," Mina said. "From a group called Luck Gods Watch. I've never heard of it."

"They have a website, too," I said, feeling numb and disturbed at once. "Is this a live feed?"

Mina nodded. "It says they're at a club downtown called Pantheon."

Deuce already had the car in gear.

❧♡♧◇♣☙

There was a line outside the club that went halfway down the block, but my Valentines and I marched past them and right up to the bouncer, flaring charm so hard he didn't bother to check our IDs. He just opened up the velvet rope and gave us a deferential nod as we passed. The music hit us before we were even in the door, its bass rattling cars and its squealing guitars causing passersby on the sidewalk to wince.

At the entrance I paused to survey my crew. Every Valentine was behind me except Ten. All were armed. All bore the same expression of grim determination.

"What's the plan?" Cobe asked, as if he'd plucked the words from my mind. In truth, there was no plan. But we needed one. Every time I'd confronted Mom in the past, I'd barely survived. And though she was probably still recovering from the wound Molly had given her, she'd also had more time to develop her power. But I'd also had time to develop mine.

"You hold off the sycos and whatever other Spades happen to be there. I'll handle my mom."

Cobe's eyes narrowed. "You're going to kill your own mother? Do you really have the stomach for that—" he added a grudging, "Your Majesty?"

"I'm going to capture her." I snapped. "And we're going to help her. *Not* kill her."

"But if she's about to kill one of us—?"

"Cobe, stop inveighing, please." I said.

Cobe frowned. "Stop *what*?"

"Stop arguing," Deuce said. "Jeez. Use context clues, my man."

SAT in the morning, and I'd barely studied for days. This was so not how the prep guide said things should be. But nothing mattered now except getting Mom back safe.

"Hey. You going in, or what?" a twenty-something with many piercings barked from the line from behind us.

My eyes flicked back to Cobe. "Just follow my lead," I said, and pushed through the doors to enter the venue.

We passed down a hallway and emerged into what looked like an old theater with the seats removed. A balcony stretched overhead with colored lights affixed to the front, shifting in time with the ear-splitting music. The dance floor —or mosh pit, whatever it was called—teemed with young people gleefully skipping or jumped or jostling one another in time with the music, headbanging and taking every possible occasion to run into, punch, or kick one another. A haze hung over the entire scene, fog that gave me the pins-and-needles prickle of bad luck.

As I ventured further into the space, I saw quite a few audience members had retreated from the dance floor to sit against the wall, looking pale and ill. Others huddled in the booths that lined the wall, coughing and shivering.

The musicians on the stage, a guitarist, bassist, and drummer, were all skinny, tattooed, and shirtless, playing their atrocious music with the fervor of lunatics. At the center of the stage stood a figure who could only be Mom— but she was Mom out of a nightmare.

A gas mask covered her face. The black marks on her hands faced the crowd and glowed, a black benediction, as if she were figure off some grotesque prayer candle. Even in the flowing black dress she wore, I could see she'd lost weight since the last time I'd seen her, to the point where she was almost skeletal. She stood amid the din and chaos with a perfect stillness so eerie it sent a shiver through me. I was closer to her than I'd been in months. But seeing her, I somehow felt she was farther away than ever. I expected to feel relieved, seeing her alive after what happened last time we met. Instead, I just felt afraid. For her. For me. For all of us.

*One, two...* I started to count the gyrating, dancing bodies passing in front of me, then stopped.

*Queens don't count,* I reminded myself. *They fight.*

I drew the gun from my hip, aimed it at the ceiling, charmed to ensure the bullet wouldn't ricochet off the roof and hurt someone, and pulled the trigger.

The report of the gunshot seemed to pull the oxygen from the room. There were a handful of screams, then a breathless silence as people whipped their heads around to find the source of the sound. Spying me, the crowd shrank back. A few screamed again, or ran. A couple of meathead types forced their way in my direction, ready to confront me, I guess—but when they saw the rest of the Valentines flanking me, armed to the teeth, they retreated fast.

The band's music slowed and stopped, like a wind-up toy with its gears running down.

Mom took a microphone from a stand. It squealed as she brought it to the place in the gas mask where her mouth should have been.

"Aggie. You shouldn't be here," she said in a flat, muffled voice.

"Neither should you," I said, defiant at first, then pleading: "Come home."

She shook her head. "You know I can't."

"Well you can't stay like this," I shouted. "Look at you!"

"I have to finish my servitude, Aggie. I've told you that. It's the only way."

I noticed dark-clad figures making their way through the crowd, surrounding us. Several had the same curly, dark hair —the clones Mom had bought from the sylph, Bartholomew

Barth. Another was probably Mom's lieutenant, Shade, though his gas mask made it impossible to tell for sure.

"Well, I can't let you run around hurting people and making them sick, Mom," I said.

At those words, the pips on my hands throbbed with longing. *Yes, stop her,* they seemed to say. *That is* the work *you must do.*

Mom tilted her head, a creepy mannerism that wasn't her own. "You can't stop me," she pointed out.

Another hulking figure in a gas mask came up alongside her, put a hand on her shoulder. I didn't even want to know who *that* was—but he was certainly a bad luck god. Just the sight of him sent prickles up my spine.

"This isn't you," I said, my voice going shrill with desperation.

"I'm many things, Aggie," she said sadly. "I always have been. You just haven't seen it."

"You have to fight it."

"No," she countered. "You have to let me go."

Suddenly, I didn't have the breath to respond. Tears stung my eyes. My hands quaked. My teeth gritted together, on edge as anger and frustration warred with the grief inside me.

"I'll never give up on you," I finally managed to say.

"Aggie," Deuce said at my shoulder. It was a warning. We were completely surrounded by those black clad figures in gas masks, as well as regular members of the crowd, who watched the drama with fascination.

The hulking bad luck god on the stage knelt and placed his hand on the shoulder of one of the concertgoers. A shiver went through her body and she shoved the person next to her, who kicked the person next to him. A contortion of violence began washing through the crowd like a wave.

"The Berzerker Touch," Mina gasped.

That was a Clubs dow, a power of the Blackovers, not the Morbus.

"Who is that?" I asked, staring at the tall, masked man on stage. A Club with that much power... was it Thad, the king? No. This one was taller. Leaner. Then I recognized the tattered, gray-black cloak he wore. But it was impossible. Gallo was dead. Jack had killed him months ago.

But there wasn't time to wonder. The contortion of violence rippled through the crowd, coming toward me and the Valentines, and I was profoundly aware of how outnumbered we were.

"Back to back!" I shouted. "And no guns."

Most of the concertgoers were innocent people who'd been swept up in this battle and were being used as pawns. I didn't want any of them getting killed, and certainly not by us. But before I could say all that, they'd fallen on us, a nasty surge of bodies, all butting heads, kicking feet, and swinging fists.

Without charm to blunt the attack, we'd all have died. But I flared with all my might, and judging from the red gleam that came off us, everyone else did, too. And it had an effect. A woman charging me stumbled, giving me a chance to sweep her front leg and make her fall. A big man tripped over her, landing hard on one knee. While he was still off balance, I cuffed him in the side of the head and he toppled sideways. Another man, skinny and with a shaved head, leapt over him and came at me brandishing a broken beer bottle. His face was familiar, and after a moment I placed him as the neo-Nazi from the rally in the park. The realization made my anger flare as well as my charm. He swiped at me with the bottle, but I dodged the strike and managed to nick his forearm with my knife. His weapon fell from his grasp and he reeled away, hissing, to be swallowed up by the crowd.

That was three I'd taken out.

*No, stop counting them.*

We were holding them off, but it wouldn't last. I looked up again to find Mom standing on the stage, both hands raised, hex coming off her in pulses so strong I could feel them in my chest. If I could just stop her, we'd have a chance. I had to get on that stage—but a sea of violent bodies roiled between us.

Mina was fighting just to my right, doing admirably despite having one injured arm.

"With me," I shouted, touching her shoulder, and she followed me into the fray.

"Come on!" she called, and the other Valentines streamed behind us, forming a phalanx. Together, we drove through the crowd, toward the stage.

Then, a man in a gas mask loomed in front of me. He held a wakizashi, a Japanese short sword, in each hand. Hex rolled off him powerfully. This was the one I thought was Shade, my mom's second in command. He hesitated for a second when he saw me, which confirmed my suspicion. At some point, Mom had probably instructed him not to hurt me. At least, I hoped she had. But his pause lasted only a moment, then he was coming at me, blades flashing.

"I'll take him. You get to your mom," Mina said, shouldering past me. Before I could argue, she was ahead of me, meeting Shade's assault, her traditional Korean blade flashing against his short katanas *one, two, three* times, then she shot in as if for a wrestling takedown, locked onto one of Shade's legs with one of hers, shifted her body, and brought him to the grown—a deft use of one of the Jiu Jitsu moves I'd not yet mastered. The way cleared, I hurried past them toward the stage.

But I'd only gone a few strides before another hulking figure blocked my path. Up close, that tattered, dark cloak and long hair looked more familiar than ever. My suspicions were confirmed when the figure swept his gas mask back to reveal that handsome face—with one eye patched.

I sucked a breath and whispered, "Gallo."

His only response was a darkly crooked grin.

I lunged at him, a half-hearted, probing thrust. Instead of using the mace he held to block it, he mocked me by slapping the flat of my blade aside with his hand—then soundlessly laughed in my face.

"Let me," Deuce said. Shouldering past me, he dove at Gallo's feet, mirroring the move Mina had used to take out Shade. To Deuce's credit, Gallo did stumble and fall to one knee. But the Heart Slayer would not be toppled so easily. While Deuce heaved and grunted, Gallo dropped an elbow into his ribs then stood and kicked Deuce aside, stepping free.

It was enough distraction, however, that I was able to shoot past. Before Gallo could turn and grab me, I'd darted between two more clones and off into the crowd. With his big frame, Gallo wasn't able to follow.

Beaten and buffeted, shoved and scraped by the failing, moshing crowd, I somehow managed to reach the foot of the stage. I hauled myself up and stood before Mom.

Her hands were still raised, the hex light burning from her palms. Behind the glass eyeholes of her gas mask I could see her eyes were shut, as if she were entranced by the power flowing through her. I opened my mouth to call her name.

Then I stopped myself, pausing to look back.

I could see the knot of red in the crowd, but from what I could tell, only three of my Valentines were standing. The rest had been brought down or dragged away.

I'd trying reasoning with Mom before. It hadn't worked.

And I wasn't just her daughter now, I realized. I was a Valentine queen, too. I had a responsibility to my suit. And so I closed my mouth. And I closed my fist. And I stepped forward and punched my mom in the face.

She went down faster and harder than I'd expected, the back of her head banging against the stage. My heart seemed to fall with her, stuttering in my chest.

"Sorry!" I said.

But the feeling in the room changed instantly. Without the oppressive force-field of her hex, it felt like I could breathe again.

I stepped toward Mom, taking a pair of golden handcuffs from my back pocket. I'd nabbed them from the Valentines armory for just this occasion. Gold was known to mute luck power, and if I could just get these onto Mom's wrist, maybe—

*Ow.*

Pain, like a bee sting.

I looked down to see a dart, its body and fletching protruding from my chest. I stumbled backward, looking around, and spied my assailant. He emerged from the wings of the stage wearing a gas mask and a white doctor's coat, and he held a black gun with an air cannister on the top.

I plucked the dart from my chest and threw it down,

plumbing my body for any signs of a toxin. Dizziness. Confusion. But I felt fine.

I brandished my sword and advanced, but the masked doctor neither fled nor brought up his gun again. He merely cocked his head, and I had a feeling he was smiling behind that mask.

"Greetings, Aggie. I am Doctor Gabardine," he said, his voice so muffled behind the mask I could barely hear him.

"You're another of my mom's minions, right?" It wasn't a hard guess. I could feel hex radiating from him—less then had come from Mom or from Shade, but it was there.

"Minion," he tutted. "I saved your mother's life. Now I'm about to save yours."

He took a step toward me and I raised my blade, touching its point to his sternum. Undeterred, he drew from his belt an instrument that looked like a metal blade with a pistol grip. A medical bone saw. He brought it up and dashed it against my sword blade, knocking it away from his chest.

"You want to fight? Good. It'll be interesting."

It *would* be interesting, I thought, but not for him. Tired of banter, I advanced, flaring charm.

Only, no charm flared. The warmth in my hands, a feeling that had become as familiar as my own heartbeat, was gone. I looked at my left palm and saw that the light in my pip had gone dark.

"Oh, I forgot to mention," Gabardine said. "That dart contained a solution of gold. Your charm will be repressed for several hours, at least. So about that fight we were having…"

Seconds ago, I had been a goddess queen.

Suddenly, I was just a teenage girl facing a much larger

man. He strode toward me, swinging widely and methodi-cally with his saw, like a baseball batter warming up.

I held the sword out in front of me in a hand that now felt numb with no charm to warm it. When the saw met my blade, the weapon clashed out of my hand. The next stroke sliced my arm. The saw was so sharp it barely hurt; it just made my stomach turn and my toes curl as a fat drop of blood plopped at my feet. I stumbled backward. The next slice nicked my elbow as I tried to cover up and defend myself.

I glanced around for help. Mom still lay on the stage, oblivious, maybe, but not unconscious. She lay spread out, as if mid-snow angel, her black pips flaring once more. She hadn't bothered standing up, but she was radiating hex again. The room seethed with it. I looked and saw no glimpses of red among the riotous crowd.

No help was coming. Not from the hearts. Not from Mom. Not from anyone.

I back-pedaled across the stage as Gabardine advanced, swinging his infernal saw like a farmer hacking wheat with a scythe.

I'd reached seventeen before I realized I was counting his slices.

Seventeen. My age.

The same age Joan of Arc was at the battle of Orléans, I remembered from AP history class. Maybe without powers, I was just a teenage girl. But Joan had been a teenage girl, too. And we were both warriors.

This time as Gabardine swung I stepped in, blocking his swinging arm and driving a knee into his crotch.

He crumpled, falling heavily to his knees, breath hissing in and out of his mask.

"I don't need luck to kick your ass," I said.

I ripped his mask off to see a smug, handsome face wracked with pain.

Before I could kick in his perfect white teeth, the air in the room shifted again. The effect was pronounced enough to nauseate me. The light changed, too, the colored columns of stage lights suddenly muted and suffused with a deep, pulsating purple.

I wheeled to find something had appeared just behind me at the center of the stage. A black obelisk. I could see the markings on it. Glyphs I couldn't read that nevertheless evoked thoughts of blood. Plague. Human sacrifice. And there was a familiar marking on there, too, repeated over and over.

Spades.

The voice inside the monolith rang in my mind. *Hello, Aggie. Welcome to the end,* it said.

Then out from behind the obelisk there emerged a figure. Small. A sprite? No. A little boy. A boy, with black pips on his hands. Hex hummed around him like a dark halo.

I squinted, trying to make out his features in the shifting stage lights.

For a second, I knew only that he was familiar. Then I placed him. It was the little boy Cleo the leprechaun had been taking care of, the one she had left in Deuce and Mina's care at the Hearts mansion while I went on my queen trial. But it couldn't be. That boy had been lucky, but he hadn't been a god. And he hadn't been evil, as far as I could tell. But an ominous feeling of hex hung around this kid, powerful as a lightning storm.

"Junior?" I said.

He blinked at my recognition, but did not smile.

"Sorry," he replied.

Before I could answer, *for what?* his hex flared, hitting me in the form of a stomach cramp so painful it doubled me over and left me gasping.

"It's a trap," the boy said, apologetic. "It was his plan. He's making us—" the boy glanced over his shoulder at the Spades obelisk, then seemed to think better of what he was saying and went silent.

The boy. The obelisk. Mom. Gallo. An army of possessed berserkers... We were grotesquely outgunned. I had to get my Valentines out of here, but a scan of the room revealed no exit signs. And no Valentines either, although the crowd still convulsed with violence, which gave me hope that at least some of them were still fighting.

I tried my charm again. Still, nothing. I couldn't help but think about all the things I could do with my power intact. Make an electrical breaker trip, plunging us into darkness. Cause a light fixture to fall from above and smash the obelisk. Make one of the guitar amps spark into an electrical fire, which would trip the sprinkler system, spraying the berserkers and making them snap out of their trance. My queen power could do any of those things. But I didn't have it.

What remained was my smarts, which, let's be honest, were formidable. But right now, my mind felt horribly empty.

The boy advanced on me. He held no weapons, but even with only his pips, he made a menacing figure, glaring at me with lowered brow like a little horror movie antichrist.

"Junior," I warned. "Whatever you're going to do, don't do it."

He continued toward me, undeterred.

"Junior!" I scolded, but still he came, his hex making the air around him crackle like static electricity.

His hex was so powerful I could feel it disrupting my brain, my ability to reason. As he drew close I panicked, stepped forward and shoved him. As I did, I somehow bonked him in the face.

He stumbled backward, and suddenly he looked like nothing but a stunned little boy.

"Junior?" said a low voice, then Gallo the Heart Slayer leapt onto the stage and knelt before the boy.

"It's you," he whispered. "What are you...? Where's your mom?"

*It's his kid,* I realized. *Junior is Gallo's son...*

The boy just looked at his dad, impassive. Blood snaked from his nose from where I'd banged into him, and Gallo swiped at it with one thumb, not so much removing it as smearing it across his upper lip.

Then Gallo turned to me, a protective rage in his eyes like none I'd ever seen.

"It's not my fault," I said quickly. "The kid is a Morbus. He..."

But one look at the Heart Slayer told me he wasn't up for an explanation. He was out for blood. And he strode toward me, swinging his spiked mace lazy circles.

I backpedaled a few steps, then hit something solid. Wheeling, I found Gabardine behind me, the bone saw glinting in his hand and a maniacal grin on his face.

He swiped at me with his saw and I dodged *one, two, three, four* of his blows—pretty good when he had luck and I didn't.

Before I could bolt and jump off the stage, Gallo grabbed me from behind.

I opened my mouth to say something clever, but he brought his massive knee up and slammed it into my pelvis. Pain rose in me, burning like a sun, and I collapsed to my knees with a whimper. He backhanded me. It stung, but I knew it could have been far worse. His closed fist would have knocked me out for sure. He was toying with me.

Gabardine kicked me from behind, his foot sending a shock of pain through my spine. As I fell forward, Gallo smacked me again, sending my sprawling across the stage, stars shooting across my vision. I tried to count them, but I couldn't even find the number one.

More pain shot through my body. Kicks, I guessed.

I tasted blood.

A foot stomped my left hand into the floor and I screamed, pain exploding from each finger. I balled up, the hand cradled to my chest, and shutting my eyes, just waiting, waiting for the pain to be over. But it got worse, throb-by-throb.

There were more blows, maybe, and more kicks, but my consciousness hardly registered them. My thoughts drifted.

To my dad. A doctor. He could have healed me, if he were alive.

To my mom, who would have helped me if she were herself. But she was so, so not herself anymore.

To Jack. Jack, who would have saved me, if... if...

It dawned on me incrementally that I was no longer being beaten, though the shouts and grunts, thuds and clashes of weapons still rang out around me. With great effort, I forced my eyes open and looked up.

Through blurred vision, I saw a red shape standing over me. A man. And as my vision came into focus, I saw that he was fighting, taking on Gallo, Gabardine, Shade, and an army of berserkers all at once, fighting like a cornered wolf and somehow, somehow, holding them all off.

"Aggie," he shouted. "If you can move, get to the back door. Get out! Now!"

I tried to obey. With a wheeze, I managed to get to my hands and knees and crawl like a baby toward the wing of the stage, leaving a trail of drooled blood behind me.

Looking up, I saw the exit sign, which seemed to float over a metal door in the distance. As I made my way toward it, grunting with each motion, and the sounds of fighting followed me: taunting, cursing, and the clink of metal-on-metal. I passed the edge of the curtain. Reached the foot of the exit door. Then from behind me there came a shout of pain. I collapsed with surprise, rolled on my side and looked back. My defender still stood over me, red sport coat flapping as he fought. Then he took a blow, stumbled backward and fell, hitting the metal door hard.

But it was not Jack I saw there, his face pale and contorted in pain, not Jack who had fought with all his being to defend me.

It was Deuce.

And he lay next to me now, a bone saw protruding from his chest.

# 45

## AGGIE

I couldn't count. I couldn't breathe. Pain washed over me in waves that had my hands shaking and my brow dripping sweat, and yet I felt as numb as if I were packed in ice.

With a trembling hand I reached out and grabbed the handle of the bone saw; the impulse to pull it out was stronger than the tug of *the work* had ever been. But Deuce grabbed my wrist and breathed.

"No, no, no."

He was right, of course. If I'd been thinking clearly, I'd have realized immediately that yanking the weapon free would just make him bleed out and die.

"Just... charm... me..." he hissed through bloody teeth.

I started to tell him I had no charm. But that would only make him despair, wouldn't it? So I just took his hand, slick with blood, and pressed my face against his shoulder. He trembled as shock set in. I held him, my chest heaving with silent tears.

I wanted to call for my mom, but when I inhaled to shout, the pain in my ribs felt like fire. And she wasn't herself anyway, she wouldn't answer.

I blinked against Deuce's shoulder, my eyelashes brushing his sport coat as I counted the blinks. A random memory came. Dad used to do this to me, when I was a girl. Butterfly kisses.

I reached twenty-three blinks and stopped. Not because I didn't want to start counting again. But because the energy in the room changed. I shifted so I could look up and saw four figures looming over me. Gallo. Gabardine. Shade. And the boy. Between their legs I glimpsed Mom, still lying on the stage, staring up at the lights and hexing. Mad. No help at all. The obelisk was in my vision, too. Somehow, it had moved closer than it was before. It had unaccountably moved positions, like an object in a dream.

The stone tower spoke to its minions.

*There is no greater work,* it said. *Than the sacrifice of a god. Strike them down, and revel in the hex.*

Weapons raised, hovering over us, ready to kill.

I was too beaten to even roll over, too exhausted to brace myself.

A roar came from Gallo's throat as he readied his mace to strike. But before he could bring the weapon down, *something,* some beast, leapt on his back, causing him to stumble sideways.

The other dark gods turned as more of the monsters

swept in and leapt on them as well, savaging them with claws and teeth. Grunting in pain, I managed to shift enough to see one clearly, and was disgusted to see it was in fact human. Or humanoid, anyway. The things moved on all fours, much more quickly than a human or even a dog, eerily fast. But they were indeed shaped like men and women, clad in dark leather armor. In the colored light of the concert hall it was hard to tell, but their faces looked slightly purplish. Their teeth—many now glistening with blood—were sharper than a human's, as were their fingernails. Some carried weapons. Oddly shaped, barbed swords. Short, jaggedly tipped spears. Chains with spikes imbedded in them. Gloves covered in razor blades.

They came on as fast and thick as a swarm of hungry ants. The wrongness of their movement and the brutality of their attack turned my stomach. And everyone—sycos, clones, civilians, and dark gods alike—fell back at their onslaught.

"Goblins," Deuce hissed next to me.

I might have blacked out for a moment. My head spun, my vision wavered. I felt outside of my body, then had the sensation of being sucked back into myself. I was being lifted, held like a baby in strong arms.

"Who did this to you?" his familiar voice growled in my ear, low and rough with emotion. I forced my eyelids open. When my vision came into focus, I saw him. Of course it was him.

"Jack," I whispered. I wasn't answering his question, I was saying his name. But he didn't understand.

"What Jack?" he demanded.

"Gallo."

"Impossible. He's dead."

He looked across the room and I saw the moment he spied his old nemesis. He paled, a fire sparking behind his eyes.

"Do it, Aggie," he said fiercely. "Make me your king and I'll avenge you."

"I..." I hesitated. Before I could formulate an answer, someone called my name.

"Aggie!" It was Mina.

Cobe, Dubs, Adelie and Abraham bounded up on the stage behind her. Blood streamed down Abraham's face and Mina's knuckles were mangled and steeped in crimson, but they all seemed to be whole.

"I'm okay," I breathed, responding to the concern on Mina's face.

The others had already put their backs to me and were fighting, holding of a resurgent phalanx of clones. Over their heads, I could see Mom getting to her feet, roused from whatever strange trance she'd been in. Already the balance of hex in the room shifted with her rise, like a changing of tides.

Beyond her, Gallo had seen us and was coming our way. That brutal killer, coming for me.

"Aggie," Jack said urgently. "Name your king,"

"Yes," Cobe added pointedly. "Name your king."

King and killer. Killer and king. Those were the words, the questions that had swirled around my mind for weeks. Now, amid all this chaos, I shut my eyes, leaned against Jack, and counted his heartbeats.

*One, two, three...* would I make it to twenty-three before Gallo arrived? Before the clones broke through our defenses? *Four, five, six...* This puzzle. This test. There had to be a way through it. A solution. Every equation, every riddle, every test had a solution. Only I didn't have luck enough to find it. *Seven, eight, nine...*

"Aggie," Jack shouted. "Come on. The window is closing."

I knew what he meant. The window of opportunity. The chance for me to make him king, to grant him the power he needed to protect us before Gallo and Mom and the boy and the army of clones crushed us.

But for some reason, my uncharmed brain got hung up on the idea of an actual window. The one in King Michael's bedroom. The one I'd found open on the night Michael was found dead. Something had always bothered me about that window, and I'd never quite been able to pinpoint what it was.

*The window is closing.*

I thought of one of my vocab words: *steek.* To close. Make fast. That was one of my OCD ticks, too. Shutting things. Making sure they were shut and locked. I always made sure windows were closed before I went to sleep.

Always.

"I checked that window," I said aloud.

No one seemed to hear me. The rest of the suit was caught up with fighting off clones. Mina knelt next to Deuce, charming to keep him alive, but he was too pale. He was dying.

"What?" Jack said, irritated.

"I checked the window. I don't really remember doing it, but would never have gone to bed without checking it," I said.

Jack frowned.

I went on, "which means, it was opened from the inside."

"What are you talking about?" Jack glanced uneasily toward Gallo once more.

When he looked back to me, our eyes met.

And what I saw in them then confirmed something I'd wondered about, dreaded, and longed for, all at once.

Jack did have feelings for me. Real ones. I realized in that moment what I hadn't quite believed before—that a boy like him could love a girl like me. But it was obvious now, his concern, his caring plain as writing on his face. Cupid's arrow or no, he had genuinely loved me.

He would not have abandoned me to become the king's wife, the bride of a man he hated.

He would never have let me marry Michael unless he intended on killing him all along.

"It was you," I whispered.

"What—?" he started, then some unspoken communication passed between us and he stopped. He understood what I was saying. And his silence, the look on his face, the agony of a good boy caught doing something terrible, told me all I needed to know.

"Aggie," he said, his voice so low only I could hardly hear it over the din of the fighting. "Yes. Okay? I've been meaning to tell you, but... I came back in after everyone was asleep. I snuck through the house, into the bedroom, and I killed him while you were sleeping, then I went out the window. Okay? I did it for you. I wasn't going to let you be his wife, not even for one night. Not after what he did to Aubra."

I wanted to speak, to answer. But I had no breath. And no words. Not even vocab ones.

Finally, I managed to say: "So the shimmer I saw. That must've been... Seemor?"

Of course Jack would have left that little sprite creeper to watch over me.

Jack nodded his affirmation, another puzzle piece clicking into place. It was so obvious. I'd been blind.

"We can rule together, Aggie," Jack pressed. "It's what the Ace wants. It's what I want. Everything I'm doing is for that —for us. For us to become king and queen—of everything."

I felt his fervency. The arms he held me with trembled with it. His voice shook. His eyes burned with earnestness. "It can be perfect, Aggie," he finished. "Just say the words. Make me your king."

Jack Valentine. His eyes, the blue of hottest flame. His lips as red as blood. His face, the visage of an angel. I took him in, as if for the last time. I could feel the dark gods drawing closer, the impact of their attack seconds away. I wished I were still counting, but I'd lost count. I'd lost track of everything.

"For my king..." Despite the pain of breathing, I spoke loud enough for everyone to hear. "For my king... I choose... Deuce."

## AGGIE

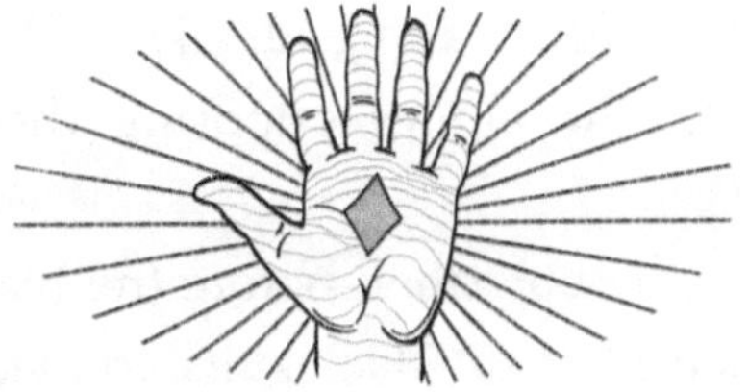

For a second after I said Deuce's name, I thought Jack would drop me. Pressed against his chest as I was, I felt him deflate as the air left his lungs. He looked into my eyes and I braced myself for anger. What I saw instead was a different emotion. Hurt. And something else much harder to name. Much deeper.

His lips moved as if he would speak, but he didn't. Instead, he slowly knelt and set me down on the floor next to Deuce.

"Jack..." I whispered, but I didn't know what to say next. Part of me wanted to take it back, to say *never mind, you can be my king.* Another part wanted to apologize. But there were no words, so social script to follow in this uncharted territory. And there was no time to talk, anyway. Battle raged all around us.

Cobe's face twisted with rage.

"Deuce?" he demanded. "You're kidding. He's the second lowest ranking Valentine. When Ten gets back…"

But I wasn't listening to him. I was watching Jack as he drew his sword and charged into the fray, snarling and hacking and hexing with such ferocity that the enemies, both clone and god, parted and fell back before him. Most of the concert goers had already fled to the exits, and the few remaining huddled in corners of the room or in booths or under tables, hiding and coughing.

But the tide of the battle had shifted. The goblins seemed to be fighting alongside Jack, and with their combined efforts, the clones opposing them either died or ran.

On the stage, the boy stood before the black obelisk and spoke into a microphone. "Black suits, to me," he said, with and air of authority that was creepy coming from a little kid.

Gallo had been about to meet Jack in battle. At the boy's words, his grin of blood-lust wavered, and he looked up to the stage like a dog at a master whose command he was loathe to follow. But he only hesitated for a second before laying into Jack with a snarl. Their weapons clashed, and I was sure with Gallo's power and strength, he would take charge of the duel in seconds. But instead Jack, in his rage, pushed his enemy back toward a set of doors that led into another room.

I looked at Deuce. His breathing was shallow and his skin pale, but his eyes, looking back at me, were bright and clear. I realized now that the saw jutting out of him was more in his shoulder than his chest, the wound serious, but perhaps not deadly—if we were lucky. I took his hand and tried charming. My power stirred then, just a little, and I watched some color return to his cheeks.

"Did you mean it?" he asked. "About me being king?"

"Are you ready to be king?" I countered.

His laugh turned into a cough. "Definitely not."

"Well, I meant it."

He grew serious. "Then I'm ready."

Me as queen? Deuce as king? Maybe Cobe was right. Maybe I was destroying our suit. But from somewhere inside me, maybe from the well of energy where the urge for *the work* emanated from, I knew this was right.

I knew from my reading that kings didn't need to undergo a trial like queens did in order to ascend to their new rank—a bit of systemic sexism I intended to remedy. But I wasn't sure if I could elevate Deuce without the obelisk present and without the Ace's blessing. I had to try, though. It took luck to survive with a serious wound, and having king power was the best chance Deuce had. And so, I squeezed Deuce's hand and let the charm flow. As I did, I shaped it with intention: *make Deuce our king.*

*But,* I silently amended, *keep me as high queen, okay?*

I was a feminist, after all. I wasn't about to hand the highest power in the suit to a male, not even Deuce.

The charm worked through me, making my body tingle and my hands burn pleasantly. There was a moment of resistance I'd never experienced before, like pushing on a stuck door, as if the luck magic were fighting me. But I pushed again, focusing and hardening my will, and the resistance gave way. Energy poured through me, bright and hot and liquid, illuminating every cell and synapse of my being. It was charm on a vast, macro scale, charm like I'd never felt it before.

Deuce sucked a sharp breath beside me. When I let go of his hand, his pips glowed so brightly they hurt my eyes. His skin, which had been pallid with blood loss, now glowed with ruddy vibrance.

Mina came to my side, catching her breath. "We have the chance to get away," she said. "We should take it."

She was right, I saw. The battle between the remaining clones, black suits, and goblins had shifted to a smaller, adjoining bar space, where Jack was dueling Gallo. *We should stay. We should help him*, I thought.

And yet, though I felt better, the ache in my ribs told me I couldn't keep fighting. And I'd led my Valentines into a meat grinder already. I couldn't ask them to risk their lives for Jack, who had betrayed our suit by killing Michael.

I wanted to help Jack. But I had to be queen first.

Of course, he wasn't my only concern. There was Mom, too. I'd searched for her long enough that I wasn't going to let her go now, when she was so close.

My gaze swept to the stage. I found her on her feet, standing before the obelisk with the rest of her suit—Gabardine, Shade, and the boy. *They're multiplying*, I thought. *Not good...*

The men were holding off a half-dozen attacking goblins while mom stood by the obelisk, hexing.

Our eyes met, and I waited with held breath for her response. The tiny, tight-lipped smile she used to give me at our little shared jokes. The look of frowny reproach she saved for when I'd really screwed up. Maybe even a tear of remorse. But the expression she gave me wasn't her own. It was that of a wild thing. A deer watching a hiker, taut and wary.

*She's not her,* I thought again. *I'm losing her...* The thought left me feeling bleak and alone, as empty as Mom's stare.

"Parent!" I called.

I thought I saw something, just for an instant. A flicker of recognition. A subtle twitch of her lips or a tiny quirk of her eyebrows. Then she startled, as if at the call of some voice only she could hear. She turned to the obelisk. She shouted something I couldn't hear, then she and all her fellow Morbuses reached out and touched it the stone column, and in one surreal instant, they were all just gone, blinking out of existence, leaving nothing behind but an empty stage.

"Mom," I said, at once pleading and lamenting.

"Mina is right, Your Majesty," Cobe barked in my ear. "Let's go."

I glanced toward the other room once more, where Jack was fighting for his life. Then I glanced to Deuce. The pain in his face reflected the conflict I felt within myself. He was sweating, his breathing was shallow, and his shirt was soaked with blood.

*God save the king,* I thought. *And in this room, I am the god.*

"Alright. Let's go," I said, struggling to my feet as Dubs and Mina helped up Deuce.

And for the second time that day, I left Jack behind.

## 47

---

## JACK

**H**ex and charm together should defeat hex alone, Jack told himself, as his sword clashed against the steel handle of Gallo's mace. And yet, he couldn't quite seem to get the upper hand.

*Distracted.* His mind kept flashing back to Aggie. The way her lips had looked when she formed the name *Deuce*. Her hand, clasping onto Deuce's.

Maybe she didn't want Deuce romantically. Maybe her decision was just a rejection of the bad luck pulsing through Jack's left hand. Still, it hurt. And it infuriated him. His mind couldn't help but dart down a thousand different rabbit holes, imagining whispered secrets, subtle looks, stolen kisses. Of course there was nothing secret about Deuce's feelings for Aggie. There never had been. He was always getting her coffee, helping her, trying to make her laugh. Even when Jack and Aggie were a full-on couple, and even though he was Jack's best friend, Deuce hadn't been able to stop himself from pursuing Aggie. It had been out in the open all along. It was Jack's own fault for underestimating his friend, a mistake he'd never make again.

Pain exploded through his left hand as the head of Gallo's mace clipped it. Hot blood dripped from his fingers and thudding pain raced up his arm, momentarily dimming his vision. But a surge of charm muted the pain and a flaring of hex righted his focus.

Damned Gallo. He was strong for a dead man, Jack thought, bringing his sword back up with a flourish.

Gallo paused and pointed to his eyepatch.

"Right," Jack said. "Last time we met I took your eye. This time I'm going to take the other one."

Gallo gave a bloodthirsty grin. He shook his head, pointed to the eyepatch again, then to Jack's face.

"Oh, you're going to take mine?" Jack scoffed.

Gallo nodded.

*Take it. I've seen too much already in this life,* he wanted to say.

But he was too winded to shout over the din of battle all around them. His goblins fought bravely, but with all the bad luck gods in this place, the hex was not in their favor. The clones had managed to push them back and they seemed to be coalescing around him now, the battle winding toward its final, deciding moments.

Which would be his death, if he didn't do something.

Jack spied an extension cord running across the floor, to one of the light arrays on a DJ booth. Parrying a particularly savage overhead swing from Gallo, Jack charmed, aiming his intention at the cord. When Gallo stepped into it, the thing caught his toe. Gallo barely stumbled, but it was distraction enough for Jack to lunge in. His sword tip found the meat of Gallo's quadricep and the big man halted with a grimace.

But Jack felt a change in the room, then. With two different marks on his hands, he had the strange feeling of experiencing both aspects of luck energy at once. It was something like being able to tug at both ends of a rope during a game of tug-of-war. For a second, he'd used his energy to tug the balance toward the red, toward charm. Now, hex yanked back—hard.

Before Jack could jerk his sword free from his enemy's leg, Gallo countered, bringing his mace around in a big, whooshing arc. Jack charmed and ducked so that he took only a glancing blow to the head, rather than the direct hit that would have brained him. Nevertheless, the shot was enough to drop him.

When the world spun back into focus, he saw Gallo standing over him. It was a replay of the last time they'd met. Gallo had straddled him, ready to kill, and Jack had been clever enough to strike him a nearly deadly blow instead. But now, all cleverness was lost in the spinning of his head, the nausea twisting his gut, and the thought of Aggie, those words of hers, *I choose Deuce.*

The sword Jack had borrowed from his goblins was gone from his hand, dropped when Gallo had dropped him. He reached for his holster and remembered his gun was gone, too.

Gallo hefted the mace onto his shoulder, like a lumberjack preparing to delimb a tree.

Using what meager focus remained to him, Jack tried to

look into himself, to assess what reserves of charm he had left. But it was no use. With all the hex in this place, his charm had ebbed from a bonfire to a candle flame.

Gallo grinned, raised his mace. This was a movie Jack had seen before...

Then, his own thoughts echoed back to him. *All the hex in this place...*

Jack had been working on learning to use hex, but he still used charm predominately, especially when battling against someone with hex. It was habit. Muscle memory. But charm was not the only power he had.

*Use hex. Embrace it,* he thought, though the words came from such a deep place inside himself that they almost seemed to come from somewhere, and some*one* else entirely.

It was like flipping switch inside himself, like shifting a train from one track to the other. Charm—to hex. And as Jack made that adjustment in his mind, he felt broad vistas of power open up before him. His left hand hummed to life with a numbing pain, as if he were gripping a palmful of dry ice.

Gallo raised the mace, ready to kill.

And Jack hexed, swinging his injured hand in an arc above himself—and splattering blood in Gallo's one good eye.

The black jack growled, scrubbing at his face with the back of his hand. It was quick, just a moment's distraction, and Jack had no means to counterattack. His body felt too leaden even to crawl away. Though he groped, no weapons came to hand. He kicked upward, his foot catching Gallo in the groin. But it must not have been a direct hit, for though Gallo winced, he didn't crumble.

And too soon, the blood was out of his eye. He raised the mace again.

This was it. Truly the end...

Then a blurred shape streaked in and knocked Gallo sideways. It was Varsmith.

Though the goblin priest was nearly as tall as the black jack, he'd jumped onto Gallo's shoulders, crouching like a gargoyle atop a building, glomming into him—sharp teething sinking into Gallo's head, legs locked around Gallo's neck, claws raking across his face. Top-heavy now, Gallo stumbled, then fell.

He hit the ground with enough force to shake the whole room. When he came back up, he'd gotten free of the goblin, but at that moment another change washed over the room. Hex receded, like a wave sliding down the sand. The change was so sudden and so profound Jack guessed what must have happened even without seeing it. The obelisk of spades had disappeared, and the dark gods with it.

Jack felt his charm rushing back, like the changing of a tide.

He fought to his feet, buoyed by fortune and ready to kill.

Gallo, alone and bleeding, gave Jack one last snarl, a look that promised future vengeance, then turned and fled.

# 48

## JACK

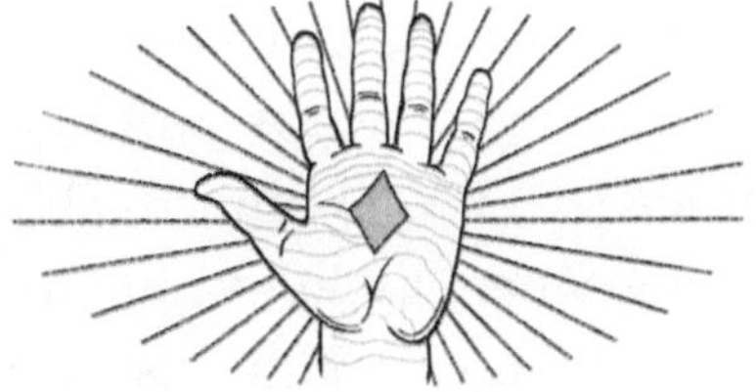

His head still ringing from the battle, his wounded hand cradled against this chest, Jack followed Varsmith and the other goblins through a pitch black tunnel that smelled of wet earth and decaying meat. The only illumination came from the golden key in Varsmith's hand, and Jack tried not to think about which leprechaun he had killed to get it. Soon they came to a low, square door. It must have been made of stone, because it made the grinding sound of a mill wheel when it moved and it required four strong goblins to push it ajar. When it was opened, the goblins stepped aside and Varsmith gestured politely for Jack to pass through first.

His training and his instincts tugged at him, reminding

him not to trust this goblin, to be wary of tricks and traps. But his pips, both the dark and the red, seemed to draw him onward. So Jack forced himself to duck through the low doorway, the coin necklace jangling as he went.

He emerged in a space that at first seemed otherworldly, and for a second Jack wondered if the goblins had somehow smuggled him through the rift. The vast, stone-walled chamber resembled the throne room of a palace, with vaulted ceilings, granite pillars, and statues of robed figures peering down from shadowy recesses. Moonlight shone through a dome high above, its shafts igniting a constellation of slow shifting dust motes and illuminating a row of tall, stained glass windows. It was a church. But when Jack looked where the alter should have been, there stood a large throne instead. And where the cross would have been hung, there loomed instead a colossal bronze rabbit's head with a smooth, empty plane where its face would have been.

Jack heard the goblins emerging from the tunnel behind him and glanced back to see that they were coming out of one of the church's burial vaults. Varsmith came and stood next to him. A macabre entrance the leprechaun key had chosen, Jack thought.

"Does the space please you, your worship?" Varsmith asked, his sharp teeth glinting in the moonlight. "We took great care in choosing a stronghold that was highly defensible but would also honor your position."

"Where are we?" Jack asked.

"Still in Detroit," Varsmith said, following as Jack walked forward, taking in the space. It held all sorts of strange touches, Jack noticed. Tapestries with obelisks on them. Statues of ancient luck gods with pips on their hands in place of saints. One of the stained glass windows depicted a bloody scene of a king being ripped apart. *The sundering of Uthule,* a glass banner at the bottom of the window read. Jack shivered. He found himself walking up the aisle, toward the black throne that waited in place of the altar. He got the sudden sense that he was walking through a dream. That the ace would appear at any moment with fire in her eyes and admonish him.

But this was no dream.

"...we brought this throne through the rift for you at great cost," Varsmith was saying. "It isn't the lord's original throne, of course. That one was destroyed when his castle was sacked. But goblin scholars have worked hard to recreate it with as much accuracy as possible. I think you'll find when you sit on it..."

Jack noticed that each of the chair's legs were in the shape of obelisks, and each had a different mark upon it—heart, diamond, spade and club.

He sat, sinking into its soft red leather seat. It was surprisingly comfortable, and at the release of his joints, he felt something inside his chest release, too, though he wasn't sure if he would fall asleep or cry.

*Aggie.*

*She'd passed him over.*

*She'd chosen Deuce.*

Pain clenched in his gut, like the hot twisting of magma in the earth.

Of course, Aggie was afraid of him. Afraid of what he'd become. Afraid of his transformation and of what his growing power would mean for her friends in the Valentines. Deuce was a weak, safe choice. Easily understood and easily controlled—even by a queen who was only a high school girl.

Of course, it scared her that he had killed Michael. How could she understand that Michael's demise had been of Michael's own making, and a long time coming? She might have been angry that he hadn't told her the truth sooner, that he'd played along with the charade of searching for King Michael's killer. But the sham investigation had given her an excuse to bring him back into the Valentine house, and it had given him a chance to spend time with her. To make her feel comfortable enough, he'd hoped, to choose him as her king. He thought he'd have a chance to pin the assassination on someone else, or at least make her understand why he did it.

And Galen... Jack had not been the one to kill Galen, though he doubted he could convince Aggie of the truth now.

Yes, he understood every reason why she was afraid, why she'd passed him over and denied him the power he was due. But that didn't make the pain he felt any less. For she was denying the love they shared, too.

*She will have to marry him,* Jack thought. *Marry Deuce and not me...*

At every breath he felt pain, like a great knot of barbed wire in his chest. *I'm closer to what I've wanted than ever before,* he thought with a bitter smile. *And I'm more miserable than ever.*

And yet the only way was forward. There was no going back.

In a game of chess, if you couldn't take the queen, what would you do? You'd take every piece *but* the queen. Leave her defenseless and alone.

*When everyone else is gone, when it's just her and me...* he thought, but the rest of the thought didn't quite coalesce.

"Your Worship?" Varsmith said, and Jack realized the goblin must have been talking for a while. The rest of the goblin horde was there, too, their dark, yellowish eyes gleaming in the dim light as they knelt, watching him. Waiting.

"You are our god," Varsmith said. "What is your command?"

What was his command? What should his next move be? Gallo had emerged as Rachel's companion to ruin the Spades suit for him. And his advancement in the Hearts was blocked, at least for now. That left the Diamantes and the Blackovers...

Jack's gaze drifted across the goblins' faces again. He saw their adoration. Their avarice. Their fervency. *They would do anything for me,* he thought. *So let's see what they can do...*

# 49

# MOLLY

Molly had spent the night in Diamond Queen's penthouse apartment, one of the finest in Monaco. The next morning, DQ informed Molly she had arranged a dinner with the Kleppers and the Diamantes to celebrate the impending merger—and Molly was to be the surprise guest of honor.

To prepare, Diamond Queen had taken Molly shopping and brought her to her own personal stylist, where she'd gotten a manicure and a haircut and color. They'd picked up smoothies together and drank them in the back of DQ's limo while blasting one of the goddess' unreleased singles. Then they'd returned to DQ's penthouse apartment, where the superstar had decked Molly out in glittering jewelry and three stylists gotten Molly all dressed and ready. It reminded Molly of the makeover Aggie received when joining the Valentines, a story that, when she heard it, had made Molly ache with envy. Now, she was the one living the fairytale.

Yes, she felt like a princess. But as she and DQ rode the mirrored elevator to the 49th floor of Odeon Tower, her nerves and insecurity returned.

"Why are you doing this for me?" Molly asked DQ, for perhaps the third time.

The superstar crossed her arms and looked Molly up and down. "I'd like to say it's just to keep the merger on track. But hell, kid, I'm a Leo. I'd do it just to see the look on Danusia's face. I love the girl, but I like to keep my suit members on their toes. You'll find that out soon enough."

Molly smiled nervously. As she did she felt a warmth in her hands, as if she were holding a mug of tea. She looked down at the red diamond marks glowing there. Pips, Aggie called them. God, it felt good when they glowed.

DQ leaned in to Molly conspiratorially. "Want to learn a trick of mine?" she said.

Molly nodded.

"Okay. Now don't go blabbing about this to Rolling Stone or anything," DQ said. "I don't want to be known as one of those stars who's obsessed with self-help affirmations or any of that malarkey."

She crossed her arms over her chest and placed the palm of each hand on the opposite arm, then turned to face the elevator's mirrored wall.

"Go ahead," she prompted, and Molly followed suit. "Now look at yourself in the mirror, and as you speak, feel the luck power flowing into your hands. Repeat after me. I am worthy. I am beautiful. I am powerful. I am lucky. I am a goddess."

Molly spoke the words, the star's incantation, and as she did she felt an incredibly satisfying warmth radiate from her palms and into her body, a feeling like the intoxicating heat of liquor in your chest, but healthy, joyous. Tears welled in Molly's eyes. She blinked them away and looked at herself.

The patch of dry, reddish skin on her chin and neck wasn't gone entirely. Even under the perfect makeup job DQ's stylists had done, it was still visible, a subtle stain. Maybe it would never go away completely, Molly thought. But it didn't matter. Because her eyes shone like arctic ice. Her skin radiated light. Her hair was sleek and perfect as something out of a priceless painting. Light seemed to dance off her body, like she was some sort of a metaphysical disco ball, a celestial being. Like she was a diamond.

DQ gave Molly a smile. "How does it feel?"

"Good," Molly exhaled, nodding.

"Good," DQ echoed. "You're my girl now, little Black-Eyed Pea. This is just the beginning. I know none of this seems real, and you probably don't feel like you deserve all this, but—"

"No," Molly interrupted, catching her own eyes in the mirror. "I *do* deserve it."

The elevator chimed and the doors whooshed open.

The two demigoddesses strode through a small crowd of lavishly dressed people, and DQ swept a pair of champagne classes from the tray of a passing waiter.

They found the rest of their suit members out on a huge veranda with an incredible view of the city and the ocean beyond. It boasted a pool, complete with a waterfall and a two-story slide.

*This is the life I was meant to live,* Molly thought wistfully.

Danusia was talking to the senior Klepper, who was clad in a white suit, and Seth, who despite the elegant surroundings wore a pair of camo cargo shorts and a tattered tank top with a Union Jack on it. Seth caught sight of Molly before anyone else and gave her a grin.

"I'm sure we can get past this one sticking point and close this deal," Danusia was saying. "I'm having my team drawing up a list of other potential CEOs now. Or in a pinch, I would be willing to—"

"The sticking point," Diamond Queen interrupted grandly, "is unstuck."

Everyone turned to DQ and Molly. If the Queen of Diamonds had been counting on a reaction from Danusia, she must have been disappointed, because the Jill's face remained completely expressionless as she took Molly in. But Tristaine and Tina-Ten's jaws dropped.

"Our Molly has agreed to accept the position of CEO," Diamond Queen said. "And we already have our PR team working on the announcement. We ought to get quite a lot of press out of it—she'll be the youngest CEO in Fortune 500 history."

"Right," the elder Klepper muttered. Clearly, he wasn't in favor of Molly's elevation to the role of CEO, either.

But Seth was nodding and clapping. "That's so dope."

Molly smiled at him and gave a little wave, showing everyone the diamond that glowed on the palm of her hand. And at last, the look of shock and rage Molly had been waiting for appeared on Danusia's lovely face.

**50**

---

**AGGIE**

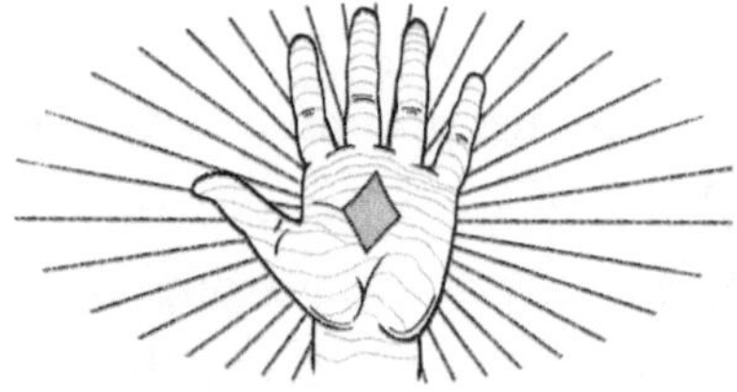

The SAT!

I sat up from the floor of the Valentine mansion master suite where I slept, every muscle and bone in my body protesting with pain at the movement. The clock on the bedside table read 7:16AM. I still had time to get to the 8AM test—if I hurried.

As I rose, a pair of heads popped up—one from the bed and one from the floor on the far side of the bed. It was Mina and Deuce. We'd given Deuce, the most injured of us, the bed for the night while Mina and I bunked on the floor on either side of him to keep watch. Ironically, after looking us both over, the Valentine medic had stitched Deuce up and pronounced that as long as he kept it clean, the stab wound in his shoulder was probably less serious than the beating I'd taken.

But after what had happened to King Michael, we weren't taking any chances.

"You've gotta be kidding," Deuce rubbed his bleary eyes. "You're seriously going to take a test today... after... you know... yesterday?"

"Do I look like I'm being facetious?" I demanded.

Mina side-eyed him. "She's Aggie. Of course she's not going to miss her test."

"Couldn't you register for a later date?" Deuce asked.

"And risk missing the early admissions deadlines?" I said. "Never."

Deuce laughed, shaking his head. "Okay, fair. But you're going to quit with the vocab words after the test, right?"

"What? Is my sesquipedalian vocabulary becoming irksome?" I chirped.

Deuce just groaned and stood up from the bed. "I'll brew some coffee."

"And I'll snag some breakfast bars," Mina said.

❦

The trip to the testing center passed as a series of long yawns between sips of coffee. Deuce, demoted from driver to DJ because of his injury, insisted on playing Mozart.

"It makes you smarter," he claimed.

"It makes *babies* smarter," Mina said. Then added, with some irony, "Your Majesty."

Deuce shook his head in wonder. "I'm never going to get used to that."

"Technically, we have to get married before..." I felt my

face flushing and went silent. Honestly, I hadn't thought about that aspect of making Deuce king yet. Marrying Michael had clearly been a formality, nothing more. But Deuce was one of my very best friends. It would be different. And... weird.

But when he glanced over at me from the passenger seat, I could see the gratitude in his face. Deuce was one person who'd never have tried to become king—had never tried to move up in rank at all. Which made him the perfect choice. He would be a nice king. A sweet king. A good king.

Whether two of us were strong enough to keep our crowns—that was another question.

At the testing site we said our goodbyes. Deuce as already feeling tired and Mina promised to get him settled in back at the mansion then come to pick me up when I was finished. They wished me luck—without a hint of humor—and left.

Like a sleepwalker, I went through the motions of getting checked in, finding my testing cubicle, sitting down. The place was utterly silent except for the buzzing of an electric clock on the wall, the breathing of my fellow students, and the occasional click of a computer mouse or creak of a chair.

It made me think of mom. Of how she'd described being kidnapped by the Spades obelisk and kept in a small, silent room as a part of their brainwashing processes. Which, in turn, made me think of the last time I'd seen her. How she'd been. Not possessed as she'd been initially after her imprisonment. But definitely not herself. At some point, would I have to accept that she just wasn't her anymore, that she would never be herself again?

No. I'd never accept that.

And yet, people kept changing, didn't they? Molly had

become obsessed with popularity and had gotten weird to the point where she literally stabbed my mom in the back. Claudette had gone from being a bully to being sort of a friend. And Jack... *Jack.* Had he changed? Or had I just been blind to the truth about him from the beginning? Selfish. Reckless. Obsessed with his own destiny. Those were all ways I'd heard him described, early-on. All warnings I'd ignored.

And yet here I was, thinking about him again. Missing him.

But how could things ever be like they were between us now that I knew he'd killed King Michael even as I slept in the same bed?

I could love so many things about Jack. His beauty. His dry humor. His dogged loyalty to his friends. The way his fingertips slipped down the inside of my arm when we kissed. But I could never love a killer. Could I?

I blinked and realized I'd been staring at the reading passage for God knew how long without even grokking the first sentence. *Jeez, girl. Focus. Stick to the strategy. Seventy-five seconds per question.* I started reading. But halfway into the first paragraph, I was thinking of Jack again. Of that night in his apartment when we were drinking to summon Lorcan. Of that first time I took his hand at the Clubs brewery. Of our first kiss.

*No,* I shook my head, trying to snap myself back into the present.

But then I thought of Galen. Jack had confessed to killing Michael, but not him. Galen was a boy, a two. He was no threat. Had Jack really killed him, too? No. Maybe I'd been naïve before, but I still couldn't believe Jack would do something like that, especially when he didn't have a motive.

Which meant there was still a killer out there somewhere.

*Okay. Really. Focus.*

But my stomach gurgled loudly. I was hungry, I realized. After last night's battle, one measly breakfast bar wasn't going to cut it.

*Ignore it. Read.*

I tried. But I was nervous now, counting words instead of reading them.

I groaned, my head falling into my hands. From all around came a chorus of *shhhh* and I looked up to see the proctor watching me with a corvine look of warning. I scrubbed my hands over my face and turned back to the passage on the screen.

My whole body ached from the beating I'd taken. I was starving. Thirsty. Heartbroken. Traumatized. Preoccupied. Lost.

My choices were to give up, fail the test and lose my shot at going to a great college, or...

I flared charm, the power coursing through me like liquid fire. And I started clicking answers without even reading them.

My heart beat faster at the wrongness of what I was doing. Aggie Van Der Graaf would never, ever cheat on a test. But I wasn't just Aggie Van Der Graaf anymore, was I? I was Aggie, demigoddess, Queen of the Valentines.

And queens fight to win.

# 51

## CLEO

Cleo stepped through the leprechaun tunnel door and into the dim interior of a truck stop diner. The place was mostly empty. A few taciturn men in Carhart coats or dingy overalls sat alone, regarding cups of black coffee and plates in various states of emptying. Cleo was not just the only leprechaun in the place, she was also the only woman, except for a waitress with dark circles under her eyes. And Carlotta, the former Blackover.

Although they were technically sisters in arms now, the sight of Carlotta still sent a shiver through Cleo. The woman might have given up her queenhood, but she still had luck power, and Cleo imagined an aura of ill luck and ill deeds still clung to her.

Still, she pretended to be at ease as she pulled chair from the table, turned it around and sat in it backwards, as she preferred to do.

"Well..." Cleo started, prepared to lead with a joke about Carlotta's lack of friends, since she sat alone. But Carlotta cut her off.

"I'm sorry."

The leprechaun stiffened. "About what?"

"About the boy." At those three words, the usual piss and vinegar drained out of Cleo, she felt herself slump forward against the chair back. She usually fought hard to keep up an impenetrable veneer in front of others, even her fellow Shastaryan. But some griefs were too keen to hide.

"Yeah," she said. "It's a hell of a thing. All I wanted was to save him from the life of black luck. But he ended up touching that damned Spades obelisk because of me."

Carlotta took a slow sip of coffee. "The obelisk might have been calling to him for some time. It might have found him with or without you. You shouldn't be too hard on yourself."

Cleo shook her head bitterly. "No. It's my fault he's what he is," Cleo said. "Somehow, I'm going to make it right."

Carlotta nodded. "Then you're in the right place."

Cleo knew the *place* she referred to wasn't this Detroit Coney Island, a greasy spoon out of an out of an Edward Hopper painting. She meant the order. The Shastaryan.

Cleo hoped she was right. She had joined the order almost five years before. She'd opposed the existence of luck gods on principle, back then. Now that she'd had numerous occasions to see them in action, she hated them even more, although she'd done little enough as a Shastaryan member so far except move some items from place to place and go to a few meetings. After what had happened to Junior, however, she had a feeling all that might change. Alone, one leprechaun would have little recourse to get the boy back. But working with the Shastaryan, maybe there was a chance...

Cleo glanced around for the waitress, who was nowhere to be seen. "Jesus, what do you have to do to get a cup of coffee around here? Do a pole dance?"

"Everything comes when it is meant to," Carlotta said.

Cleo fought not to roll her eyes. If there was one thing she couldn't stand, it was philosophizing. To some, the Shastaryan became like a religion. She supposed it made sense, as it involved gods—or at least, the downfall of gods. Still, it rankled Cleo to see a former queen of ill fortune spouting platitudes.

At last the waitress appeared and set a cup of coffee down in front of Cleo. She offered a menu, but Cleo waved it away, and the waitress departed.

Carlotta was looking at the time on her phone. "Where the hell is she?" she muttered.

Cleo didn't bother asking *who*. In truth, she was beyond caring who Carlotta had invited. She'd have much preferred to be elsewhere, to keep chasing after Junior. When he was spirited to Detroit she'd had to take a leprechaun door to follow, but she'd had no way to visualize his actual location, so she couldn't find him. No doubt he'd have been in the middle of a nest of hex gods anyway. Instead she'd come here, to a restaurant she'd eaten at once with her no-good brother, and called Carlotta.

Now, she took a sip of bitter coffee. She preferred it with

cream and sugar, but was punishing herself by drinking it black.

"I heard your old friend Jack Valentine is trying to shoot the moon, get all the power of all the suits for himself," she said.

At this, Carlotta's expression darkened. She sipped her own coffee, but didn't answer.

"Why not let him do the work for us?" Cleo continued. "Let him wipe out all the other gods, gather up their power. Then all we have to do is take him out and it's finished."

"We could," Carlotta said. "But by then, Jack would no longer be a demigod. He'd be a true god. Nearly unstoppable."

"They beat Uthule the first time around," Cleo pointed out.

"Sure," Carlotta said. "But before they did, he wiped out armies. Laid waste to continents. He unleashed such horror on the other side of the rift there are still peri who will kill you just for saying his name. No, the only choice is to stop him soon, while he's still building his power. Him and all the other luck gods."

"Well, as long as I can help Junior along the way, you can count me in," Cleo said. "But it's going to take more than just the two of us and a handful of peri, most of whom are stuck on the wrong side of the rift..." Cleo trailed off as bell above the front door dinged.

The young woman who entered wore a red coat over a white turtleneck, and one of her arms was in a sling. Her dark hair was cut in a chin-length bob, and her lipstick was the color of an overripe strawberry. She probably only stood five feet tall and was slender enough that a hard breeze might have made her stumble. But as she caught sight of them and strode toward the table, Cleo saw the power that was in her. With every step she remained perfectly over her center of gravity, as only a dancer—or a fighter—could be. A feeling of charm came with her, as if she were riding in on a warm breeze.

The young woman reached their table, pulled out her chair and sat with perfect posture and a small, impertinent smile. Cleo had seen her once before, but she'd barely noticed her among all the other gods that day. Now that she got a good look at her, the wee woman was impressive.

"Cleo," Carlotta said. "Meet the leader of the Shastaryan. Warrior. Assassin. Double agent."

The woman reached out to shake Cleo's hand, the light from the heart on her palm glowing red.

"Yes, we've met," the woman said. "I'm Mina Valentine."

*The adventure continues!*
*Order King of Clubs: Luck Gods Series book 4 today!*

***One more thing! I have a FREE Luck Gods book for you. The Thief and the Lucky Boy** is a novella that takes place in the luck gods story universe just after **Girl of Hearts** and before **Mother of Spades**. It's a really fun story, and it tells how Cleo met her little kleptomaniac protégée, Junior. Sign up for my e-newsletter and grab your free ebook copy of **The Thief and the Lucky Boy**.*

*And if you enjoyed this book, please take a moment to review it on Amazon.*

*Did you notice any typos, errors or omissions in this book? Let us know by emailing them to: j@jgabrielgates.net.*

*Thanks again for reading, and good luck.*


*• J. Gabriel Gates*